Dear Reader:

   Moonspun Magic is the last novel in the Regency Magic Trilogy, first published well over a decade ago. I've rewritten the novel just a bit, and dressed it in a new cover.

   You've already met Rafael Carstairs, the mysterious sea captain who worked against Napoleon in *Calypso Magic*. He's a civilian now and traveling to see his twin brother, Damien Carstairs, Baron Drago, in Cornwall. In the middle of a moonless night, Rafael rescues a young girl, Victoria Abermarle, from smugglers, only to find that she's trying to escape his twin, who tried to rape her.

   What's a retired spy to do with a young girl whose nubile self and sizable fortune are both threatened by his own brother? He does the noble thing, finally. He marries her. And that's just the beginning of their adventures. . . .

   Step into this whirlwind of intrigue, shattering secrets, and black-souled villains that sets brother against brother and pits good against evil. Revisit all the characters from the three Magic novels and see what mischief they've been brewing since *Midsummer Magic* kicked things off in 1810 Scotland.

   Write me and tell me which of the Magic novels you like the best. Do enjoy all of them.

Catherine Coulter

MOONSPUN MAGIC

Catherine Coulter

A SIGNET BOOK

SIGNET
Published by New American Library, a division of
Penguin Group (USA) Inc., 375 Hudson Street,
New York, New York 10014, USA
Penguin Group (Canada), 90 Eglinton Avenue East, Suite 700, Toronto,
Ontario M4P 2Y3, Canada (a division of Pearson Penguin Canada Inc.)
Penguin Books Ltd., 80 Strand, London WC2R 0RL, England
Penguin Ireland, 25 St. Stephen's Green, Dublin 2,
Ireland (a division of Penguin Books Ltd.)
Penguin Group (Australia), 250 Camberwell Road, Camberwell, Victoria 3124,
Australia (a division of Pearson Australia Group Pty. Ltd.)
Penguin Books India Pvt. Ltd., 11 Community Centre, Panchsheel Park,
New Delhi - 110 017, India
Penguin Group (NZ), 67 Apollo Drive, Rosedale, North Shore,
Auckland 1311, New Zealand (a division of Pearson New Zealand Ltd.)
Penguin Books (South Africa) (Pty.) Ltd., 24 Sturdee Avenue,
Rosebank, Johannesburg 2196, South Africa

Penguin Books Ltd., Registered Offices:
80 Strand, London WC2R 0RL, England

Published by Signet, an imprint of New American Library, a division of Penguin Group (USA) Inc. Previously published in an Onyx edition.

First Signet Printing, July 1999
10 9 8

PUBLISHER'S NOTE
This is a work of fiction. Names, characters, places, and incidents either are
the product of the author's imagination or are used fictitiously, and any resem-
blance to actual persons, living or dead, business establishments, events, or
locales is entirely coincidental.
    The publisher does not have any control over and does not assume any
responsibility for author or third-party Web sites or their content.

For Anton C. Pogany
our first *New York Times* bestseller—
August 1988

Prologue

Charlotte Amalie, St. Thomas
August 1813

A harmless necessary cat.
—SHAKESPEARE

Rafael felt rage, then fear in equal measure. To die alone in the West Indies, so far away from home, from Cornwall, all because of his own stupidity, all because he'd trusted the wrong man.

He fought the fear, the fear that engendered the paralyzing helplessness, and tried to stir the rage to full flame. The man whose life he'd saved eight months before in Montego Bay had betrayed him. The man, Dock Whittaker, was a French spy.

And now Whittaker was going to kill the English merchant captain who had spent the past five years of his life beleaguering the French at sea, slipping through their lines in Portugal, infiltrating their ranks in Naples.

Dock Whittaker had two other men with him, both of them wharf scum, men who would murder for a mug of rum. All had cutlasses, the blades silver-bright and deadly. All were silent, simply moving toward him in a three-quarter circle, making him retreat into filthy Stoner's Alley away from the waterfront of St. Thomas harbor. The night was black, the street quiet, even the drunks asleep; the only sounds coming to his ears were the steady breaths of the three men coming inexorably toward him.

To kill him. He didn't want to die. He strove for contempt to control the deadening fear.

"You're scum, Whittaker, lying bastard scum. This is how you repay the man who saves your damned hide? Or was that all of a piece to lure me in? Listen, both of you"—he spoke to the other two now, his eyes following their slow, determined movements—"Whittaker can't be trusted. Do you want knives in your backs in some dark alley because of this bastard?"

"Captain," Whittaker said very quietly, "I am sorry about, well, this ending, shall we say? But I am loyal to Napoleon, to no one else. And when one is loyal to one master, one must sometimes pretend loyalty to another. Surely you of all people know that. You are just the same as I, after all."

"The day I am the same as you is the day I'll take up residence in hell. What is your real name, Whittaker, Pierre or François Something?"

That struck, and Whittaker jerked his head back. "My real name, Captain, is François Desmoulins. Bulbus, Cork, watch him closely . . . I've seen him fight. He's fast and deadly. Now, Captain, you have hurt my cause quite enough. Henri Bouchard, a brilliant man, and trusted by Napoleon himself, wanted me to be certain you were really the ruthless, hell-bent privateer in the employ of his majesty. And the Black Angel, I believe my compatriots named you in Portugal. You have interfered mightily, Captain, but it's over now. I have no more doubts. I followed you, Captain, to see

Mr. Benjamin Tucker. I couldn't hear much, but I saw you give him papers. Yes, it's over now."

Three more feet and his back would be pressed against the wall of the Three Cats brothel. He looked up for a brief instant, picturing several of the girls leaping from the upper windows to his aid, wearing the flimsiest of negligees. It almost made him smile. In reality, and this was reality, he had about three steps to live. He could taste the fear in his mouth—metallic, cold.

"I will take two of you with me," he said easily now. "You, Bulbus, you trust this French scum? You're not French. I'll pay—"

"Shut up, Captain," Whittaker said sharply. "Ah, there is something else. That English earl—Lord Saint Leven—I will have to kill him and his wife, of course. I cannot be certain that you didn't involve him or indeed, that he wasn't already involved long before he boarded the *Seawitch*."

The fear left him; rage flooded him. Kill Lyon and Diana? Oh, no, that wouldn't happen; he wouldn't let it.

He judged the distance, his chances of taking Bulbus before Cork gutted him or Whittaker sliced his cutlass through his chest. There was no chance. He would go down, but he would take two of them with him. One of them would be Whittaker. It was his only way to save Lyon and Diana.

Suddenly fate made a perverse turn and Rafael's savior appeared. It was a mangy black tom with a long ragged tail, a bush of whiskers, and a torn ear. Rafael acted.

The cat was meowing loudly, and he was between Rafael and his three attackers. Rafael dropped suddenly to the ground, rolled and grabbed the cat as he came up to his knees and threw the yowling, furious tom into Whittaker's face. The tom, enraged, clawed furiously, and dug in.

Rafael was on Bulbus, his fist going hard and low into the man's groin. He saw the silver arc of the cutlass, and elbowed Cork in his fat belly. He heard the cutlass clatter to the cobblestones at the entrance to the alley.

Whittaker was screaming and the mangy tom, bless him, was shredding his face.

Bulbus was breathing hard, and his pocked face was flushed with pain and anger. "You bastard," he grunted, but Rafael took a quick dashing leap to his left and smashed his fist into Bulbus's mouth. He dragged the man's sword arm, twisting until he heard the bone snap. It was a sickening sound and Bulbus groaned. He heard Cork behind him, going after his fallen cutlass. There was nothing he could do about Cork, at least not yet.

He heard Whittaker cursing in French, saw the tom go flying off his chest and land lightly against a pile of trash at the end of the alley. His tail was full and wiry and he was hissing. Rafael wished he could command the tom to leap again on Whittaker's chest.

Whittaker drew a pistol. He was beyond caring if anyone heard. He was ready to kill and damn the cutlasses.

Rafael grabbed the cutlass and sent it smoothly into the air. Whittaker was pointing the pistol at him. Both men were frozen in place. Rafael saw the finger squeezing at the trigger. He saw himself falling, not feeling any pain, simply falling and falling.

He heard a sharp thud. He saw Whittaker's face . . . bewilderment, confusion. He saw the cutlass sticking out of his chest.

"You're dead, Whittaker," he said.

Whittaker just looked at him.

"You're too stupid to know it."

Whittaker opened his mouth, but no words emerged. Slowly he fell forward. He never loosed his hold on the pistol. When he landed on his face on the alley ground, the pistol exploded, its loud report muffled by Whittaker's body. Rafael felt a moment's pity for the man who would turn Whittaker over.

Bulbus was lying on his side, moaning and holding his broken arm. Cork was standing, half-crouched in the alley entrance, the cutlass now in his hand, staring at Whittaker, then at Rafael.

"Don't," Rafael said. "Don't do it. Did Whittaker pay you? No, I didn't think so. He's dead. It's over. Go away."

Cork nodded slowly, cast a disgusted look at Bulbus, stuck the cutlass back through his belt, and melted into the shadows.

Rafael slowly turned and looked toward the back of the alley. He began whistling for that tomcat.

Montego Bay, Jamaica August 1813

It was infernally hot, as always. The room was stifling, for Morgan had a fear of drafts, just like the Prince Regent, Rafael was thinking as he pulled his shirt free of his sweaty back for a moment. He faced the man whose career it was to direct his movements in the Caribbean. Morgan looked insignificant with his receding chin, his bald spot just like a monk's tonsure, his faded eyes, his round shoulders. Nonetheless he was a master strategist and Rafael held him in great respect. But at this moment he was feeling only frustration and anger at Morgan's intransigence.

"Damnation, Morgan, it was an uncomplicated attack, nothing more. Whittaker is dead. The scum he hired didn't even know who he was or who I am, for that matter. He didn't—"

Morgan held up a hand and Rafael fell silent.

"Enough, Rafael. You know as well as I that it is over now. Whittaker's attack was the crowning touch, if you will. Your identity is now known and your, er, usefulness is over."

"Just like that?"

"Yes. Do not forget the French attack on the *Seawitch*. LaPorte was instructed to see you to the bottom of the sea. I thank God he is as incompetent a captain as his brother is an arms merchant."

Morgan fell silent for a moment and reached for his ever-present glass of lemonade. "To the Black Angel," he said, giving Rafael a smile meant to soothe and conciliate. "You did excellently. Lord Walton, my contact in the War Ministry in London, agrees with me, naturally. Go home, Rafael. You have avenged your parents' death. You are still alive. Return to Cornwall."

Rafael paced the long, narrow room. It was filled with Morgan's books. They overflowed from the floor-to-ceiling bookshelves. They were stacked on the floor, on the chairs, even on top of an overturned wastebasket.

Morgan eyed the young man thoughtfully. He was a fine man, a fine captain, and his courage in the face of overwhelming odds bordered on the reckless. Morgan liked him. He sometimes wondered how this

was so when Rafael Carstairs was so bloody handsome, but he'd discovered that most men liked Rafael, despite the fact that their women stared at him
with longing bordering on lust. Morgan grinned.
Thank goodness his daughter was in Kingston, visiting her aunt. If she were here, Lucinda would oggle
Rafael until he turned red.

"You have saved many lives during the past five
years. You have aided England immensely."

Morgan was in his gentle, cajoling mood, Rafael
thought, his eyes narrowing. Damnation, he didn't
want to quit now. But he'd known, oh yes, deep
down he'd known after LaPorte's attack that it was
over. Then Whittaker. That piece of treachery still
enraged him.

"LaPorte is disgraced. Three of their ships against
your one. I should have liked to see it." His voice
sounded a bit wistful and Rafael was forced to smile,
remembering that night.

"LaPorte couldn't navigate in that storm," Rafael
said. "I sent a cannon broadside, he fell back, and I
slipped the *Seawitch* between the other ships and was
away before they could regroup."

Morgan finished off his lemonade and reached for
a letter opener. He twirled it with some skill between
his fingers. "I also heard about your two passengers.
Lucien Savarol's daughter and an English earl. What
is his name?"

"Lyonel Ashton, Earl of Saint Leven. Incidentally,
Lucien Savarol's daughter, Diana, is now the Countess of Saint Leven. Lord, if I'm forced home, I shall
probably see them in London." He grinned suddenly.
"I married them, you know. My first experience in
that sort of thing. I was more nervous than they
were."

Morgan laughed, showing the wide space between his front teeth. "Is it true you had them jump overboard? They spent a week alone on Calypso Island?"

How, Rafael wondered silently, did Morgan know all this? It was obvious he was just affirming his information. "True. I believe they enjoyed themselves immensely. I wasn't worried for them. Diana Savarol was raised here, after all. That young lady is a born survivor." He smiled, remembering the day he had returned to rescue them. He'd seen them through his spyglass on the beach, Lyon naked, holding Diana in his arms, her arms and legs wrapped around him. His timing had not been of the best.

"My days of adventuring are over," he said now, aloud. He sighed, turning to face Morgan. "I do miss Cornwall."

"Go home, Rafael. Go home and pick up your life. Perhaps your brother has changed over the past five years."

Once, when Rafael had been deep in his cups, he'd told Morgan of his brother, his identical twin brother born thirty minutes before him, Damien Carstairs, fifth Baron Drago. He wished now that he'd kept his drunken mouth shut.

"Probably not," he said.

"He is now married, is he not?"

How did Morgan know that? The information the man gleaned was frightening in its scope. "Yes. A baronet's daughter from Dorset. Elaine Montgomery. She brought him a huge dowry."

"I will tell you something, Rafael. Miss Montgomery's father, Sir Langdon, isn't a fool. I know about him—quite a lot, as a matter of fact."

"Somehow that doesn't surprise me."

"Yes, well, the fact is that he didn't just hand over the dowry to your brother. The settlement was made in yearly payments. He protected his daughter."

Rafael could only stare at him. "You are bloody frightening."

Morgan merely laughed. "I knew your father. Did I tell you that? No? Well, now, your father was a strong man, fierce, loyal, something of a feudal lord in the modern world. You are much like him."

"Thank you, sir. Oh, yes, I will sail to Spain before returning to England. I wish to visit my grandparents. Surely there is some information of value I can take to our people there."

Morgan shook his head. "I don't want you anywhere near Spain. Postpone your trip to your grandparents. Another year or so and Napoleon will be dead or incarcerated. His ill-fated Russian campaign did him in. He lost most of his experienced officers and veteran soldiers. Now he has nothing but raw recruits, boys most of them. It will all be over soon, Rafael."

Rafael hated to admit that Morgan was right. He felt as if he'd been abruptly cut adrift. He walked to one of the narrow windows and stared out toward Montego Bay at the ship-dotted harbor beyond the squalid town.

"The damnable bastards," he said under his breath, staring unseeing out of the window. He would never forget the day he'd learned his parents' ship had been attacked and sunk by the French.

"I myself will be returning within the next six months to London," said Morgan. He rose and automatically straightened his cravat, which didn't need straightening. Didn't the man ever rumple or sweat?

Morgan extended his hand. "Perhaps the both of us will cut a fine figure in London. What do you say, Rafael?"

"I don't plan to go to London. The city never interested me. Too big, too noisy, and too many utterly useless people doing utterly useless things."

Morgan grinned. "Well, I wish you would reconsider. I do just happen to have a message for you to take to Lord Walton."

"I should have known. For someone who is no longer useful, I have experienced a fine resurrection."

"Yes, I should think so. Now, shall we have a glass of Jamaica's best rum? I have it from the Barretts' plantation. It's so smooth, your throat will think you've cocked up your toes and passed over."

Rafael smiled. There was nothing else to do.

1

Drago Hall, St. Austell, Cornwall, September 1813

What bloody man is that?
—SHAKESPEARE

She heard the footsteps. *His* footsteps, eerie echoes down the long eastern corridor, closer, nearly to her door. Now they were slower, as if he were hesitating, but only for a moment, only long enough for her to feel a spurt of hope. Then louder, a lengthened stride, as if he were now hurrying. So close now.

Victoria stared straight ahead in the darkness. She sat up in her bed, her movements as silent as the clouded half-moon outside her window, terrified that somehow he would know that she was awake, that she was aware he was there. Her eyes never wavered from the bedchamber door.

The footsteps stopped. He was standing in front of her bedchamber door now. She could see him extending his hand, see his fingers flexing about the brass door handle, clasping it, squeezing it inward.

Nothing happened.

She wished she could see the large, old-fashioned brass key in the lock, her protection, her only protection against him.

She heard the door shake as he squeezed the handle, then, in frustration, shook it hard.

Why wouldn't he go away? Oh, please, make him go away.

The key rattled loudly in the lock. He was exerting great pressure. Suddenly the heavy key fell to the floor, making a loud cracking sound on the bare wood, like a pistol shot. She jumped, stifling a cry.

There was no sound now. She could see his face changing as he came to understand the sound, see him becoming slowly enraged as he realized that she had locked him out. The door was strong and thick as Drago Hall itself. It wouldn't yield.

She held her breath, waiting for him to call out.

Her heart pounded—loud, fast strokes. Could he not hear her heartbeat? Feel her fear of him?

She could see his gray eyes, darkening now, dilating with anger and cold in the night gloom of the vast eastern corridor. In the daylight they would be as light and clear as Ligger's newly polished silver.

"Victoria?"

His voice was soft and compelling. She stuffed her fist in her mouth, not moving.

"Open the door, Victoria."

Now the master's voice, threaded with steel but still quiet, soft-sounding. She'd heard it rarely, normally directed at servants, and they'd been frantic to obey. She remembered once he'd turned on Elaine and spoken to her in that tone. Bright, strong Elaine had cowered.

What to do? She couldn't answer him. Perhaps he would believe her asleep. The thought of him believing that she was deliberately disobeying him made her flesh crawl.

She'd come to live at Drago Hall at the age of fourteen after the marriage of her first cousin, Elaine Montgomery, to Damien Carstairs, Baron Drago. Victoria, starved for affection, had adored him then, seen him as the hero, the perfect gentleman, and he'd treated her with careless affection, giving her the kind of attention he occasionally bestowed on Elaine's pug, Missie, or his small daughter, Damaris.

But no longer.

When had he begun to look at her differently? Six months ago? Nanny Black had teased her about being "late to grow on the stalk." Whatever stalk was in question, evidently Damien now believed her grown enough. She wanted to yell at him, scream at him to leave her alone. She was his wife's cousin, for pity's sake. Didn't a man owe loyalty and fidelity to his wife?

The minutes passed. He said nothing more. Her heart continued to pound in slow, loud strokes. The door handle rattled again suddenly, then abruptly stopped. Her breath caught in her throat. She heard his footsteps going away now, fainter and fainter down the eastern corridor.

She remembered suddenly the summer that one of his hunters had hurt its leg in a trap. He'd shot it. Then walked away, tossing his gun to one of the white-faced grooms.

She had to do something. Because if she didn't, he would win. He would trap her and do just as he pleased with her. She would tell Elaine, she had to tell her cousin. Even as the thought sifted through her mind, she was shaking her head. Tell Elaine that her husband wanted to ravish her young cousin? She swallowed, picturing her humiliation when Elaine laughed at her, shook her head, and berated her for spouting such ridiculous, such *mean* nonsense. And she would. Unlike her husband, she was loyal and faithful.

She couldn't stay here at Drago Hall. Not now.

Victoria lowered her face into her hands. She was shaking, but there were no tears. The feeling of helplessness was paralyzing. No, she thought, shaking her head, no. How could he want her? It made no sense. Elaine was beautiful, with her lustrous black hair and her pale green eyes, and accomplished, her fingers nimble with needlework and the keys of the piano-forte. And she was carrying his child, his heir, as he said every day now, as if saying it over and over would produce the male child he wanted. Elaine was his wife; *she* had no deformities. Surely he knew about her leg; Elaine must have told him. Victoria touched her fingers to the ridged scar on her left thigh, probing lightly at the now relaxed flesh, the smooth muscles. Once, when she was fifteen, she had run away from a teasing Johnny Tregonnet, run too hard and long, and Elaine had seen the result—muscles knotting, bunching beneath the jagged scar. She'd tried to be kind, but she'd been repelled at the sight.

How could he possibly want her? She was ugly, as defective as that poor hunter he'd shot.

Very slowly Victoria eased down under the goose-feather quilt. The night was long. She was cold, inside, so cold, and she was afraid.

She thought of David Esterbridge, but four years older than her almost nineteen. He'd proposed to her three times since the previous January. He was kind to her, generously persistent, weak, and the only child under his father's thumb. She didn't love him.

But what else could she do? At least David would protect her. She would make him a good wife. Yes, she would. She would marry him and he would take her away from Drago Hall.

Away from Damien.

There were eight men in the beam-ceilinged drawing room of Treffy, the small hunting lodge owned by the old infirm Earl of Crowden. The caretaker had died and no one had told the old earl's steward. The steward wouldn't have cared in any case, for Treffy was falling apart and the old earl's heir surely wouldn't want the expense of putting it to rights. The lodge had been built in 1748, in the boring time of George II, and it was small by the standards of the time, boasting only seven rooms. It was, further, too isolated for most tastes, set in the middle of a thick maple-tree thicket. It was only three miles from the town of Towan, and Towan but half a mile from Mevagissey Bay. There was always the smell of the sea in the air, a feeling of dampness that lingered on clothes, and on the seats of chairs, and in the bed linen, what there was of that left.

The eight men weren't concerned about dampness that night, or about any other lack of Treffy. In three minutes it would be midnight. They were ready, prepared for the upcoming ritual. Each had a preassigned position, each was to be standing facing the long table.

Rites and rituals, that was what the Ram demanded. Nothing was spontaneous. All actions were governed by rules, rules that the Ram had made and continued to make or change or modify when it suited him.

All eight men were dressed in black satin robes,

their heads encased in black satin hoods. There were slits for their eyes and holes for their nostrils. There were no mouth openings. The satin was thin enough so that their speech was easy and not slurred. Their moans were perhaps muffled a bit, and that was as the Ram wished it.

The Ram had a book, a thin bloodred-vellum-covered book that only he could read. It was his guide, he would say. No one questioned the Ram anymore.

All enjoyed the wickedness of anonymity.

All were enjoying the spectacle of the fifteen-year-old girl who was lying on the scarred old oak table, her hands and feet pulled away and bound easily but securely with soft leather cords. She was clothed only in a long black velvet gown, her feet bare and clean, thank the powers.

She wasn't particularly toothsome, one of the men had remarked, but the Ram had only shrugged and said, "Her body more than compensates for the plainness of her face. You will see. She is also a virgin, as the rules state she must be."

What the Ram didn't say was that he had duly paid the girl's father ten pounds for her virginity.

And so they were waiting. The Ram had said that midnight was the hour she was to be broken in. They'd drawn lots from the pottery bowl, an ancient piece the Ram said had come from a ship of the Spanish Armada, blown to bits by Queen Bess's sailors, and wrecked off the shores of Cornwall.

The Ram very calmly walked to the table, bent down, and kissed the girl full on the mouth. She whimpered, but no more. She'd been fed enough drug to do nothing more. Slowly the Ram walked to the end of the table. He freed her ankles, and slowly, as if to a strange cadence, he pushed her legs up, bending her knees until her feet were flat on the table. He told her to keep her legs open.

He looked at one of the men, the one who had drawn the first lot, and nodded. Johnny Tregonnet was ready, more than ready, he was eager, and he was rough as he drew up the girl's gown, baring her to the waist.

The Ram had once stated, "A woman's uses are below her waist. Her breasts are nothing but a distraction."

No one knew if he had taken this from the red-vellum guidebook or from his own capricious nature. No one really cared, though a sight of really full breasts would have titillated some.

She bled as she was supposed to. Not copiously, for she was a peasant girl. The Ram remarked that peasant girls were like the stolid, gritty animals they tended. He then motioned for two of them to hold her legs wide, for she was growing tired.

She was deeply asleep from the drug when the eighth finished. It didn't matter, said the Ram easily. It was better that a woman remain silent. It was a blessing.

The men were relaxed and drinking steadily now. This part of the ritual was a bit of an annoyance. To drink their brandy, they had to turn their faces away, lift their hoods, drink, then lower the hoods back into place before turning back to face the others. Each turned to look at the girl upon occasion. She lay in the shadowy light from the fireplace, now lightly snoring from the surfeit of drug the Ram had fed her.

The Ram sat a bit apart. He drank sparingly. He'd given them this girl to keep them in line. None of them, he mused many times, had the depth of spirit to truly become part of the rituals that nurtured a man's soul. They were allowed to plow a girl only when he deemed it proper, and at no other time. He'd quoted from the book on that point: "The man's sex is to prove to the female that he is the dominant, the master, the superior of the species."

The Ram told them further that such proof wasn't all that necessary in terms of repetition, for women knew themselves mastered, knew themselves the inferior, knew themselves the weaker.

Several of the men doubted that sincerely. Particularly the two who were married. The Ram, as if sensing their recalcitrance on this point, said strongly that the drug didn't diminish the female's knowledge that she was mastered, it merely kept her from voicing her beliefs too loudly, which would be an irritant.

No one knew that the girl's father was ten pounds richer from this night. That was the Ram's private counsel. It would have lessened their sense of wickedness if they'd known.

Vincent Landower wondered aloud if the girl could be pregnant. He looked at her as he spoke. She was still snoring, her legs splayed, the velvet bunched below her breasts. He thought a pregnant woman as appetizing as a gutted trout. And he voiced aloud his revulsion.

The others laughed, but the Ram didn't. He said it would be interesting, his voice pensive, if she were. Which one of them would the child resemble?

"Perhaps our leader," said Johnny, guffawing loudly. "Yes, a Ram. That would shock the neighborhood!"

The Ram ignored that bit of levity and said after a few moments, "We will not meet until the first Thursday of October. At that meeting you will enjoy a surprise. That evening, after the surprise, I will tell you of our plans for All Hallows' Night."

Paul Keason, who had drawn the fourth position, felt in private moments that any emphasis on satanism, on cults, and on warlocks and covens was bloody nonsense. He didn't want to be a budding satanist or warlock. He wanted to push the limits of what was wicked and unlawful and leave it at that. He suspected that most of the men felt the same way. But to achieve what it was they wished, they had to pretend serious interest in all the Ram's rites and rituals, which were becoming more elaborate and complex as time passed. All Hallows' Night was a night for an innocuous party, that was all. He looked at the Ram, relieved that he couldn't see his expression. Then he recalled the promised surprise. Another girl, more than likely. Perhaps he would draw the first lot instead of the fourth. He looked over at the Ram, sitting silently, looking as dignified as one could in the ridiculous black hood and long full robe. He wished the Ram hadn't made that particular rule. No one was supposed to know who any of the others were, which was silly. All of the men knew each other, with or without the hoods.

But no one knew the identity of the Ram.

The Ram saw that the girl was slowly regaining her senses. She was twisting a bit and ruining the artistic position he'd arranged her in after the eighth had spilled his seed in her. He frowned. He didn't appreciate her detracting from the solemnity of the group, from their quiet fellowship. He waited a few more minutes, then raised her head and fed her a bit more of the drug in a cup of brandy. The brandy trickled down her chin. He shut her jaw. She would sleep now through the night. He rearranged her limbs to his liking.

At precisely one o'clock in the morning, each of the eight rose, placed his right hand on top of the red-vellum book, raised his left hand over his heart, and feeling like a complete fool, recited the speech the Ram had taught him. It was blessedly short, so despite the amounts of brandy consumed, it wasn't beyond any of the men's capabilities.

"We are the masters of the night. We extol each other and our power. Only we know of ourselves. We are silent. The world knows only of our deeds, and they are awed."

The Ram nodded gravely when the recitations were finished. He said his own speech alone, his voice going deep to give the words a more moving, vibrant timbre. He was the Ram and he was the master of masters. The name suited him. He nearly forgot to keep his voice disguised, so moved was he at his own performance.

2

The Blue Boar, Falmouth, Cornwall, September 1813

> *To dispute with a drunk man is to debate with an empty house.*
>
> —PUBLILIUS SYRUS

"You drink any more of that swill, and Flash and I will have to bury you here."

Rafael cocked a black brow at Rollo Culpepper, his first mate and longtime friend. "Swill, my dear fellow? This is the finest French brandy. Old Beaufort assures me he smuggles only the best. Just another little bit, I think. Lindy!"

"More like a bloody keg," Flash Savory said, observing the huge snifter Rafael was holding. He wondered if he could snatch the snifter without Rafael knowing it. A pickpocket of the first order from the advanced age of five in London's gin-soaked Soho, Flash still boasted many unusual talents, but convincing his drunk captain to leave the alehouse wasn't among them. He knew why the captain was getting drunk as a lord, knew as well as Rollo did. The captain was feeling cut loose and useless after five years of danger, excitement, and doing things that made a difference to the war. That was it: the captain no longer felt that he mattered. Whatever he did now wouldn't change or alter what was happening in France or in Italy or in Portugal. And he was back in Cornwall, back where his damned twin brother, curse his eyes, lived and lorded it over everyone. A bloody shame about that Whittaker being a French spy and telling folk about the captain. Ruining everything he did. Flash felt a shiver of fear remembering that Whittaker—or whatever the bloody Frog's name really was—had nearly succeeded in killing the captain. Well, he'd lost, damn him. And Flash was now caretaker of the mangiest, most perverse, most randy damned cat that ever sailed quite happily aboard a ship.

"Lindy!"

Flash tried wheedling. "Now, Captain, don't you know that old Hero doesn't sleep well when you're not aboard? He meows and carries on, and the crew can't sleep either, what with all his bloody racket, and—"

"Flash, go away. Now. You and Rollo just go away."

Rollo leaned forward, resting his elbows on the tabletop. "Look, Rafael—"

But Rafael wasn't looking at him. He was grinning at Lindy, a toothsome barmaid whose ample endowments were difficult to ignore even if a man were sober and bent on abstinence.

"Ye want more, do ye, my fine lord?"

"I'm not a lord, Lindy. I'm not an anything now. No, wait, that isn't true. Hero needs me, won't sleep without me, you see."

Rollo snorted and Flash's fingers suddenly started

itching. He didn't understand it until he saw the prosperous-looking merchant come into the taproom with his bulging pockets. He forced his attention away from those bulging pockets back to his captain, and stuffed his itching fingers into his own breeches' pockets.

"Well, tonight you don't need this Hero," said Lindy, and poured him more brandy.

Rollo snorted again, then clamped his lips shut. They'd managed to limp the damaged *Seawitch* into Falmouth harbor the previous day. She'd been crippled in a freak, very vicious storm just a day beyond the Channel. Rollo guessed that Rafael, in addition to his other worries, wanted desperately to continue to St. Austell, to Drago Hall, but the papers he was carrying were bound for London, and according to Morgan, they were urgent. He looked at Rafael's abstracted expression and knew the captain was trying his best to bury his unhappy thoughts in a brandy grave.

" 'Tis a comely man ye are, Cap'n. Aye, comely." Lindy ignored both Rollo and Flash, her full attention on Rafael.

"Balm for a man's soul," Rafael said, and downed the remainder of the brandy. "More balm, Lindy."

"It grows quite late, Captain," Rollo said. "Flash is right; you should come back to the ship and—"

"I suggest the both of you nursemaids take yourselves back to the *Seawitch* and sleep with that blasted cat." He smiled vacuously up at Lindy. "I shall spend the night here in Beaufort's very comfortable inn. It is comfortable upstairs, isn't it, Lindy?"

"Unbelievable comfort, Cap'n."

"There, you see?"

Rollo threw up his hands.

Flash withdrew his still-itching hands from his pockets and looked wistfully toward the steadily drinking, quite inattentive merchant. The urge to lighten the merchant's pockets wasn't as strong as it used to be, thank the powers. He'd be twenty in four months. Rafael had promised him that when he became twenty, all urges toward criminality would disappear. He believed Rafael implicitly.

"Ye're a divil, Cap'n," said Lindy fondly. She ran light fingertips through Rafael's thick black hair. "Aye, a divil."

Rollo rolled his eyes. "Come on, Flash, let's get back. He'll be all right." The two men left the Blue Boar, the prosperous merchant, and their sodden captain.

"He'll be all right," Rollo said again.

"He might not be the divil," said Flash, a gamin smile lighting up his thin face, "but he'll feel the very divil tomorrow."

"Aye, but his night will be pleasant enough."

"Not if he keeps drinking that vile swill."

"I daresay that the girl, Lindy, will know when he's had enough."

Lindy, at that very moment, was gently prying the snifter from Rafael's long fingers. "It grows late, Cap'n. Me feet are weary."

Rafael looked up at her, but his eyes didn't range farther north than her bosom. "And the rest of you, my girl?" His look was lazy, his voice drawling.

She chuckled, and stroked her fingers over his jaw. "Ye come with me, me fine lad, and I'll show ye."

As Rafael followed Lindy upstairs, he devoutly prayed that his major working parts wouldn't shut down and leave him humiliated as well as drunk. Lindy paused a moment, turning to face him from the step above. His face was on a level with her bosom. He leaned forward and kissed the soft white flesh.

"Ah," said Lindy, and pressed his face close. He was right and randy, this lovely man. The moment he'd come into the Blue Boar, she'd known she wanted to bed him. It was the way he looked at her that made her know, simply know that he was a man who was generous with a woman, a man who enjoyed a woman's body and her pleasure. The fact that he was one of the most beautiful men she'd ever served unwatered brandy to made her leap of faith final. His body, she had observed during the long evening, would be as magnificent as his silver-gray eyes. Ah, yes, she would enjoy him thoroughly.

She smiled as she slid her hand down his body. When her fingers closed about him, she said softly, with immense satisfaction, "Aye, ye are a divil."

Elaine Carstairs, Baroness Drago, looked at her younger cousin across the breakfast table. It was an altogether lovely morning, the sun bright, a nip of fall briskness in the air. "What is wrong with you, Victoria? You are always up beforetimes. Is there something you wish from me?"

It was late, Victoria knew, and Elaine, now six months pregnant, didn't rise until at least ten o'clock in the morning. And Victoria had waited in her locked room until she guessed Elaine would be in the breakfast room.

"Well, Victoria?"

Yes, Victoria wanted to shout at her suddenly, *I want you to keep your husband away from me.* But she only shook her head and bit into her now-cold slice of toast.

"I must say that you don't look yourself. I am the one increasing, and here you are with shadows under your eyes looking quite awful. I hope you aren't sickening with anything."

How to tell her cousin that she hadn't slept, that fear of Damien had made her cower like a helpless creature in her bed, afraid even to answer the maid's knock.

"I trust you are well enough to take Damaris riding? The child could talk of nothing else when I visited the nursery this morning. If you call that prattle of hers talking, of course."

"Yes," Victoria said, looking up from her plate of congealed eggs. "I'll fetch her in just a little while."

"Victoria! Really, what is wrong with you?"

"What's this? You aren't well, little cousin?"

Victoria felt the small amount of breakfast form a hard knot in her stomach at the sound of Damien's smooth voice. She forced herself to take a deep breath and look up at him. "I am well," she said, her voice cold, stilted. "I will take your daughter riding."

"Excellent," said Damien. "I do believe I will join you. We will ride to St. Austell, if you like. I have business there."

"She looks awful," Elaine said, not mincing matters. "If she is sickening, I don't wish her to be near Damaris."

Damien Carstairs, Baron Drago, walked to where Victoria sat, stiff as a stick, in her high-backed chair. He leaned down and looked at her closely. Victoria forced herself to remain still. She could do nothing. Not here, not now.

"Didn't you sleep well, Victoria?"

"Yes," she said. "I slept very well. Very deeply, in fact."

"Ah. That explains much, and yet it doesn't, not really."

Elaine's voice was suddenly high and shrill. "Be certain not to overdo, Victoria. You know how terrible your leg looks if you push yourself too hard."

Victoria wanted to thank her cousin. "Yes, it does look horrible, doesn't it? Ugly and disgusting. Yes, that is quite true."

But Damien, to her chagrin, only smiled. He flicked a careless finger across her pale cheek, then straightened.

"Is there anything you wish in St. Austell, my love?"

Elaine shrugged. "I am thinking that perhaps Victoria should remain here today. We are having a party, and Ligger could use her assistance. The silver, you know."

"I know," said Damien easily.

"Perhaps you don't wish to attend the party, Victoria," Elaine continued to her cousin. "There will be dancing, and I don't wish you to be placed in an embarrassing situation."

She knows or she guesses something is amiss with her husband, Victoria realized in that moment. She is trying to give Damien a disgust of me. Victoria prayed for her success. "You're right, Elaine. I shall help Ligger with the preparations. My leg is feeling particularly bothersome this morning. Dancing would doubtless embarrass all of us. I will keep Damaris and Nanny Black company in the nursery."

Damien gave his wife a lazy look that was neatly belied by his voice, which brooked no further arguments. "Victoria will ride this morning, with Damaris and myself. She will attend the party and the dancing. I shall help her choose a gown, my dear. Perhaps one of yours that is no longer of any use to you. Now, if there is nothing more of grave importance, I shall be with Corbell. The stables, Victoria, in half an hour."

"But I need her to help—"

"Half an hour."

Victoria raised her chin. "I'm sorry, Damien. I will be riding with David. Damaris will be our chaperon," she added with a nod toward Elaine.

"Yes," said Elaine quickly. "That will be fine. I do wonder when David will speak to you, my dear."

Damien stared at his wife. "David Esterbridge," he said slowly. "So, that is the way of it, hmmm?"

"Yes," said Victoria, "that is the way of it."

Damien smiled suddenly, nodding to his wife. "Well, this is very interesting, yes indeed."

Both women watched him stride from the breakfast room. The instant the door closed, Elaine rose and splayed her fingers on the table. She said in a low, hard voice, "You are wise to accept David Esterbridge. He is suitable. It is time you left Drago Hall."

Things were moving rapidly, too rapidly. Victoria had always known that she hadn't a sou, and it hadn't been important. But now it was. She would have to tell David that she was poor, wretchedly poor, that she would bring him nothing. Squire Esterbridge appeared to Victoria to be a man of stern and rigid fiber, with even more fibrous notions of what was due to his family. Surely he couldn't want a daughter-in-law with nothing to recommend her but the Abermarle name, her blue eyes, and her straight teeth. She simply couldn't bring herself to believe that he did want her in the Esterbridge family, even though David had assured her at the beginning of each of the three proposals that his father was desir-

ous of having her for a daughter-in-law. She lowered
her head. She would speak to David, make him fully
aware of her concerns before she accepted his pro-
posal. Perhaps she was making problems for herself
where there should be none. Surely David was certain of his feelings and of his father's attitudes
toward her, for they were of long enough standing.
She was worrying for naught. Perhaps, she thought,
more optimistic now, just perhaps Damien, once he
realized that he wouldn't gain his ends, would provide her with a dowry.

She left Elaine with a brisk step and went to the
nursery. Nanny Black merely gave her her usual
dour nod and straightened the pink velvet bow on
the little girl's riding hat.

"You wish to be my chaperon, Damie?" Victoria
dropped to her knees in front of the child, carefully,
of course, favoring her left leg.

"David?"

"Yes, David is riding with us. We will go to Fletcher's Pond and feed Clarence and his family."

"Yes, yes, yes, Torie!"

Victoria ruffled Damie's black curls, thinking that
she was the picture of her father. Except there was
no cruelty in her clear gray eyes. Only innocence and
eagerness and an only child's occasional petulance.

Victoria rose gingerly to her feet, feeling the slight
strain in her left leg from the kneeling position. Nothing but a twinge, but it made her realize that this
was something else she and David had never dis-
cussed before.

"Come on, Torie! Come! Come!"

"Little terror," said Nanny Black fondly.

"I'll bring her back after luncheon," Victoria said.

"Come along, Damie, and we'll fetch Cook's picnic basket." She took Damie's small hand and together they walked downstairs.

Victoria came to a startled halt at the foot of the wide staircase. There was David, standing very still, looking up at her. He was but four years her senior, ruddy-complexioned, his eyes dark brown, his hair a darker brown. He was slight of build, no masculine compliments coming to mind upon viewing him, but he was kind to her, always had been, and was soft-spoken. She had always liked him.

He was wearing buckskins. Victoria said immediately, "How very natty you look today, David. Doesn't he, Damie?"

"Natty," said Damaris.

David wasn't smiling, nor did he smile now. He said only, "Are you ready?"

She searched his well-known face, feeling a moment of unease. She simply nodded.

"Must the child come today?"

"Come! Come!"

"Well, yes, I promised her, you see. I didn't know that you would mind. She will be feeding the ducks, David. It will occupy her."

"Enjoy your outing, you two."

Victoria forced herself to stay calm and turn easily at the sound of Damien's voice. He was standing in the doorway of the drawing room, his arms crossed over his chest, his head cocked to one side, studying them.

"Papa," said Damaris, but she didn't release Victoria's hand.

"You make certain your cousin doesn't let you fall, my dear," Damien said, not moving. "Esterbridge," he said, nodding to David. With those words he turned and walked down the back hall toward the estate room.

"Come!" said Damaris, tugging at Victoria's hand.

"Yes, Damie."

David walked a bit ahead of them toward the stables, and Victoria wondered at him. It occurred to her vaguely that his mustard-yellow riding jacket wasn't a felicitous color for him. It made him look bilious. A wifely thought, she decided, and kept her mouth shut.

Toddy, her mare, snorted when she saw Victoria. True to her habit, Victoria withdrew two cubes of sugar and laid them on her palm for the horse to eat.

"Come!"

"I'll give you a leg up, Victoria," David said, and followed action to words. Once Victoria was settled on Toddy's back, he handed her Damaris. The child was squealing with delight and excitement. David didn't seem at all amused.

"Sit still, love," Victoria said, encircling the wriggling little body firmly with her arms. She watched the stable lad, Jim, give David the food basket.

They rode down the long drive, eastward toward Fletcher's copse and pond. There was no opportunity for them to speak of private matters with Damaris chattering constantly. The day was warm and clear, only scattered clouds dotting the blue sky.

"It's a lovely day," Victoria said finally, smiling toward David.

"I suppose," he said.

"I must speak to you."

He looked at her now, and she saw his hand jerk unexpectedly on his horse's reins. His stallion snorted, danced sideways, nearly unseating him. Her

eyes widened, but she said nothing more until he
had his horse under control.

"Almost there!" shouted Damaris.

"Yes, love, very nearly." What was wrong with
David? He was looking at her oddly. Then she saw
Damien in her mind's eye, standing there so smugly,
looking at them, and she felt a sense of foreboding.

They dismounted near Fletcher's pond. David
lifted Damaris down, gave her several slices of bread
from Cook's basket, then watched her until she came
to a halt a good three feet from the edge of the water.

"That's quite far enough," Victoria called. "Ah,
there's Clarence. You can begin their feast, Damie."

The squawking of the ducks was very nearly deafening, and Damaris was completely oblivious of the two
of them. Slowly David placed his hands around Victoria's waist and lifted her down. Victoria smiled up at
him and lightly laid her hands on his coat lapels. "I
will marry you if you still wish it," she said, no preamble coming to mind, just the bald essence of the matter.

He stared down at her, saying nothing. Finally,
"Why now, if I may inquire? You've turned me
down every time I've asked since January."

Oh, God, what to say? It hadn't occurred to her
that he would wonder at her sudden agreement,
more fool she. She could hear her own voice reciting
to him, *"I must leave Drago Hall before Damien ravishes
me and I can only do that by marrying you and I don't
love you but I swear to make you a good wife."*

"More bread!"

David watched her pull more slices from the paper
wrap and toss them to Damaris. When she turned
back, wiping her hands on her riding skirt, he felt a
surge of immense longing for her. Until he remembered. "Well?"

"I think we should suit, David. There are a few concerns, though, and something I really must tell you."

"What is this *something*?"

"Well, first, I am concerned about money. I haven't any."

"Damien would provide a dowry, you must realize that. He wouldn't wish to appear niggardly and petty, and he would were he to simply send you off with only the clothes on your back."

"Your father—"

"My father wants you. He is adamant, in fact, and has been for a very long time."

That was a shock. "But why?"

David shrugged.

"Certainly he has always been kind to me, but a daughter-in-law shouldn't arrive on his doorstep as poor as a vicar's mouse."

"I think I've already answered that. Now, Victoria, there is something else you should tell me, isn't there? You do intend to tell me more, do you not?"

She cocked her head to one side, wondering at him. He wasn't behaving as he normally did in her company. Damien, she thought. Damien had something to do with this. She said aloud, blurting it out, "What did Damien do? Did he tell you anything?"

"So," said David. He laughed. "So, it is all there, for anyone to see. God, how blind I've been."

"Blind? What are you talking about? What did Damien tell you?" She closed her eyes a moment against the ugly twisting of his lips. "It was not really so bad, was it?" Had he told David of her leg and its ugliness?

"I wouldn't have imagined it, nor would my father. I did think that I knew you, Victoria. But you deceived me. Made a complete and utter fool of me."

"What are you talking about?"

"Dear God, I don't believe you. I didn't want to believe him—no, I didn't. How could you? He even told me about your mother. Inherited tendencies and all that, he said, trying to find excuses for you."

Victoria gaped at him. "My mother? What is going on here, David?"

"You've as good as admitted it, damn you, Victoria. You actually believe I would still want you? Just you wait until I tell my father. He'll change his mind about you quickly enough."

She tried to calm herself in the face of his utterly wild and unbelievable words. "David, I truly don't understand what this is all about. I haven't admitted anything." He gave her a stony stare. "David, what did Damien tell you?" Her hands felt clammy, and she was becoming cold, terribly cold.

David laughed, a very unpleasant sound, but Victoria was too distraught to hear the pain in it. "Used goods, my dear, very used. Even by the baron. Your cousin's husband. How could you?"

"Used goods," she repeated slowly, and she suddenly had the image of Molly pouring used bathwater back into the buckets to take them to another family member. She nearly giggled aloud. "Used goods," she said again. "How ridiculous that sounds."

"The baron hopes you're not with child, but he isn't certain, and said he couldn't let me marry you in good faith with the possibility that my heir could be a bastard. He wanted to warn me, to advise me, and I hated him for spewing out such filth about the girl I wanted to make my wife. But it isn't nonsense. Are you with child, Victoria? Is that why you wish to wed me now?"

So very cold, and so alone now. She nearly laughed aloud seeing herself as used goods, as some sort of package now retied with old string. Damien hadn't wasted time on irrelevant things. He'd gone immediately for the jugular. And David had lapped up all he'd said. She raised her chin and said only, "No."

"No what? You have played me false, madam. I am leaving now and I don't wish ever to see you again."

He sounded like a bad actor in a melodrama. She shook her head, trying desperately to clear it of extraneous images and thoughts. What had happened, what was happening, was real and it was now and it would affect her the rest of her life. "None of it is true, David. Damien lied to you."

"Like mother like daughter," David said. "That's what he thought, anyway. And your mother was a trollop."

"Torie! Thirsty. Come!"

Victoria ignored Damaris. Anger flowed through her now. "Don't you dare speak of my mother like that. None of it is true and if you believe it, you're naught but a fool, David, a credulous, naive fool."

David said nothing. She watched him untether his horse with jerky movements, then quickly mount. He stared down at her. "Lies, Victoria? Tell me then why you wish to marry me. Not for love, that is certain."

No, she didn't love him, and he saw it in her eyes.

"God, that I could have been so deceived in you."

She told him the truth. "I wanted you to protect me from him."

"Torie, I'm thirsty." Damaris was tugging on her riding skirt.

"Why? Has he tired of you already? Does Elaine know and want you out of Drago Hall? Are you pregnant?"

"I haven't done anything. He is the one."

"Torie, what's the matter? David's yelling."

"Hush, love. David—"

"Good-bye, Victoria. If only . . . Oh, the devil. Find another witless fellow to cozen."

He dug his heels into his stallion's sides. Victoria stood swaying slightly and watched him gallop erratically through the maple trees.

"Where's David going?"

"Away, Damie. Yes, away." She turned slowly, took the child's hand, and walked to the edge of the pond. The water looked appealing, dark green and endlessly calm. It was also only two feet deep, she thought, and began to laugh at herself. She was more of a fool than David.

"Why are you laughing, Torie?"

"Laughing? Is that what I was doing? Well, I suppose there is really nothing else to do."

3

It is easy to be brave from a safe distance.

—AESOP

Victoria fisted her hands, coming fully out of the shadows on the first-floor landing when she heard the lilting strains of a waltz coming from the ballroom below. A small act of defiance. Damien was there, and she was safe, at least until the ball was over. How she wished at that moment that she could have him in her power for but five minutes. Let him plead with her, beg her not to harm him. But it was a fantasy and he would never be in her power; it was not the way the world worked. No, Damien was in the ballroom laughing, dancing, knowing that he had threatened her and lied to David—and not caring.

Damaris, thank the powers, had finally fallen asleep an hour before, and Nanny Black had plaited her wispy gray hair, picked up her Bible, and retired to her own narrow cot. Victoria leaned against the wall, taking the weight from her left leg. Her shoulder touched the edge of a portrait. She turned, startled, to see a long-ago Carstairs in periwig and purple satin holding a dog uglier than Elaine's pug, Missie. She moved away from the portrait, drew a deep breath, and tried to think clearly, but Damien's face, his words, his fierce hands, intruded.

Two hours before, he'd caught her just outside her bedchamber. He was dressed in evening clothes and he was smiling at her. A victor's triumphant smile.

"So, my little Victoria, you're not coming to the ball?"

She knew she shouldn't show him her fear, but it was difficult. "No," she said. "No, I'm not."

"I daresay Esterbridge isn't coming either."

She couldn't help herself. "You're a lying bastard, Damien. How could you be so despicable?"

He was still smiling as he stepped toward her, and she quickly jerked sideways. She wasn't fast enough. He trapped her against the wall, a hand on either side of her face. "No more running, eh? With that leg of yours you're not fast enough. Now, enough of your missishness, my dear. As for Esterbridge, the thought of that knock-kneed sod bedding you—well, consider that I have done you a favor."

He lowered his head and his hands came down to grasp her shoulders. "No!" His mouth covered hers and her cry was buried in her throat. She felt his tongue stabbing against her closed lips.

He raised his head. His look was determined. "If you lock your door against me again, Victoria, you will regret it."

"You lied to David. You said horrible things about my mother."

"Why, yes, I did, didn't I?"

"Dear God, I hate you. You will not touch me again, Damien."

"I am touching you right now." His hands came swiftly down to cup her breasts. "Victoria . . . you're soft and full. I—"

She twisted wildly. "Let me go."

Damien stared at her, feeling her trembling fear of him, and felt a surge of desire so strong it shook even him. He easily pictured her naked beneath him, struggling, but for naught, of course. No woman had ever reacted to him as Victoria was doing. It was immensely exciting, this chase, and her capture was inevitable. He said easily now, "At least I am a man, my dear, not a sniveling weakling like Esterbridge. Did I tell you I came upon him one day? Ah, yes, he was mauling a village girl. No finesse at all. Now, I am accounted a good lover. I will teach you things, show you how to please me."

She stared at him, her eyes dark and frightened in the dim light.

He laughed softly. "Why, my dear Victoria, do you fear me seeing your leg? Is that what this is all about? I shan't repine, no matter how ugly it is. Indeed, if I am repelled, then you can return to your narrow virginal bed that much sooner. Of course, you won't be a virgin then, will you?"

"I'll kill you, Damien."

He laughed, enjoying the wild excitement pounding through him. "Do try, little Victoria. I shall enjoy your efforts."

There came the sound of male footsteps. Damien slowly took two steps back. "Tonight, Victoria. Tonight I will come to you. Ah, good evening, Ligger. What is it you want?"

"Her ladyship sent me to find you, my lord."

Damien merely nodded. "Later, my dear," he said softly, only for her hearing.

She was afraid to look at Ligger. Had he truly come with a message from Elaine? Finally she looked up. Ligger's expression was wooden, his rheumy eyes unblinking, but he didn't move from his position until the baron had turned on his heel and walked away.

Ligger merely nodded, then slowly shook his head. He said very quietly, his voice emotionless, "You'd best not be alone, Miss Victoria." He followed in the direction of the baron.

Victoria opened her eyes and shook herself. The waltz was over and the orchestra was now playing a country dance. I am not helpless, she thought. I must act. I cannot let this continue. She pushed off against the wall and strode to her bedchamber. There was only one choice, she knew.

She quickly stuffed clothes and underthings into her sturdy valise, the one she'd brought with her five years before. Suddenly she stopped cold. She had no money. She wouldn't survive a day without money. She thought of Damien's study, a large airy room filled with fine Spanish leather furnishings, the one room in Drago Hall that was his own private lair. Even Elaine didn't venture into his study without his permission. He would have a strongbox there, in his big mahogany desk.

But where to stay tonight? Where would she be safe from him? She smiled. She would sleep in the nursery. Beside Damie, with Nanny Black just beyond a thin partition, her ubiquitous Bible beside her bed. And she'd be gone before dawn tomorrow.

But where?

Victoria straightened over her valise. That, she decided, she would consider before she fell asleep.

She carried her valise and cloak to the nursery. No one saw her. If Damien came to her bedchamber tonight, and she knew that he would, he would find her gone. What would he do? He would not, she guessed, try to drag her out of the nursery, even if he discovered her there. Even Baron Drago could not go that far.

She wrapped herself in her cloak and pressed against the edge of Damie's small bed. The child's even breathing calmed her.

She slept in spurts and roused herself at four o'clock in the morning. Upon jerking awake, her first thought was of Damien. What had he done when he'd found her gone? She shivered. It was cold, the air damp. She kissed Damie's soft cheek, tucked her securely in a cocoon of blankets, and left the nursery. She crept down the stairs, feeling her way, for it was dark as a pit. She lit her candle only when she had firmly closed Damien's study door.

In the bottom drawer of his desk, she found the strongbox. She had no qualms about forcing the lock with a hairpin. It came open, and she calmly counted out twenty pounds. There, she thought. It wasn't really stealing; after all, she'd been Damaris' nursemaid since the child had been born. She would return the money after she'd found a position.

She was quietly and intently replacing the strongbox when she chanced to see a pile of letters tied in a black ribbon. The top one wasn't folded properly, and she saw her name—Miss Victoria Abermarle—in a sentence written in black ink in a small cramped hand. Frowning, she pulled it out and smoothed it on the desktop. She sat in Damien's chair and brought the candle closer. It was a letter to Damien from a solicitor, Mr. Abner Westover. She read it slowly, then read it again with a growing sense of unreality.

She finished it a third time, and tucked it neatly back into the pile with the others. My God, she thought, this was incredible. At least now she knew exactly where she was going. London. To Mr. Abner Westover.

She realized her hand was shaking, not from fear, but from pure, clean rage. The bastard.

Rafael mounted his new stallion, Gadfly, that he'd purchased the day before from Viscount Newton, and clicked the white-stockinged bay forward. The stallion was strong, a good sixteen hands high, and was sweet-tempered to boot. Rafael didn't know if he could handle a stallion that was a devil, and he hadn't been stupid enough to try. His legs were used to the rolling deck of the *Seawitch*, not clamping about the belly of a horse.

"Let's go, boy," he said near Gadfly's twitching ear. "It's to London we're going." Rafael had bidden goodbye to his crew earlier, and to Hero, of course, his scruffy savior.

"You'll be careful," Rollo said.

"No more brandy," Flash added, trying to pet a struggling Hero.

Rafael merely grinned. "Keep the repairs going," he said. "I'll be in touch as soon as I can." He absently rubbed Hero's chin. "Keep our Romeo here safe. I don't want him to be a dog's sport."

"Ha," said Flash. "I pity any beast who'd take him on."

Rafael grinned as he remembered Flash's further descriptions of Hero, his temperament, his morals, and his character. Hero the Plague was his favorite epithet. He sighed, gently tugging on Gadfly's reins to turn him onto the left-branching road out of Falmouth. He didn't want to go to London. He didn't particularly want to see Lord Walton. He wanted nothing more to do with any of it, now that they had seen fit to dismiss him. Well, that wasn't really what had happened. It was simply that he'd ridden on the edge too long and had been found out. It was bound to happen, and it had. At least he was still whole-hide. He wondered, though, very often, what he was going to do with himself now. Something that mattered, something that would make him content.

He would be riding quite close to Drago Hall. The temptation was great, but even as he smelled the familiar sea air and took in the countryside, he knew it wouldn't be wise to stop. Not yet.

He would return and then he would remain.

He reached Truro by noon and stopped at one of his favorite inns, the Pengally. He wasn't at all surprised to be greeted by the host, Tom Growan, as Lord Drago. So, he thought, even though five years had passed, he and his brother still looked alike. He had halfway hoped that Damien would have gained flesh, gone bald, lost a tooth or two. He laughed at himself. He corrected Growan.

"Master Rafael? By all that's holy, is it really ye, lad?"

"Aye, Tom, it's really me, the black sheep."

"Nay, boy, don't prattle like that. Come along, and the missis will feed ye up right and proper."

The missis fed him and hovered. All the while, Tom questioned him, as bold as brass, no reticence at all in Cornishmen.

"I have business in London, Tom, but I'll return shortly. Aye, I'll build my own place. Er, how is the baron?"

Tom merely shrugged. "About the same as ever, I suppose. Don't see him all that often, not anymore."

Tom talked on, but Rafael didn't glean any satisfying information. He took his leave and rode out of Truro, heading east. He would ride within miles of Drago Hall. He felt something deep stir inside him as he neared St. Austell. Boyhood memories flooded him. Most of them good until he remembered his sixteenth year.

The year he'd realized his twin hated him. The year his twin had proved his hatred.

God, Rafael thought, and spurred the tireless Gadfly forward. He rode hard until he reached Lostwithiel, and stopped there for the night at the Bodwin Inn. There was no lovely barmaid there, but there was stargazy pie, a treat he hadn't enjoyed for years. But he found that the pilchards, with their heads poking out of the crust, took him aback for a moment. He'd become a faintheart, he thought, and shoved a particularly loathsome pilchard head beneath the crust. He took to his bed early. Tomorrow he would ride until he dropped.

He left early the next morning and didn't stop until he'd reached Liskeard. Gadfly was sweating and blowing hard. He didn't want to change horses so it meant a good rest for Gadfly. He spent several hours exploring the old town with its Norman towers and ancient cobbled streets. Later he swung Gadfly toward the sheltered south coast, remarking the palm trees, the balmy breezes, and thinking of the similarity to the Virgin Islands.

It was almost nine o'clock in the evening and he

was nearing Axmouth. The night was cloudy, with but a sliver of moon, and very warm for the end of September. It was a night for smugglers, he thought, grinning to himself. He wasn't tired and decided to push on. The curiosity from his youth brought him to a sheltered cove just south of Axmouth. He dismounted and quietly tethered Gadfly to a palm tree. Soon enough he heard voices, low yet perfectly distinct. He smiled, staying perfectly still, listening.

"Eh, a good haul, Toby."

Brandy, no doubt, Rafael thought, peering through the thick bushes toward the beach. Excellent, very expensive French brandy. He wasn't stupid; he made as invisible as he could and made not a single sound. Smugglers were a funny lot. If threatened, they were violent. He had no intention of announcing his presence.

"My Gawd, Bobby, did ye hear that?"

Rafael blinked. He'd made no noise.

"By all that's holy, 'tis a female. Up there, Bobby. Hey, wait, ye!"

A female? What female would be out here?

He heard a scream, then sounds of a scuffle. He sighed deeply.

"Hold still, missy. Gawd, she's a beauty, Toby. Just look at that pretty face."

"Aye, she is. Guess we'll have to take her to the Bishop. He'll want her, that's for sure."

"But—"

"Shut yer trap, Bobby. She ain't for the likes of ye. A proper little lady, she be. Why be ye here, missy?"

"Please, let me go. Who are you?"

"Now, that be right funny, missy. Just who do ye believe us to be? Frogs mybe?"

"We hopped right over the Channel, that's what ye believe?"

"I saw the lights and thought perhaps I was near Axmouth. I didn't know . . . are you smugglers?"

"The missy's got a rare wit, Toby. Aye, rare. It's a pity."

Rafael gently pulled his pistol from his belt. He walked quietly toward the furiously struggling female and the two smugglers. He'd heard of the Bishop. The man was a mystery, for no one knew his identity, and he'd been in charge for so many years now that Rafael had assumed he was long dead. He thought with a twisted smile that if the girl was as pretty as the men thought, the old Bishop just might adopt her. Surely he was too old now for much more.

"Ye be sure she's alone, Toby?"

"No," Rafael said very firmly, "she's not alone. She's with me. Let her go, lads."

Victoria abruptly shut her mouth, relief flooding through her. The man Toby loosed his hold on her and she stomped on his foot with all her strength. He yowled and let her go. She stumbled to the ground and lay there panting.

"Now, boys, I suggest that you take yourselves off to the Bishop with your booty. Surely there's no reason to upset him and tell him about this little mix-up. She shouldn't be here, and I promise you she won't be here again. It's obvious she knows nothing about you, and I promise you she'll say nothing about any of this."

"And who be ye?" Bobby demanded, his wits gathered again. He bent as evil an eye as he could manage at the tall man who held the gleaming pistol.

Rafael stepped closer into the light cast by the single lantern.

"Gawd, it's the bloody baron. Ain't it, Toby?"

My twin again, Rafael thought. So they were afraid of him, were they? "Go along with you now. You're safe enough, at least if you obey me."

Victoria felt her blood run cold. All her efforts, all for naught. He'd found her. He'd saved her. What to do? She came up to her knees, staring toward Damien. He wasn't dressed as he usually was. He looked as much a smuggler as the two villains who'd grabbed her, in his long black cloak and gloved hands.

"Lookee, Baron, we have no bone with ye, but this girl here—"

"I know her," Rafael said with great untruth. "She won't say a word. Now, go. You have much to do, I imagine."

Still they hesitated, and Rafael stood quietly waiting for them to finish. "Don't you trust a Cornishman, lads?"

"Aye, oh, aye," said Toby. "Come on, Bobby, leave the baron be."

Victoria watched them disappear into the shadows, their lantern swinging between them. She leapt to her feet. Unfortunately, her leg, weary from the hours of walking and the scuffle, crumpled beneath her. She fell to her knees, swallowing the moan of pain from the cramping muscles.

"Are you all right?"

Damien's voice, sounding concerned. Dear God, he was coming to her.

She screamed at him, "Stop! I won't come with you, do you understand me? I won't."

She forced herself to rise, grabbed her now very dusty valise, and ran. Pain from her leg sang through her body, making her gasp, but she didn't slow.

"For God's sake, I won't hurt you." Bloody chit,

he'd saved her, and here she was trying to escape him.

Rafael was tempted to let her go. She was probably here to meet her lover and had stumbled onto the smugglers. She was clumsily running, limping badly. obviously she'd hurt herself.

"Stop being a fool," he shouted after her.

Victoria turned suddenly to see if he was gaining on her, and her leg collapsed. She fell on her face against the weedy ground. She lay there listening, knowing it was all over for her now. He was coming closer.

"Please, please," she said, not looking up at him, "leave me alone. I won't come back with you, I won't."

Rafael stood over her crumpled figure. She was quite young; he could hear it in her voice. As for how pretty she was, he couldn't tell. She'd drawn her cloak closely about her, the hood over her head. "Whatever are you talking about?" he asked reasonably, dropping to his knees beside her.

He reached out his hand to help her, and she shrank from him. She raised her face, and even in the shadowy light from the moon, he read terror in her eyes.

"I won't hurt you."

"Liar. That's all you've wanted to do. Now you've caught me, damn you."

He stilled, even as she tried to roll away from him. "Who are you?"

Victoria vaguely heard his ridiculous question, but her pain was too great for her to say anything at the moment, her pain and her despair. Odd, but his voice sounded a bit different, a bit less smoothly polished, like his clothing.

She said finally, "What game are you playing with me now?"

"I'm not playing any game. I'm simply trying to get you away from here safely. Where is your lover? Why isn't he here?"

"I don't have a lover, and well you know it."

Rafael shook his head. He was missing something here. "Look, miss, I haven't the foggiest notion of what you're talking about. You're hurt. Let me help you."

She'd come up on her knees, but the spasms in her thigh intensified. She fell sideways. She curled up, and sobs broke from her throat. She'd tried so hard. So very hard.

He wished he could make out her features more clearly in the darkness, but no matter for now—he knew fear well enough when he heard it. She was becoming hysterical. This was all he needed, he thought with growing impatience. The girl had the nerve to come out here, of all places, and now she was falling apart. He tried to make his voice calm and soothing. "I will tell you again. I won't hurt you. Now, let me get you someplace warm and safe. You're already hurt."

Victoria sucked in her breath. He sounded impatient with her, but not angry. She didn't understand him. She felt his hand touch her and she flinched.

She raised her face to look at him. "How did you find me? I was so quiet, so careful."

"Find you? I wasn't looking for you. What is the matter with you? Did you strike your head?"

"Please, stop lying. You've won. There's nothing more I can do. Certainly I can't run from you, and well you know it."

"I'm not lying. Did you sprain your ankle?"

It was too much. He was toying with her, like a mouse in some perverted game. "I can't stop you," she said, defeat in her voice, defeat and weariness. "Will you simply leave me here when you're done with me?"

"Done with you? Done what with you? Did you hit your head? Can you tell me your name?"

"Stop it! God, I hate you."

Rafael slowly got to his feet. He tucked his pistol back into his belt. He said more to himself than to her, "Save a woman's life and she raves like a bedlamite. Look, miss, even if you hate me, even if you want me to leave you here, I'm not such a villain. No more of your hysterics, if you please. I'll take you into Axmouth. There's an inn there that will accommodate the two of us."

"No. Dear God, have you forced other females there?"

"Forced other—" He broke off. She had to have hit her head. She was making no sense at all. "It would help if you told me your name."

"I won't make it easy for you, Damien. I will go nowhere with you willingly."

Damien.

"My God," he said softly, the truth hitting square between his eyes. His twin after this girl? He said very slowly, firmly, "Shut up and listen to me, all right? Good. You believe I am Damien Carstairs? Baron Drago?"

"Of course you are. Stop mocking me."

"Well, I'm not. Mocking you, that is. As it so happens, I am his twin, Rafael Carstairs. Now, who the devil are you?"

"His twin?"' She stared at him fully now. She

knew that Damien had a twin, she'd even seen a portrait of him as a young boy. But he'd never shown his face at Drago Hall since she'd arrived there five years before.

"Yes, his twin. I gather my brother wanted you and you were trying to escape him."

Victoria drew a deep, steadying breath. "Yes. Then you came along. I thought you were Damien. You look just like him."

"Looks, as well as people, can be deceiving. Now, who the devil are you?"

"I'm Victoria Abermarle, Elaine's cousin. I've lived at Drago Hall for five years now."

Rafael grinned down at her. He dropped to his knees and thrust out his hand. Tentatively she took it. "Hello, Victoria. I have this awful feeling that I've just dropped into a bloody mess. However, one thing at a time. Will you come with me? We'll see to your ankle. You sprained it, did you not?"

She shook her head. "No, I shall be fine. I don't think it wise for me to accompany you, sir."

"No choice, sorry. I can't very well leave you, and you can't walk an inch. Do you have a horse somewhere?"

She shook her head. "No. The mail stage stopped some ten miles back. I wanted to keep going. I was afraid."

"Of Damien?"

"Yes. He tried—"

"I understand." And indeed Rafael did understand. His damned brother hadn't changed. In fact, it appeared that he'd grown a good deal worse. His wife's cousin.

Without any more hesitation he grasped her under

the arms and pulled her up. She didn't struggle. But
once on her feet, he saw the pain on her face. He
simply stood there holding her up.

"I'm sorry, truly. It's just that—"

"I can manage." He swung her up in his arms.

"My valise," she said. "I can't leave it."

He sighed, held her close, and leaned down. "Have
you every damned piece of clothing you own in
here?" he asked as he heaved it under one arm.

"Yes."

"And iron-handled hairbrushes as well?"

She smiled, her first smile in many a long hour.

He walked carefully through the undergrowth to
where his horse was tethered. "We have a problem.
I also have a valise. Well, I shall have to call on all
my ingenuity, won't I?"

He lifted her up onto the saddle. "Can you hang
on?"

"Yes, of course."

He grinned at the insulted snap of her voice.
"Here, take your valise."

It took a few more minutes of concentration and
then he swung up behind her. "Swing your leg
over."

It was her bad leg. She tried, and gasped as the
muscles screamed in protest.

"Very well, I'll hang on to you. We'll go very
slowly." He added, "I'll fetch you a doctor in
Axmouth."

"No!"

"Prickly, aren't you?"

Victoria didn't answer. She was concentrating on
staying on the horse's back. The muscles in her leg
knotted and pulled and throbbed.

"Fate," Rafael said, staring between his horse's ears, "is a bloody strange thing."

"Yes," she said, "yes, it is."

He tried bits of conversation with her, but she was silent, and he guessed from her unnatural stiffness that she was in pain. But why didn't she want a doctor?

When they came into Axmouth, Victoria forced herself to speak. "Mr. Carstairs, if you will take me to this inn you spoke about, I will be fine."

"Will you?"

"Yes. Then you may go about your business."

He sighed deeply. "What am I to do with you, Miss Abermarle?"

"Nothing. I will see to myself."

"Just as you did so very well tonight? I don't suppose you've ever heard of the Bishop?"

"Well, yes, I have. Before tonight, I thought he was just one of those Cornish legends."

"Evidently he's still very much with us. He isn't at all a man of sterling reputation."

"I know," she said on a weary sigh. "I suppose I should thank you for saving me."

"Yes, you should."

"Thank you."

Rafael pulled the tired horse to a halt in front of the Sir Francis Drake Inn. He wasn't known here, thank God. "Do you wish to be my sister or my wife?"

He felt her go perfectly still.

"Quickly, it must be one or the other."

"Sister."

"Very well."

A stable lad was there, thankfully, and Rafael

tossed him their valises. Slowly, careful not to hurt her, he dismounted, Victoria close against his chest. Her arm was around his neck. "Good girl," he said against her ear.

If the innkeeper didn't believe them to be related, he didn't say anything. He did, however, assign them adjoining rooms, a fact that made Rafael shake his head at the cynicism of his fellowman.

He carried Victoria into her small bedchamber and gently eased her down onto the bed. A maid stood close by, lighting a branch of candles.

"You may go now," Rafael said over his shoulder. He didn't turn, for he was staring down at Victoria Abermarle. Even dusty, a smudge of dirt on her cheek, her hair wildly disheveled, he saw that she was a beauty. And young, as fresh as a new winter snowfall. Chestnut hair, thick and lustrous, and blue eyes—not a faded, washed-out blue, but a vivid dark blue. No wonder Damien wanted her.

Victoria, in her turn, was looking up at him. He was so much like Damien, even those silver-gray eyes of his, that she flinched unconsciously in fear. Even in the light, she saw but one major difference— this man was deeply tanned. Unfortunately, the tan would fade.

"You are so like him."

"Yes, as I told you, we are twins. Now, I am off to fetch you a doctor for your ankle."

"No, please don't."

He heard the anxiety in her voice and frowned down at her. "Why ever not? You are obviously in pain. At least the doctor could dose you with laudanum."

She shook her head. "Please, just leave me. I'll pay you for your trouble. I'll leave in the morning."

Rafael said abruptly, "Have you had your dinner?"

She shook her head.

"Nor have I, and I'm hungry."

He strode to the door and left her alone.

Victoria stared about the bedchamber. It was spartan, with only the single narrow bed, a rough-hewn dresser, and a very old armoire in the far corner. There was a small circular table against the single window, two chairs beside it. A commode and a washbasin were, thankfully, close by. She forced herself to rise, gritting her teeth at the protesting muscles in her leg. She washed her face and hands and removed her cloak.

Rafael quietly opened the door to see his young charge clinging to the bedpost, breathing hard, her head lowered.

He noted on a purely male level that her body seemed to be as lovely as her face. Slender, tall for a girl, and as soft-looking as sweet butter.

"Come," he said, "let me help you. Our dinner will arrive in a few moments."

Victoria closed her eyes a moment, getting a grip on herself.

Rafael didn't move. He said only, "Can I assist you?"

He could see the quiver in her shoulders, see her arguing with herself. To trust him.

She decided in his favor, for she nodded.

Without another word he picked her up in his arms again, carried her to the table, and gently set her down on one of the chairs.

He moved away from her and sat in the opposite chair. He saw her lean her head back, close her eyes, and knew she was trying to control the pain.

"May I call you Victoria?"

"If you wish. I suppose it isn't any more improper than all of this."

"No, you're right about that. Call me Rafael."

"That is an odd name."

"Surely you must know that my mother was Spanish. It was her wish."

"Yes, I suppose I did know. But Damien never spoke of you, at least in my presence."

"No, I don't imagine that he would. Ah, our dinner."

He helped the serving maid with the tray. Delicious smells of roast lamb curled toward Victoria's nostrils and her stomach rumbled.

Rafael grinned. "Not a moment too soon, I'd say. Do you also like mashed potatoes and peas?"

Her stomach answered for her. He smiled and served her.

Under the cover of the table, she massaged her thigh. Slowly the muscles began to ease, the painful spasms growning more tolerable. As she gained control of the pain, she began to see everything more clearly. For all she knew, this twin could be as bad as his brother, or even worse.

They ate in silence.

"Where are you going?" she asked finally, wiping a drop of gravy from her lower lip.

"To London. Unfortunately, my ship is in Falmouth under repair, so I couldn't sail there."

London.

"I have business in London," he added.

She met his eyes. "So have I."

Rafael cracked a walnut between his long fingers. "Oh? Were you planning to walk there?"

"No, I have twenty pounds. Rather, I have eigh-

teen pounds now. I didn't realize the cost of things.
I shall have to be careful."

"Did you steal the twenty pounds?"

Her eyes flew to his face, but his concentration was
seemingly on the walnut meat.

"Not that I blame you, of course. I wonder what
Damien will do. I wonder what he has done already.
I assume he would know you're long gone."

He looked up at that moment and saw her go perfectly white. He felt like a bounder, scaring her like
that.

"You didn't stop at Drago Hall?"

"No, I didn't. Look, Victoria, I can't leave you here.
Do you have relatives in London? Anyone who could
take you in? Were you going to someone?"

She shook her head and at the same time said
quickly, "Yes."

"Ah."

"I will pay you for this room and for the meal.
How much was it?"

"Eighteen pounds," he said mildly. He poured
himself some thick black coffee, warmed his hands
on the mug, and sat back in his chair, at his ease.

"You're not a gentleman."

"It appears to me that you haven't experienced
many gentlemen in your life thus far. Actually, I suppose I am, but I also understand that it would be
difficult for you to judge. Now, what am I going to
do with you?"

"I'll leave tomorrow. Alone."

"With your eighteen pounds?"

"Yes."

"The devil you will," he said. He rose and stretched,
then turned toward her, his features softening.

She felt herself go rigid with fear.

4

Comparisons are odorous.
—SHAKESPEARE

"My God," Rafael said, coming to an abrupt stop. "Did he frighten you so much, then? You believe I am like him? You're afraid of me?"

"No. Yes. Go away."

"Very clear. Thank you."

"It is just that you look so very alike and—" She stopped and drew a deep breath. "I'm sorry, it's not your fault."

"But you're wondering if blood runs the same in twins? Bad blood or good blood?"

She raised her face at his serious tone. "No, really not. Indeed, I've never known twins before."

"Nor have I, for that matter. Suffice it to say I am not Damien. I would appreciate it if you would stop your comparisons. Now, does your ankle still pain you?"

"No," she said, wishing he would simply drop the subject. "Really, I'm fine now. I want to go to bed."

That, he thought, careful to keep his features expressionless, was an excellent idea. He was frankly surprised at his reaction to her. He'd certainly met and bedded more beautiful women. Not that she wasn't lovely, of course. It was just that— Oh, the devil. He didn't know what it was about her. Lord knew he wasn't in the market for a damned wife. *Wife?* He was losing his mind, that was it. He shook his head at himself, saying as he did so, "Shall I order up a bath for you?"

Victoria felt sweaty and dusty. She knew that warm water would soothe the muscles in her leg. She nodded gratefully. "I must look a skelter-patty."

"No, just something of an urchin."

She was still sitting in the chair when he returned some five minutes later. "It will be up soon," he said, sitting across from her. "Did you eat enough?"

"Yes. The lamb was delicious, the carrots not over-cooked, the potatoes—"

"All right, I'm not your nanny. Now, tell me about the baron."

"There's really not all that much to tell. I simply couldn't let him come into my room and—"

Her voice faded into the wainscoting, and Rafael didn't push.

"All right, we'll leave that for the moment. I gather you have no wish to return to Drago Hall?"

"I will never go back there. Never."

"What about your cousin, Elaine?"

"I don't know," Victoria said, lowering her head, her eyes on her clenched hands.

"You didn't speak to her, then, about her husband's behavior toward you?"

"No, I did not. You see, Elaine is increasing. The baby is due after Christmas. So I really couldn't upset her, not in her condition. I really didn't know what to do. I think, however, that she has guessed something. She became more curt toward me."

Looking at her, Rafael didn't doubt it. But still, the thought of a man taking advantage of a young lady under his protection made his stomach turn. Her jaw was stubborn, he saw. She'd refused to stay and become a victim. She'd escaped with but twenty pounds. Yes, very stubborn. He admired that.

"Here's your bath. We will speak some more when you're finished. I trust you have a dressing gown in that valise?"

"Why?" she said, looking at him blankly.

"Because," Rafael said with exaggerated patience, "I wish to speak to you about what we're going to do. I have no wish to frighten you again."

"Oh."

He nodded and walked to the adjoining door. He said over his shoulder, showing his white teeth in a roguish smile, "I too have a dressing gown."

"I am exquisitely relieved," she said, showing her own white teeth. He gave her a mock salute and strode into his bedchamber, closing the adjoining door behind him.

Victoria didn't undress until the maid had left. It was more a habit than anything else. Ever since Elaine had seen her leg with its knotting muscles she didn't want to feel another's pity or revulsion. She spent fifteen minutes in the hot water, feeling the muscles loosen and relax. She sighed deeply, and leaned back against the copper tub rim. She started up when she heard a light tap on the adjoining door.

"Victoria? Are you ready for me?"

"No," she called, "not yet."

"Is your ankle all right?"

"Yes, please, I'll just be a moment."

He should have fetched a doctor, Rafael thought, staring at the closed door. But she seemed to have eased during their dinner. He turned back into his room and sat down, waiting. He was tired, weary to his bones. He was a long way from Falmouth and Lindy and it was a long way to London. A very long way.

When she called to him, he was half-asleep. He blinked his eyes and wits awake and went to her. She was seated again in her chair, her nightgown covered by a very prim schoolgirl muslin dressing gown that was tied by a ladder of blue ribbons to her chin.

"How old are you?" he asked.

"Nearly nineteen. December the fifth."

"In that maidenly casing you're wearing you look like a little girl. Didn't your cousin, my dear sister-in-law, clothe you properly? Aren't you to have a Season? Meet gentlemen, attend endless balls, and all that?"

"No, and I didn't expect to," she said with no regret that he could detect. "You see, I thought I was the poor relation until I just happened to see—"

Her eyes widened as she realized what she'd given away. She ducked her head down, color rising on her cheeks. Stupid fool.

Rafael sighed. Trust, he supposed, was an elusive sort of thing. Not given lightly. And after all, he was the spitting image of his brother.

He let the fish gently off the hook. "You said you are going to London."

She nodded.

"You said you had business there. Relatives also?"

"No, no one. But you already guessed that, didn't you?"

He said very patiently, "Listen to me, my child; a young lady doesn't go alone anywhere. Look what very nearly happened to you tonight."

"I shall be more careful in the future."

"I applaud your courage, but your naiveté will bring you low."

"I might not be of your advanced years, but I am not all that naive."

"If not naive, then stupid."

"That is unkind of you. I think I would rather fit the pattern card of naiveté than stupidity."

He grinned and said without further consideration, "All right, I'll escort you to London."

"Escort me? Are you certain? Are you jesting with me?"

"Do I sound like I'm carried away with hilarity?"

"No. Rafael, you don't mind, truly?"

He winced at the plea in her voice. "No, I don't mind. However, what am I going to do with you once we're there?"

Her chin went up. "I have someone to see there. After I have seen him, I shan't have to worry about money. I will be able to see to myself."

Rafael wasn't either naive or stupid. "So you discovered you really aren't Elaine's poor relation?"

She paled under his interested gaze.

"I won't tell my brother. To tell you the truth, Victoria, there's little love lost between us. Now it's your turn for some home truths. Go ahead, I'm listening. You stole twenty pounds—"

"Yes, from Damien's strongbox, in his study. I will pay it back. It was then that I saw a packet of letters. One of them wasn't folded quite properly."

"And you unfolded it?"

"I saw my name written on the unfolded part. It

was to Damien from a solicitor in London. I'm not poor. I'm really quite well-off, it would appear. At least I hope I still am."

"Damien is your guardian?"

"I don't know. I suppose so. He has never spoken of anything to me. No one told me I had any money. I guess it is from my mother's side of the family. Father had the good name, you see, but few farthings in his pockets."

"I imagine that Damien has been making free with your funds," Rafael said quietly, more to himself than to her. "Hopefully he has shown some good sense in his financial dealings." Rafael sat back in his chair and steepled his fingers, lightly tapping them together.

"I don't think so. The letter from the solicitor said something about his concern with the principal. I don't know anything more."

"So you were going to leave Drago Hall even before you knew you were an heiress?"

"Yes. I really don't know if I'm what you would call an heiress. There is money, that's all I know."

"You planned to escape with a paltry twenty pounds?"

"I had no choice. In my position, what would you have done?"

I would have beaten him senseless, Rafael wanted to say. But of course he was a man, a very strong man, not a young girl dependent on a man for the roof over her very head, the same man who also wanted to make her his mistress.

"I would have perhaps done the same."

"No, you wouldn't have. You're just trying to make me feel better. Less naive, less stupid."

"Victoria, you couldn't very well have coshed him

on the head or planted your fist in his face. You did very well until the smugglers."

"If it weren't for a kind Fate, I should be a morsel on this Bishop's plate."

Rafael had never before been a kind Fate. It wasn't the worst thing a man could be. He grew thoughtfully silent and she watched in fascination as he began again to tap his fingertips rhythmically together. He was thinking that he was a bachelor, that he knew absolutely no proper female in London. He was at an impasse. Suddenly he remembered Lyon Ashton, the Earl of Saint Leven, laughingly telling him of his tartar great-aunt, Lady Lucia Cranston. She lived in London, the old martinet, and tried to govern his life whenever he was within firing range. She had, Lyon said, decided that he and Diana Savarol would match up perfectly. And damn the old lady's hide, she'd been right.

"I know what to do now," he said, straightening.

At his smile, she said, "It is something proper, I trust, sir?"

"Pure as the driven snow. My idea, that is."

"Well?"

He grinned as he rose. "I think I'll leave you in a bit of suspense. We'll leave early in the morning." He paused, looking at her carefully. "I will hire a carriage."

"I can ride."

"It would take us three days' hard riding to reach London, perhaps even four."

Victoria thought of her leg and the inevitable strain. She knew Rafael wouldn't think she was suffering again from a sprained ankle. Nor could she see herself limping into the solicitor's office. She sighed. "All right, a carriage, then. And, Rafael, I shall pay you back."

"Of a certainty you will," he said. "With interest from your immense fortune."

"It might not be all that immense."

"We shall see."

"I shall see. Once you've escorted me to London, you can be on your way and well rid of me."

"We shall see about that too."

He turned slightly at the adjoining door. She was still seated in the chair, her profile turned toward him. Why the devil did he have this near-compulsion to kiss her and smooth her hair and tell her he would give his life to protect her? She had a very stubborn jaw.

Elaine sat in front of her dressing table, rhythmically brushing her long hair. It was thick and black as a raven's wing and it was her vanity and a source of great pride. She saw her husband enter her room and said, "I simply don't understand it, Damien. How could Victoria be so ungrateful? Damaris is carrying on and Nanny Black can't quiet her." She was studying him closely in the mirror, alert and watchful, but his expression didn't change.

"I have sent out men in search of her, my dear," he said, yawning. "We should hear something soon." What he didn't tell her was that he was certain Victoria had seen the tied letters that were beneath the strongbox. He'd discovered that fact but a few minutes before, and felt his jaw clench with helpless rage. Damn, he should have burned the letters, but who would have thought—? Well, he would find her. He said now, disinterested as a clam, "In fact, you seem so very worried, my dear, that I intend to join the search on the morrow. I believe it likely she has gone to London."

"But she had no money."

"As a matter of fact, she took some twenty pounds from my strongbox."

"That little thief. After all I've done for her, and she a worthless cripple."

Damien merely shrugged.

Elaine continued with her brushing, calm again, watchful. "I wonder," she said, again studying her husband's face in her mirror, "why she ran away."

"I imagine it was that pitiful bore David Esterbridge. He was after her, you know. Perhaps she was escaping from him."

"I can't think that is true. Don't you remember? She was talking of David as if she'd made up her mind to wed him. I truly don't believe David could be responsible for her running away."

"That isn't what David told me. Evidently she changed her mind. I wouldn't put it past the stupid boy to have frightened her, mauled her about with no finesse and all that."

"Lord knows she should take him. He's probably the only chance she has at a decent match."

"But then you would lose an excellently suitable companion for Damaris, would you not?"

"Why do you believe she's gone to London?"

"Let me just say I believe it her only alternative."

Elaine wanted to probe, but he was removing his dressing gown. He was quite naked. She watched him climb into her bed. She closed her eyes, but she could see his member swelling, feel his hands, so knowing, his hands.

"I am breeding, of course," she said in a thin voice.

He laughed. "Indeed. Your shape has become rather unusual. But I shan't repine. I wish my son to know his father."

He would make her want him, she thought as she slowly set down her brush. He would make her lose control, forget things, ignore what she more than guessed. God, she hated Victoria. The little viper, betraying her in her own home. Had Damien already bedded her cousin? Was Victoria in fact pregnant and Damien had sent her away? To London? Was he going to set her up there as his mistress? She shook her head even as she walked toward the bed. He wouldn't do that, he couldn't.

"Elaine?"

"You are so certain it is your heir I carry?"

"Yes." He patted the pillow beside his. "If you are not, then we will simply have to continue trying. Come now, Elaine. I believe I want your very warm mouth tonight."

"All right," she said. "Yes."

Victoria resigned herself to a long day of boredom. Rafael, curse him, was riding, and she was alone in the bouncing carriage. The carriage was an ancient, very musty excuse for a vehicle and it was as poorly sprung as Nanny Black's single chair that had belonged to her mother's mother. It was pulled by two singularly independent bays, each wanting to pull in a different direction. The driver, Tom Merrifield, a spare, balding man of fifty with a bland expression and equally bland outlook on his fellow humans, took the carriage and the bays in stride, having agreed in the fewest words imaginable to drive them to London and enjoy something of a holiday with Rafael's money, then return carriage and horses to Mr. Mouls in Axmouth.

Victoria wondered how long it would take her to get her money from Mr. Westover. This excursion would cost her dearly, though Rafael hadn't said a word about the carriage cost or Mr. Merrifield's demands. She tried to pay attention to the passing scenery, but the movement of the carriage wasn't all that comforting to her stomach.

As for Rafael, he thought of many things that day. Tom Merrifield, that man of so few words, was a robber, and that was what Rafael had told him. Tom cracked a smile. "Nay, 'tis London, ye know. Now, there be a place I have no wish to go."

But he'd agreed, of course, after Rafael had offered him an exorbitant amount, and called him a bloody robber.

"It's all a simple matter of which hat a man wants and what is available," said Tom Merrifield, and spit.

It amused Rafael to realize after some hours that his thoughts continually went to the girl who rode in the carriage some distance behind him. He found himself turning every once in a while to assure himself that she was there, and safe. Which of course she was.

He thought of the inevitable problems that would arise very quickly upon their arrival in London. Victoria was so certain that she could simply wend her innocent way to the solicitor and claim her inheritance. If Damien were her guardian, he would probably be in control of her and her money until she was twenty-one, perhaps older. In complete control of her, according to the laws of the land.

When they halted for lunch, he watched her closely

and was reassured. She bubbled on about a poet named Coleridge, a fellow he'd never heard of.

"He is still alive, you know," Victoria said, chewing on a strawberry. "I think he lives in the Lake District."

He let her prattle on. Let her enjoy herself for the time being, at least. Lord knew she was in for a crashing fall in London.

"Are you tired, Rafael?" she said at last, shoving her plate back.

"Tired? Why ever should I be tired?"

"Well, you have been so very quiet."

"You've done all the talking. Since I am a gentleman, I would not interrupt you."

Victoria hoped he was teasing her, but she wasn't certain. "You aren't regretting our trip, are you?" she said at last.

"Yes, but no matter." He shrugged and looked out the inn window to see Tom Merrifield talking to the ostler. He wondered if the ostler knew he was talking to a damned bloody robber. "Are you ready, Victoria?"

Because of excellent weather and an equally excellent pair of horses Tom had bargained for with Rafael's money—an excellent bargain—Rafael kept them on the road until they reached Broadwindsor.

He didn't know the innkeeper at the Bisley and he felt his hands clench at the man's leer.

"Your sister, sir?"

Victoria, bless her innocent heart, was giving her attention to the particularly fine molding that was three centuries old and, Rafael suspected, bug-ridden.

He kept his voice calm, though he gave the innkeeper the look that had brought many a recalcitrant sailor into line. That's right. I should like the rooms to adjoin," he added. "One can never be too careful about protecting a lady."

The innkeeper drew himself up at that, and crisply called out for a lad.

The private dining room Rafael hired for the evening was small and rather airless. The furnishings were as ancient as the moldings, Rafael thought as he helped Victoria into her chair. She'd changed from her girlish gown into yet another, equally girlish gown of pale pink muslin. They were served boiled beef, stewed tomatoes, and a kidney pie. He told her she shouldn't wear pastels.

She didn't rise to his bait, and simply agreed with him, which made him frown. "I wish you would prattle a bit. What's the matter with you?"

She smiled. "I'm just a bit tired. I'm not used to so many endless hours of travel in a closed carriage."

Rafael said finally, "If you would like to ride with me tomorrow, I can arrange a mount for you."

Instant color brightened her cheeks and her eyes. "Oh, yes, thank you, Rafael. It's so very boring, you know, to ride alone. And it was quite hot."

She prayed her leg wouldn't betray her. It was just one day, after all. She took her first enthusiastic bite of the kidney pie. "You said you haven't been to Drago Hall for five years. Where have you been for all that time?"

"Here and there," he said easily.

"What countries are those? Or perhaps they are capitals?"

"I am a sea captain. My ship, the *Seawitch*, is docked in Falmouth this very moment, undergoing repairs. If she hadn't been damaged in a storm, I shouldn't have met you."

Victoria forgot all about her dinner. "*Seawitch*," she said, savoring the word. "You are so very lucky. Now I must call you Captain Carstairs."

He was peeling a ripe peach. "No, not anymore. My first mate, Rollo Culpepper, will take her over now. I'm going to return to Cornwall and become a landed gentleman."

She leaned forward, cupping her chin in her hands. "Five whole years with your own ship. The excitement of it all. Whilst I was trailing about Drago Hall becoming a very boring person, you were sailing everywhere. Did you go to China?"

"China?" He smiled and handed her a slice of peach. "No, not China. I did, however, just return from the Caribbean."

"You're a merchant?"

"I suppose you could say that. I do owe my improved fortune to trading."

"Come, Rafael, you are being entirely too close-mouthed. Please, tell me of your adventures."

"Victoria, you're not boring."

"No? Well, I am certainly nothing compared to you. Come on, now, tell me."

He described Tortola to her, and St. Thomas. He told her of mangos and how they tasted. He mentioned Diana Savarol and Lyon, the Earl of Saint Leven. "I married them at sea," he said, grinning in fond recollection. "Perhaps we will meet them. Who knows?"

"How could that happen? We will go our own ways when we reach London."

"Well, not immediately. Have you no curiosity, Victoria? Don't you wish to know where I'm taking you in London?"

She grinned, an impish grin that brought out a dimple in her right cheek. "I decided that I should act uninterested in the entire matter. That way, you would tell me all that much sooner."

He handed her another slice of peach and watched her eat it. A drop of peach juice trickled down her chin and he leaned forward and dabbed it off with the tip of his napkin. Victoria didn't move. She cocked her head to one side, merely staring at him.

He said abruptly, "You remember the Earl of Saint Leven I mentioned?"

"Yes, and Diana, his countess."

"I'm taking you to the earl's great-aunt, Lady Lucia. I have never met the lady, but Lyon told me all about her."

Victoria chewed that over in silence. "What if she doesn't want to take me in?"

"I shall be my charming self. How could a lady, any lady, refuse me?"

"I certainly wouldn't," she said with alarming candor, "but that is no test, surely. Oh, dear, what if she doesn't like me? She doesn't know me either, Rafael."

"Don't worry before you have to," he said, wiping the peach juice from his fingers.

"Why do you and Damien dislike each other?"

He stared at her. "That is a disconcerting habit you have."

"Oh?"

"Yes. You ask a question entirely out of context. Does your victim usually spurt out an answer before thinking?"

She sighed. "No, just Damaris."

"Who is Damaris?"

"Why, she is your niece. She is three years old and could easily pass for your daughter as well. She loves me and I miss her dreadfully."

"I didn't know."

"Obviously the reason you didn't know is that you and the baron haven't spoken. For five years?"

"A bit longer, actually."

"Why?"

"Don't pry, Victoria. A lady strives to keep impertinent comments and questions behind her teeth."

"David did too."

He blinked. "Who is David and what did he do too?"

"David Esterbridge, the son of Squire Esterbridge."

"I remember him. He was a paltry boy, as I recall, always whining when he lost at a game. Of course, to be fair, he was somewhat younger than I. What does he have to do with anything?"

She sat back in her chair. "I believe that that is an impertinence."

"Not when you brought it up, ma'am."

" 'Ma'am,' am I? Well, I suppose you are right. What I meant was that I could draw a question out of my hat and David would immediately spring for an answer."

"How old is Esterbridge?"

"Twenty-three."

"Ah, so he was a suitor?"

"He was, that's true."

"What happened?"

Victoria wasn't about to tell anyone of that dreadful debacle. Rafael was regarding her, at the best, with mild interest. She said only, "I had decided to marry him, to escape, you see, from Damien and Drago Hall. Unfortunately, it didn't—well, we determined that we wouldn't suit."

"I pray you won't stop now, my dear. I'm fairly crackling with interest."

Victoria raised her chin and her eyes flashed with remembered anger and hurt, but she managed in a nicely distant voice, "It was a boring denouement, truly. He didn't really want to wed me, nor I him."

Rafael gave her his best incredulous expression.

It was an excellent ploy, and Victoria found herself quickly filling in the silence. "It's odd. According to David, it was his father who wanted to have me for a daughter-in-law. Perhaps he knew I wasn't a poor relation, perhaps he wanted my money."

"I doubt that sincerely. Damien, whatever his failings, never would make free with information that was of a private nature, and your money would have been very private."

"Yes," Victoria said, "perhaps. I think it was for the best. I didn't love David, you see. It would have been unfair to him had I married him."

"Oh? He wasn't the one to break things off?"

"Well, perhaps. A bit. Somewhat, I guess."

Rafael laughed. "Well done, my girl. If you learn more such definitive words, I pray you will tell me."

"Maybe, if it pleases me to do so."

"I begin to believe that a girl raised in Cornwall has a sufficient measure of wits. You please me, Victoria."

She ducked her head at that compliment and fiddled with her napkin.

"As for David Esterbridge, he's what I'd call meager, no shoulders, you know. Not at all a sterling specimen."

"That's what I thought, but I felt ashamed to be so very unkind in my appraisal of him."

"As for you, you would have made his life a misery."

"Misery. You make it sound as though I am some sort of termagant—"

"No, not at all. But you are strong-willed, are you not? I venture to say that most other young ladies, finding themselves in such an untenable situation as you did, would have succumbed."

Mollified, Victoria smiled, just a bit. "One has to be a bit strong-willed if one is much alone," she said without a shade of self-pity.

He was glad that he'd asked her to ride with him on the morrow. He rose, scraping back his chair. "It's late. I wish to leave early. I shall see you to your bedchamber."

Victoria frowned over at him. Had she said something to anger him? She didn't think so, but her experience with men wasn't all that impressive. She followed him to her room, where he left her with a nod and a curt good night.

By the following afternoon, she knew she'd made a grave mistake in judgment.

5

*Pain will force even the truthful
to speak falsely.*
—PUBLILIUS SYRUS

Victoria gritted her teeth against the painful spasms that rippled in her thigh. She'd realized, all too late, of course, that an entire day of riding might prove too great a strain. She hadn't thought. She nearly laughed aloud, remembering how she'd been so anxious to ride the entire distance to London.

She closed her eyes, willing herself to control the pain. The mare, sensing that her rider was losing control, snorted, flinging her head up, and wheeled to the left.

"Victoria. Pay attention to your mount."

She set her jaw and brought the mare under control. She should have broken it off when they'd stopped for lunch. But then, she'd felt only a tightening, not really any pain.

It was only early afternoon, a warm, blue-skied day in Somerset. But Victoria was beyond basking in the lovely day and the sweet-scented grass of the fields beside the road. At a particularly vicious spasm, she knew she had no choice.

"Rafael," she called. He was riding a little way ahead of her, and at the sound of her voice, he pulled up, turning in his saddle.

"I think I should like to ride in the carriage for a while."

He grinned. "Your bottom hurt?"

If only that were true, she thought, not taking offense at his outrageous remark. "No. It's just that I would like to ride in the carriage now."

His grin fell away and he looked at her with lowered brows. Did she look different? Was her voice shaky?

He said with appalling frankness, "Do you need to relieve yourself?"

"No."

"Well, then, why? I thought you wanted to ride all the way to London. Your bottom is sore, isn't it?"

This time, she wasn't too much of a fool to grasp at the proffered straw. "I am sore. I've never ridden so long and at such a pace."

Still, he continued with that steady look of his. She was pale, and there was something in her eyes that wasn't quite right.

"Please."

"Very well." He wheeled back and waited for the carriage to round the bend just behind them. Victoria was relieved. He wasn't paying her any attention at the moment. Slowly, painfully, she managed to slide off the mare's back. She clung to the mane, willing her leg not to collapse beneath her.

"Giving your mare a kiss?"

"Only in the morning. She's too sweaty now."

"That's better. Pull over, Tom, our lady wishes to ride in the carriage."

"Aye," Tom called. "Ye wish to lead the mare, or will ye tie her to the back?"

"The back, I think."

It wasn't a great distance, only a few steps. She had only not to disgrace herself for six steps. Tom opened the carriage door. Victoria looked at the door, then back to Rafael. Thank God, he was tying the mare to the back of the carriage, on a long lead, paying no attention to her.

She managed to make it to the door, then grasped it when her leg collapsed.

"Miss? What be the matter with ye?"

"Nothing, Tom, really."

He snorted in obvious disbelief, then hefted her up into the carriage without ceremony.

Victoria sank onto the soft cushions, stretching out her leg. Automatically her fingers went to the tortured muscles and began to knead them.

Rafael's face appeared in the doorway. "Are you all right?"

"Certainly," she said. "Go along. We still have some hours of daylight."

He frowned a bit, but nodded. "Very well."

She watched him stride back to his stallion and gracefully climb into the saddle. To be free like that, she thought. Never to fear others seeing your weakness, never to feel the ghastly pain.

Her fingers went back to the knotting muscles.

Three more days, she thought, three more days of riding in this bloody carriage. She wouldn't be such a fool as to ride again. Well, perhaps in the mornings. Yes, until they stopped for luncheon.

If Rafael wondered why she rode her mare only

until they stopped for luncheon each day, he said nothing. She was, after all, a lady, and ladies didn't have a man's endurance. He found her appetite for his adventures insatiable, and over dinner each evening he told her of places he'd visited and things he'd done. He told her about his grandparents and the immense parcel of cousins, aunts, and uncles who all lived in Spain. He told her of America, its vastness, its mix of people, from the Boston merchants and their whaling ships to the Virginia planters and their huge numbers of slaves. He told her of the Mediterranean and the incredible Rock of Gibraltar, and the pirates from North Africa who still preyed on unwary ships. He told her of Jamaica, of the Barretts and the Palmers, and how the sugar plantations were run. He always tired before she did.

"Enough," was his invariable ending, and her invariable response was a disappointed sigh. Had she been so bereft of companionship, then? So very alone? Very probably, he thought, until Damien noticed that his little cousin-in-law had become a tempting morsel.

Victoria wasn't at all stupid and she soon realized that the places he told her about in the most detail were where English soldiers and Napoleon's men fought. He'd been much more than a simple sea captain, it was obvious to her, but she held her peace. Perhaps he was still involved in activities of a secret nature. If she pried, he might not tell her any more of his more innocuous adventures.

Their last night was spent in Basing. Rafael managed a private dining room, despite a boxing match that was being held nearby. Victoria, he quickly discovered, had become too quiet for his taste.

"You're scared, aren't you?" he said finally, pouring her another glass of wine.

"A bit. And excited. I've never been to London before. What if this Lady Lucia isn't there, Rafael? What if she takes me into dislike? Or you?"

"Don't worry about it. Here, have some lamb. It looks quite nice."

She ate little. Rafael began a tale of how he'd met his valet, Savory, who had remained with the *Seawitch*. "I met him when he was only fourteen years old. His nickname when I met him was Flash, and it still is what he is called. 'Flash,' because by his eighth year of life he was the fastest pickpocket in all of London, he told me."

"Goodness, a criminal."

"Well, I suppose so. He was quite good, only I was just a bit faster. While he was pinching my money, right out of my coat pocket, mind you, I just happened to sneeze. I shall never forget the look on his face when I had my arm around his neck."

He was grinning with the memory, and Victoria leaned forward, fascinated. "However did he become your valet?"

"I made him a deal. He agreed to be my valet for three months. If he disliked it, I would pay him twenty pounds and turn him loose again on the innocent of London. He liked it. He is an excellent friend, and thankfully, an excellent sailor. I do believe that's what turned the trick, and not my sterling personality. I do wonder occasionally if he will leave me once I tell him I won't be putting out to sea again."

"Back to being the Flash of London?"

"I hope not. I think I might have him join us in London after I send Tom Merrifield back to Cornwall. I'll tell him it is the ultimate test of his lawfulness."

It rained only when they'd reached the outskirts

of London. But Victoria was too excited to be forced back into the carriage. Rafael found himself smiling at her enthusiasm, but said firmly, "I don't wish you to take a chill, nor do I wish to present you to Lady Lucia looking like a drowned rat."

He bundled her back into the carriage, turned up his collar, and pulled his hat firmly about his ears.

He began to doubt his own judgment when, upon arriving in Grosvenor Square and asking directions from a soaked sweep boy, he saw the imposing facade of Lady Lucia's town house. What if she wasn't in residence? What if Lyon were wrong and she turned up her nose at him? He swore. He had all Victoria's worries, then some.

"It's beautiful, isn't it, Rafael?"

"I want you to remain in the carriage. I will speak first with this Lady Lucia. Don't move, Victoria."

His knock was answered by an imposing butler of advanced years and equally advanced dignity. "Sir?"

Rafael identified himself and asked to see Lady Lucia.

"She is tatting, sir, and doesn't wish to be disturbed."

"Tatting? Good God, man, what the devil is that?"

Didier unbent a trifle. "It is something Lady Lucia despises, a form of needlework. She considers it in the nature of a penance." Realizing he'd spoken too frankly to an absolute stranger, Didier frowned down his nose and added, "Should you like to leave your card?"

"No, tell the lady I am providing a new penance. Whatever sin or sins she's committed, tell her that this penance will be more than adequate for her needs. That is the new penance in the carriage." He waved toward Victoria's face. "It is urgent that I speak with her, as you can see from the rain dripping off the lady's nose."

Didier pondered. Her ladyship was growing a bit drawn in the withers. She was punishing herself with the endless irksome tatting because she'd read the entire batch of new gothic tales from Hookham's all in a week. He'd gently suggested that the tatting could wait for a snowy winter day, and she'd frowned at him and told him to stick his nose back in Cook's business.

A new penance, was it? He looked toward the carriage through the drizzle and indeed saw a lady's face.

"Very well, sir. Please come in."

Lady Lucia was bored. Drat that overbearing Didier anyway. And the tatting looked like no scarf she'd ever before encountered. Lyon and Diana hadn't yet returned from the West Indies, but the Earl and Countess of Rothermere were due in London sometime soon, and the earl's father, the Marquess of Chandos, as well. Ah, well, not too many more days filled with boredom, baiting Didier, and the ghastly tatting.

When Didier appeared in the doorway, she frowned at him. "Don't say it, Didier, I'm in no mood for more of your impertinence."

"A new penance has arrived, my lady."

"Eh? What the devil are you talking about? Have you finally fallen into your dotage? About time, I say."

"No. A gentleman is here, a Captain Rafael Carstairs, and a young lady is very nearly here."

She brightened. "A captain, Didier? A captain of what, pray?"

"I haven't the foggiest notion of his antecedents, my lady, or of his current affiliations."

"Dratted academician Show him in."

Lucia's eyes widened when the very handsome man came striding into her drawing room, a black greatcoat swirling about his booted ankles. He was somewhat wet—only to be expected, of course, since it had been drizzling for hours now. She quickly stuffed her tatting beneath her chair cushion and rose.

Beautiful eyes, she thought, a pale silver gray. Lovely thick black hair, and a presence to make even old Mrs. Ackerson's heart do a double beat.

Rafael regarded the proud old woman. She did look a terror with her very straight carriage and her gimlet eyes. "My name is Rafael Carstairs, ma'am. Thank you for seeing me. I married Lyon and Diana."

Lucia didn't blink. "You're really a vicar, then?"

He grinned at the disbelief and disappointment in her voice. "No, ma'am. I am captain of the *Seawitch*. I sailed Diana and Lyon to the West Indies. Lyon told me all about you. He said that if he were ever in trouble, you were the one to save his hide. I'm in trouble, ma'am, and desperately need your help."

"All ears, Didier? Fetch some brandy for Captain Carstairs."

"The penance in the carriage, my lady?"

Rafael laughed aloud. "That is my problem, ma'am. Her name is Victoria Abermarle and she is very young and I don't know anyone in London to take care of her."

"Fetch Miss Abermarle, Didier, and see to Captain Carstairs' horses and carriage."

"First, madam, the brandy."

Rafael had but a few minutes to prepare Lady Lucia for her treat. He wondered how much of the truth was in order, and decided to put forth only the skeleton of the situation. It wasn't even enough for a worthy skeleton, he thought, after telling her that Victoria had run away from her cousin's home because she'd been unhappy, and although he himself had never met her, he'd saved her from smugglers and brought her with him to London.

"That's not all of it by any means," Lucia said comfortably, "but it will suffice for now. Ah, here is my penance. Miss Abermarle? Come here, child, and let me have a look at you."

Victoria faltered. She swallowed and took three steps forward. "Yes, ma'am." She dropped a curtsy. Lucia nodded, pleased with her grace.

"Come closer, child, I won't eat you. Victoria, eh? A nice name, a bit stiff and formal, of course, but it will do. Now, who are your parents?"

"Sir Roger Abermarle and Lady Beatrice, ma'am."

"There are Abermarles in Sussex. Your kin?"

"No, ma'am. My parents lived in Dorset. I have no relatives except for a cousin in Cornwall."

"Ah, well, no matter. Sit down, child. You need something invigorating. Didier, some Madeira. Where the devil is that cursed man?"

Rafael met Victoria's startled eyes and smiled.

"You're a beauty," Lucia said suddenly. "I trust your nature is as lovely as your countenance."

"I will vouch for her good nature, my lady," Rafael said. "As I told you, I have been her escort."

"Very improper, of course, but it can't be helped now. Hmmm."

Didier appeared, and his impassive features softened. Her ladyship was primed and ready for a new adventure, he saw. This Carstairs fellow seemed honest enough, and the young lady—well, a bit travel worn and— "I shall bring in some tea and cakes directly," he said, and left.

"Well, I say," Lady Lucia said. "He left before I could tell him to bring some Madeira."

"Tea would be wonderful and I am terribly hungry," Victoria said, then shut her mouth.

I shall have the truth, all of it, out of her in no time at all, Lucia thought, pleased. The girl had about as much guile as Diana Savarol. No, she thought, grinning, not Savarol. The Countess of Saint Leven. She rubbed her hands together. No need to probe now. Captain Carstairs was smooth as a pebble underwater, and likely wouldn't give away much, but the girl— She couldn't wait. She trusted that the very handsome Captain Carstairs wasn't married.

After generalities over tea and delicious lemon cakes, Lucia said abruptly, "Captain Carstairs, you will return here for dinner. Eight o'clock, mind, no later. As for Miss Abermarle, I will see that she's made comfortable. You may go now."

Rafael, stifling a grin at the agonized, very frightened look from Victoria, nodded and took Lady Lucia's hand. "Thank you, ma'am. Very much."

Of Didier he asked quietly in the entranceway, "I need some rooms. What can you recommend?"

Within an hour Rafael was possessed of rooms on Courtney Street, only fifteen minutes from Lady Lucia's town house.

As for Victoria, she was looking wide-eyed at the lovely bedchamber. "Ah," said Lucia, "this is Grumber. She sees to all my needs, doesn't talk much, and always screws her mouth up like she's just eaten a lemon. Don't mind her. She's not a bad sort at all. Grumber, this is Miss Abermarle."

"Hello, Grumber."

"Miss."

"Now, Grumber," said Lucia, "don't turn your nose up at Miss Abermarle's clothing. We shall improve on those silly girlish muslins in no time at all. My dear, you shall take a rest now, and Grumber will come for you in good time to change for dinner."

Lucia made her way to the door, only to stop abruptly and say over her shoulder, "My dear, is the good captain married?"

"No, ma'am. He has just come home from the sea, I gather."

"For good, I trust," said Lucia. "Rest now, my dear."

With that command, Victoria was soon left to her own devices. She stood in the middle of the room thinking vaguely of the unexpectedness of fate. "Well," she said aloud to the empty chamber, "this can't be worse than Damien or that Bishop smuggler person."

She removed her shoes and stretched out on the very comfortable bed. Very quickly she was enjoying the sleep of the innocent.

Lucia, a strategist of the first order, carried the gown to Victoria's bedchamber. She heard the splashing of the bathwater and grinned. She knocked lightly, then opened the door and entered.

Victoria gasped until she saw Lady Lucia.

"Oh, ma'am."

"Don't drown yourself, my dear. I'm not Captain Carstairs. Now, just finish your washing. I've brought you a gown left by my niece, Diana Savarol. Did Captain Carstairs tell you about her?"

Victoria, routed utterly, nodded even as she continued with the bathing sponge on her left knee. "Yes. ma'am."

Lucia looked at the very slender shoulders showing above the edge of the tub. "How bountiful is your bosom?"

Victoria couldn't help herself. She laughed. "Not excessive bounty there, I'm afraid, ma'am."

"Pity. Diana, as my nephew Lyon was wont to point out, is very amply endowed. I fear this dress won't fit you. Well, no mind. We will go shopping tomorrow for you."

"But, ma'am, you don't know me."

"We'll remedy that in short order, don't you think? Of course you do. As Didier will tell you, if he's in one of his moods, you are providing me with much-needed entertainment. Now, my child, out of that tub. I will leave you. Grumber! Do come and be of some assistance."

But Victoria very firmly told Grumber she didn't need any assistance.

"Your hair, miss," said Grumber, and her pained voice told Victoria that she was in dire need.

"Can you come back to me, then, Grumber, in about thirty minutes?"

"Very odd," said Grumber to Lucia a few minutes later. "Are you certain that Miss Abermarle is a lady? Her speech is certainly ladylike, but not wanting me to help her?"

"You're right, of course. Here, fasten the pearls for me. Thank you. Well, perhaps the child is simply modest. I love a mystery, don't you, Grumber?"

"Harrumph," said Grumber, sour to the core.

"Get into the spirit of things. That face of yours would curdle the milk."

Lucia wasn't at all surprised to find Victoria Abermarle quite a beauty. True, the high-necked yellow silk looked more appropriate for a sixteen-year-old, but that would be quickly remedied. She looked briefly toward the clock on the mantelpiece. A good half-hour until Captain Carstairs arrived. Plenty of time, yes indeed.

"Do sit down, Victoria."

Victoria sat.

"Now, my dear child, you must trust me. Will you?"

"I suppose so, ma'am."

"Excellent. Tell me how you met Captain Carstairs."

Victoria chewed on her tongue.

"No, please don't tell me he's a longtime friend or semirelative or any of that nonsense. If I'm to help you, it must be the truth. Now, onward, my child."

And Victoria, unused to such lightning tactics, succumbed without a whimper.

"I thought the captain looked a bit familiar," was the first thing Lucia said after Victoria, twenty minutes later, finally fell silent. "I knew his father, the former Baron Drago. A handsome man, a very strong man who wrung the withers of many a hopeful female before he married a noblewoman on a trip to Seville. I didn't know, however, about this twin business."

"As I told you, ma'am, Rafael isn't at all like his twin, Damien. He's good and kind."

Ah, thought Lucia, what proximity will do when the gentleman acts a gentleman and is a handsome devil to boot.

At that moment Didier appeared in the doorway. "Captain Carstairs, my lady."

Victoria stared. Rafael was dressed in severe black evening clothes, his equally black hair brushed, all whiskers gone from his chin. He looked immaculate, powerful, and absolutely breathtaking. And he looked so much like Damien that she felt frozen to the spot.

Lucia thought the same things about the captain's physical endowments, but she had the benefit of many more years in her dish. "Well, Captain, you are on time. I like a man who is on time."

"My lady," Rafael said smoothly. He kissed her veiny hand. "Victoria, you're looking none the worse for our adventure."

"Hello," she said, then blurted out, "Grumber arranged my hair for me."

"Ah, an excellent result." He grinned at her, showing his white teeth. "Come along, Victoria. Stand up and curtsy or whatever a lady is supposed to do, and I will kiss your hand."

She did. His grin faded only when he placed a light kiss on her wrist. He felt the quiver of her smooth flesh and his eyes widened.

He didn't look closely at her for many minutes.

"Will you keep her, ma'am?" he asked Lucia without preamble. He'd gotten her measure quickly enough, and planned not to disappoint her.

"I believe so, Captain," said Lucia, enjoying herself so much the tatting was destined to remain under her chair cushion for many a long week to come. Hookham's, also, would be bereft of one of its best customers.

It was over an excellently prepared first course of carrot soup, and turbot of shrimp sauce, that Rafael said, looking squarely at his hostess, "I assume that Victoria has told you everything?"

Victoria choked on her carrot soup.

"Why should you think that, Captain?"

"Your cellars are excellent. Why? Well, you aren't one to mince matters, ma'am. Victoria is of a trusting nature, once she accepts a person."

"Yes, of course. First, I suppose, you must see to this solicitor of hers. What is his name, my dear?"

"Mr. Abner Westover," said Victoria. "But, ma'am, I intend to see him myself."

"No."

"No."

"I am not a silly child." She looked from one to the other. "It is too bad of both of you."

"Hush, child, and listen. I could accompany you to Mr. Westover's offices, but it would be more strategically sound were Captain Carstairs to do it for you."

"Correct observation, ma'am," said Rafael, his eyes gleaming. The old lady was sharp as a tack.

"But—"

"Victoria," Rafael said, then paused as John, the footman, directed by Didier, served the lavish second course of stewed kidneys, roast saddle of lamb, boiled turkey, knuckle of ham, mashed and brown potatoes, and something he thought was rissoles.

"Good Lord," he said. "My stomach believes it has gained nirvana."

Didier poured a superb bordeaux.

"Tell Cook that Captain Carstairs is pleased, Didier."

"Yes, certainly."

Rafael held his peace until the three of them were happily involved with knuckles and kidneys. "Now, as I was saying, I don't imagine that Damien will simply bide his time in Cornwall. Once he discovers the twenty pounds missing, he is certain to notice that you also saw the letters."

"He will hotfoot it to London, my dear, particularly if he has been misusing your inheritance. The captain is right."

Victoria's face became as white as her napkin.

"Now don't you worry. You will be safe with me. It's a pity you're not older, but no matter."

"Perhaps even if she were twenty-one, ma'am, it wouldn't be enough. We have no idea as yet what the terms of her father's will are."

"You are quite right, my boy. Didier! Bring some of that Spanish port I laid down twenty years ago. I do believe it ready for drinking. No, Captain, the ladies won't leave you. I drank port with my father and have a great fondness for it. I believe you gentlemen have convinced females that it's unladylike to drink port so that you may have all the more."

"Ma'am, you wound me."

"I just happen to have some in the pantry, my lady."

"Oh, you do, do you? You are a great deal too smart, Didier."

"Certainly, ma'am."

Didier turned at the doorway and said calmly to Rafael, "Her ladyship has the finest cellars in London, sir. You will see shortly."

"That is true enough," said Lucia. "I begin to wonder when the two of us will begin to resemble each other. I have heard it said that people who are together for a great many years do begin to look alike, and, horror of horrors, think alike."

"Will you soon look like Flash, Rafael?"

"Don't be impertinent, Victoria."

"Flash? What is this?"

Victoria giggled, and Rafael said, "My valet, ma'am."

"A former pickpocket, ma'am."

"You two won't bore me, I see. Ah, here is the port. My dear, you shall try just a bit."

Rafael kept his opinion to himself, but frowned when Didier poured the rich port into Victoria's glass. Under his fascinated eye, Didier very calmly added water.

He already acts the doting husband, Lucia thought, quite pleased. The coming days stretched out pleasurably in her mind. This quite likely would be far more interesting than the best gothic novel.

Rafael left shortly after tea that evening. Before he took his leave, he said to Victoria, "I won't be able to visit the solicitor tomorrow. As I told you, I have business here, and it cannot be put off."

"What sort of business is so urgent?"

"Victoria, don't pry."

She looked quite ready to do so, but Lucia interrupted, saying to Rafael, "I shall expect you for dinner tomorrow evening, my boy. Don't worry about Victoria. I am taking her to my modiste."

"Excellent. I'll bid you good night then, ladies. Ma'am, my profoundest thanks for your assistance."

Lucia grinned at him. "Yes, my boy, my assistance. In all matters."

"You terrify me."

"I'll walk you to the door, Rafael," said Victoria.

"No, Victoria," he said shortly upon reaching the front door. "Mind your own business. All right?"

"Very well, but I don't want to."

"I see that you don't."

"Where did you get your evening wear? Surely it wasn't packed in that small valise of yours."

"Didier is a fount of information." He lightly touched his fingers to her cheek. "Don't worry, Victoria. Everything will work out, I promise you."

She turned her face slightly and rested for a brief instant against his open palm. "You're very good to me."

Rafael felt a surge of protectiveness so great that he stepped away from her as if scalded.

"Good night," he said, and was gone in the next instant.

Victoria cocked her head, wondering at his abruptness. Didier, with as many years in his dish as Lady Lucia, said gently, "Take yourself to bed now, miss. You will see the captain soon enough."

As for the captain in question, he was walking as fast as he could toward his rooms on Courtney Street. He was thinking furiously that he much preferred feeling good honest lust for a beautiful woman, not this other thing that made him profoundly afraid.

6

I will find you twenty lascivious turtles ere one chaste man.

—SHAKESPEARE

"Captain Carstairs," Lord Walton greeted Rafael as he shook his hand. "It's been a long time, sir, too long. Welcome home. Allow me to express the government's thanks on the excellent job you've done."

Rafael merely nodded, and seated himself in a welcoming leather armchair in front of Lord Walton's mahogany desk. Lord Walton had aged, he thought. His hair was grayer now, thinner on top, and there were more lines of worry on his face. But the intelligence in his eyes was as formidable as ever. He waited until Lord Walton had finished Morgan's packet of information. He studied the office, admiring the drawings of racehorses clustered on one wall.

"They are Caverleigh Arabians," Lord Walton said. "My grandson named that last one, the strong-shouldered bay. He's only seven and already racing mad."

"They are quite excellent, sir," Rafael said. He knew little of racehorses.

"Would you like a brandy?"

"No, I thank you, sir." He made to rise.

"Actually, Captain, not quite yet. Please, relax. I wish to thank you on behalf of all Englishmen for your fine work over the years. Do not distress yourself that your usefulness is over. It is not. However, in this particular instance, you won't be required to disguise yourself and sneak in and out of difficult situations. I understand that you intend to go home to Cornwall."

"Yes, that's right. I'm not the Baron Drago, as you well know. I intend to build my home in Cornwall, however."

"That is what Morgan wrote to me." Lord Walton paused a moment, then said, "The smugglers still abound there, you know, droves of them. I fear if their rate continues to soar, they will become a national institution."

"Evidently the Bishop is still alive."

"So I understand. However, smuggling doesn't particularly concern me today. It is something else, something a bit more insidious, a bit more evil, if you will."

Rafael sat very still, waiting. He watched Lord Walton lightly rub his fingertips over his temples.

"We don't have a Bishop in this group. This man calls himself the Ram."

Rafael laughed. "Ram? Good Lord, what pretentious nonsense."

"I agree, but there you have it. Captain, have you heard of the Hellfire Club?"

"Yes, it was active in the last century, in the seventeen-seventies, perhaps eighties, I believe. A group of dissolute young noblemen bent on outdoing each other in wickedness and perversion. Satanism, as I recall, was their object, new and varied sorts of satanism, that and the raping of as many young virgins as the bounders could capture."

"That's right. What we have in Cornwall is a revival of the Hellfire Club, with this Ram as its leader. It's still a small group, not more than ten men as its members. Unlike their predecessors, they eschew the more outrageous trappings and perversions of satanism, and get on with the ravishing of young virgins. To be honest about it, Captain, we would not be at all interested in this group were it not for the rape of Viscount Bainbridge's daughter. He, I will tell you, is active in the ministry and is so very enraged he can scarcely see straight. I promised him that I would ask you to look into it."

"A viscount's daughter? That wouldn't seem very intelligent of them."

"Not at all. Evidently it was a mistake. They kept calling her by another name—Mally or something like that—and this Ram fellow fed her some drug to shut her up when she began screaming her head off. When she came to her senses, she was clothed again, and was propped up against an oak tree some four miles from her aunt's house near St. Austell."

"So the daughter was visiting a relative and wasn't known in the area?"

"Exactly right. We also know that this group of idiots dress their role—black robes and hoods, the girl said. They also drew numbers for the order to rape her. The Ram directed it all with evidently superb orderliness. Would you see what you can discover about this group, Captain? Find out who this damned Ram is?"

"I assume that this Hellfire group has raped other girls?"

"Yes, I had a man down there for two months poking about. The normal procedure is to pay a father a goodly amount for his young daughter's virginity. That way, there can be no complaints."

"That is truly quite disgusting."

"Indeed. Unfortunately, my man didn't accomplish a great deal, just learned the group's method of operating. He also made up a list of some local young men who appeared to him prime candidates for this kind of wickedness."

Rafael grinned for the first time. "Actually, I could name you the young men on that list right now. The point is to prove it, then make certain they stop their activities."

"Exactly. And as a local young man from a fine family, you already have entrée into every circle in the area. I would appreciate it, Captain, if you would look into the matter. Find out who this Ram is and notify me. I promised Viscount Bainbridge I would provide him the Ram's name. He wants to kill the fellow in a duel. I agreed. A man should have the right to protect his family, and if that fails, he should have the right to avenge the wrong done him."

"Would it be possible for me to speak with the viscount's daughter?"

Lord Walton shook his head decisively. "The girl has been shamed. To speak with you, a stranger, of what happened to her would be impossible for her. All the information comes from the girl's mother."

"A pity," said Rafael. "Does she recall where she was taken?"

"A house near St. Austell, off in some wooded area, she thinks. She was out walking her aunt's dogs, had outstripped her groom, and was nabbed. She didn't see anyone's face, just heard voices."

"Any other name besides Ram?"

"I don't know, my boy. Bainbridge refuses to make the girl speak of it again. I suppose I do understand his feelings. Will you undertake this for us, Captain?"

"Were there any incidents involving other sorts of crimes? Murder? Robbery?"

"Not that I know of. If they hadn't mistaken Bainbridge's daughter, we wouldn't now be involved. It is most distasteful that a man would sell his daughter's virginity, but not against the law. Well, Captain?"

"Why not?" Rafael said, and stood. He shook Lord Walton's hand and added, "Morgan is coming home as well."

"Yes, I know. Unfortunately, he is coming home because of his wife's health. She's dying, you see."

"No, I didn't know. Morgan and I never spoke of personal matters."

"Morgan is a private man and one of great talent. Well, there is naught we can do about it, Captain. You will keep in touch with me about this affair?"

"Certainly."

The two men parted amicably. Lord Walton wandered to the window in his office and stared down at the street below. Carstairs was a young man to admire. If he managed to uncover the identity of the Ram, there just might be a title in it for him. He watched Carstairs stride across the street, tall and strong, a ladies' man indeed, he thought, remembering the report he'd received on just how Carstairs had managed to discover a woman spy in the West Indies. Although the report was one of Morgan's gems of emotionless dryness, much like the man himself, it had still been clear that the woman had told Carstairs all her secrets in his bed. This Hellfire Club business was another matter entirely, though. He wished Carstairs luck.

As for Rafael, the moment he left the War Ministry, his step lightened and he shucked off his fatigue. He didn't question why, merely enjoyed the feeling of anticipation.

He felt more than anticipation when he first saw Victoria standing in Lady Lucia's drawing room. My God, he thought, staring at her, she is exquisite. Her gown was new, of course, and suited her to perfection. It was a pale blue satin slip over a net frock. It was cut low over her bosom, with short sleeves decorated with small knots of blue ribbon. The skirt was trimmed with a flounce of blond lace and more judiciously placed knots of blue ribbon. Her breasts looked very white against the blue satin. Her hair, sparkling with red and deep brown highlights in the candlelight, was fashioned in a braided coronet atop her head with soft looping wisps framing her face and trailing down her neck. She looked elegant and not at all sixteen years old.

"Rafael, I'm so glad you're here." She gave him a curtsy and twirled about. "Do you like my gown? Aunt Lucia positively snarled at the woman until she agreed to alter this one for her immediately." She twirled about again, laughing and saying over her shoulder, "Aunt Lucia ordered the woman to take off the rows of grape blossoms and cockleshells, but the lace is nice, don't you agree?"

"You look fine," he said finally. "You don't look at all fussy. I'm glad there are no cockleshells." He nodded toward Lucia, saw that the old lady was smiling benignly at him, realized what she must be thinking, and drew himself up.

He didn't look again at Victoria, but seated himself beside Lucia and engaged her in vacuous conversation.

"It didn't rain today."

"No, my boy, it didn't. There were several hopeful-looking clouds, however."

"You did not overtire yourself, ma'am?"

"It was fatiguing to rid the gown of the cockle-shells."

He ground his teeth, aware that Victoria was looking at him like a wounded doe. "Victoria looks lovely."

"Indeed she does."

"Rafael," Victoria blurted out, "what did you do today?"

"Stop twitching about," he said shortly. "Ladies are to appear calm and not at all nosey."

Victoria eyed him closely. He was behaving oddly. "Whatever is wrong with you? Didn't your business go well? Did you suffer reverses? Isn't that what it is called?"

He grinned at that. "No, no reverses. I shan't tell you, Victoria. Search your mind for other conversation."

"Very well. Will you take me riding tomorrow afternoon? In the park, so I may see all the fancy people? Aunt Lucia tells me it's the thing to do."

"*Aunt* Lucia?"

"I insisted, Captain," said Lucia. "Now, we need to discuss what to do about Victoria's come-out."

"Come-out? But she's here for a short time only, ma'am. Surely you can't mean to—"

"Ah, Didier. Is dinner ready?"

"Indeed, my lady. Cook has outdone himself. I venture to say it is because Miss Victoria slipped into the kitchen this afternoon when she smelled his baking scones. He is French, you know," he continued to Rafael, "and like all his countrymen, prone to flattery."

"I didn't *really* flatter him, Didier. The scones were delicious."

"It is the result that is important, my dear. Now, let's see what Louis has concocted for our pleasure."

Louis had prepared the most incredible vol-au-vent of lobster that had ever caressed Rafael's taste buds. The wine sauce was so delicate that it defied description. Conversation consisted primarily of praising Louis as the three of them made their way through the fillets of turbot *à la créme*, the French green beans, the salmi of grouse and the hare, boned and larded, with mushrooms. It wasn't until John, the footman, had removed the apricot blancmange that Lucia, drawing a deep, very sated breath, mentioned the Earl of Rothermere and his impending visit to town. "Do you by any chance know him, Rafael? Philip Hawksbury."

"Hawk?" Rafael said, utterly surprised.

"You know him, do you?"

"Yes, certainly, we met in Portugal, when I—" He broke off, realizing he'd nearly given himself away. He retrenched quickly under Victoria's wide-eyed look. "I was sort of in the army," he said. "I had heard that Hawk sold out."

"Yes, his brother died and he was the heir. He did his duty."

"It's been a long time," said Rafael, swirling the delicate white wine in his glass.

"He's married."

"Hawk, married? Good heavens, I remember him saying that—well, never mind. Who is she, ma'am?"

"Her name is Frances, she's a Scot, and a vivacious, entertaining girl. They have two children, a boy and a girl. Philip's father will also accompany them, I understand. He is the Marquess of Chandos, you know."

"Philip?" said Victoria.

"Philip or Hawk, my dear. I'll never forget the time Frances and Hawk's former mistress—well, I suppose that tale isn't at all appropriate for Victoria's unwed ears."

Victoria, leaning forward, her elbows on the table and her chin propped up on her hands, gasped, "What, ma'am? Oh, do tell me. Former mistress? What happened?"

"Victoria," Rafael said in his father's voice, "you will be quiet now."

"But, Rafael, whatever was his wife doing with his mistress?"

"Former mistress."

"It still seems odd to me. It doesn't seem at all proper to me that a gentleman would do that sort of thing after he is married." Her eyes lowered instantly, her thoughts so clearly written on her face that Rafael wanted only to wipe Damien and his atrocious behavior from her mind.

"Some men aren't honorable," he said. And some wives, he thought, are such cold, frigid creatures that the husbands in question are forced to mistresses. He wondered about Hawk's wife. Two children. Good heavens. He realized with a start that he was twenty-seven years old. He simply hadn't thought about a wife and children during the past five years. He looked at Victoria, and felt that ill-disguised fear. Fate, he thought. Minding his own business, doing nothing at all untoward, only to have himself firmly captured by a little ragamuffin who had become a damned beauty.

"I should say they wouldn't be, to do such a thing," Lucia was saying. "Honorable, that is."

"Well, no more of that, ma'am. Victoria, tomorrow morning I shall see your solicitor. And if it pleases you, we will ride in the park in the afternoon so you can show off your fine new plumage."

"And show you off as well," she said, admiration plain in her eyes even though her voice was teasing.

As she had the previous evening after tea, Victoria walked with him to the front door.

"You will take care, won't you, Rafael?"

"Take care? Is your solicitor rabid?"

"I don't know," she said slowly. "I'm just afraid."

Once again, he touched his fingers to her cheek. "Don't be, Victoria."

At precisely ten o'clock the following morning, Rafael entered the office of Mr. Abner Westover.

A black-coated clerk looked up as he came into the office and his eyes widened. He jumped to his feet. "My lord. You're back again? Is something wrong?"

Rafael paused deliberately, knowing full well that the clerk thought him his brother. So, Damien had come to London as quickly as all that, had he? And immediately he'd come to the solicitor. Rafael wasn't really surprised; it suited his own plans.

"I wish to see Mr. Westover," he said easily.

"Certainly, my lord. Just a moment, if you please."

Rafael stared around the outer office, noting the musty smell and the very few small windows. He shuddered, thinking of Victoria coming here.

"My lord, welcome. You bring good news, I hope?"

"Mr. Westover," Rafael said, nodding as the man beamed him a fulsome, yet worried smile.

"Has the young lady, Miss Abermarle, been found as yet, my lord? The thought of ransom, it's infamous. Do you have need of more funds?"

Rafael felt anger surge through him. How could his twin resort to such a thing? Well, if he'd tried to ravish Victoria, nothing was beyond him. So he'd gotten more money from Victoria's estate, had he? For her ransom, curse him to hell.

"No, I have no more need of funds," he said. "What I should like to have you tell me—again, if you please—are the exact terms of Miss Abermarle's inheritance."

"But the young lady—"

"She is safe now. I recovered her." That, at least, was the truth.

"Thank God," said Mr. Westover. "The terms of her inheritance, my lord? I thought you understood that—"

"Again, if you please, Mr. Westover."

"Certainly," Abner Westover said, his voice a bit uncertain at his lordship's behavior. He looked briefly at his clerk whose chin quivered in excitement, and said abruptly, "Come into my office, my lord."

Dignified, Rafael thought as he seated himself comfortably in a leather chair across from Mr. Westover. He watched the narrow-shouldered man search with prissy deliberation through a pile of folders on his desktop. "Ah, here it is."

"Go ahead."

Mr. Westover carefully placed a pair of spectacles on his nose. "As I told you, my lord, I'm concerned with your, er, use of Miss Abermarle's funds. As I have indicated, the principal wasn't to be touched—the interest, invested in the funds, providing sufficient money to provide for her upkeep. However, I have grown gravely concerned during the past six months, as I have written to you, that—"

"Mr. Westover," Rafael interrupted smoothly, "I understand your concern. No more of the principal will be touched. How much is in the trust for Miss Abermarle?"

If Mr. Westover was surprised at the baron's strange lapse of memory, he gave no sign of it, saying only, "Thirty-five thousand pounds, my lord. It was, of course, nearly fifty thousand pounds, until you removed the fifteen thousand for the ransom demand."

"I see," said Rafael, so furious with his brother that he could scarce think straight. Victoria was an heiress. But she wouldn't be for much longer if Damien remained her guardian.

"When does the money come to Miss Abermarle?"

"Upon her twenty-fifth birthday or upon her marriage." Mr. Westover fussed with some papers, not looking up. "Of course, any gentleman applying for her hand must have your permission as her guardian."

Rafael could well imagine that no gentleman, no matter how innocuous or well-placed, would ever gain Damien's permission to marry Victoria. He knew he couldn't ask how his brother happened to become Victoria's guardian. That would be going too far, even for Mr. Westover.

"Can you tell me how you managed to save Miss Abermarle?"

"Of course," said Rafael. "Smugglers had taken her. It was a relatively easy matter to retrieve her." It was at least the truth, Rafael thought. "Incidentally, Mr. Westover, the fifteen thousand pounds weren't needed. The funds will be returned to Miss Abermarle's trust."

"Excellent, my lord. I had thought that— Well, never mind now. I will say only that you have relieved my mind greatly."

But Rafael knew what the man had wanted to say. He was honest, and distressed at Damien's misuse of his young client's inheritance. What the devil should he do now? he wondered, rising. He shook Mr. Westover's hand and took his leave. He was deep in thought when he suddenly heard a man shout, "Good God. As I live and breathe. It's the infamous pirate."

Rafael jerked about to see Philip Hawksbury, Earl of Rothermere, standing across the street, waving at him.

"Hawk," he said, grinning. They met in the middle of the street, shaking hands, to the raised ire of a hackney driver.

"Come along, old fellow," said Hawk, clapping Rafael on his back. "Lord, what a long time it's been. What are you doing in London? Where are you staying?"

Rafael said, "Haven't you seen Lucia?"

Hawk looked dumbfounded. "How do you know Lucia? No, Frances and I are at Hawksbury House.

We are dining with her this evening. But how do you know Lucia?"

"There is much to tell you, Hawk. Let's go to Cribb's Parlor and I'll fill you in."

The two gentlemen found a table in the corner of the taproom and ordered ale. "I can't wait to meet your wife, Hawk. So you've been properly caged?"

"True enough," agreed Hawk easily. "Now, Rafael, tell me all about what you've been doing. And how you know Lucia."

Rafael sat back in his chair and told him everything; there was no reason not to. After all, Hawk knew all about Rafael's work for the government. Since Victoria was staying with Lucia, there was no excuse not to tell him of her. Nor did he spare the details of his brother's infamy. Hawk was very intelligent and Rafael rather hoped to get his opinion on how to proceed. "So, when you yelled at me, I had just left Victoria's solicitor. And that, my friend, is how things sit at this moment."

"Fascinating, Rafael. As I recall, your presence always relieved tedium. So it continues. And you've got the young lady at Lucia's. A pity about your brother. But wait—Lyon is married. It's almost too much to take in, all your news. Frances and I met Diana, of course."

They were drinking their third mug of ale when Rafael said honestly, "I think I just might need your assistance, Hawk. I have the proof that my brother is a damned bounder. And Victoria must be protected somehow."

"What do you think of the girl?"

Rafael looked into the mug of ale, swirling the gold-brown liquid about. He said thoughtfully, more to himself than to Hawk, "She's lovely and quite in-

telligent. She's got courage and strength, although at
the moment she's every reason to be afraid. She is,
in short, an admirable girl and well, a darling."

"Ah."

"Ah what, curse you, Hawk?"

"Marry her."

Rafael met the earl's eyes. He wouldn't have been
overly surprised to see the word "Fate" written
across Hawk's forehead. "I suppose," he said slowly,
"that it is the only thing to do. Actually, I had already decided it best, not five minutes before you
shouted at me."

"At least you've had the chance to get to know
her," said Hawk. "Much different from my experience. Lord, I shall never remember without a profound shudder Frances's disguise. You will like
Frances. She's a real trooper."

"Did you bring your children?"

"No, little Alexandra is too young, and as for
Charles, he gets vilely ill in a traveling coach. One
of the realities of married life, old man. Incidentally,
you must meet my father, the marquess. No doubt
about it, Rafael, once he learns of your dilemma, he
will stick his oar in. He's a great plotter, curse him."

"As subtle as a battering ram, like Lucia?"

"The two of them with their heads together would
be enough to send Napoleon scurrying back to
Russia."

"Lucia just happened to mention last evening
about Frances and your former mistress saving the
day. Needless to say, Victoria was all ears."

"They attacked me, the both of them. Frances
slammed her fist in my belly. Ah, what a time that
was."

More time passed with reminiscences. "Good

Lord," Rafael said suddenly. "I promised to take Victoria riding in the park."

"Well, Frances and I will see both of you this evening. Rafael?"

"Yes?"

"Take care of the little one."

"Oh, indeed I shall." But Damien was in London. And it worried him, even though there was no way Damien could know where she was or whom she was with. Damien didn't even know that his errant twin had come home.

Rafael was abstracted, a completely unacceptable companion, Victoria thought, looking at him from beneath her lashes. There were more ladies and gentlemen in the park than Victoria ever could have imagined. Since Rafael knew no one, their perambulations were uninterrupted.

"Careful of that landau, Victoria."

She automatically brought her mare closer to his stallion. He merely nodded and fell again into his own thoughts.

"Do you like my new riding habit?"

"Yes."

"And the hat? They dyed the feather to match the blue velvet. It's royal blue, you know."

"Charming."

"My boots are the finest Spanish leather."

"Nice."

"And my chemise is covered with lace."

"Yes, very good— *What?*"

"There, at least I've finally gained your attention. Now, Rafael, I have had quite enough of your secrecy. I'm not a nit-witted child. Tell me about Mr. Westover and your interview with him. Am I an heiress?"

"Not if Damien continues with his machinations."

"What does that mean?"

"It means, Victoria, that you're better off not knowing, and—"

"Rafael, I am the key to all of this. If you don't tell me everything, I shall go visit Mr. Westover myself."

She watched a muscle jump in his jaw. He wasn't, she realized, a man who took orders easily, or ultimatums. She watched, fascinated, as his beautiful gray eyes, almost silver in the afternoon sunlight, narrowed on her face. "You, my girl, will do exactly what you're told. Do you understand me?"

She grinned at him. "No, I'm so silly and stupid, I don't understand anything."

"Victoria, I'll—damn you, stop laughing at me. I am but trying to protect you and—"

"I see. Protection to a gentleman means keeping me in blinders. I'm not a block of ice to melt in the sun, Rafael."

But he had no intention of telling her that Damien was here in London. He didn't want to see the fear in her eyes again.

"No," he said finally, "but you're a pushing sort of female who wants manners. Suffice it to say that I have everything under control now. Have you now had enough of the *beau monde*?" He swatted her mare's rump with his gloved hand, not even giving her a chance to answer.

Her grin dropped away and she frowned after him. Protecting her, was he? Well, she would see.

The laughter at the dinner table made Victoria forget all about Damien and her anger at Rafael and his cavalier treatment of her.

The Countess of Rothermere, Frances Hawksbury,

was engaging and amusing and Victoria thought her the most beautiful woman she'd ever seen. As for Hawk, or Philip—she wasn't yet certain what to call him—he had much the look of Rafael. Tall and strong, dark-haired, but his eyes were a startling green, not a silvery gray.

Lively spirits continued to flow as consistently as the fine wine from Lucia's cellars.

Suddenly Rafael said to her, "I believe you've drunk quite enough, Victoria. Didier, is there any lemonade?"

She'd sipped her way through but one glass, while— "You're the one to begin in the lemonade, Rafael. That is at least your third glass."

"I am a man and much more used—"

"I do believe I have heard something along those boring, quite obnoxious lines before," Frances said. "Come, Rafael, Victoria isn't two-and-ten, you know."

"Thank you, Frances. However, the good captain is fond of giving orders."

"Well, old boy, I suggest you succumb gracefully or pack your valise," said Hawk. "Frances, love, turn your cannon elsewhere. Damn, I wish my father were here."

"Why?" Rafael asked.

"He has the knack of changing a particularly uncomfortable subject, leaving all the principals with their dignity intact."

"Look, Victoria, it's not that I think that you are starting on a career of drunkenness, but you're not used to wine, are you?"

That was true, but she wasn't a fool. "No more than a bottle a day. On a good day."

"I see," said Lucia, at her most stately, "that I must

intervene here. It is a case of compromise, I believe. Didier, half wine and half soda water. Is that agreeable to both parties?"

Rafael grumbled. Victoria shot him a look and said, "Since the good captain looks ready for apoplexy, I agree."

Rafael gave her a crooked smile.

"Excellent," said Frances. "Now we may continue with our gluttony and our conversation. Wonderful sirloin of beef, Lucia. Victoria, do you enjoy racing?"

"Oh, yes," Victoria said, sitting forward in her chair, her spoonful of giblet soup hovering between her bowl and her mouth, "but I haven't ever really been to a real race. Once, when I was a little girl, my parents took me to a cat race in the south of England near Eastbourne. It was marvelous."

Frances was the only one who had never attended a cat race. She smiled and said, "I will watch the cats race and then you must come to Newmarket in November. Flying Davie will run and win, I have no doubt."

Horse racing was the topic until the ladies left the gentlemen to their port. To Victoria's surprise, Lucia seemed willing to forgo her nightly glass of port.

"In company, my dear," said Lucia, guessing her thoughts, "one must bow to convention. Frances, why don't you take Victoria upstairs and fix her hair? You are on the verge of losing a braid, Victoria."

"She wanted us to have a chance to speak alone," Frances said as the two ladies mounted the staircase. "It's said that she's a regular tartar, but I find her the most interesting and charming lady of my acquaintance. She saved my life, you know."

"What? When?"

Frances smiled. "I would very likely have died in

childbirth. Lucia booted out the idiot doctor and saved me and my daughter. I suppose I would do just about anything for her."

While Victoria chewed over this bit of information, Frances continued in a laughing voice, "And then she proceeded to give Hawk instructions on the care of pregnant ladies. He later swore to me that he had no intention of ever sharing my bed again." She shook her head and said fondly, "Silly man."

"And has he?"

Frances grinned. "I should add that Lucia also gave him a lecture on how not to make me pregnant. That was later, of course, and he was ecstatic."

"Oh," Victoria said doubtfully.

"Dear heavens, I shouldn't be speaking like this to you."

When Victoria was seated at her dressing table, Frances standing behind her and arranging the errant braid, she said, "I suppose you're worried that I'm taking advantage of Lucia."

"Not at all. If Lucia has accepted you, and she most certainly has, it is quite good enough for me. But tell me, Victoria, what is all this about your inheritance? Hawk told me just a bit of it, curse him."

Victoria's eyes narrowed. "Rafael—a more obstinate man I'll never meet—won't tell me a blasted thing. It is too bad of him, Frances. He's acting as though I am a wilting rose who will lose all her petals if hit with the raw truth."

Frances's hands stilled. The light was more than dawning. It was fully risen. Her precious husband obviously knew much more than he'd let on to her. She would gave him a piece of her mind.

"Captain Carstairs is a very fine man," she said mildly, continuing again with her braiding as her mind flew to various possibilities. "Hawk thinks very highly of him, I know."

Victoria sighed. "It's true. He is good and honorable. If he hadn't come upon me, I shudder to think what might have happened. I owe him a great deal."

Frances slipped in the final fastening. "There, all done." Victoria stood and Frances hugged her. "Everything will work out all right. You will see."

"Well, I trust you're right, Frances, but I fully intend to do something myself. I'm going to see my solicitor tomorrow. He will be in no position to be a dictator like Rafael."

Frances knew Victoria wasn't one to sit knitting in a corner whilst events swirled about her. "If you don't mind," she said finally, "I shall accompany you to the solicitor."

"You won't tell your husband or Rafael?"

"No, neither of them deserves our confidence. Now, my dear, do you sing? Play the pianoforte?"

7

*He who would have the fruit
must climb the tree.*
—THOMAS FULLER

It didn't matter that the morning was dreary and
damp, the air thick and cold. Victoria had made
up her mind. She had to see Mr. Westover herself.
She had to know about her inheritance, then make
her plans. She couldn't abuse Lady Lucia's hospitality forever, after all. She frowned as she leaned back
against the cracked leather squabs in the ancient
hackney. She would not further tolerate Rafael's
whims—treating her as if she were an idiot or, worse,
a helpless young lady.

If the hackney driver had thought it odd that a
young lady, quite alone, wished to go into the City,
he gave no sign, just spat on the roadway and made
a noise that sounded, at least to Victoria, like affir-
mation. She didn't want to admit it to herself, but
by the time the driver neared Derby Street, she was
beginning, if not to regret coming, at least to be con-

cerned about the four pounds she'd placed in a hand-kerchief inside her reticule. There was so much noise all around her. From the hackney window she saw hawkers everywhere, each of them shouting at the top of his lungs, hoping, she supposed, to gain the custom of the hordes of shiny, black-coated men whose heads were buried from the drizzle and cold inside wide-rimmed black hats. There was another element that made Victoria clutch her reticule firmly to her side. Men slouched in alleyways, eyeing the passing hackney with assessing and utterly cold expressions. Most of all, it was simply a depressing sight. In her new walking dress of lemon bombazine, the spencer of equally bright lemon color, she felt like an exotic specimen, a parrot in bright plumage surrounded by ravens.

Every few moments she heard her driver curse or shout at a recalcitrant who got in his way. There was so much traffic, the street itself full of drays, more hawkers, wagons filled with huge kegs of ale.

Just because you've never before been in a city of any size, you needn't act like a provincial. It's an adventure, not something to cower about. And that, she told herself firmly, was that. There wasn't the slightest reason to cower against the smelly squabs. After all, Frances would come shortly, in her own carriage, and they would laugh and talk and Victoria would doubtless feel like a fool for all her alarms.

The hackney pulled to a halt in front of a narrow-fronted building, just like its neighbors, and Victoria, her money in her hand, jumped out and paid the man.

"Ye don't wis' me to wait, missy?"

"No, thank you. A friend is coming for me."

He gave her a long look, then shrugged and clicked his miserable-looking horse forward.

It had stopped drizzling for the moment. Victoria stood there staring around her, wondering at this vastly different world from the one she knew. It was the avidly curious looks from several men that recalled her to her mission. She carefully lifted her skirts from a mud puddle and walked up the shallow steps to the solicitor's office.

The clerk, upon seeing the somewhat wet but nonetheless elegant vision, was palpably taken aback. He gaped at her, dropping the piece of paper he was holding.

"I wish to see Mr. Westover," Victoria said in an imperious tone that would have pleased Lady Lucia. "Please inform him that Miss Victoria Abermarle is here."

"I—well, I don't know, miss—you're a lady, and, well, ah, you know—"

Victoria frowned down her nose at him, drawing on one of Lucia's intimidating mannerisms. "Tell him that I am waiting, if you please."

"Er, yes, miss, right away."

Mr. Westover, hearing of his unexpected visitor, was out of his office in a flash. "Miss Abermarle?"

She nodded and smiled at him, waiting.

"Such a relief that you are again safe, miss. Where is Lord Drago? Isn't he with you?"

I must tread carefully here, Victoria thought, *I must go very carefully.* "Lord Drago?" she asked.

"Of course. He was here just yesterday to tell me he had managed to rescue you from your kidnappers. So dreadful for you, my dear Miss Abermarle, but the baron— Well, all's well, eh?"

Rafael pretending to be Damien? Very clever of him. He must have gotten all the information he wanted. But what was this about kidnappers? If that had been Rafael's tale, she mustn't make a liar of him.

"I'm perfectly all right now, Mr. Westover. I'm here merely to review with you the terms of my inheritance."

Mr. Westover stared at her in obvious consternation. "This is unusual, a young lady, here, alone, I'm not certain—"

She interrupted him smoothly. "The baron suggested it was time I met my solicitor, the gentleman who was taking such good care of my inheritance. As the baron told me, it is my money and I should know all the, ah, stipulations. Don't you agree, sir?"

"The baron said— Well, that is pleasant news indeed, I suppose. It's irregular, very unusual, I say, but I suppose I have little choice now."

Victoria gave him a brilliant smile. "Thank you." She walked past him into a high-ceilinged office that smelled comfortingly of leather and ink and decades of closed windows. She waited as he dusted the leather chair in front of his desk with his handkerchief, then sat down.

"I will tell you, Miss Abermarle, that I don't approve of this, any of it. However, since you're here"—he realized he would have to physically heft her out of the blasted chair—"and the baron approves of your being here, I will give you the general terms of your inheritance."

He did, spicing his discourse with many pauses and disapproving looks. He wasn't stupid and was beginning to realize that the baron would have more

likely suggested his ward visit a cockfight than her
solicitor.

"Twenty-five," she repeated, feeling her heart sink.
Her money wasn't hers until she was twenty-five.
She wouldn't be nineteen until December. She wasn't
a fool. Although Mr. Westover had been quite careful
in his choice of words, it was clear to her that Damien was making free with *her* money.

"Yes, twenty-five, Miss Abermarle, or upon your
marriage, as I said," said Mr. Westover.

Marriage.

"With my guardian's permission?" Was that why
Damien had told those lies to David Esterbridge? He
wanted no husband to take over her money?

"Naturally. I, er, do believe, however, after seeing
Lord Drago yesterday, that you need have no concern about the disposition of your funds in the
future."

Certainly she wouldn't. It had been Rafael to reas-
sure the poor gulled man. Where was Damien?

She rose and extended her hand. Mr. Westover,
after regarding that small gloved hand with surprise,
finally shook it. He saw her out, ignoring his clerk's
gape-mouthed interest.

It had stopped raining, and there was even a sliver
of sun coming from behind the heavy gray clouds.
Victoria stood on the top shallow step looking about
for Frances's carriage. She was growing nervous,
aware that several rather disreputable men were eyeing her as if she were the Christmas goose. Where
was Frances? She saw a curricle approach and
heaved a huge sigh of relief. Then she blinked in
surprise. She felt her pulse quicken. It was Rafael.

"Rafael." She waved wildly at him. Let him be

angry with her, she thought. She'd found out what she needed to. There was nothing he could do to her, after all. Perhaps rage a bit, but nothing more dire than that.

The curricle came to a smooth halt beside her, and she lifted her eyes to his face.

"Well, Victoria, what an unexpected surprise this is. I see you've discovered Mr. Westover."

He sounded odd, somehow, not really angry, more relieved.

"Now, Rafael, I told you I would. It was too bad of you not to tell me anything. Did Frances send you after me?"

"Frances? No, I was actually coming to see Mr. Westover myself. Again. However, now that I've found you, my dear, I believe I will see to you myself."

"All right. You're not angry, are you?"

"I? Angry? Actually, Victoria, I'm very pleased."

She watched him jump gracefully down from the curricle. His clothing was natty, his Hessians glossy. "Come, my child." He held out his hand to her. "May I say that you look none the worse for your adventure? Indeed, that's a new gown, is it not? Very charming."

She cocked her head at him, a half-smile on her lips. "We're going back to Lucia's?"

"Lucia's? No, actually, I don't believe so. I would like to spend some time alone with you."

It was in that instant that Victoria realized it wasn't Rafael. He wasn't tanned, for one thing. That, and something else, something she couldn't define, even to herself. Her eyes widened and she took a quick step backward, unable to help herself.

"Come along, Victoria."

He grabbed her arm. "Damien," she whispered, so frightened she could scarcely think straight.

"Yes, you little fool. I thank you for falling so neatly into my hands. My brother, eh? I shall look forward to hearing how you met Rafael. What a shock to hear that he is here in London and that he has you in tow."

There were so many men about. She opened her mouth to scream, but Damien slammed his palm over her mouth, pulling her inexorably toward the curricle.

She began to fight him in earnest, kicking out as much as her narrow skirt would allow, flailing her arms wildly, her fingers trying to score his face. He was stronger than she had imagined. She was panting, trying to jerk away so she could call for help. She saw that men were staring, but they were making no move to assist her.

His arm about her waist tightened, squeezing the breath out of her.

Suddenly Victoria heard the most welcome sound in the world.

"Victoria! What the devil."

It was Frances. She felt Damien's hold loosen just a bit in his surprise, and she managed to jerk her mouth away from his hand.

"Help, Frances! Help me."

Frances didn't hesitate. She gracefully jumped down from the carriage. "Mullens," she said, "your pistol, please." She very calmly took the pistol from her driver's nerveless hand.

Damien was trying desperately to haul Victoria into his curricle, no easy task since the seat was so high off the ground.

"Let her go," said Frances, pointing the pistol. "I

take it you are not Rafael Carstairs, but Baron Drago. Release her, sir, or I will shoot you."

Damien felt immense rage, and frustration so mighty he wanted to do violence. He looked at the woman holding that damned gun, and shouted, "If you do, you will likely hit this little slut."

"No, I am an excellent shot. You would look rather alarming without one ear. But at least in the future Victoria would know it was you immediately and not your brother. You have one second, Baron."

Damien cursed, then, seeing no hope for it, shoved Victoria away from him, sending her sprawling to the muddy gutter. He climbed into his curricle and was gone in the next moment. He shouted over his shoulder, "I will see you again, Victoria."

Frances, smiling slightly, handed the pistol back to Mullens. "Victoria, my dear, are you all right? Come, let me help you rise. Oh, dear, you are quite wet and filthy. No harm done. All is well now. I am dreadfully sorry that I wasn't here sooner."

Victoria forced herself to draw deep breaths, Frances's easy flow of words soothing her. "Thank you, Frances," she said, and rose. She stood there vaguely aware of all the people standing about gossiping about her, and none of them had done a thing to help! "I was a fool," she said. "I thought it was Rafael."

"I know. I did too, at first." She chuckled as she helped Victoria into her carriage. "I couldn't imagine what the good captain had done to make you so angry. And vice versa, I might add."

She boosted Victoria into the carriage and said to the unmoving Mullens, "Lady Cranston's, if you please. Come, Mullens, everything is fine now, don't frown so, and you needn't tell his lordship, though from your sour expression I would wager my next quarter's allowance that you will do so."

The carriage bowled forward. Frances, looking at Victoria's white face, said, "I thought you'd rip the skin off his nose. You were splendid."

"Yes," Victoria said, slowly, "I was holding my own, wasn't I?"

It was unfortunate, in both ladies' opinion, that Rafael was waiting at Lucia's town house.

Didier, unruffled, told them of that piece of news.

"Let us go upstairs," Frances whispered to Victoria. "There's no reason to draw fire."

"Hurry, Frances."

But they didn't make it. Rafael, hearing the noise, emerged from the drawing room to see Victoria, wet and filthy as his original ragamuffin, held against Frances, who was nearly as frowsy.

"What the hell."

"Good morning, Captain," Frances said, all bland confidence. "If you will excuse us for a moment, we will be down again presently."

"The devil you will. Victoria, what happened to you?"

Then he saw her eyes. Saw the fear and the shock. Dear God, what had happened?

Frances released her, and waited, a twinkle in her eyes, to see what would happen now. Sure enough, in but another moment Rafael strode to Victoria and took her into his arms. "What happened? Tell me."

"It was Damien," she said, burying her face against his shoulder and wrapping her arms about his back. "I thought it was you. But he wasn't at all tanned. There was something else about him, but I don't know what it was. He tried to force me in his curricle. There were so many men about, but none of them would help me. Frances came along just in time." She raised her face and tried for a smile. "I don't see why Frances would ever have any need of a former mistress to help her."

"Ah, but I did," Frances said easily. "That is a story I will tell you one cold winter's night."

"She told him she would shoot his ear off if he didn't let me go."

But Rafael wasn't amused. "You went to the solicitor's office, didn't you? And Damien was there as well?"

"Yes, outside. I had already spoken to Mr. Westover. I learned the provisions of my inheritance."

He wanted to shake her and to hold her very close. It was an unsettling dilemma. He compromised, saying harshly, "I trust you have learned your lesson, Victoria. You will do as I tell you in the future, do you understand me?"

He felt her stiffen, but didn't release her. He said over her head to Frances, "Thank you. As for you, Victoria, you will go upstairs now and bathe. I don't want you to catch a chill." He remembered belatedly that Frances was also a bit frayed and damp.

Frances, who wasn't at all remiss in her faculties, said, "Don't worry about me, Rafael. I shall take myself back to Hawksbury House. Victoria, I will see you later today. All right?"

Victoria nodded.

She was still held close to Rafael. She felt his warmth and his strength and wondered how it could be that he was so very different from his twin. Didier gently closed the door behind Frances. It was only then that Rafael roused himself. "I'll help you," he said. "Come along now."

She allowed herself to be led upstairs to her bed-chamber. Grumber was waiting stoically, no discernible surprise on her face at the sight of the young miss.

"You look grubby as hell," Rafael said, flicking his fingertip over a slash of mud on her cheek. "Clean her up, Grumber. I'll be downstairs with Lady Lucia."

"It will take a while," said Grumber.

"Keep her warm."

With those words, and one final searching look at Victoria, Rafael took himself back downstairs to Lucia, who was in close conversation with Didier.

"I gather you now know as much as I do," he said to Lucia.

"I'm not certain, Captain," said Lucia, as bland as Cook's giblet soup. "I did gather that it was your brother, Baron Drago, who came upon Victoria?"

"Yes," Rafael said in a savage voice. "She went to the solicitor, by herself, I might add, and Damien came upon her when she was leaving. She thought at first that he was I, but he wasn't tanned, you see, and he was forcing her."

"Yes, my dear boy. Oh, dear, here I thought Victoria was still in her bed, with the headache."

"In any case, Frances saved her hide. Damnation—pardon me, ma'am—but it is too much. I told her I would handle everything. Why couldn't she have simply left things alone?"

Lucia walked to the sideboard and calmly poured Rafael a snifter of brandy. "Very good for temper," she said, handing it to him.

"You know," she said after a moment, "I suppose I should tell you why Victoria went to Mr. Westover's office. She isn't a child, Rafael, and it is her right to know about her inheritance. You were high-handed, you know, all with the best intentions, I'm sure, but the result was the same. Now, as for your twin, it appears that he isn't at all stupid. I doubt it will take long to find out that Victoria is here. And he is her guardian, with the law on his side. He could force her removal, could he not?"

"No, I won't let him."

"But he has the law on his side."

"I know." Rafael sighed. Well, he might as well get it over with. He would propose to Victoria. Marriage would protect her, and there was no reasonable way Damien could refuse permission to his own brother. She would have to obey him, high-handed or not, once she was his wife. His mind made up, Rafael was impatient to get it over with. He trusted that Victoria was at least somewhat fond of him.

He knew his own feelings tipped the scales to beyond mere fondness.

He was to find himself thwarted. Hawk and Frances arrived shortly after Victoria emerged from her bedchamber, over an hour later, bathed and changed. He couldn't prevent a frown. She looked sweet and fresh and utterly guileless, not at all the same girl who'd come into the house, her face as white as January snow.

The entire matter was rehashed over luncheon for Hawk's benefit. And the Marquess of Chandos arrived just after luncheon and demanded an equal hearing.

To Rafael's surprise, Victoria asked him quietly if she could drive with him in the park.

"It's raining again," he said.

"Oh, well, in that case, can I speak to you in the music room?"

"All right."

He hadn't intended to propose to his future wife in a damned music room, but he rapidly saw his alternatives deteriorating. He followed Victoria into the room and closed the door behind him. He watched her walk to the pianoforte and run her fingers over a few keys. He drew himself up, prepared to declare himself. The good Lord knew he had right on his side.

But he didn't have the chance.

Victoria turned suddenly, and without preamble, said, "I wish you to marry me, Rafael. I wish it to be a marriage of convenience, with benefits to both of us. The benefits to me are obvious. For you, I wish you to know that I will give you half my inheritance."

He stared at her, unable to remember when he'd been so taken aback. She'd beaten him to the punch. He felt at once deflated and irritated. As a lady, she should have waited, should have let him do the proposing. Here she was demanding a ridiculous marriage of convenience. Well, so much for her fondness for him. It was on the tip of his tongue to tell her that if he married her, all her money, not just half, would become his automatically. He didn't say it.

Before he could reply, whatever that would have entailed, she continued, more quickly, more uncertainly, "As I said, it would be a marriage of convenience. I won't try to curtail your activities. You will be free to do whatever you wish to do. I swear, Rafael, I won't hang on your sleeve or make you uncomfortable."

"I see," he said finally, turning away from her to walk to the long bay windows. He stared at the blurring streaks of rain on the windowpanes, and said over his shoulder, not looking at her, "When did you come up with this idea?"

"While I was bathing."

"Ah. What makes you think I would be in the least interested in such a proposition?"

She was silent.

"A wife is an immense responsibility, Victoria. A responsibility of a lifetime. We scarcely know each other."

"You're right, of course," she said, and he heard the defeat, the utter helplessness in her voice. He felt like a damned bounder. He had planned to marry her, and here he was making her a supplicant. He was grinding her under, breaking her utterly, and it wasn't well done of him.

"I'll marry you," he said.

He turned as he spoke, and saw the leap of joy and relief in her expressive eyes. "Your eyes are very blue at this moment," he said.

"They change. Sometimes they even cross, particularly when I'm scared."

"Well, they're not crossing now."

"No."

"There is just one matter, Victoria. I refuse to have a marriage of convenience."

She stared at him.

"If we marry, when we marry, you will be my wife and we will be as intimate as a husband and wife should be. Do you agree?"

She thought of his strength, his warmth, the gentleness of his hands on her back but hours before, when Frances had brought her back. She tried to picture him naked, but she wasn't all that certain what a man looked like completely unclothed. Then she thought of her leg and blanched. He would see her leg. What if he were repelled, as Elaine had been? It was a thought she simply couldn't handle at the moment. She would think of something. *Tell him now. Tell him the truth.* But she couldn't. She was a coward, a bloody coward.

"Well, Victoria, do you agree?" Why was she hesitating? Did she find him unattractive? Did she fear having him bed her? He frowned. It wasn't a possibility he was used to.

"Yes," she said finally, "I agree."

He rubbed his hands together. "Very well. We will wed as quickly as possible. I'm glad it's settled, for I expect Damien to appear here at any time."

He saw that fear in her eyes again.

"You won't have to see him. Now, let's tell everyone. I imagine that Lucia will know precisely what to do. Special license and all that."

"There is no one to give me away," she said, her voice a bit wistful.

"The marquess would be delighted."

"He is a very nice gentleman, isn't he?"

Rafael agreed and the two of them went back to the drawing room to receive congratulations from people who weren't at all surprised at their announcement.

The marquess was delighted at the prospect of acting Victoria's parent, and said quietly, "My dear, you appear to be an utter delight. It will be my honor."

"Delight?" Rafael said, hearing this. "I'm not certain, sir. She does, however, require a strong hand."

Upon their departure, Frances said to Victoria, "You see, Victoria, everything worked out just as it should."

"I suppose so. I pray so. Rafael is very—well—"

"Virile, handsome, a devil?"

"Yes, you're right. I suspect he will be a handful."

"If ever you find yourself in need of lessons or advice on dealing with such a man, I shall be at your beck and call."

Looking at Hawk from beneath her lashes, Victoria didn't doubt for a moment that Frances had much experience dealing with gentlemen who were handfuls.

8

*More belongs to this marriage than
four legs in a bed.*
—THOMAS FULLER

Lucia didn't wonder even once why Rafael was
loath to leave her town house. Perhaps those with
lesser mental acuity might believe it was because he
was playing the ardent lover with his betrothed, but
not she.

When Didier appeared at precisely three o'clock
the following afternoon in the door of her drawing
room, she took one look at his face and said to Rafael,
"Well, my boy, I imagine the baron has duly
arrived."

"Yes, my lady," Didier said, only a single flick of
an eyelid to show his surprise.

"Do show the baron in," Lucia said. "Then inform
Miss Victoria that she is to remain in her
bedchamber."

Lucia knew they were twins. However, seeing the
two men together was still something of a shock, so

alike were they. Mirror images standing there, facing each other.

"Brother," Rafael said, not moving from his position beside the fireplace.

Damien gave Lucia a curt nod, then said to his twin, "I was rather hoping you would remain with your ship and take your merchandise to China."

"Unfortunately China was never a port of call. I imagined you would discover Victoria's whereabouts quickly. You didn't disappoint me."

"There is only one Lady Lucia in London," Damien said, proferring Lucia another nod and an ironic bow. "You, my lady, I must thank for seeing to the comfort of my ward."

"Baron," she said only. To Rafael she continued, "I shall leave you alone now. If there is anything you wish, you have but to ask Didier."

"That stately old fossil who answered my knock?"

"Yes," Lucia said, "he is the one." She left the drawing room, wishing she could leave the door open, but of course she didn't. Sometimes, she thought, it was most provoking to have had manners drummed into one from such an early age.

The two brothers eyed each other in silence. It was like looking in a mirror, Rafael thought. It was as if he could raise his left hand to his jaw and the image facing him would automatically do the same thing. He hadn't forgotten that another man laid claim to his face, his features, to eyes the identical silver-gray color—no indeed—but to see that man after so long a time, to see *himself*, it was disconcerting.

Damien said, "It has been a long time."

"More than five years. Yes, a very long time."

"I had hoped that you would have changed, but you haven't. If it weren't for your tanned face, no one would know us apart. I've never liked sharing myself, so to speak."

"It is difficult, I agree."

"I have come for my ward," Damien said.

Rafael, who had pictured this inevitable meeting at least a half dozen times in his mind, now moved to the sideboard and poured himself a brandy. "Brandy?"

"No."

"Well, brother, I trust I find you well?"

"As you see, Rafael. I am quite well."

"And your doubtless lovely wife? Her name is Elaine, I believe? Is she well?"

"Yes, certainly. I want Victoria, Rafael. I don't want difficulties with you. Nor do I wish to extend this conversation beyond what it must be. Have her fetched."

"I don't think so, Damien. I believe any court in the land would agree that you have abused your position as her guardian."

"You're being quite ridiculous, of course."

"Do you really think so? Shall I tell you how I happened to meet Victoria?"

Damien merely shrugged, as if bored. "If you wish," he said. But Rafael knew better. His twin was nearing an explosive point, his frustration and rage clear to Rafael. This time, however, he was dealing from the winning hand.

"Remember as boys how the smugglers and their activities always drew us out of the hall at nights? Well, I was riding near the coast just south of Axmouth and felt that old excitement. I rode down near the beach, and sure enough, there were two smugglers on their way to meet some fine French brandy, I suppose. It turned out that the smugglers had caught a very frightened girl. I saved her. It was Victoria, of course, trying to escape you."

"She stole twenty pounds. Any court in the land would be shocked at such behavior of a ward toward her guardian."

"Perhaps. But then again, twenty pounds is a very paltry amount compared to fifteen thousand pounds, is it not?"

Damien stiffened almost imperceptibly. "Ah, so you visited Westover, did you? Or did Victoria give you that information?"

"No, I visited him first. He took me for you, of course, and his concern over Victoria's, er, kidnapping was profound. I suppose you decided it was a very easy way to increase your coffers. After all, what chance would an eighteen-year-old girl have against you, Baron Drago?"

Damien said nothing.

"I assured Mr. Westover that Victoria was now quite safe and that the fifteen thousand pounds would be returned to her trust."

"You have no power at all in this matter, Rafael. None at all. Get me the girl, now. I have been patient with you, but my patience is wearing thin."

"Mr. Westover," Rafael continued, ignoring his brother's words, "was relieved that I—rather, you—had undergone so honorable a change of heart. He now believes you back on the path of guardian righteousness."

"Though you have been gone from England's shores for many years now, brother, surely even you remember that a guardian holds the only power. And I will continue to hold absolute power over her until she is twenty-five."

"Or until she marries," Rafael said very quietly.

"There was only one gentleman who showed any interest, and he cried off."

"David Esterbridge, I believe?"

"Yes."

"A paltry excuse for a man, that one. However, you assume that no other gentleman will want her? She is something of an heiress, after all."

"You may be certain that I will be well on my guard against fortune hunters."

"Indeed, you will be so very careful that she will reach twenty-five unwed and unfortunately quite poor?"

"I have no reason to continue this with you, Rafael. It's none of your affair. Now, if you don't tell me where she is, I shall find her myself."

"Oh, I will tell you. She is upstairs in her bedchamber. With Lucia, I imagine. Waiting for me to tell her that you are well and finally gone."

"I will tell you one last time, brother, she is my ward. I will have the constable fetched if you continue with this."

Rafael gave his twin a very lazy smile. "What constable would remove a girl from her betrothed?"

Damien felt rage, and the blood of his rage pounded at his temples. "My God. You would marry her, you bastard, just to thwart me?"

"You think so little of Victoria's charms, brother? Well, it is of no consequence. Indeed, she has already agreed to marry me. The wedding announcement is in today's *Gazette*, I believe. I had assumed that the announcement would be the way you would discover her whereabouts. Well, no matter now. The wedding is this Friday. As Victoria's guardian, I am formally asking your permission to wed her."

"I do not give it."

"Your own brother? You believe your own flesh and blood a fortune hunter? Hardly kind of you, Damien." Rafael paused, giving Damien a long look. He said quietly, "If you require a scandal, I will give it to you. Indeed, I will rock the land with a scandal. Now, my pleasure at seeing you after five years is about what I expected, except that you have become even more of a rotter. If you weren't my brother, I would kill you for what you have done to Victoria, doubt it not."

"You damned bastard."

"The fifteen thousand pounds, Damien. See that it is returned to Mr. Westover by Friday. Trust me, if you don't return the money, I will make your life a misery. You might even find yourself in Newgate."

Damien couldn't think straight. His fury was so great he was shaking with it. His damned brother. He cursed long and fluently. Rafael didn't move, merely looked at him, his expression remote. The gods were against him. And he wanted that money, wanted the money as much as he wanted to bed Victoria. Now both would be lost to him.

No. He would think of something. He had to.

"The fifteen thousand pounds—you want it for yourself."

"Don't paint me with your own brush, Damien. But as for the fifteen thousand pounds, it will be mine. As her husband, all her earthly goods belong to me."

"I will give you this round, Rafael," he said, turned on his heel, and strode from the drawing room.

Rafael stood quietly, staring toward the empty doorway. "Damien, it is the final and last round," he said. He heard the front door slam. Such a damned pity, he thought, remembering the two young boys, so alike they could even fool their parents. But Damien had changed. Or perhaps it was he himself who had done the changing. Perhaps Damien had always been as he was now, and Rafael just hadn't wanted to see it. Until they were sixteen. He shook himself. The memory was faded now.

"Are you all right, Rafael?"

He looked up to see Victoria slithering into the drawing room.

"Yes, of course."

"I saw him leaving from my bedchamber window." She shivered. "He looks so very much like you. It's frightening."

"Come here," he said, and opened his arms to her.

She paused but an instant, then grasped her skirts in her hands and skipped toward him. She fitted herself against him and rested her cheek against his shoulder.

"Thank you," she said. "You've saved me."

His arms tightened about her back. He breathed in the jasmine scent of her hair. So sweet and innocent she was. Gently he lifted her chin with his fingers. He smiled down at her, and kissed her.

He felt her surprise, then a slight quiver of pleasure. To awaken her was a heady thought. He lightly touched his tongue over her bottom lip, nothing more. Not yet. He didn't want to scare her. He had all the time in the world. He said as he raised his head, "No more fear, Victoria. We shall deal well together, you and I."

She gave him a dazzling smile. "Yes," she said, "yes, we most certainly shall. Even though you're a handful."

He arched a black brow. "I beg your pardon?"

"Frances said she would give me advice on how

to deal with you if you became too much of a handful for me. She, you know, has had a good deal of experience, married to Hawk."

He laughed. "Poor Hawk. How the mighty have fallen."

"Somehow I don't believe your Hawk minds at all."

"No, he doesn't, does he?"

Bishop Burghley, a very old friend of Lady Lucia's, presided over the very private wedding. A bluff, florid-faced man, he carried out his part with superb theatrics, his booming baritone overshadowing the vows of the handsome Captain Carstairs and his lovely young bride.

Victoria was at once excited, scared, and filled with anticipation. She gazed up at Rafael when he quietly repeated his vows. He was kind, gentle, and he would be a good husband. He was also stubborn and occasionally autocratic. He would come to care for her, she would try very hard to make it so. And he didn't want a marriage of convenience. Surely that meant that he wanted to make it a true commitment to her, to their marriage, to their future.

She heard a slight movement behind her, but didn't turn around. Only the Hawksburys, the Marquess of Chandos, Lucia, and her servants were in attendance. Perhaps, she thought, Lucia was dabbing her eyes with her handkerchief.

"Your vows, my dear."

Victoria started. The bishop was looking benignly at her and Rafael was grinning. "Say you'll have me, Victoria."

"I will—I do," she said. "Oh, yes, I do."

When Bishop Burghley completed his exhortations

on the sanctity of marriage, he said in his most genial voice, "You may kiss your bride, Captain."

"I will do my best," said Rafael as he lifted the gauzy veil.

Victoria raised her face to his and felt his lips lightly touch her closed mouth.

"Hello, wife," he said.

His words were drowned out by the applause of their friends and the servants and the rounds of congratulations. They both turned as one, and in that instant Rafael met his brother's eyes. Damien was standing at the back of the drawing room, his arms folded over his chest. He was wearing morning garb and Hessians. It was an insult.

Rafael felt Victoria stiffen beside him and gave her a quick hug. "There is nothing he can do, Victoria. You remain here and I will get him on his way."

Hawk found himself staring from Damien to Rafael and back again. "Good Lord," he said to Frances, "they are like two peas in a pod."

"And one a dangerous pea," she said.

"Rafael will rout the bounder," said the marquess.

"Well, brother, I see that you have indeed bound yourself to her. A pity, for you, that is."

"What the devil are you doing here, Damien?"

"It occurred to me that you didn't know the truth of things. I wanted to speak to you before you made the mistake of your life, but you weren't here last evening." Damien didn't add that he'd looked everywhere for his twin and had been furious at his failure to find him. And he hadn't been in time this morning. They were already married. He continued, "Being your loving twin, I was seeking only to spare you disappointment and humiliation."

"Get out, Damien."

"Afraid of the truth, Rafael? Perhaps you already know the truth. Of course, it isn't the first time, is it, that we have shared the same girl?"

"No more filthy references to Patricia. That is over and done with. Now, come with me to the library. I wish to get this over with once and for all."

Damien followed him willingly enough, casting one final glance at Victoria, who was staring at him, her face as white as the Valenciennes lace at the throat of her wedding gown. He smiled at her and gave her a small salute. It was both a threat and a promise, and Victoria knew fear.

Rafael closed the library door. "Now, Damien, the only reason I didn't kick you out is that I want to know if you have returned the fifteen thousand pounds."

Damien ran a negligent finger over his coat of pale brown superfine. "Oh, yes, indeed I did. I wouldn't want my own brother not to have all that is his due upon his marriage to that little slut. To palliate your disappointment, perhaps."

"Do you want me to kill you?"

The Rafael of today wasn't the Rafael of five years before. Damien wasn't fooled by those softly spoken words. He believed him, believed that Rafael would kill, believed that his life had led him to know death and fighting. "Not at all. What I want is for you to know the truth."

"What truth is that, damn you?"

Damien walked away from his brother, saying over his shoulder in a calm, nearly disinterested voice, "I assume that Victoria told you what a blackguard I am?"

"Yes, I managed to pry it out of her. It wasn't

difficult. When I rescued her, she thought I was you."

"An excellent actress," Damien said, turning to face his brother. "She always has been."

"You have five minutes, Damien."

"Very well, Rafael. You haven't married a shrinking little virgin. Indeed, it's true I wanted her, but I love my wife. It was Victoria who did the seducing. Why do you think she married you? It is because you are my imprint. But I digress. I bedded her, yes indeed. She wanted it so much I couldn't have stopped her if I had been a saint, which I'm not. She is a slut and a wanton, Rafael. Her passion exhausted me, I admit it. She escaped when I refused to divorce my wife and marry her. Her disappointment has become hatred, her hatred her revenge, using you. Against me."

He had no time to say anything more. He saw his brother's arm, then felt a searing pain in his jaw when Rafael's fist connected. He fell back, hitting his hip against the large desk.

"You damnable liar. God, I can't believe that even you would sink so low."

Damien stroked his jaw. It wasn't broken. He wanted to smile, but he didn't. He forced himself to shrug. "I just wanted to spare you a horrendous surprise this night. You remember David Esterbridge? I told you he cried off. It's true. He discovered that Victoria was my mistress. He was struck down, poor boy, but considered himself well free of her. I myself wondered if perhaps Victoria weren't pregnant and that was why she even considered Esterbridge. You must ask her. I tried to be careful, but as I said, she is so very passionate, so very eager. I sometimes forgot myself. Do you know that once she followed me into the old portrait gallery? I took her just beneath the portrait of Grandfather, against the wall." Those words were scarcely out of his mouth before Damien quickly skirted the desk, making it a barrier between him and his furious brother.

"Get out," Rafael said. "Your lying filth has taken you beyond your five minutes."

"I only wanted to spare you, it's true. Now that I've done my duty, I will return to Cornwall. Do you also plan to bring your bride there?"

"Get out."

Damien shrugged. "*Au revoir*, then, Rafael. Perhaps I shall see you at Drago Hall?"

Rafael said nothing. His rage was so great that he didn't trust himself to speak.

Damien smiled. "If only Grandfather could tell you now what he saw. Well, you will discover the truth soon enough."

"Get out before I kill you."

Damien's smile grew wider. "You must ask her which of us she believes the better lover. Brothers in all things—share and share alike, hmmm?" Since he wasn't a man bent upon his own death, Damien quickly removed himself from his brother's presence, leaving his damning words in the silent room.

Rafael watched his brother stride to the library door, open it, and leave.

He closed his eyes a moment, trying to regain his control. Poor Victoria. That sweet, innocent girl, having to defend herself against a man like Damien. The filthy, lying sod.

He forced himself to walk to the library door, open it, and pass into the entrance hall. Damien was gone, the bastard.

"You've been so kind to me," Rafael heard Victoria saying to Lucia. "Not at all a tartar."

"My dear," Lucia said in high good humor, "you didn't give me the right circumstance. Now, if you could but remain with me to do a proper come-out, you would see me fly my tartar colors quickly enough. When and if you meet Diana, she will tell you that I'm an impossible old lady."

"Somehow I don't think so," Rafael said, taking Lucia's hand between his two large brown ones. "Thank you, more than I can say, for helping us." He leaned down and kissed her. He grinned at the light flush on her parchment cheek.

"Laying it on a bit strong, aren't you, my boy?"

"Not I, sir," Rafael said to the Marquess of Chandos.

"Lucia has been a bothersome old busybody for as long as I can remember, and that is more years than I care to count."

"Unfortunately, you old goat," Lucia said, "I have yet to equal your ploy with Frances and Hawk. Masterful. You see, I am the soul of generosity. I'm willing to give you your due."

The marquess chuckled. "It's true. I will also admit that you weren't guaranteed the opportunity to truly test your own doubtless ruthless abilities. Rafael and Victoria were all too easy to match up."

"That we were," said Rafael, pulling Victoria's hand through the crook of his arm. He said quietly to her, "Did I tell you that you look quite lovely? The gown becomes you, but I can't say much about that wretched veil."

"I believe the purpose of a veil is to keep the bridegroom from expiring from shock and fleeing through the nearest door before the vows are finalized."

Rafael briefly thought of Damien's damning accusation. He tightened his hold on Victoria's hand. A pity that Damien was his brother. He hoped that when he'd struck him he'd at least loosened some of his teeth.

"Whatever is the matter? Are you just now realizing the enormity of your situation?"

He grinned down at his bride. "I am a very lucky man. That's what I was thinking."

But Victoria wasn't at all certain of that. Rafael could be very smooth when he wished to be, just as he was now with those glib words of his. She wondered what had passed between him and Damien, and found herself desperately wanting to know. She wasn't granted the opportunity until after she and Rafael had dutifully toasted each other with Lucia's finest champagne.

She said without preamble, "Rafael, why was Damien here? Surely he didn't believe he could prevent our marriage?"

He'd hoped, of course, that Victoria wouldn't inquire. A stupid hope. "He just had more ire and filth to spew over me. Nothing at all pertinent to anything. Now, my dear wife, I do believe it time for you to change into your traveling clothes."

This was the first Victoria had even thought about traveling anywhere for a wedding trip. "Good heavens. Where are you taking me?"

"The marquess has very kindly offered us the use of one of his country estates in Dorset. It is called Honeycutt Cottage, near the town of Milton Abbas. Does that please you?"

"Oh, yes. Yes, it surely does." She paused a moment, cocking her head to one side. "I forgot all about Mr. Westover, Rafael. Mustn't we see him so that I may legally transfer half my inheritance to you, as I promised?"

"Actually, I visited with Mr. Westover yesterday afternoon. Everything was taken care of. Papers signed and all that. There is nothing you need do now." He didn't add that Mr. Westover had been shocked that Rafael was the baron's twin brother, his lips a nearly invisible line when he realized that Rafael had pretended to be Baron Drago.

"I don't understand. Since it is my inheritance, shouldn't there be papers for me to sign?"

Well, Rafael thought, Victoria wasn't stupid. But how to tell her that all fifty thousand pounds was in his hands? He'd instructed Mr. Westover to draw up a document for his signature, allowing a generous allowance for Victoria, to be paid by him quarterly. He said now, "No, only I needed to sign papers. I'm your husband, you know."

"But—"

He lightly touched his fingertip to her soft mouth. "Upstairs, then, madam, but know I will drink champagne until you return."

"I shall be quick about it. I don't wish a weaving husband this soon in our married life."

Rafael watched her leave the dining room with a light step. She paused a moment to say something to Frances. He saw her shake her head, laugh sweetly, and nearly skip out of the room.

She was a darling. She was his wife. He decided at that moment that he would put half her inheritance in a trust fund for their children. It was a fair solution, one that should please her. The last thing he wanted was for her to think that he'd married her for her money. Thanks to Dame Fortune, he'd amassed quite a respectable amount of money for himself during the past five years.

He turned from his thoughts to see Lucia looking at him thoughtfully. "What is it, ma'am? Have I unknowingly committed some indiscretion?"

"No, my boy. It just occurred to me that since I'm a nosy old woman, perhaps I should play stand-in for Victoria's mother."

He looked at her, at sea.

"Victoria is a quite charming, quite innocent girl. Perhaps I should speak to her of the more intimate side of marriage."

"Ah," said Rafael. What Lucia could know of that was beyond him. She'd never been married. "Trust me," he continued in a very smooth voice, "to see to her properly. She will be all right, Lucia. I'm not a clod, you know."

Lucia nodded. "I don't suppose that you will tell me about that meeting with the baron?"

He stiffened. "No, ma'am. Suffice it to say that my brother is a very disappointed man, and disappointed men tend to spew nonsense in their frustration."

Lucia saw his hands clench into fists. She would have given up reading her gothic novels for a week if she could but discover what had passed between the two brothers.

A half-hour later, Lucia watched Rafael hand Victoria into the carriage. He spoke a moment with that impudent fellow from Cornwall, Tom Merrifield, then climbed into the carriage. A dear sweet girl, Lucia thought, waving. She hoped she would be happy with Captain Carstairs. She turned at the sound of Frances's voice.

"I think we should have at least one waltz," the countess said. "Where is Didier?"

"Here, my lady."

"Very well," said Lucia, her eyes going to the marquess. "Well, old man? Do you think you are up for some jollity?"

"With the awesome Didier at the pianoforte, I shall shine and my consequence will make even you, my dear Lucia, appear a charming gazelle."

"Good God, Father," said Hawk. "You insult Lucia with much more creativity than you accord to me."

"If 'village idiot' applies, my boy, there is no need to embellish upon it."

9

I am bewitched with the rogue's company.

—SHAKESPEARE

Fifteen minutes after Tom Merrifield had tooled the carriage away from Lady Lucia's town house, Rafael said abruptly, "I have a confession to make."

A confession was better than nothing, Victoria supposed, wondering at his strange and unusual silence of the last ten minutes. "What is it?"

"I get vilely ill riding in a closed carriage. Most unmanly, I know, but since you are my wife, and I will stick to you like a limpet, I feel I can admit my weakness."

Victoria looked at him with thoughtful concern, but he saw the dimple deepen in her left cheek. "Now that I look at you closely, you are turning a rather peculiar shade of green."

"Don't," he said, and in the next instant smashed his fist against the ceiling of the carriage. Tom obligingly pulled the carriage off the road. "Later," Rafael said as he leapt out of the carriage. Victoria leaned

forward, watching him standing very still at the side
of the road, breathing in deeply.

A pity only his stallion, Gadfly, was tied to the
back of the carriage. The thought of riding alone
again wasn't pleasant. Well, there was no hope for it.

Victoria grinned. She'd wondered, a bit miffed,
why her new husband hadn't been at all loverlike.
Well, now she had her answer. How could he be
such a good sailor and get ill in a carriage?

"It isn't at all fair, you know," she called out as
he turned toward her. "Now I am to be stuck with
my own company."

"Think all sorts of marvelous things about me, Victoria. Think about tonight, and what delights await
you."

"You're outrageous. Hush, Tom will hear you."

"Tom never hears a thing unless it involves the
word money. Now, we'll stop in an hour for luncheon. All right?"

She nodded.

Lunch at the Green Eagle passed pleasantly
enough. Rafael had recovered his healthy color and
upon her eager request told her another of his adventures, this one of his meeting with a whaling captain
in Boston harbor, a treacherous old man who'd tried
to blow up the *Seawitch*.

"Why, Rafael?" Victoria asked, sitting forward in
her chair.

"Later, my dear. There, I've given you something
mysterious and exciting to think about this afternoon,
since I'm not available to you."

It was only when he handed her into the carriage
again that he leaned down and kissed her full on the
mouth. Victoria, startled, froze, but only for a moment. His mouth felt wonderful, warm and sweetly

tangy from the wine he'd drunk at luncheon. She felt an immense urge to return his kiss, and did, coming up to her tiptoes. When his tongue lightly glided over her lips, she opened to him eagerly.

Rafael slowly pulled away and looked down at her, his gaze intent. Her cheeks were flushed.

"Oh," she said.

He lightly touched his fingertips to her cheek, then helped her without another word into the carriage.

She was warm and loving, he thought with a pleased smile as he mounted Gadfly. His wedding night would doubtless prove enjoyable, for both of them.

She is so eager for it—a wanton, a slut.

Rafael shook his head. Good God, what the devil was the matter with him? He wouldn't believe his brother's filthy words. He was an idiot to even remember them. He motioned to Tom to increase their pace.

He didn't call a halt until they reached Minstead and the Flying Goose. He saw the tiredness on Victoria's face and felt guilty. But he wanted to reach their destination in two days. He wanted to be alone with her and get to really know his bride. He wanted her to laugh and to love him. He rubbed his hands together, smiling.

Despite her weariness, Victoria was excited. It would be a night for mysteries to be solved. She wanted to become a woman, and though she wasn't at all certain what was involved in such a transformation, she was eager to learn.

And she knew that she would have to tell him about her leg. Oh, please, she begged her conscience, not tonight. She didn't believe he would be repelled, but she wasn't at all that certain. Her conscience warred with her uncertainty, rendering her markedly silent during their dinner.

Rafael was content to watch her. She's nervous, he thought, immensely pleased. He fully planned to go very slowly with her, to lessen her inevitable virgin's pain as much as he could. He spoke easily of inconsequential things, willing her to relax in his company, to smile with him again, perhaps even to tease him.

"Do you like your ring, Victoria?"

"Oh, yes," she said, smiling at him. "The sapphire is exquisite."

"The stone nearly matches your eyes, though it isn't as brilliant."

It occurred to her at that moment that she hadn't thought to buy him a wedding gift. Not that fifteen pounds would have purchased all that much. She would simply wait until she had enough money of her own, then she would find him something very fitting. She didn't know him well enough as yet to know what that something would be.

"Would you like to retire to our rooms now, Victoria?"

She swallowed. "All right."

"Shall I send a woman up to you? Or will you allow me to play your lady's maid?"

"No, I'm used to seeing to myself."

He walked beside her up the dimly lit stairs of the inn. He'd ordered adjoining rooms, feeling himself a considerate fellow. He patted her shoulder and left her at her bedchamber door.

He smiled over his shoulder at her. "Knock on my door when you wish me to come to you."

"All right," she said again. *Tell him. You must.* But she said nothing. Later, she thought, she would tell him later.

There was warm bathwater awaiting her, and she smiled toward the adjoining door, wondering when

Rafael had ordered the bath for her. She undressed swiftly and stepped into the tub.

Rafael slowly undressed, folding his clothes neatly, as was his wont. Every few minutes he looked toward the adjoining door, wondering if Victoria was still in the tub. The thought of her naked made him harden instantly. His wife, he thought with satisfaction. His *wife*. He thought again of fate, of the unlikely set of circumstances that had brought them together. Just a bit over two weeks before, he hadn't known she existed.

It was another ten minutes before a light, very tentative tap came on his door. He nearly bounded into her room, he was so excited. He forced himself to calm, and slowly opened the door. There was but one branch of candles on the small table beside the bed. Victoria was standing in the middle of the room, her glorious chestnut hair loose down her back. She was covered from neck to toe in a beautiful confection of peach silk, a wedding gift from Frances. She looked so exquisite he could only stare at her.

"Well," he said finally and with great inadequacy, "did you enjoy your bath?"

She nodded shyly.

"You're beautiful, Victoria."

She looked at him fully as he spoke. He was wearing a rich burgundy dressing gown. His feet were bare. "As are you, Rafael."

He grinned. "A crusty old salt like me?"

"There is nothing crusty about you."

"Come here, Victoria."

She walked to him without hesitation and he gently took her into his arms. He held her, not caressing her as yet. She smelled so good, he thought, inhaling her jasmine scent. Slowly he stroked his hands down her back.

"You're not nervous, are you?"

She thought of Damien and his groping hands and stilled for just a moment. She shook her head against his shoulder. "No, not with you."

"Well, I'm nervous," he said, nibbling on her ear. "You will be gentle with me, won't you, Victoria?"

She giggled, just as he had hoped she would. "I'll treat you with the greatest circumspection," she said, and leaned back against his arms to look up into his face. Lightly she touched her fingertips to his jaw, his lips. Slowly he leaned down and kissed her. Softly, not demanding, just a gentle exploration. Again she responded to him without hesitation, just as she had when he'd kissed her this afternoon. Her response made him draw in his breath. He wanted her very much. "Victoria," he said against her mouth.

She felt his hands cup her and lift her against him. He was hard against her belly, and she felt a bolt of heat deep inside.

He was nibbling her ear, kissing down her throat. She arched her back against him, throwing her head back. She thought vaguely that she should tell him about her leg, and opened her mouth, but he kissed her, his tongue lightly touching hers, and she forgot about her leg.

She felt somehow insistent and wild, and she gasped with the power of it. "Rafael," she said, her voice filled with surprise.

He heard the excitement in her voice, and trembled himself as he picked her up in his arms. "You don't weigh much," he said, and pulled her more closely to him. He felt her breasts, full against his chest, and nearly ran to the bed.

"Lord, Victoria, you're driving me over the edge."

"The edge of what?" she said, staring up at him as he eased her onto her back.

"I want you very much." He forced himself not to touch her, not yet.

Victoria wasn't at all certain what this wanting entailed, but she knew she wanted as well. Wanted to touch him, kiss him, feel the length of his body against hers. Unbeknownst to her, her eyes glittered with excitement, and something else he recognized—desire.

She was so eager for it.

He shook his head. Good Lord, he wanted his wife to desire him. He didn't want her to fear his lovemaking. He straightened and stepped back from the bed, his eyes never leaving her face. Slowly he untied the sash around his waist and shrugged out of the dressing gown. "I know you've never seen a man before, Victoria. I want you to look at me, get used to me, and know I won't hurt you."

Victoria stared at him. He was magnificent, silhouetted by the flickering candlelight. Shadows played over the thick black hair on his chest and over the ridged muscles over his flat stomach. She felt her heartbeat increase, felt the spurting warmth intensify, just looking at him. Her eyes moved downward and widened. Without conscious thought, her hips lifted, and her legs parted.

"Rafael," she whispered, and she opened her arms to him.

He came to her then, lying beside her, propped up on his elbow. He looked down at her, his eyes as stormy a gray as the North Sea in the dead of winter. "You like what you see, Victoria?"

"You're beautiful," she said, and kissed his throat. "I can't imagine a man more beautiful than you."

You are my imprint—that is why she married you.
"Can you not?" he heard himself say in a distant voice. Then, furious at himself, he yanked at the ribbons of her nightgown. She began to tremble. When he pulled the silk apart, she felt the chill air on her breasts. He was staring down at her and it increased her own excitement to a near fever pitch. She couldn't imagine feelings like these, but she didn't question them. He was her husband. He lightly touched his hand to her breast and she gasped. "Very nice," he said, lifting her breast, feeling its weight in his palm. He could feel her pounding heartbeat against his hand. He heard himself say, "You're not afraid, are you, Victoria? Of me touching you like this?"

Since she'd never felt anything like this in all her nearly nineteen years, she couldn't think clearly enough for the moment to answer him. She closed her eyes, feeling him caressing her breast, making her want to scream with the sensations.

He lowered his head and nuzzled her breast, his warm breath caressing her.

"You're perfect, Victoria." He suckled her, and she arched upward, unable to help herself. "Yes," he whispered, his breath hot against her flesh, "utterly perfect."

His words brought her a moment of sanity. She wasn't perfect, she was flawed. His hand was moving downward now and she knew that soon she would be naked and he would see her.

He pulled the nightgown aside. She heard him suck in his breath. His hand roved downward, coming to rest on her belly. She felt a nearly uncontrollable sensation, lower, just below his long fingers. She wanted him to touch her, wanted— His hand went instead to her right thigh, kneading the smooth flesh, the sleek muscles.

"Does that please you?"

She groaned, her head back. His hand wedged between her thighs, his fingers coming nearer to where her need was becoming nearly unbearable.

"You're soft, Victoria, and warm." His fingers lightly touched her. "Hot," he said, kissing her, even as his fingers found her. Suddenly his fingers left her, left the burning need, and she wanted to tell him not to stop, tell him— His hand neared her left thigh and her breath flattened, and she stiffened.

"Rafael, please, douse the candles."

Even as she spoke, she was pulling away from him.

"Why?" His own breathing was ragged, but he also felt strangely apart from her. "I want to see you, all of you. Don't become missish on me now, Victoria."

"No. Please, Rafael, there is something I must tell you. Please, wait."

His hand left her thigh and came to rest on her belly, holding her there, holding her still. He felt an awful foreboding. "What is it?"

"Something I should have told you before we married," she said, her voice coming in small, gasping breaths.

He felt sick, and his belly cramped. Damn her, he knew what she would say, and hated her, himself, and Damien. His desire died a swift merciless death.

He watched her jerk the nightgown over her stomach and legs, covering his hand.

Dammit, no. She couldn't be a wanton, a slut, his brother's eager mistress. Not Victoria, his innocent, utterly guileless wife.

He forced himself to say in a light, teasing voice, "What could you possibly have to tell me? Something that will make me despise you? Don't be silly, Victoria."

"I hope it will not. I was just so afraid of what you would think. I've been a coward. I'm sorry, truly."

He couldn't bring himself to look at her. Slowly he drew the silk over her breasts. Just as slowly he drew up and rose to stare down at her.

"Virgins bleed the first time," he said, his voice distant.

Victoria didn't understand what was happening. He'd left her. She looked at him and saw that he was no longer swelled and eager. "I don't understand," she said, confusion in her voice and in her eyes.

"I didn't want to believe it," he said slowly, feeling more miserable than he had in his life. "I would have wagered my life on your honesty, on your innocence." He laughed harshly, grabbed his dressing gown, and flung it on. "God, to think that I could be such a fool. You are a wild little slut, aren't you? You should have had me douse the candles much sooner, my dear girl. Perhaps, just perhaps I wouldn't have missed what I wouldn't have been able to see for my own eyes."

"I don't understand. Surely it's not all that awful. I couldn't help it, truly, Rafael. Why are you so angry?"

"Dear God, would you have screamed and faked a virgin's pain? You might have forgotten, though, you were so excited, so anxious for me to take you. There will be no comparisons, Victoria. Damn you to hell, you perfidious bitch."

He turned on his heel and strode to the adjoining door. She stared after him, flinching when he slammed the door behind him.

Had Damien told him of her ugliness, made it sound worse than it was? What did he mean about comparisons, and blood, a virgin's blood? She remembered clearly Damien's look before he and Rafael had left for the study. What had Damien said to him?

Victoria suddenly felt very cold. She felt cold deep inside. It was her wedding night and her husband had left her. He'd told her she was beautiful, he'd caressed her until—

Her hand went to her left thigh, her fingers lightly rubbing the ridged scar. She felt suddenly unclean, her body an object to be despised. She had disgusted him, that was clear. But why? He hadn't seen her leg.

Slowly she lowered her face to her hands but she didn't cry.

"Are you ready?"

Victoria forced herself to look at her husband. Those were his first words since he'd slammed his door on her the previous night. She'd eaten her breakfast alone. She hadn't even known where he was. Her husband, her loving husband who hated her.

"Yes," she said. "I'm quite through now."

"Come, along, then." He paused, taking in her pale face. Was she writhing in guilt for what she had done to him? Suddenly the fact that they would be alone at Honeycutt Cottage—for how long?—struck him as insanely funny. But what man wouldn't want to be alone with such a passionate little slut? *Except she is your wife.* It occurred to him that he could have their marriage annulled. *But what if she is pregnant with Damien's child?* The child would most certainly look like him, if it weren't the picture of Victoria, and what court would grant him an annulment when there was a child in his image?

He cursed softly, turning away from her. He would strike her if he remained in the same room with her.

He heard her rise and push in her chair. He didn't look back, merely walked out of the room and the inn. He mounted Gadfly, waiting for Tom to assist her into the carriage. At least he wouldn't have to see her today.

He watched her walk toward the carriage, her head lowered. Tom was holding open the carriage door. Suddenly she looked over at him.

"Rafael?"

"What?"

His voice was impatient, and she heard the underlying anger. She shook her head. How could she ask him in front of Tom: Why do you suddenly hate me so? She shook her head, defeated. "Nothing."

"Good."

When he halted for luncheon, he simply led her into the inn and left her. It appeared that he despised her so much he couldn't even bear to share a meal with her. During the afternoon she went from self-pity to rage. "He can't do this to me," she said aloud. "He's behaving horribly. I won't allow it."

Although the marquess's directions had been adequate, there were a number of roads that wound about without sign markers, and they didn't reach

Honeycutt Cottage until nearly six o'clock that evening. It was set back from the narrow country lane behind a black wrought-iron gate. The drive was lined with lime and oak trees. It was a charming ivy-covered Georgian house, two stories, with many chimney pots on the slate roof, and of a cozy size.

When the carriage pulled up in front of the double front doors, a woman emerged, wiping her hands on a voluminous apron.

She gave Victoria a curtsy when she stepped out of the carriage. "My name's Mrs. Ripple. And you are Mrs. Carstairs?"

How odd that sounded, Victoria thought with mild shock. She nodded.

"You must be exhausted, you poor child." She nodded toward Rafael, then continued, "Come in, my dear, and I will show you to your room. I just received word yesterday from the marquess. But everything is in readiness for you. Yes, your man is bringing your luggage."

Victoria didn't wait to see if Rafael would follow her. She assumed that he wouldn't. She trailed after Mrs. Ripple up the narrow stairs to the second floor. At the end of the corridor the housekeeper threw open the door and announced that this was the master's suite. Victoria's eyes went to the large, stark-looking bed, and shuddered. Mrs. Ripple kept up her enthusiastic monologue, and Victoria followed her into the adjoining bedchamber. It was very feminine, with quantities of pale blue ruffles on the spread and canopy. The furnishings were a combination of a soft cream and the same pale blue, the thick carpet swirls of blue and cream. Victoria regained a few wits, realizing that Mrs. Ripple had paused and was looking at her.

"I beg your pardon. What did you say?"

"You're weary, my dear. Why don't you rest? You and Captain Carstairs can dine in an hour. Is that all right?"

"Certainly. Thank you." Anything was all right with her at the moment. She wanted only to lie down, close her eyes, and stop thinking and feeling.

"Get up."

The curt orders quickly penetrated and Victoria jerked awake to see Rafael standing beside her bed.

"It's time to dine."

His expression was implacable, his eyes as bright as polished silver. She shivered.

"Do you need Mrs. Ripple?"

"No."

"I will see you in the dining room, then." She watched him stride from her room.

When she entered the dining room, a very small, intimate room paneled with dark wainscoting, her husband was standing next to the table, a glass of wine in his hand.

He downed the rest of the wine in one gulp, motioning her to sit down. Very well, she thought, squaring her shoulders. No more cowering.

Unfortunately, she had to hold her tongue until finally Mrs. Ripple had left them.

"Beef?"

"Yes, thank you."

"Potatoes?"

"Yes, thank you."

"You didn't change your gown."

"No. I didn't feel like it."

"Stewed vegetables? Green beans, I believe."

"No."

"Your hair looks as if it hadn't seen a brush in a fortnight."

She opened her mouth, and he quickly cut her off. "I know, you didn't feel like combing out the rat's nest."

Victoria forced herself to eat three bites of everything, though the beef was stringy, the potatoes half-boiled. She drank a glass of wine. Rafael said nothing and neither did she. She was ready for the offensive when Mrs. Ripple entered the dining room. She looked from one of them to the other, her gaze bright.

Victoria sighed, thanked the woman, and rose.

Rafael didn't even look up.

"Good night," she said, and marched from the room.

Fortunately, her anger didn't have time to burn itself out. She heard Rafael's footsteps not an hour later. She waited ten more minutes, then opened the adjoining door without knocking.

He was standing with his back to her, staring down at the sluggish fire in the grate.

"I have had quite enough of this," she said in a clear voice. "For some reason that I can't fathom, you now despise me. I have come to ask you if you would like to have this farce of a marriage annulled."

Rafael slowly turned to face her. "Annulled?"

"That's right. I can't imagine spending much more time with a man who can't bear my company."

"It's a pity, but I fear that our marriage can't be annulled."

"It can, most certainly."

"I don't believe I could prove that I hadn't been intimate with you, madam. After all, you aren't a virgin, and I doubt that even you, with all your glibness, could pretend that."

She stared at him blankly.

"Are you also pregnant?"

"Are you insane?"

He sliced his hand through the air. "Stop it, Victoria. Stop your damned lies. How many men, besides my twin, have you bedded?"

She released a long breath. "So," she said very slowly, "that is why Damien wanted to speak to you. May I ask what he told you, exactly?"

He said brutally, "He told me that you seduced him, that you were so eager he took you once in the portrait gallery, against the wall, that you were a slut, a wanton. God, madam, your eagerness last night proved it."

She could only stare at him. Her tumbling thoughts straightened themselves out. So his rage of the previous night had nothing to do with her leg. He had believed his brother's lies. She said aloud, her voice as cold as ice, "So, because I wanted to become your wife, you thought me a slut? You believed your brother and his lies?" Suddenly she laughed, a raw, ugly sound that made him start. "You believed him because I was enjoying your caresses and kisses? It is too much, Rafael. Goodness, if I'd known, I would have shrieked and fought you and fainted. You're a fool. You may keep half of my money. After all, I do have the protection of your name, as little as that means. I'm leaving tomorrow. I'm returning to London. I will see Mr. Westover. Good night."

She turned on her heel and stomped through the adjoining door.

"You are in the same situation, Victoria," he shouted after her. "You haven't a bloody sou. Are you so damned ignorant that you don't know that a wife's money becomes her husband's upon her marriage?"

She stopped in her tracks. She turned to face him. She said slowly, "I don't believe you. It's my money, not yours."

"Believe it," he said. "You are as poor as you were when you punished Damien by running from him. How much is it you still have? Fifteen pounds? I wager that won't get you all that far."

"I don't believe you," she repeated. No, she wouldn't believe him, she couldn't. It couldn't be possible.

"I suppose," he said brutally, "that you could sell your body. You are young enough and beautiful enough to find yourself a generous protector. Unless, of course, you're pregnant. Are you with child, Victoria?"

Her fingers closed around a particularly ornate Chinese vase sitting in isolated splendor on a table. She saw red, whirled around, and hurled it at him.

10

It is not enough to aim, you must hit.
                              —ITALIAN PROVERB

Rafael ducked quickly enough to save his head, but not quickly enough to spare his upper arm. The vase struck hard and bounced off, shattering against the wooden floor.

He unconsciously flexed his arm, saying nothing. Victoria was standing rigid as a stone, her eyes on the floor, on the shards of vase.

He heard himself say very calmly, "You have an excellent arm and a good aim."

"I wish I had a pistol."

"If you did, and you had the gall to aim it at me, I would thrash you senseless."

"A man's threat," she said, "just as a man uses his strength to ravish an unwilling woman. You are all despicable. I had believed you different, more fool I. Good-bye, Captain Carstairs. You needn't see me off in the morning." She gave him a mocking salute and turned the door handle.

"Don't do it, Victoria."

She simply shook her head, not looking back at him. Then, abruptly, he was behind her, his hand pressed against the door above her head. She stood perfectly still, knowing that sooner or later he would tire of this game of his and allow her to leave.

"I don't understand you, Victoria," he said, and she heard the bafflement in his voice. "My God, I didn't believe anything Damien had spewed out, until—"

She said nothing. It should have occurred to her sooner, much sooner what Damien had done. After all, his slander had worked well with David Esterbridge. Why not employ the same device with his brother?

"You yourself told me. You said you had a confession, something you should have told me before we married. You don't intend to deny that now, do you?"

"No, I don't deny it," she said dully, still facing the door. "I did have something to tell you. But it isn't important now."

He looked down at the top of her head, frowning ferociously.

"What would you possibly have to confess to me if not the fact that you weren't a virgin? If you will recall, I was nearly to the point of initiating you into lovemaking. Initiating. God, that's a jest on me, is it not?"

"So that is what you were talking about," she said, more to herself than to him. "I did wonder. I didn't understand."

"Stop your infernal playacting."

"I wish to go to my room now. I must pack my things."

"I told you, you won't get very far with a paltry fifteen pounds."

"It isn't your concern. I stole twenty pounds and you managed to steal fifty thousand. You have made yourself quite a bargain, Captain. Surely you should be content with your gain." She shook her head and laughed. "I was the fool, an utter fool to believe you different from your brother."

Something wasn't right here. He didn't move his hand from the door. "I'm not like my brother," he said.

"Are you not? He's a ruthless, lying bastard. You chose to believe him rather than believe me, your wife. That tells me quite enough about your character, or lack of it."

"Very well, then. If you weren't going to confess your lack of virginity to me, what was your confession? What could you possibly confess that would have aught to do with anything, particularly in the midst of our lovemaking?"

"Be content, Captain. You are now a much richer man than you were but two days ago."

He felt primed for violence, his frustration was so great. He grabbed her shoulders and turned her savagely around to face him. "What was your confession?" He ground out the words, shaking her.

"Go to the devil," she said very precisely and very calmly.

He frowned down at her. He said slowly, thoughtfully, "I can prove what your confession was or was not. I can prove to myself that you are a virgin. Or that you are not."

"Don't touch me, Rafael."

"I am touching you. You are my wife. I can do just as I wish to you."

He lowered his head and tried to kiss her, but she jerked away and his mouth landed in her hair. He grasped the knot of hair at her nape and held her. He kissed her hard, trying to force her mouth open.

She began to fight him, hitting her fists against his chest. When his tongue thrust into her mouth, she bit him. He lifted his head, anger and pain coursing through him. She was pale, her eyes dilated.

"So, you are no different from your brother. You would force an unwilling woman. You're an animal."

She swiped her hand across her mouth to remove the feel of him, the taste of him, and he saw the disgust in her eyes.

Her action enraged him. "You little hypocrite. You were so wild for me last night, I doubt you will play the unwilling maiden for long. You felt only my fingers on you last night, not my mouth, not that you needed that, you were already so hot and—"

She lost control. She drove her knee into his groin.

He gasped, stared at her, knowing the pain he felt now would soon be unbearable. "I wish you hadn't done that," he said before he groaned and fell to his knees, his hands clutching at his belly.

Victoria didn't wait another instant. She was through the adjoining door, slamming it behind her. There was a key in the lock and she quickly turned it. Slowly she stepped back. She was trembling. She didn't know how long she had stood in the middle of her bedchamber, not moving, when she heard him striding toward the outer door of his bedchamber. Her eyes flew to the door that gave onto the corridor, and she ran quickly to it. She turned the key just as she heard his footsteps stop on the other side.

Rafael's fist was raised to pound on the door.

Slowly, as reason returned, he lowered his arm. He said very quietly, "Open the door, Victoria."

"No." Then, louder, "No." In that instant she pictured herself lying terrified in her bed, Damien calling to her from behind her bedchamber door. It was too much.

"I will kick the door in if you don't open it this second."

Very quietly Victoria fled across her bedchamber to the adjoining door. She unlocked it and slipped into his bedchamber, locking the door on his side. Her heart was pounding, but she was smiling grimly.

Her sense of triumph disappeared but moments later. Dumbly she watched the hall door open, watched him stride confidently into the room. He closed it behind him. "I thought you just might try something like that. No more escape for you, Victoria. Don't even try it. Another thing, dear wife. You try to unman me again, and I will tie you down and show you not a whit of consideration. Do you understand me?"

She had lost. She felt an overwhelming sense of helplessness. Futile, she thought. Everything I try is futile. She looked at his angry set face from across his bedchamber. Slowly she sank to her knees. She crouched against the wall, her head buried against her thighs. She didn't cry; the pain was too great, her sense of loss too overpowering.

Why didn't she simply tell him about her leg? But she knew the answer. He had believed his brother's filth. She didn't owe him an explanation. He didn't deserve it. He deserved nothing. She didn't even hear him walk to her, she was so lost in her own misery.

Rafael stood over her, his hands on his hips, his

legs spread. She deserved a beating, he thought, but the sight of her huddled on the floor against the door unnerved him. Slowly he dropped to his knees beside her.

"What was your confession?"

She felt his hand on her upper arm and flinched away. But he didn't release her. "What was your confession?" he repeated. "You will tell me—something—or you will spend the night here on the damned floor. I mean it, Victoria."

To his surprise and chagrin, she shook her head, not saying a word.

"So, you can't even think of a convincing lie."

Suddenly she raised her head from her folded arms and said, "Are you a virgin, Rafael?"

"What the hell does that have to do with anything?"

"Are you?"

"Don't be ridiculous, Victoria, I'm a man."

"And a man always wins, does he not?"

"I didn't," he said, bitterness filling his voice. "Not this time, not with you."

She looked him straight in the eye. "Are you going to rape me?"

He sighed. "No, I'm not like that."

"I don't want to spend the night on the floor. May I go now to my room?"

"Not until you tell me this confession of yours."

She gave a brittle laugh. "Very well, I will tell you, all of it. I am really known as the trollop of St. Austell. Damien was only one lover in a very long line of men. There were so many, it's difficult for me to remember—I began quite young, you know, perhaps as young as you, a man. I was, ah, not more than fourteen when this very virile stableboy took me into

the loft. I shall never forget how he kissed me,
how—"

"Stop it."

Rafael jumped to his feet. "Get out," he said finally. "Get out of my sight."

I have won, at last, she thought as she forced herself to rise. Her leg, cramped from the position, knotted, and she had to grasp the door handle to keep
from falling.

Rafael didn't notice. He'd turned away from her.

She gave him a last bitter look and slipped into
her room. She didn't lock the door. There was now
no need.

Very early the following morning, Victoria quietly
opened her bedchamber door, looked up and down
the corridor, and slowly pulled her valise out of her
room. It wasn't much heavier, she thought with a
sad smile, than it had been when Rafael saved her
from the smugglers. How very long ago that seemed.
A lifetime, at least a lifetime of feeling. As quietly as
she could, she crept down the corridor to the staircase. She paused a moment, staring down into the
gloomy entranceway. Of course Mrs. Ripple wasn't
up and about yet. She prayed Tom slept in the house
and not in the stable.

Quietly, slowly, she made her way to the oak front
door, unlocked it, and slipped through into the chill,
foggy early morning. She pulled her cloak more
closely about her and half-dragged her valise toward
the small stable set at a right angle to the cottage.

She had every intention of taking his stallion,
Gadfly.

Her chin went up. She also intended to go to London, to Mr. Westover. Surely Rafael had lied about
her inheritance. Surely it could not simply all be his,

just because of a few words spoken by Bishop Burghley. No, nothing could be that unjust. She'd had the
long night to refine her plan. She wasn't stupid and
knew well enough that her leg could bear only three
hours of riding a day. It would take her at least four
days, then, to return to London. And that, she
thought now, a bit uncertain, would most certainly
eat up her fifteen pounds.

She slipped into the warm, dark stable. She
smelled leather, linseed oil, hay, and horse. Comforting smells. She found Rafael's stallion, and spoke
softly to him, wishing now she'd had the nerve to
fetch some food from Mrs. Ripple's kitchen. As she
slipped a bridle over the stallion's head, her wedding
ring sparkled in the dim light. The beautiful sapphire, circled with small perfectly cut diamonds—
Slowly she smiled. She had more than fifteen pounds.
She would hock the ring.

She eyed the saddle, then squared her shoulders
and hefted it onto the stallion's broad back. He
snorted, dancing a bit to the side of his stall.

"Hush," she said. "Please, don't move, that's right.
Hold still now, Gadfly. Good boy."

She tightened the girth, then slowly led the stallion
from the stall. She managed to lift the valise to the
saddle and slip the leather handles over the saddle
pommel.

"Hold still now, boy. We'll be gone in just a
moment.

"I doubt that, Victoria."

Victoria whipped around to see Rafael standing in
the doorway of the stable, his arms crossed over his
chest. He was wearing only a pair of breeches and a
white shirt. His feet were bare.

For a moment she could think of nothing to say.

She'd been so quiet. She laid her cheek against the saddle, willing him to magically disappear, willing him to be a nightmare.

But he didn't disappear, of course.

"How? I was so quiet."

"It occurred to me that you weren't in an excessively intelligent frame of mind. Only a female would decide to run away with fifteen pounds. You have proved your stupidity by this stunt."

"Oh, I have more than a paltry fifteen pounds." The instant she spoke, she wished she'd kept her mouth shut. She eyed the stallion's back and gauged her chance of climbing into the saddle and running Rafael down.

"Don't try it, Victoria. As to your meager fortune, I already checked. You didn't try to steal my money. Of course, that would have meant creeping into my bedchamber. I couldn't see you doing that. After all, I might have awakened, and then you would have shortly found yourself in my bed, on your back."

She forced herself to straighten and face him fully. There was a good twenty feet between them and it gave her courage. "Why are you doing this? Why aren't you delighted that I wish to leave and be gone from your life?"

His right hand slashed through the air. "Were you going to sell my stallion once you reached London?"

"No." Actually, she now realized that she probably would have thought of that, sooner or later.

"If you managed to make it to London, of course, which I strongly doubt. No smugglers, not here, in any case, but there are bandits, Victoria, who would be ecstatic to come across a delightful morsel like you."

"Why would you care?"

"After, of course, they raped you, they would probably kill you."

"Why would you care?" she repeated. "Then there would be no question that all my money would be yours."

"There is no question of that now, with you quite alive."

"I don't believe you. It would be too unfair. No, you are lying to me."

"My feet are cold," he said. "Come along back to the house."

"No, I'm not going anywhere with you."

He heard the panic in her voice and it bothered him. It made him feel guilty as hell. Damn her, she'd lied to him, she didn't deserve any consideration.

"Come here, Victoria."

"No. And since you appear to be so very concerned about my lack of funds, I fully plan to sell my ring. Perhaps you will be good enough to tell me how much of my money you paid for it?"

"About a thousand pounds."

"Poor Rafael," she said, trying for a credible sneer, "now you have only forty-nine thousand pounds left. Believe me, there will be much less for you when I am done."

"Actually, there will shortly be a good deal less for me. I intend to have Mr. Westover draw up papers for half your inheritance to go into a trust for our children."

She drew up, astounded. "I don't believe you. Damien would never have—"

"Don't compare me with my brother again, Victoria."

"I don't believe you," she said again.

She stared at him, watching him walk toward her, and something deep inside her snapped. With a broken cry, she kicked up, trying to thrust her foot into a stirrup. Then his arms closed around her waist and he was pulling her back. She yelled, calling him the few names she knew, and heard him laugh.

The stallion whinnied and jerked away from them both. In the next instant she was lying on the floor of the stable. Rafael grabbed the panicked stallion's bridle and began soothing the animal. With quick, efficient movements he removed the saddle and her valise. Then he led Gadfly back into his stall, still speaking low to him. He didn't look at her until he'd calmed his horse and closed the stall door.

"Stand up, Victoria. Don't make me carry you."

Slowly she came up on her knees. The muscles in her leg were tightening, she could feel them, and knew she must ease them. She must stand up.

He watched her slowly rise. Bits of straw clung to her cloak, her face was pale, and despite himself, he thought her beautiful and so very desirable, that his groin ached. He picked up her valise and turned away from her. "Come on," he said over his shoulder.

Another exercise in futility, she thought, trailing after him. She saw him wince when his bare foot hit against a sharp pebble, but he kept going.

She found herself studying him, his strong, straight back, his long legs. His thick black hair was disheveled. And she remembered, so very clearly, how she'd felt when he'd kissed her and caressed her on their wedding night. Such feelings she'd never imagined. She shook her head at herself. She was a fool. Evidently she should have showed more hesitation, more maidenly fright. It simply hadn't occurred to her not to act naturally with him. Didn't men want honesty? She sighed.

Mrs. Ripple was in the kitchen when Victoria followed Rafael back into the house. Her step was quicker up the stairs. She didn't want to be caught in such an unexplainable situation by the housekeeper. "Oh, yes," she could hear herself saying, "I was running away from my husband because I responded too freely with him on our wedding night and he believed his brother and thinks me a whore."

She wondered vaguely if she would ever forgive him for believing his brother's lies. And all because she'd wanted to become his wife and all because she was terrified that he would be repelled by her leg.

"Go back to bed," he said, and left her at her bedchamber door, the valise at her feet. He turned suddenly. "Don't try such a stunt again, Victoria. You wouldn't like the consequences, I promise you."

She took off her clothes, pulled a cotton nightgown over her head, and crept into her bed. She had to think, to decide what she would do now, but she was wretchedly tired, and within a few moments she was sound asleep.

Rafael quietly opened the adjoining-room door. He saw her huddled in the middle of her bed. What the devil should he do now? His marriage, begun with such promise and confidence, had fallen about his head in a shambles. He left the adjoining door open and walked back into his own room. He flung himself down on his own bed and pillowed his head on his arms. He stared at the white ceiling. He had to know, damn her, he had to. But he couldn't rape her. He'd been honest about that. It wasn't his style; indeed, he had nothing but contempt for men who treated women in such a callous fashion. No, he couldn't do that. What he had to do, he decided finally, was to seduce her. Then he would know once and for all. *And if she isn't a virgin? What will you do then, you stupid sod?*

He wouldn't think about it. He would simply deal with it if it happened. *But what is her grand confession? Whatever could a supposedly young innocent girl have to confess in the middle of lovemaking, for God's sake?* He found himself trying to remember her exact series of responses to him. Had she acted at all surprised when he'd first kissed her? He could feel her trembling against him, feel her part her lips.

Had he really expected her to shrink from him? Had he wanted her to be shy and frightened of sex so he could play the gallant, patient lover? Was he such a fool to have seen himself in the part of her mentor, her gentle husband who would teach her according to rules of his own creation to enjoy sex with him?

Of course, he remembered Patricia then. So sweet, so innocent, he'd thought, and he'd been so passionately in love with her, his sixteen-year-old heart filled with her. With all the restraint of a boy desperately in love, he'd taken her, so afraid that he would hurt her, his sweet, virgin love. She'd cried and whispered that he had hurt her, and he'd begged her forgiveness. And he'd believed with all the fervor of his sixteen years that he was the only man—man, ha!— she wanted. And then he'd found her with Damien. How his brother had laughed at him.

Rafael couldn't bear those memories, memories that he'd firmly believed were long dead. Until Victoria. He rose quickly, dressed, and left the house. He rode Gadfly until the stallion was lathered and blowing with fatigue.

It was near noon when he returned. Luncheon was laid out in the small dining room. Victoria was seated there, listlessly playing with a thin slice of ham on her plate. She looked up briefly when he entered, then just as quickly lowered her head again.

"Captain. Would you like some luncheon?"

He forced a smile for Mrs. Ripple and nodded.

When she took herself from the room, he forced himself to eat a bit of ham, which was incredibly salty, and buttered potatoes that tasted rancid. The silence was deafening.

He could hear himself chewing the bread, which was alternately crunchy and doughy.

"Victoria," he said finally, slowly laying down his fork.

She said nothing.

"Would you care to drive into Milton Abbas and see the sights?"

She could only stare at him, completely at sea. "Why?"

"We are on our wedding trip," he said, his voice smooth as velvet. "Surely we should find some enjoyment."

Victoria had already thought ahead to the long empty hours facing her. There was nothing more he could do to her. "All right."

"Excellent," he said, and took another bite of ham. "Perhaps we can have something to eat there."

There was a moldering old mare in the stable, but Victoria preferred riding even that relic to sitting in the closed carriage. The afternoon was clear, the sky light blue dotted with white clouds. They left Tom

Merrifield chatting with Mrs. Ripple, that good woman flushed with pleasure at his attentions.

The weather provided conversation fodder for a good five minutes. When it ran dry, Rafael looked at her profile for a moment, then drew a deep breath and said, "If you shouldn't mind too much, tomorrow or perhaps the next day we can continue to Cornwall. I wish to stay at Drago Hall for a week or two, that is all. Just to give me enough time to find the land where I want to build my home."

"Perhaps you will find a house already there that you like," she said, closing her eyes against the awful return to Drago Hall and Damien and Elaine.

She hadn't refused outright to go to Drago Hall, and he wondered about that. He'd expected her to be horrified when he told her. He looked at her and saw that she was smiling. At what? Damien?

"That appears to please you," he said, and she heard the suspicion in his voice.

"Yes, it does. I have sorely missed Damaris. I have cared for her a good deal since her birth."

"Yes, I remember your mentioning her now. You would not mind staying at Drago Hall for a while?"

She chewed on her lower lip, staring between the old mare's ears.

"Your position would be quite different, you know, from before. I assume you were at Elaine's beck and call."

"Yes, but I didn't mind. After all, until a very short time ago I believed myself a poor relation."

"Now you are my wife."

He sounded possessive, and that surprised her. She said nothing.

She felt his hand lightly touch her arm, and she

turned to face him. "You are mine, Victoria," he said
again. "I want no more strife between us."

She looked at his hand, his long fingers. "The strife
was of your making, Rafael."

"That is true. I wish now to unmake it."

"Do you truly mean it?"

He dropped his hand from her arm. The hope-
fulness in her voice shook him, made him hate himself, and his deception. Well, it was what he wanted.
He wanted her trust. He wanted her to smile again.
He wanted to make love to her and then he would
see.

"Yes," he said, "I truly mean it."

11

I do desire we may be better strangers.
                              —SHAKESPEARE

The problem, Victoria thought objectively, was that she became besotted when he was with her, notably when he basted her, just as Mrs. Ripple would a birthday ham, with his particular brand of charm. She disliked feeling this way immensely. Rafael didn't deserve anything from her after what he had done. She sighed.

He had, in the most sincere manner possible, asked her for a truce.

When he wasn't with her, as he wasn't now, she remembered his awful words on their wedding night and her two feet were firmly planted in blunt reality. And his afternoon charm had worn off a bit, like rice powder.

Victoria knew she wanted to believe Rafael had changed from a bitter and vindictive man to the charming and loving man she'd ridden with all afternoon. After all, an olive branch was an olive branch, and he'd offered it so charmingly. She sighed again as she slipped her blue silk gown over her head. And she had unbent so completely to him, grabbing that olive branch with great alacrity. And for more than just a little while. He quite simply blinded her with his charm.

At least now, away from him, she thought, viciously forcing the last button, she could see things more clearly. She sat at her dressing table and picked up her hairbrush. She frowned at her face. Why? Why had Rafael changed?

It was miserable to be constantly at war with each other. But he had started the war. Since that was the case, she supposed he believed he could just as easily and quickly end it.

She leaned closer to the mirror as she threaded a dark blue velvet ribbon through the curls atop her head. In the soft candlelight, flashing beacons of red and blond and deep brown shimmered through her chestnut hair. She decided that she looked well enough.

She paused a moment, turning slightly toward the mirror behind her dressing table. Perhaps it was the candlelight or the high ceilings of her bedchamber that gave off strange shadows and shades, but she realized with a start that she looked not just well enough. She looked well beyond acceptable. She stared a moment at her bare shoulders and nearly bare bosom, pushed upward by the stiff band of material beneath her breasts. White, she thought. She looked very white and soft and very female. And Rafael would think so.

And that was why he wanted to make peace with her.

He wanted to take her to bed.

He wanted to know if she was a virgin.

How could a man know that? she wondered, turning away from the mirror. Could a woman tell if a man were also a virgin?

Victoria pulled back her shoulders and headed down the winding staircase to the small drawing room on the first floor. Rafael was waiting for her there, a snifter of brandy in his hand. He looked remarkably handsome in his severe black evening garb, offset with the snowy white linen. A man shouldn't be blessed with such a silver shade of gray eyes or with such thick long lashes.

Then he smiled at her and she felt like a very cloudy day that had just been given a strong dose of sun.

"You look lovely," she blurted out.

Rafael blinked, for words of a similar nature had been on his tongue, ready to fire off. "Thank you," he said, grinning. "You're not such an affliction for the eyes yourself. You look enchanting in that shade of blue."

She merely nodded at his compliment, seeing him with new eyes. He was her husband, yes, he was, and he also looked quite determined and steely behind that layer of charming nonsense he was spreading so smoothly.

"Would you care for a glass of sherry?"

She nodded again. When he handed her the crystal glass, his fingers lightly touched hers. His flesh felt warm and smooth and hard. She willed herself to show no reaction. She should, she thought bitterly, as a virgin, jump out of her skin with maidenly fright whenever he even came near her. If he touched her, she supposed she should shriek with downright horror. She did nothing, merely stood quietly and silently, sipping her sherry.

At that moment, Mrs. Ripple appeared in the doorway, a smile on her wide mouth that showed the space between her front teeth, to announce dinner.

"She always smiles when she tells us to come to a meal," Victoria said. "It makes me feel like the sacrificial lamb. I wonder what she has concocted this evening."

"I just hope it's recognizable," Rafael said as he offered her his arm. She grinned and he decided that the truce was going well. So he looked lovely, did he? That made him want to smile. No woman had quite told him that before. As for his wife, he was honest: she looked immensely pretty, both in and out of that blue silk. As a man with some experience with women, he knew she'd spent more than a usual amount of time on her appearance. That pleased him. The night ahead would progress nicely, he hoped, and not become the desert of the past nights.

There was no conversation between them until Mrs. Ripple, having served them, left them alone in the small dining room to face the dinner.

"I believe it's beef," Victoria said. "Boiled."

"Yes, but it won't be too dry. All the fat is on it."

Whatever was on it, Victoria ignored the platter and took a helping of boiled potatoes and carrots. She began to eat without thinking about the taste of boiled parsley.

"She does try very hard," she said after some moments.

"Yes. If we were fat folk, she would be the perfect cook."

"Rafael?"

"Hmmm?" Rafael didn't look up. He was at the moment intent on cutting off a large ridge of fat from a slice of beef.

"How can a woman tell if a man is a virgin?"

His fork clattered to the plate. He looked at her perfectly serious face in blank surprise.

"I beg your pardon?" he said, buying himself some time. What the devil was she up to now?

"I asked you," she said patiently, "how a woman can tell if a man is a virgin."

"Your dinner-table conversation is unusual. Is this the first sign that you have embarked on an improper career?"

He was smiling at her, and that devastating white-toothed smile robbed his words of insult. Victoria didn't take offense, she merely shrugged. "There's no one else to ask."

"You want to know how a woman can tell if a man is a virgin." He toyed with his fork a moment, a long moment, and said finally, "A woman can't tell, at least she can't tell from any physical signs. I suppose if the man were particularly inept, she could guess that he was. Without any prior experience, that is."

He had watched her closely as he spoke. He wished he knew what was going on in that head of hers. He was quickly to find out.

"Is it the same with a woman? A man can't tell physically? He can only guess, if she is inept?"

So that was it, he thought. Hadn't she bled with the first man she'd been with? Hadn't it hurt her? Very well, he would tell her the truth, even though she probably already knew. It didn't matter if it were her plan to pretend virginity. He wasn't a fool. He said calmly, crossing his arms over his chest, "Actually, a woman is fashioned physically to prove her virginity."

"How do you mean?"

"I mean," he said, feeling anger stirring, despite his intentions toward peace, "that a woman usually has a stretch of skin inside her that is broken when the first man enters her. When it's broken, she bleeds. Also, there is pain because the woman's passage isn't used to having a man's member inside, and depending on the size of the man, it can, I suppose, hurt a great deal."

She paled as he spoke, but he didn't regret speaking so bluntly. Damn her, if she wanted him to be crude about it, he would oblige her. First, though, he said, his voice harsh, "Do you understand?"

She heard the incredulity in his voice, the suspicion, the anger, and nearly smiled at the image of his olive branch fast withering. "I suppose so," she said finally. It didn't sound at all pleasant, this lovemaking business. As to his male member, she had no difficulty at all remembering Rafael's their wedding night. If memory served, he was quite large and she supposed that meant that it would hurt a good deal. He would thrust that part of himself into her. All of it? In the light of day, without him touching her, it was truly a ghastly thought. She didn't like it, not one bit. But then she remembered more of her wedding night and the wild uncontrol Rafael had made her feel. None of it made any sense, none at all.

Rafael said in a coldly stern voice reminiscent of his father, "Don't even try it, Victoria. I'm not an idiot, nor am I blind. I remember hearing once how a bride, to keep her husband believing her virtuous, had a vial of chicken blood with her on her wedding night. She screamed when he entered her and then smeared the chicken blood on her thighs. Unfortunately for her, she didn't get away with it. Her husband wasn't pleased when he found the vial beneath her pillow, some chicken blood still in it. Nor would I be pleased."

"Chicken blood," Victoria repeated. "She used chicken blood?" She burst out laughing—she couldn't help herself. It was too ludicrous.

"Look, Mrs. Ripple has made some baked chicken. On that plate there, the greasy-looking hunks of meat." She hugged herself and laughed harder. "At least it's not boiled like the beef."

Rafael stared at her.

"I should go to the kitchen immediately. You must tell me how much I would need. Ah, but I am beset with the problem of a vial. Surely Mrs. Ripple would have something of a useful nature about. If not a vial, then a—a what, Rafael? An empty wine bottle? No, much too large." Tears streamed from her eyes, she was laughing so hard.

"Stop it, Victoria. Now."

She sniffed, hiccuped, giggled, then managed to pick up her napkin and gently dab at her eyes. "Forgive me," she said at last. "You're an amusing storyteller, Rafael. Have you other tales I should enjoy as much as that one?"

"I could finish that one, if you wish."

He didn't wait for her to reply, merely continued in an emotionless voice, "The husband sent the wife off to a godforsaken estate in Northumberland. Sure enough, in six months she birthed a bastard. He refused ever to see her again."

"I don't think I like that story after all," Victoria said. "It doesn't end well."

"Doesn't it? Should he have divorced her? Wrung her neck?"

"No, he should have asked her why she did it. I would assume that he had some affection for her."

"She played him false and lied to him. He knew enough."

"What happened to the child?"

"I don't know."

"So," Victoria said, sitting back in her chair, gazing at her very lovely husband down the expanse of dining table, "this is what you think I'm doing to you? You are afraid I'm with child? A bastard?"

"I hope that you're not."

"Your twin's bastard? How difficult that would be. After all, the child would resemble you. Whatever would you do?"

"Victoria, shut up. I want no more of this from you."

"Oh, I understand now. Of course, if the child were yours, it would be born nine months after you committed your sexual act. Any earlier, the good Lord help me, and there is yet another bastard to populate the earth."

"Victoria, I told you to be quiet."

"Your peace offering is growing more tattered and unrecognizable by the moment, Rafael."

"I'm not used to ladies asking me the symptoms of virginity. Surely it's not all that proper a topic of conversation."

"Little we've spoken of would qualify, I think, as proper."

She began to pare the warm skin off a peach. He watched her graceful fingers. "Untouched by Mrs. Ripple's housewifely hands," she said.

He poured himself another glass of wine. In silence.

"I have chanced upon some proper conversation," she said at last as she chewed on a peach slice. "Here it is. It will be difficult returning to Drago Hall. Perhaps Damien won't want us there. I can't imagine that he would ever wish to see either of us again. After all, Rafael, you did take what he must have seen as his fifty thousand pounds."

"Whatever else Damien is or has become, he never could tolerate any sort of scandal, particularly if he were the one in the middle of it. It would cause a great scandal for him to refuse shelter to his own twin brother." Rafael smiled, a rather nasty smile. "And you can be certain that everyone would know of it if he did refuse."

"I don't understand why you wish to stay there."

"I told you. Drago Hall would be a base of sorts. I wish to find a site for my future home."

His home, she thought, not theirs. "There are comfortable inns about."

"I haven't been in the house of my birth in many years. It was my home as well, you know, just as it was yours for five years."

"I have nothing at all against Drago Hall. It's just the inmates that are trying."

"You become vehement now. Why is that, I wonder. You weren't when I first told you of it this afternoon."

"Was I not? Well, perhaps I had other things on my mind. Would you care for a peach slice? No? I shall finish it off in that case. It's very sweet. Mrs. Ripple told me all the fruit is from the cottage orchard. Is it—"

"Victoria, do shut up."

"It took me a goodly amount of time, and, I might

add, being away from you, but I also determined why you wanted so very much to make peace with me."

He stiffened. "I'm really quite tired of your prattle. Would you like coffee in the drawing room?"

"No. Nor would I care to climb into your bed. If you but had some physical flaws, Rafael, I should have understood your motives much sooner."

"That is the oddest compliment I have ever received. I can't thank you for it. Nor, I might add, do I understand what you mean."

Victoria rose from the table. "It matters not. Do you play piquet?"

"Yes, certainly. At sea, one learns all sorts of interesting games to pass the time."

"Well, I suggest we ask Mrs. Ripple for a deck of cards. It is either that or doubtless we can begin to argue in earnest."

"I don't wish to argue with you."

"I don't wish to return to Drago Hall."

"I'm sorry, Victoria, but we must. Truly, I won't allow anyone to treat you—"

"—with less consideration than you do?"

"Your mouth glides on well-oiled wheels."

She sighed. "I suppose so. You're a constant contradiction, Rafael. It's difficult to keep pace with you."

"Not really. I'm just a man, Victoria, and now I'm a husband, your husband."

"Just what is that bit of obvious information supposed to convey? That I am to come to heel? I won't let you forget yourself again, Rafael." She'd spoken calmly, a layer of contempt in her voice, but all the same, as she'd spoken, she was backing up until her shoulder touched the doorframe.

"Why not? As I recall with great clarity, you couldn't get enough of me fast enough." His white-toothed smile wasn't lovely now, it was predatory.

She forced herself to smile in return. "That's true, but now I realize that a virgin is supposed to behave according to certain rules—rules, I am certain, that men came up with centuries ago. You touch me, Rafael, and I am to shudder with disgust and shriek with outrage. Have I got that right at last?"

He said nothing for a long moment. Finally he said easily, "Let's play piquet now."

"What is so very odd about all this is your anger. It would seem to me that you, as a man, would feel very pleased at my reaction to you. Shouldn't it make you feel a good deal of masculine pride? Make you crow about your prowess as a lover? You're a contradictory, perverse creature, sir, truly you are. Shall we play piquet?"

"You expect me to answer yes or no and ignore what you just said?"

"You do it to me with great regularity."

"I had not realized what an impertinent mouth you have, Victoria."

Then he must be quite slow-witted, she thought. "Ah, you wouldn't have married me had you realized it?"

"Yes, but I would have at least been prepared for the shrew, and not caught off guard."

"I imagine that you can ignore anything you wish to, Rafael. After all, you managed to come away with the spoils. Fifty thousand pounds. Perhaps you can even buy a moldering estate somewhere in the north and send me there. Then you have my money without my company."

"You will cease pushing me, Victoria, and you will

stop your nonsense about the fifty thousand pounds."

He wasn't smiling, and his face, without a smile, looked stern indeed. Forbidding. She bowed her head and turned on her heel. "I shall ask Mrs. Ripple for a deck of cards," she said over her shoulder, not looking at him.

She paused in the doorway, but didn't turn to face him. "Oh, Rafael, is a virgin supposed to play piquet well? Or is she to stutter and flutter about helplessly? Perhaps shuffle the cards badly? Make stupid plays?"

She was doing him in quite nicely, he thought, at once angered at her and admiring. She had guts, his wife. It was her other qualities he was concerned about. He managed to say easily, "I have never played piquet before with a virgin. I should say, though, since a female's goal in life is to procure a husband, she would play badly so that he would win and thus feel superior."

"She, of course, could then act admiring?"

"Ah, yes, indeed. How well do you coo, Victoria? Can I assume that you have been a virgin at least part of your female life?"

Amazing how just one short series of words could be the final straw. She said with amazing calm, "The truce is over, Rafael. I wish you would go to the devil and roast yourself."

She turned away from him, shoulders squared; then, as if she thought her exit too slow, she grasped her skirts and fled the entrance hall up the stairs.

He raised his hand, then dropped it to his side. He'd done it. Ruined things again. His damned mouth. He cursed softly, grabbed the brandy decanter from the sideboard, and strode to the small, very masculine study at the back of the cottage.

He wasn't at his best the following morning. The steaming bath Lizzie brought up had helped a bit, at least the hot water helped unkink his stiff muscles, but his head felt like a lead pipe was wrapped about it.

He'd awakened at dawn, cramped in the chair in the study, and staggered to his bedchamber. He moaned. He didn't want to think about it. He didn't want to think about anything.

It was Tom who saved his life. "You look a bit underground, sir," he said as Rafael drew in deep breaths of fresh morning air. He grunted and kept breathing.

"My ma taught me a marvelous recipe for the morning after. Should you like me to prepare you some?"

Rafael felt a shaft of hope. He nodded.

The potion was brown and thin and tasted of vile, thankfully unknown ingredients, but was possessed of remarkable restorative powers.

"Dear God, Tom Merrifield, I am in your debt," Rafael said not ten minutes later. He wrung Tom's hand.

Tom gave him a commiserating grin. "The brandy, sir, can be an assassin, that's certain. Did Miss Victoria also imbibe?"

"No," Rafael said, "no, she didn't. I do believe I'm even ready to face Mrs. Ripple's notion of breakfast fare."

"Lots of eggs, sir. 'Twill do you good," said Tom. "Another of my ma's suggestions."

Rafael wondered at Tom's sudden loquaciousness. The Cornishman had been a niggardly jailer of his words since Rafael had hired him. He said, "Mrs. Carstairs and I will be riding in about an hour, Tom."

At least Rafael hoped he could talk Victoria into accompanying him. How many peace offerings was a man allowed, he wondered as he walked back to Honeycutt Cottage, before his wife cracked his head with a poker? But she had provoked him, she had indeed.

All her ridiculous questions about virginity. Damn her beautiful eyes. And her near-hysteria about the chicken blood.

Victoria had just seated herself at the dining table when Rafael came into the room. He smiled at her, trying for a markedly winsome smile. All he could do was try. Hopefully she wouldn't notice the blood-shot eyes.

Victoria, for an instant, felt again like a cloudy day with the sun dashing through. She drew herself up. "Good morning, sir," she said, trying not to become besotted with that smile of his.

"Good morning. Would you like me to serve you?"

What the devil was he up to now? She stared at him for a moment, then shook her head.

"No, I'm not really very hungry this morning. The bacon looks soggier than the toast, unfortunately. It looks to become a lovely day."

"Yes, that is true. Ah, Victoria, would you like to explore the countryside with me? That Norman church in Milton Abbas, I wager it is worth seeing."

"For religious or archeological reasons, Rafael?"

"Neither."

"For cozying-up reasons, then."

"What do you mean?" The scrambled eggs were more than a bit on the runny side. Rafael eyed them tentatively, then decided to follow Tom's ma's advice. He scooped a pile onto his plate.

"Another olive branch."

"If you, Mrs. Carstairs, would simply practice keeping your mouth shut, we could have a truce to last fifty years."

"You shan't gain your truce in that manner, Rafael. However can you eat eggs that are so underdone?"

"I wish that you would keep your attention on your own plate, if you please. Now, why not look at it this way. Perhaps we can be friends during the day, and save up all our venom for the evenings. Half and half. Never be boring that way."

"Something so predictable would have to become boring."

"Not with your mouth, madam."

She sighed and took a bite of buttered toast. The butter, at least, was delicious. "You want to know something, Mr. Carstairs?"

"Fire away."

"I have never been an ill-natured person in all my nearly nineteen years. You have a grand capacity for making me absolutely furious."

He looked much struck. "Come to think of it, neither am I. An ill-natured person, that is. What do you suggest we do about it?"

"It is quite simple, really." He leaned forward at her quite serious tone. "All you must do, Rafael, is to trust me and believe me. I am your wife, if you would but bring yourself to remember that one small fact."

"You can prove to me quite effectively that I can trust you and believe you."

"No, you must trust me fully and completely before we consummate our marriage."

"Consummate? Wherever did a nice young girl like you hear that word?"

"I found it one day in the dictionary. I was looking up 'consumption,' as I recall. Elaine's aunt died of it and I wondered what the symptoms were."

"All right. There is another way, then. Tell me your confession."

She toyed with the spoon in the honey pot. Thick, smooth, and golden. At least Mrs. Ripple couldn't make the bees produce soggy honey. She should tell him her confession, but she couldn't bring herself to. All of it was inextricably tied together. It would, however, make him feel a total and complete bounder. That thought brought a smile to her lips. His chagrin just might be worth the sacrificing of her principles. Since when, she wondered, frowning at the honey pot, had her lame leg become a principle? Surely that made no sense at all. Nothing she'd done since she'd met this man made much sense.

"You ate all your eggs," she said finally.

"Yes," he said. "Arguing with you made me forget what I was eating. Would you ride with me?"

"Why not? Will you be charming? Until the sun sets, at least?"

"At the very least," he said, and rose from his chair.

12

We are easily tricked by those we love.
—MOLIÈRE

When Rafael lightly clasped her shoulders, drawing her closer, Victoria was too surprised to move. When he lifted her chin with his forefinger and kissed her on her closed mouth, she simply stared up at him, still unmoving.

After but a moment he raised his head and looked down at her. He smiled, lifted his hand, and gently caressed her jaw with his fingers.

"The sun hasn't set yet," he said. "We still have some minutes before it's evening and time to argue."

"Why did you do that?"

He shrugged. "You're beautiful, your mouth is very soft, you taste sweet, and you're my wife."

"I see," she said. Victoria wanted him to kiss her again. She wanted him to pull her against him so she could feel the length of him against her. She wanted that so very much, but she did nothing. He would doubtless be repulsed by such trollop behavior were she to show the slightest interest in his lovemaking. His mouth was beautiful and firm and he tasted more delicious than she possibly could. It was difficult to keep such things to herself.

"You will just stare at me, Victoria? You'll say nothing more?"

She shook her head helplessly. Unconsciously she lifted her hands to his shoulders and arched her neck back. Her lashes swept down over her eyes.

Her invitation was clear. He kissed her again, gently, but he felt the response in her and marveled at it. She kept her mouth firmly closed. He ran the tip of his tongue along her lower lip, probing lightly, and he felt her shudder. His arms closed tightly around her back. He deepened his kiss.

It was the moan from deep in her throat that made Victoria's eyes fly open. She was trembling, awash with wild, uncontrolled feelings, and she didn't know what to do about them. She just wanted more of Rafael. She wanted— No, stop it. She felt his hands glide down her back to cup her bottom. She felt him lift her, fit her against him. She felt him against her belly, and she cried out—surrender, desire, a plea in her voice.

Rafael slowly slid her back down his body, not releasing her even when her feet touched the floor. "Should you like me to have Lizzie fetch you a hot bath?"

"Bath?" Her eyes were vague, her voice thin.

"Yes," he said, releasing her, "a bath. Should you like a bath before dinner?"

He knew well enough that she wanted him. He was nearly in the same state himself. It was just that he knew how to exercise control over himself, and evidently she didn't. It was that simple. Her mind wasn't functioning as yet and he watched her try desperately to regain control. He waited, wondering what she would say, what she would do.

What she did surprised the devil out of him.

Victoria drew her hand back and swung, slapping him as hard as she could. "I hate you." Her voice sounded as if she were in pain.

Rafael rubbed his hand over his cheek. "I merely asked you if you wished a bath. Why did you strike me?"

"You used me. God, you wanted to make me wild so you could hate me and despise me. I won't let you do that again, Rafael, I won't."

He watched her in silence as she whirled about into her bedchamber, slamming the door behind her. He heard the key grate in the lock.

He had meant just a simple sweet kiss, that was all. It was her response, instant and hot, that had made him do more than he'd intended to do. He hadn't meant to humiliate her. He'd pulled back because— He wasn't sure. He was honest enough with himself not to close himself up in a complex lie of his own making just to soothe his own conscience. He would have to think about it. Marriage, he thought as he strode into his own bedchamber, marriage was a mess, a bloody complicated mess.

What was her damned confession?

Victoria sent Mrs. Ripple a message through Lizzie. She had no intention of facing her husband across the dining table, at least not this evening. He'd done her in yet again. It was because he'd caught her off guard. If she'd but known that he was going to kiss her, she could have prepared herself, made certain that she would show nothing but absolute disinterest. Even when he fitted her against the length of him?

She bit her lip, remembering the shadow of those feelings, feelings so intense, so powerful, that she'd been utterly helpless. Was she a trollop? Did a trollop have such feelings?

No. Now he was making her wonder about herself, damn him. She'd felt nothing but revulsion with Damien, and simply nothing at all with David. It was Rafael Carstairs who seemed to have the magic that made her crazy with need and passion, at least she supposed it was passion. She might as well admit it. She wanted him, desperately, whatever that entailed. All it entailed.

She finished her bath and wrapped herself in a warm towel. It was going to be a long evening.

Downstairs in the dining room, Rafael was sitting at the table in splendid isolation. He'd botched it again, royally, he thought as he forced himself to eat a reasonable portion of Mrs. Ripple's rabbit stew. How could anyone ruin a stew? he wondered. After all, it was prepared in a pot, all of it. How could the potatoes be raw and the carrots overcooked?

He stayed at the table, a bottle of port at his elbow long after Mrs. Ripple had taken the stew remains to what he hoped was a final interment. He had no intention of drinking himself into insensibility again. He thought about Drago Hall and his brother. It was a deeper division now, with Victoria as his wife. A chasm that would never be breached.

And he thought about the assignment he'd accepted from Lord Walton. Why, he wondered, couldn't it be something to do with smuggling? That was something he knew about, had known about since he was three years old. But a revival of the Hellfire Club? It seemed ridiculous, save for the savage rape of Viscount Bainbridge's daughter. He wondered, a crooked smile on his face, if when he arrived in Cornwall he would hear of Strange Happenings as well. Well, no matter. This group of dissolute young men would have to be stopped and the identity of the shadowy figure known as the Ram made known. Ram, Rafael thought, as in masculine animal, as in horns that represented a phallus. He determined to check the small library in Honeycutt Cottage on the morrow for any works on witchcraft and covens and the like.

He fretted with nervous energy until nine o'clock, when he took himself outside for a long walk. The night was overcast, the half-moon veiled by gray clouds that crossed in front of it in thin wisps. What to do about Victoria? He really had no idea how she, or he, for that matter, would be treated at Drago Hall. He would do his best to prevent any insults to her. He also knew that if she was Damien's lover, he was throwing her back into his brother's waiting arms and bed. He would sleep with her himself, damn her, and that way he would know where she was every night.

I want you to believe me and trust me before we consummate the marriage.

"Oh, Victoria, what the devil am I going to do with you?"

There was only the wind rustling through the oak trees to give any reply. He missed the sea, the endless days and nights, the heavy sun, the restless storms, the continuous test of man against nature. He wondered how he would settle down on land with the firm earth beneath his feet, if he ever really would. He grunted, kicking a stone out of his path.

If he and Victoria continued on their present course, she would doubtless be cheering to see him off on the *Seawitch* for a six-month voyage.

With those thoughts, he wondered if Victoria had ever been on the water, if she knew, perhaps, how to sail. She would be a good sailor, he thought, she had guts and steadiness. He determined to buy a sloop once they'd settled down in Cornwall.

He also determined before he was chased into Honeycutt Cottage by a sudden thunder shower that he was prepared to lie. Why not? He wanted her, very much, and she was his damned wife. Yes, he would tell her, straight in her beautiful face, that he trusted her, believed in her. Then he would make love to her. Then, finally, he would know.

He lit a candle and made his way upstairs to his bedchamber. It wouldn't take very much effort on his part, he thought, pausing a moment in front of her bedchamber door, to make her want him. Lord, he'd kissed her, caressed her just a bit, and she'd yielded to him as surely and completely as if he'd been fondling her for hours. He ducked his head, hearing Damien's words again in his mind. "Forget Damien," he said aloud to his shadowed bedchamber. "Forget his damnable accusations."

Rafael stripped off his clothes, folded them neatly, as was his habit, and smoothed them down over the back of a wing chair. He found himself gazing toward the adjoining door and wondering if she had locked it against him. Probably. She was angry enough to spit. Surely she'd locked the door, perhaps even pushed a dresser in front of it. The trick was, he thought, to catch her unawares. She was at her most unaware during sleep. He could make her so wild for him that by the time she was fully awake she would want him so badly she wouldn't fight him.

It was a low trick.

He was even willing to admit that it edged very near to the despicable.

If he were in her shoes, he would be so furious, at least later he would, that he would consider the destruction of his manhood the only worthy revenge.

Best wait. Test the waters on the morrow. Soften her up a bit. At least give it another try. He'd royally mucked it up today. Dammit, he was used to men's company, to their aberrations and sins. Not women's.

Of course most of the women he'd known had been like Lindy. Warm, passionate, yielding, and expecting nothing from him that he didn't want to give.

They sat across from each other at breakfast the following morning. Rafael eyed the runny eggs and the limp, greasy bacon with revulsion and helped himself to muffins that appeared edible.

Victoria was listless and Rafael saw the shadows beneath her eyes. He didn't like it, not one bit. He said abruptly, "What do you know of witchcraft in Cornwall?"

That got her attention. She paused in the act of crumbling a muffin and looked over at him. "No more or no less than most people, I suppose. There are those who do practice witchcraft, and I heard there was a coven near St. Austell. Why?"

He shrugged, took a bite of the blueberry muffin, and realized belatedly that it was raw in the middle. He manfully chewed and swallowed, then selected a piece of dry toast. He said, "You know, if we ever have an argument with the marquess, we can tell him what a marvelous cook Mrs. Ripple is. Convince him to come here and sample her delights. Revenge indeed."

"She tries very hard."

"I think I will give her a brief holiday and take over the kitchen myself. What do you think?"

"I think that between us we could cook the eggs and fry the bacon."

He grinned at her. "Let's do it." Without letting the proverbial moss grow on the stone, Rafael called out for Mrs. Ripple. She appeared, apron on, her hands dusty with flour, and Victoria shot Rafael a look. He managed to keep a straight face.

"Mrs. Ripple," he said, all affability, "Mrs. Carstairs and I are very grateful for all you've done for us. We are, as you know, on our wedding trip." Victoria shot him a look but he continued, his voice at its blandest. "Indeed, to thank you for seeing after us, we would like you to take a short holiday. My wife and I should enjoy being alone for a while."

Mrs. Ripple blinked and exclaimed, "But, sir. Who will see to you and Mrs. Carstairs? I really don't think that's at all proper. Why, the dear marquess wouldn't—"

"No, it's quite all right," said Rafael. "Truly. My wife here is a fine cook. We will be leaving on Friday. Why don't you come back Friday morning?"

Mrs. Ripple did her best to appear reticent about Captain Carstairs' plan, but within fifteen seconds she was nodding and pulling off her apron.

"I don't know how to make bread," Victoria said once they were alone again, "and that is what she was doing."

"I do," he said. At her incredulous look, he grinned and added, "Actually, I learned in Portugal.

I was on a miss—er, trip there a couple of years ago—"

"Yes, Rafael, a mission. I'm not completely without brains or hearing. I do not know how you came out of it with a whole skin. I realized by your stories—all of them in places where there is fighting—that you were not a simple ship captain. Now, about the bread?"

"You know something, Victoria? I talk in my sleep, or so I've been told. Eventually, when we come together, you are liable to garner enough information to blackmail me into my grave."

"Bread, Rafael."

"I learned to make it over a campfire, that's all. There was an old Gypsy woman who was supposed to do for us—I was with another fellow at the time. But her hands were so filthy I couldn't see myself eating anything she made, so I did it myself, with her giving me instructions. The bread wasn't at all bad, actually."

Victoria rose from her chair. "Shall we, then, sir? To the kitchen and the flour?"

She was no longer angry at him, he thought, trailing after her to the small cottage kitchen. Mrs. Ripple had already left and the bread makings were spread on the oak kitchen table.

He waited until her hands were immersed in sticky dough, then pulled her gently back against him. He slipped his arms about her waist. He lightly nipped her neck just below her earlobe. "Forgive me, Victoria," he said.

She felt his warm breath in her ear and wondered at him. Surely he was taking a chance, what with her hands covered with bread dough. No, she thought, he knew her, knew she would succumb to him as easily as spreading butter.

"I won't ever again leave you. Or stop, once I've begun loving you. Will you forgive me for being such a clod last evening?"

She drew in a deep breath. Already she was feeling warmth inching up from her toes. And his hands weren't moving. But her back was against his front and she could feel the hardness of him.

"Victoria?" His hands opened and his fingers splayed, going downward over her stomach.

She closed her eyes and leaned her head back against his shoulder. "Why did you do it last night?"

"Because I'm a bloody proper sod, that's why. You smell so sweet, Victoria, so much a woman." His teeth lightly nipped her earlobe.

"I can't do anything," she said after a full minute of sheer enjoyment. "My hands are a mess."

"That's all right. Just tell me you don't hate me."

"I don't hate you. I don't even dislike you at the moment. There must be something wrong with me."

She sounded worried, so he kissed her neck.

"I'm not going to go any further, else the bread will never make its way to the oven. All right?"

She wanted him to continue, no question about that, and damn the wretched bread. But she was a lady, she reminded herself, and a virgin, and a maiden, and all those proper things, and she shouldn't want lovemaking in the kitchen.

"All right."

He kissed her neck again, then stepped back.

"Now, the next thing we do is add a bit more water."

She did as he told her. He was delighted in a most basic masculine way to see that her hands were shaking a bit.

Their finished product, both of them agreed, wasn't a profoundly satisfactory result, but it ranked above Mrs. Ripple's efforts. They ate the hot bread in the kitchen, smearing it with sweet butter and strawberry jam.

Between bites, Rafael was telling her one of his adventures near Gibraltar, in the Mediterranean.

Victoria listened with half an ear. She couldn't seem to take her eyes off his mouth.

"Victoria, what do you want?"

She forced herself to meet his gaze. "Your story's fascinating," she said.

"You weren't paying a bit of attention to my ridiculous tale. One, I might add, that I was telling you on purpose, for it didn't involve any missions or assignments on my part, just simple trading and making money."

He paused a moment, readying to screw himself to the sticking point. So what if in the deepest recesses of his mind he was still very uncertain about her?

He said in his best calm captain's voice, "I believe you and I trust you. I want you to be my wife. I want to consummate our marriage. Now."

She stared at him, moistening her suddenly dry lips with her tongue. Rafael, although she didn't notice, found the movement of her pink tongue quite fascinating. "You have," she said at last, "made two very big statements all in one breath. I would ask you first: why? All of a sudden—perhaps because I made bread with you—you don't believe me to be a trollop?"

"That's right, but it came before the bread."

She waited, but he added nothing more. She

frowned at him. "You've perhaps decided I'm not a trollop because I eat warm bread with just the right amount of butter?"

"No." Well, he thought. If one committed an untruth, one should do it to the best of one's meager abilities. "I realized—and I am just a man, don't forget, Victoria—that you are utterly guileless and innocent as a babe. And you're right. The fact that I touch you and you melt all over me, well, that simply means that you respond to me, Rafael Carstairs, your husband and an excellent lover." He paused a moment, judging the effect of his fluency.

She lowered her eyes, saying softly, "I was thinking about that, you know. When Damien kissed me, I was repelled and horrified. As for David Esterbridge, I just didn't feel anything. I would have thought it was very distasteful if it hadn't been so very personal and intimate." She raised her eyes to his face. "It's magic with you. You're magic."

He was moved; he couldn't help himself. She sounded utterly sincere, simple honesty shining from her eyes. But could a woman respond to only one man with such wonderful abandon? An inexplicable something that existed just between two certain people? It sounded like nonsense to him. He'd responded to every woman to whom he'd made love.

He remembered Victoria before Damien had filled his ears. Not once had he doubted her virtue, but then again, not once had he kissed her or caressed her.

"I suppose it would be more accurate to say that we are magic together."

She gave him a sweet, dazzling smile and he was hard instantly. His voice sounded harsh to his own ears when he said a moment later, "And my second statement, Victoria?"

"Consummating our marriage?"

"That's a rather formal way of saying it, but yes."

"But we've barely finished our breakfast."

He shrugged, and his grin—showing his lovely white teeth—was decidedly wicked.

Suddenly Victoria was very tired about being so wretchedly helpless—at least as far as he was concerned. She felt like a puppet dancing to his string-pulling. It wasn't fair, just because for some odd and inexplicable reason he had this power over her. "I believe I should like to go riding, perhaps visit Milton Abbas again. We didn't really explore the Norman church all that completely. I am fond of old graveyards also, and I would like to find the oldest grave. We could make it a sort of contest, if you would like."

His grin never wavered. Rafael supposed he should tell her that her expression was so open, her eyes such a mirror, that her thoughts showed as clearly as if she'd spoken them aloud. He leaned toward her and clasped her hand in his. "You're beautiful, Victoria, and yes, I like graveyards. I really hadn't realized it before, but now I do. I shall have Tom saddle our mounts. Will you meet me at the stables in, say, thirty minutes?"

He still had the control, she thought. He was merely allowing her to have her way. It galled her to realize it, but since it had been her suggestion, she would be spiting herself to go against it now. She nodded somewhat curtly and took herself up to her bedchamber to change into her riding habit. It occurred to her as she buttoned her blouse that once

Rafael hd initiated her into the intricacies of lovemaking, perhaps she would lose this disconcerting reaction to him. She flushed slightly, knowing full well what would happen this evening—after dinner, she hoped. Whether or not she should believe him, well—he had said he trusted her, so that was that. If one couldn't believe one's husband, one was in a sorry situation.

Rafael won the graveyard competition. He found a gravestone with the date 1489 still legible on the worn granite.

"What is my prize?"

She looked at him blankly. "I was so certain I was going to win."

"Shall I tell you what your prize would have been?"

He was striding toward her as he asked that question, and she saw the answer in his eyes.

"No," she said. "I'm not stupid."

"Kiss me, Victoria. I will accept that as my prize." He clasped her arms and drew her gently against him. "Tilt up your head. Yes, that's all right. Part your lips just a bit. Excellent. Now, all you have to do is just respond to me as you always do, and no holding back."

She responded, just as she always did.

It didn't occur to her to do any holding back.

He held her then, not moving, forcing his hands to remain still on her back. "This is enjoyable," he said.

"Yes, it is quite a surprise that you too enjoy graveyards."

"No, I was referring to our kissing."

"I need more practice."

He stiffened at her words but forced himself to relax. He had found himself wondering why she kept her lips firmly closed when he'd kissed her before. It was as if she were completely inexperienced—and he mustn't forget that she *was*, that he had told her he trusted her, believed her. "I'll teach you everything," he said at last, gave her a squeeze, and released her. "Shall we return to Honeycutt Cottage and prepare our dinner?"

She nodded. "We mustn't forget about Tom."

"Actually, I gave him a holiday as well. He and Mrs. Ripple will return day after tomorrow, Friday morning. We will leave for Drago Hall in the afternoon."

She nodded, but she wasn't at all happy about it. Drago Hall meant Damien and Elaine, and neither of them wanted her there.

Victoria grew more and more nervous as the late afternoon dwindled into evening. She didn't want to cook. She wanted to hide. She didn't want to be near her husband, but it seemed that he was there, wherever she happened to be, and there was that *look* in his eyes that made her flush to her hairline.

"Just a light dinner, Victoria?"

She hadn't turned a page in her book for the past half-hour, but she still jumped when he spoke suddenly. "Yes, that's fine, Rafael. You came in so quietly, you startled me."

"I learned many times over that my hide depended on how quiet I was. Lyon once called me as silent as a big cat. I laughed, of course. He's the one with the name for that, not I. Don't be nervous, Victoria. You will enjoy yourself, I swear it. Remember that I'm magic, all right?"

"You have an excellent opinion of yourself, that is certain."

"I believe I should like dinner now. Fruit, cheese, and the remains of our bread?"

"But it's not even dark yet."

He said in a tone of infinite patience, "My dear wife, it isn't dark until after seven-thirty. If I kept my hands off you until then, half the night would be gone. Now, don't argue with me. Come to the kitchen."

As she rose, the hem of her skirt caught on a splinter of wood on the chair leg. It yanked her back, pulling her off balance. She fell heavily onto her lame leg. It gave way in an instant and she tumbled to the floor.

Rafael was at her side in an instant. "Are you all right? Good grief, Victoria, what the devil happened?"

She wouldn't look at him, she couldn't. She was too mortified. She'd conveniently forgotten about her wretched leg and now she'd made a clumsy fool of herself in front of him. "Nothing, I just slipped."

He helped her to her feet and she sent thanks heavenward that her leg didn't give out again. "I'm sometimes not very graceful," she said, looking down at the deep red swirls in the Aubusson carpet. "I hope you will forgive that."

He gave her a bewildered look. "You, not graceful? Don't be an idiot, Victoria. Everyone stumbles occasionally, even your perfect husband. Now, are you truly all right?"

She nodded. She didn't realize that she was rubbing her leg until Rafael said, "Would you like me to take a look? Did you bruise your leg?"

Her hand fell away as if she'd been touching a hot oven. "Oh, no, I'm fine. This is foolish, really."

He'd asked her so many times what her confession was. Now it appeared that she would have to tell him. She didn't want to. What he thought of her was still too uncertain. She was afraid.

Rafael, for his part, put down her behavior to her nervousness about bedding with him. He thought it rather endearing.

Victoria had slowly and thoroughly chewed her last piece of bread before she said, "I want you to have the lights out, please."

He paused with the slice of delicious local cheese halfway to his mouth. "It's only six o'clock. It won't matter if the lights are on or off. It won't be dark, as I told you, until after seven-thirty."

She looked ready to burst into tears. Rafael sat back in his chair and studied her. "What's wrong? Please, Victoria, there is no reason for you to be afraid of me or what we are going to do. It's enjoyable, you know, truly. I venture to say that practically all husbands and wives indulge in lovemaking quite regularly." He didn't add that once he touched her he hoped she would forget all about her nervousness in any case. Unless, his thinking continued, they were back again to her lack of virginity. He shook his head.

"What's wrong?" he asked again, this time his impatience showing through.

She flinched. "Nothing."

"All right, have it your way. Why don't you go upstairs now and bathe. I will put our kitchen to rights."

She nodded, not looking at him. As she walked from the kitchen, he thought he heard her curse. A man's curse that sounded very odd coming from her. He very nearly laughed.

After she'd gone, he found himself reverting once

again to old thoughts, and his jaw knotted. Perhaps he should toss her a vial of chicken blood when he went to her.

It was close to an hour later when Rafael, garbed only in a blue brocade dressing gown, his thick hair still damp from his own bath, knocked lightly on the adjoining bedchamber door, then opened it quietly.

He stopped short. The room was dark. He blinked to adjust his eyes and saw that Victoria had closed all the draperies, tying them together so there were no gaps.

"My God," he said aloud, torn between annoyance and amusement, "will you put a sack over my head as well?"

13

I am ready to give you satisfaction . . .
—JOHN GAY

"Victoria?"

"I'm here."

He followed the sound of her low voice and saw her finally huddled behind a wing chair in the far corner of the bedchamber. "I wondered if you wished me to cover my head. If not with a sack, perhaps a pillow cover?"

"No, please, Rafael, I want the lights out."

"Why?"

He wished he could see her expression but her head was lowered. She was wearing a filmy sort of negligee and it fired his imagination and his body. He'd wanted her forever, it seemed to him now as he stood in the near-dark with his wife behind a chair, unwilling to talk to him.

"Why, Victoria?" he said again.

"Modesty. Yes, that's it."

He said in his most reasonable voice, "There

should be no embarrassment or shame between a husband and wife. There's no reason for you to fear me. I won't hurt you. Do you believe me?"

"It's not that, truly."

He felt baffled and a bit impatient with her. He strode toward her, nearly knocking over a small chair. "This is bloody ridiculous." He drew up on the other side of the chair. "Victoria," he said, "talk to me. Tell me what is wrong. I'm your husband, you know."

"There is nothing wrong, Rafael. Please, can't we just get it done?"

Some way to talk about lovemaking, he thought. "Why, Victoria?"

She was fretting with some loose threads on the back of the chair. He wasn't going to give up, and she wondered what she should do now. He looked perfectly lovely; at least she thought he did. It wasn't so dark that she couldn't make out his blue brocade dressing gown. She imagined that he had nothing at all under that blue dressing gown and it excited her unbearably.

She blurted out "Oh, all right, I'm ugly."

"Ugly?" he repeated blankly. He remembered quite clearly his reaction the first time he had seen her breasts in the cream silk ball gown, her shoulders, slender and creamy as the creation she was wearing, a temptation to any man except perhaps a blind one. And her ankles, he thought, that time he had assisted her into Lucia's carriage, gave great promise to the shapeliness of her legs.

"Where?"

"I don't want to talk about it, Rafael. Just leave the lights off, all right?"

"It will eventually be morning, Victoria. Your draperies will undoubtedly keep out some of the light, but not all. I will see you, you know, all of you." He saw she was truly upset and was completely bewildered. He gave it up without a further thought. "It's all right, love. Come here, now. It will be as you wish."

"We can really have done with it?"

"Yes, we will have this lovemaking business behind us in no time at all."

She walked around the chair and came to a halt in front of him. She didn't look up at his face, but at the gold frogged fastenings on his dressing gown.

"They're fascinating, aren't they?"

"Yes, but it's difficult to see them clearly, for it is so very dark in here."

"That's certainly true enough. You're a puzzle, Victoria. Did I ever tell you that I'm quite adept at puzzle solving?"

He resolutely kept his hands at his sides. Not yet, he thought, not quite yet. He had to calm her, make her relax, otherwise he could envision an awful debacle.

"The only thing you're not good at is riding in a carriage."

He laughed, reached out, and gently clasped her shoulders in his large hands. "Come here."

She stepped against him without hesitation. Mutely Victoria raised her face, her lips slightly pursed. He grinned down at her and gently ran his fingertip along the outline of her mouth. He leaned down and kissed her nose, her brows, her chin. "If there is anything at all ugly about you, I will eat the stirrups off my Spanish saddle." He sifted his long fingers through her hair that fell in deep waves down her back. He lifted a thick tress and brought it over her shoulders to his mouth. He inhaled deeply. "So sweet," he said, "so very sweet."

Victoria lifted her hand and touched her fingertips to his face. "Perhaps I'm sweet, but you're beautiful."

He gave her a crooked smile to cover his embarrassment. "I'm just a man, nothing more, nothing less, and a man isn't a beautiful thing, not like you. But I am your husband and if you wish to remain blind to the stubble on my chin and the way my hair sticks up at odd angles in the mornings, who am I to disagree?"

"Please kiss me, Rafael."

His eyes turned darker as he lowered his head. He kissed her lightly, very gently. He could feel the moment she responded to him. It was a quiver that ran from her breasts down her legs. He tightened his arms around her back. He raised his head a moment and looked down at her. Her eyes were closed, her lips slightly parted, her breathing coming in small gasps. "You can hold me too, Victoria," he said. "I would like it very much."

She slid her arms around his back and pressed herself against him. She felt him against her belly. She raised her face, arching her back a bit. He kissed her again, this time gliding his tongue over her lower lip, gently probing until she opened her mouth to him. He didn't ravish her mouth with his tongue, but made gentle forays, his tongue barely touching hers. Victoria was quickly awash with the most overpowering feelings. She'd never imagined anything like this, a sort of urgency in her belly. A wanting so intense, a wanting just beyond, but she knew it was there, for her. She moaned, unable to keep silent.

Rafael was immensely pleased at her response to him. He unfastened the ribbons of her negligee and slipped it off her shoulders. The soft silk pooled about her feet.

She stared at him, her eyes wide and questioning. He said nothing, merely slipped the straps of her nightgown off her shoulders. She was standing nearly in profile to him. He sucked in his breath as the soft silk fell below her breasts to her waist. In another moment the nightgown had joined the negligee at her feet. He looked down at her breasts, full and white, made whiter still in the dim shadows of the room. Very lightly he touched his fingertip to her breast and watched her shudder.

"So soft," he said. "Are your breasts as sweet as your hair?"

He leaned down and took her in his mouth. Victoria gasped with shock, and arched her back. He felt her utter yielding to him. He held her with one arm and with the other hand caressed her breast, gently lifting it, weighing it in his palm. Only after he had loved both her breasts thoroughly did he allow his hand to glide below her waist. "Victoria," he said softly, wanting to see her eyes when his fingers found her. He wanted to see her reaction.

It was more than he could have imagined. Her belly felt as smooth as satin, and when his fingers probed and found her, he nearly lost his control. He touched her very lightly. She wanted him.

"Rafael."

He stopped, his fingers cupping her. She was trembling, nearly beyond herself, and he knew it. So responsive she was, and she was all his. He released her a moment, watching her gain control slowly. Her eyes cleared just a bit. She moistened her lips with her tongue. "I want to see you, Rafael."

"I'm not nearly so ugly as you are."

Her eyes went blank and wild. He quickly laughed. "I'm teasing you, little goose. All right, then. You want your husband?"

"Yes."

He took a step back and shed his dressing gown. He stood quietly watching her face as she looked at him. She was very thorough, more so than she'd been on their accursed wedding night. She was consuming him, he thought, with that look. No woman had ever before studied him like this, with admiration, almost adoration. It was unnerving. "Victoria," he said, and pulled her against him.

Her breasts pressed against his chest, his sex hard against her belly, exciting her to the point of incoherence. "Please," she whispered, and felt his mouth close over hers. His hands were everywhere, lifting her, fitting her against him, and she moaned and pressed herself against him wildly, wanting more but not knowing what it was she wanted. His back, beneath her hands, was smooth and curved with hard muscle.

Rafael, nearly to the end of his tether, lifted her in his arms and strode to the bed, nearly stumbling over the damned table yet again. Where, he wondered vaguely, did she think herself ugly? It was ridiculous. He laid her on her back and came down beside her, balancing himself on his elbow.

"He laid his hand on the her belly. He watched her closely in the dim light. She quivered and he let his fingers glide a bit lower.

"Rafael, I don't—"

"Don't what, Victoria?"

"I think I hurt, but I want to, and it's almost too much and I want and want—"

He found her at that moment, and she gasped,

arching upward, nearly beside herself. "Do you want me to pleasure you now, Victoria?"

She looked up at his shadowed face, turning to give him her mouth. "I don't know what you mean. Do you mean you will kiss me again?"

"Certainly, but I want to see your face—as best I can in this darkness—when you melt for me."

"I don't understand."

"You will, soon, I promise." He kissed her, deeply this time, his tongue probing into her mouth just as his finger slipped inside her. She was small, but she would hold him, for her desire was nearly peaked. He kept up a slow in-and-out motion with his finger, then withdrew and began to caress her. He felt her tremble, felt the involuntary jerking of her hips as she sought his fingers. He lifted his head just as she reached her climax. He watched the look of utter astonishment in her eyes as her pleasure overtook her. "Rafael." She screamed. He nearly cried out with her, his pleasure at her release was so great.

"Yes, love. Yes, come to me."

Slowly he eased the pressure of his fingers, soothing her, feeling the small convulsions seize her in the aftershocks of her pleasure. "I want to come inside of you now, Victoria. All right?"

"Yes," she whispered. "Yes, I think I would like that." She was surprised she could even speak. She didn't have enough power to move her fingers. She felt delicious.

He came over her and gently pulled her thighs apart. "Bend your legs. That's it."

She watched him guide himself into her, his face intent, his expression pained. She felt him come into her, felt the tightness, the stretching, the pain.

"Rafael," she said in a thin voice, pressing her hands against his shoulders.

"Just a bit more, Victoria. Relax. Don't move."

She held perfectly still, feeling him come deeper. It was odd, this feeling—another person becoming part of her. The pain became more insistent, and she gritted her teeth, not wanting him to know.

Suddenly he reached her maidenhead and he felt such a surge of relief that he nearly lost all control. His mind was whirling out of control and he blurted out, "Thank God! If Damien had had you, I don't know what I would have done."

He groaned then and with one powerful thrust drove through her maidenhead and slammed to the hilt inside her.

She screamed at the tearing pain, and bucked beneath him. He got hold of himself, barely, and lowered himself over her. "I won't move. I'm sorry, Victoria. It won't hurt anymore. I promise."

She was so small, her muscles were flexing about him, driving him mad, and she was a virgin. She was truly his and only his, before and forever.

Victoria lay perfectly still. He hadn't believed her. He had believed Damien. He hadn't trusted her. He had lied to her just so he could bed her. Her hands dropped to her sides. She turned her face away from him on the pillow.

"Is that better, Victoria? Has the pain lessened?"

She didn't look at him. She felt impaled, helpless, and angry.

"I hate you," she said quite precisely.

He stared down at her averted face, but at that moment she bucked upward, hoping to dislodge him. Instead, it sent him deeper and he felt himself go over the edge. He withdrew, then thrust deep, then again and once more. He shattered. He threw back his head, arched his back, and poured himself into her.

She felt his seed, a man's seed, she thought dully. He had truly had his way. But it had been her fault. She had wanted to believe him, had been eager for him to make love to her. She'd wanted to know so desperately what the wild feelings were, and where they led. Well, she knew now. It was short, fleeting, and terrifying because it wiped out all control, all reason. She shuddered at the pain of his entry. She still hurt, deep inside now, and it erased the lingering spurts of pleasure. She felt cold and dead inside.

"You lied to me," she said, not moving. "You lied to me and I will never forgive you."

Rafael was slowly coming back to reality as he had known it. The power of his climax had rendered him insensible. He was still deep inside her, held by her, and slowly he lowered himself over her, balancing his weight on his elbows. "What did you say?" He thought she'd said something, but he was still too brain dead to make out her words.

"You lied to me and I will never forgive you."

He stiffened, and frowned down at her closed face. "What the devil are you talk—" He broke off. Oh, God, had those damnable words really come from him? Fool, a thousand times a bloody fool.

"Victoria," he said very slowly, very carefully, "it isn't what you think."

"I assume you are done with me. Would you please get away from me now?"

"No." His voice was sharp, and she flinched. "No, you are mine now and I am your husband. Please, love, you must understand. I couldn't erase every doubt, but there was but a mere shadow of a doubt when I told you I believed you. I did believe you, truly."

She said nothing. He felt sunk in guilt and anger at himself. He rolled onto his side, bringing her with him. He remained inside her. And he felt himself growing hard once again. He strove for control. "Victoria, I gave you pleasure."

She said nothing.

He was becoming fast angry with her. "You stubborn little witch, you will listen to me. Do you discount the pleasure I gave you so quickly? Shall I make love to you again to remind you?"

"No. Don't touch me."

That order was so funny that he was obliged to laugh, which he did, deeply. "My God, I'm inside you. Don't you consider that touching? Your breasts are pressed against me and now my hands are on your bottom. Well?"

"I hate you. Let me go now."

"Where are you ugly?"

She stiffened and he could feel her withdrawal. Physical and emotional. He hated it. "Forget I asked," he said, and locked his arms around her so she couldn't pull away from him. He kissed her cheekbone. "Victoria, kiss me."

She ducked her face down into his shoulder. She made the mistake of taking a deep breath and the smell of him was enough to make her muscles clench around him. He moaned.

And began to move within her.

"No!" She began to fight him in earnest, bucking her hips upward, smashing her fists against his chest.

"Damn you, hold still." He rolled her onto her back again and pinned her arms above her head, his entire weight on her. "Don't try it, Victoria. It won't be a matter of forcing you, and you know it. Give me just one more minute and you'll be begging me to continue."

She stared up at him, knowing what he said was true, and hating both herself and him. He was moving slowly inside her and the pain was now mixed with pleasure as he moved against her belly.

"A virgin isn't supposed to feel pleasure the first time, you know. But you did, and I gave it to you. You won't forget that, Victoria. Another man wouldn't have, but I did. I saw your face when you climaxed. Every time we make love you will feel like that. And you won't forget it."

"Please," she whispered, fighting the building pleasure, "please don't shame me. Please leave me alone."

"Not a chance. Tell me you want me to continue what I'm doing. Tell me."

He eased his hand between them and found her. She cried out when his fingers touched her.

She was convulsing around him and he knew she was making him as wild as he was her. "Tell me, Victoria. Tell me you want me to pleasure you again."

She felt tears sting her eyes, tasted the salty drops in her mouth. His fingers quickened and she cried out, her back arching. He released her wrists and came up on his hands. He came into her, then withdrew, twisting and pressing, making her shudder deeply.

"Tell me, damn you."

But Victoria couldn't say anything. She was beyond reason. She looked at him, a lost, wild look, then was lost in such incredible sensation that she felt she would die of it. She was writhing beneath him, her hair tangling about her face, her fingers digging into his back.

My God, he thought, she is incredible, and he let himself go. He was sweating, breathing hard. His full weight was on her, his head on the pillow beside hers.

He pulled himself up for a moment, kissed her slack mouth, then lay down again.

"You're mine, Victoria. You won't ever forget that."

Within moments he was sleeping, a sated sleep.

Victoria listened to his even breathing. He had certainly won. His weight was great, but somehow she found it comforting, which, she thought, must surely make her a candidate for Bedlam. And he was still inside her, but less so now. She stared up at the dark ceiling. She had never imagined such feelings, such dizzying pleasure. She wondered if he would now believe her a slut for responding to him so completely, so quickly. Not a lady. Surely ladies didn't yell and carry on with such abandon.

She shuddered a bit, filled with such loathing for herself that she couldn't keep still. He moved, muttering something in his sleep, words she didn't understand.

Victoria held her breath. She couldn't bear to speak to him now, to see his eyes, to wonder what he thought. Of course Rafael always told her what he thought, so she wouldn't have to wait long for that. She realized that he was leaving her. She felt soreness and some remnants of pain deep inside. A virgin's pain and a woman's incredible pleasure.

She drew a deep breath and shoved at him. He grunted in his sleep, but rolled off her, onto his stom-

ach, his head turned away from her. Slowly she
eased away and rose. Her muscles felt as weak as
her leg when she had overexerted. That thought
made her rub her hand over the scar on her thigh.
Yes, that was what he would demand next. She could
hear him now, his voice either stern and forbidding
or charming with a hint of cajoling. *What is your confession? Is it about your so-called ugliness?*

She walked to the basin and poured cold water
from the pitcher. She soaped the cloth and washed
herself. It was dark, but not too dark. The stickiness
between her thighs came away but she saw her blood
on the cloth. Quickly she lit a single candle. It was
her blood, from her maidenhead. Well, at least he'd
told her that much, so she wasn't afraid he had irrep-
arably hurt her.

She dried herself and retrieved her nightgown
from the floor. She stared toward the bed at the
sound of his low snoring. Without making a conscious decision, she carried the candle toward the
bed. She wanted to see him. She raised the candle.

He was still on his stomach, his legs spread, one
arm bent upward, the other at his side. Her eyes
followed the beautiful taut of him, His thighs were
thick with muscle and black hair. Even his feet were
beautiful, she thought, long and narrow and arched.
She wished he would turn over. She wanted to see
all of him without him knowing it. She could spend
fifty years staring at him. He mumbled something
in his sleep, came up abruptly on his elbows, and
she froze.

She snuffed out the candle and stood perfectly still.

He said quite clearly, "Victoria."

Then he fell back onto his stomach and began snoring again.

Victoria made her decision at that moment. If she slept with him, he would make love to her as soon as he woke. She knew it. She also knew that she would want him to. And it would probably be morning and the room would be light and he would see her leg.

She flinched away from that thought. He was so perfect himself, how could he tolerate such ugliness in his wife? Her hand went to the scar and kneaded it.

She covered him, then walked from her room into his bedchamber.

The sheets were so very cold, the bed so very large and empty. What was she going to do now?

It was taken out of her hands. She woke aware that she was very warm, and she snuggled into that warmth. It was many moments before she was conscious enough to realize what was happening. Rafael was spooned about her back, his hand kneading her stomach.

"Don't leave me again, Victoria," he said, his voice rough in her ear. His fingers probed to find her, and he began a rhythm that quickly made her wild.

"I had to," she gasped, pressing her bottom back against him. She felt him hard against her. Slowly, very gently, he lifted her leg and came inside her. She felt the pleasure build, become so intense that she was crying out, unable to keep quiet. She felt his fingers, felt him stroking deep inside her, and she gave over to him.

She was sobbing with the power of it. And when he nibbled on the nape of her neck, thrusting deeper still, she found herself moving naturally against him, wanting him, wanting more. And he gave it to her.

When he felt her reach her climax, felt the incredible shudders, he let himself go with her.

"You're wonderful," he said simply, kissed her ear, and pulled her tightly against him.

He was still deep inside her.

It was still dark.

She lay awake listening to his deep, steady breathing in her ear.

14

All this and heaven too.
—MATTHEW HENRY

Rafael was smiling as he opened his eyes, a very male smile, one filled with bone-deep satisfaction.

He yawned deeply. "Victoria?" he said as he turned his head on the pillow.

She wasn't there. He sat up, fully awake now. He wasn't surprised to find her gone, not really, particularly after she'd left him during the previous night. No, he wasn't surprised, but he wasn't pleased about it either.

Where the devil was she ugly? He disliked mysteries, and as he'd told his wife, he was adept at puzzle solving. If he wasn't able to figure out the puzzle using his wits, he would use guile and cunning until the information he needed was his.

He would force it out of his wife, damn her silly hide. Ugly? Silly wench, did she have a broken fingernail?

He looked sleepily over at the clock. Nearly ten o'clock in the morning. And there was a lot of sunlight streaming through the windows. At least Victoria hadn't closed and fastened all these draperies. He threw back the covers, rose, and stretched.

After he had shaved, grunting with displeasure at the cold water in the basin, now wishing he hadn't dismissed Lizzie as he had Tom and Mrs. Ripple, he gritted his teeth and prepared to bathe himself with that same cold water. It was then that he saw the blood on his sex. Victoria's blood. Slowly he walked from his bedchamber into hers. It was still very dark despite the strong sunlight. He unfastened the heavy brocade drapes and flung them back. He then walked to the bed and pulled back the covers. Her blood and his seed were dried splotches on the white sheet. His virgin wife. She hadn't lied to him. She'd been a complete innocent.

And suddenly he remembered.

When he'd thrust through her maidenhead, he'd shouted aloud his relief—that he couldn't have borne it if Damien had had her first.

He'd also made love to her three times and given her pleasure each and every time. Immense pleasure. Of that he was quite certain. He knew that many women feigned pleasure, but Victoria wouldn't know how. She responded to him wildly for some remarkable but as-yet-unexplained reason, and he guessed it would be beyond her to feign anything.

She wouldn't be able to forget what pleasure he gave her, pleasure he drowned her in. Nor would he let her. No matter how enraged she was at him, he now knew that he could control her with sex.

It was odd, this reversal of the natural order. It was normally women's prerogative to use sex to get what they wanted from men. He grinned. Not so with his beautiful wife.

He was on the point of taking her water to add to his when he saw the washcloth in the basin. The cloth was stained with blood, as was the water in the basin. He hoped she hadn't been frightened. He closed his eyes a pained moment, remembering his story to her about the bride who had used chicken blood on her wedding night to fool her husband. No, she probably hadn't been scared to see her virgin's blood. He felt a bounder, worse, like a barbarian who had hurt and raped a vestal virgin.

He hoped she wouldn't be too angry with him this morning. He had, he supposed, meant what he'd shouted out during their lovemaking, but he was willing to lie, to say anything to make her forget those ghastly words. He thought of Victoria lying on her back, her eyes wild and vivid on his face as he plunged into her. It made him instantly hard.

He walked back into his bedchamber. If she was still angry with him, he would simply love her until she was screaming, her beautiful breasts heaving, her long legs tightening around his flanks. He tried to stop those images, for his body wouldn't be reasonable about it.

"Randy goat," he said to himself as he cleaned his teeth and dressed himself.

He ran Victoria to ground in the kitchen some thirty minutes later. She'd tied her hair back with a black velvet ribbon and wrapped one of Mrs. Ripple's enormous aprons about her waist.

"Good morning, sweetheart," he said, and pulled her against him, and kissed her soundly beneath her left ear. "You're making bread? Without me, the chef?" He turned her to face him and ignored her stone face. "I like the daub of flour on your nose," he continued in what he hoped was a loverlike tone. "Cute." He kissed the tip of her nose.

Victoria slowly pulled away from him. She couldn't quite bring herself to look squarely at him. Every step she took reminded her of the previous long night. She was very sore. She lowered her head, unaware that she was turning quite red.

He grinned at her, and gently lifted her chin with his finger. "What is this, love? You are regretting your wifely state?"

And his perfidy washed over her again, and she ground her teeth.

"We leave for Cornwall tomorrow?"

He accepted her shift of topic, and her cold voice, and nodded. "Yes, right after luncheon." He gave her one of his lovely white-toothed grins. "I can't imagine that either of us will want to be up with the sun." He didn't expect a reply, and turned to fetch himself an apron. He tied it about his waist, washed his hands, then joined her beside the array of ingredients on the kitchen table.

She was behaving with more restraint than he deserved, or hoped for, for that matter. Sleeping dogs deserved to be left alone, he thought as he kneaded the bread dough. They worked companionably, in reasonably easy silence, for another ten minutes.

"What is that, pray?"

She was staring at the bread loaf he had fashioned. He laughed. "You don't approve my artistic endeavors? Why, I have shaped a very special loaf, just for you."

"But it's—it's—"

"Too much for you, huh? Well, I call it my Statue of David, or if you prefer, the Statue of Your Husband."

She stared at the dough man and the very large phallus Rafael had molded. Besides that ridiculous endowment, there was a wide smile on the dough mouth.

"Should you like more detail, Victoria? Ribs, for instance? Teeth? Perhaps something lower, maybe—"

"No! Goodness, are you completely lost to civilized manners? You are—"

"—desirous of making love with you again, Victoria. You have this effect on me. You have flour on the tip of your nose and I'm gone with admiration and lust. Will you give me a good-morning kiss or a thank-you kiss for my artistic bread man?"

He grabbed her about the waist and lifted her. He swung her around, grinning up at her. "You know that the yeast should make our bread man even more impressive while he's baking?"

Victoria felt overwhelmed. He was impervious, oblivious of her feelings to his own shocking dishonesty. Now he was holding her off the floor, jesting with her as if nothing at all had occurred, as if they were newlyweds and very much in love, which was utterly ridiculous, at least the love part. And that ludicrous dough man. She could just imagine how he would look after baking. And she was supposed to spread butter and honey on him and place him on her bread plate?

"Rafael," she said in a very thin voice, "please put me down now."

"All right," he said, all agreeable, and slid her slowly down the front of his body. He saw her flush at the feel of him, and felt his own body respond instantly. "Ah," he said, leaned down, and kissed her. She was as stiff as the baking paddle.

For about thirty seconds.

He was an excellent lover, he knew it, and she would come to accept it soon enough. He would take her here, in the kitchen, in the bright daylight, and he would find this ugliness of hers.

"Come, sweetheart, part your lips for me. A bit more. Ah, that's it."

She felt his tongue touch hers, then retreat, licking over her lips. His hands were on her back, caressing her shoulders, then downward to mold her hips. Why him? She wondered vaguely, even as her own interest rose alarmingly.

She felt his fingers untying her apron and he yanked it off her, hurling it to the other side of the kitchen. Without pause, he released her, pulled her back against him, and his hand cupped her fully. His other hand closed over her breast. He felt the heat of her through her muslin gown and groaned softly as he kissed her throat.

"Rafael," she managed, knowing that soon, very soon, she wouldn't care that the kitchen was filled with morning sunlight, that she was dreadfully sore from their mutual ardor of the night before. She wouldn't care about anything except having him. "Please, do not—ah—"

"Now, Victoria. Here. Right here."

"No, please," she said, nearly sobbing at her own helplessness with him.

He felt the heat of her beneath his probing fingers and his hands went wild on her clothes even as he lowered her to the kitchen floor. He had no thought to finding this so-called ugliness—he wanted only to bury himself deep inside her, love her until she screamed, and melted into him. He yanked up her gown, tearing it, and ripped open her drawers, ignoring her petticoat, stockings, and slippers. He was breathing hard as he quickly unfastened the front of his breeches.

"Victoria," he said, his voice harsh, and with one powerful thrust he came fully and deeply into her. Her cry was the most beautiful sound he'd ever heard. She was small, tight about him, and ready for him. He tried to keep his weight off her, but she wouldn't allow it. She was moving upward against him, bringing him deeper, and he obliged her. He lifted himself on his hands so he could press against her, and when he did, a scream choked in her throat. She whispered his name, and in that instant he looked into her eyes, the color of the ocean just before a storm struck—turbulent blue, shifting in hue and focus—and was lost, with her.

He held himself perfectly still, no thought of sleep entering his mind this time. After a few moments of recovery he came up on his elbows and smiled down at his dazed wife. Her eyes were closed, her thick brown lashes damp against her cheeks. She was beautiful, sated, and he was still deep inside her, and she was his. Only his.

"That was very nice," he said, willing her to look at him. "Aren't I the master of understatement. Look at me, Victoria."

She did. Her lashes fluttered open and she stared up at him with such a look of hopelessness in her eyes that he immediately felt fear sear through him. "What's the matter? Did I hurt you?"

She said nothing.

"Victoria?"

She still said nothing, merely turned her face away

from him. He pulled himself out of her, and felt her
flinch. He'd known she would be sore after the previous night but he'd granted himself instant forgetful-
ness to assuage his own lust. "I'm sorry, truly. Just
hold still, don't move."

He rose, fastened his breeches, then dampened a
soft cloth with cool water. He came down on his
knees beside her and gently pressed the cloth against
her. She nearly jumped out of her skin. She lurched
up, her face flaming. "Oh, no, please, Rafael. " She
swatted at him.

"Would you please hold your tongue? Lie down.
I'm sorry the bed is made of flagstone, but just a few
more minutes, all right?" He bathed his seed from
her, rinsed out the cloth, and pressed it against her
once more. He stretched out beside her on the
kitchen floor, still holding the damp cloth against her.
"Look at me, Victoria."

If possible, she turned her head even more away
from him until he imagined that her nose was pressing against the flagstone. His eyes traveled down her
body. Her drawers were neatly split down the center
seam and his hand was inside, holding the cloth
against her. Her stockings were held up with narrow
black garters, her slippers a pale pink to match her
now-ruined morning gown. Her petticoat was spread
about her like ruffled icing on a cake.

"I didn't realize before that you were a coward.
It's a disconcerting and disappointing discovery. I believe that before a man takes a wife, her courage
should be proved. Not a deed of derring-do, mind
you, just something that will show him that he can
count on her. I can see it now—we will be attacked
by a vicious highwayman and you will conveniently
faint, leaving me to face the fellow alone. I won't be

armed, of course, because you faint at the sight of weapons, thus I am helpless against him. I can only imagine your guilt when you see me sprawled out at your feet, long gone from these earthly delights." At his final words, she felt the cloth press more closely against her.

"Will you feel guilty, Victoria? Or will you faint again at the sight of my bloody body?"

She turned her head and looked up at his smiling eyes. She said very clearly, "You are ridiculous, utterly and completely and irrevocably ridiculous, and awfully spoiled. I am not a coward, I'm embarrassed and mortified, and I want to crawl away and hide myself in a rabbit hole. You persist in doing—well doing what you are doing right now. It's shocking to me. And you persist in making me forget things, like your awful perfidy."

He whistled in admiration. "Good heavens, sweetheart, I haven't heard that many words strung all together from you since—well, I can't remember when. You have put me in my place. But I won't move my hand just yet, unless it is to caress you again." He followed words with deed and watched her eyes widen.

"Stop."

"All right," he said, and did. He watched the glint of disappointment in her eyes and smiled to himself.

She was soon back to normal, more's the pity, he thought, and said, "I don't like you. I wish you would move your damned hand and let me pull down my dress—my ripped dress."

"Your drawers are ripped as well. Don't worry, I'll buy you a plentiful supply."

She sucked in her breath. His flowing good humor

seemed inexhaustible. She couldn't compete with him.

"It's a pity," he continued thoughtfully, his hand again moving slightly over her, one finger easing beneath the damp cloth to touch her, "that it is so very difficult to gain access to your womanly self. Unlike me, a perfect man, who needs only to be unfastened, which takes but a flash of an instant. I see in the future that I will have to set aside a special lovemaking fund for the replacement of your woman's clothes." He felt her squirm and eased his pressure and the motion of his finger. She was sore, after all. And he was making her wild, on purpose, he supposed, to prove that he could control her. It wasn't well done of him. "Kiss me, Victoria, and I will let you get back to your housewifely responsibilities. Remember your marvelous bread man? I can't wait to observe you place him artistically on your bread plate." He patted her lightly, all the while chuckling, and rose.

Victoria slammed her skirts down, so furious with him she was beyond words. But her tongue was tied in knots, and it was true, her mind was in a mindless fog. She opened her mouth, observed his grin widen, and closed it. With quick, angry movements she shoveled her two loaves of bread onto the wooden baking paddle and eased them into the oven.

She looked down at the absurd dough man, shuddered, and threw down the baking paddle. "I won't bake that thing. Do you hear?"

"It's all right, Mrs. Carstairs. Why don't you go upstairs and refresh yourself? Perhaps a vinaigrette to calm your nerves? Repose yourself on the chaise longue. I will complete your duties down here. No, don't thank me. I know your gratitude is boundless."

Victoria looked at the baking paddle, hearing it thwack with satisfying loudness against his bottom, and her expressive eyes gave him a fairly accurate clue to her thoughts. Rafael quickly picked up the baking paddle and held it behind him. She was standing in front of him, her hands fisted at her sides, her hair and yellow muslin gown thoroughly mussed. She looked ready to spit. He said easily, "You want to use the paddle on me, do you? How about me using it on you? Is that what you want, Victoria? I'm not at all certain that I approve. Pain and pleasure. I suppose that many folk find it a delicious combination. Perhaps someday, if you prettily try to convince me, I'll—"

"Shut up! Ah—just be quiet."

He laughed aloud, watching her march out of the kitchen, head high, shoulders squared.

"Victoria," he called after her, "where is that ugliness of yours? I have decided that you have a malformed toe. I don't mind if you wish to keep your slippers on when we make love. It's kind of you to spare me."

He heard her steps quicken, and knew she was now running up the stairs. He turned and scooped his outrageous dough man onto the paddle and slid it into the oven.

"Tied to my kitchen," he said to himself. "A man's responsibilities never end."

The look on Victoria's face exceeded Rafael's expectations. Her mouth gaped open, her cheeks suffused with color, and she quickly closed her eyes, but of course not quickly enough.

"It doesn't please you, sweetheart?"

She swallowed, her eyes tightly closed, her lips now pursed, and shook her head.

"Look at all familiar, Victoria?"

"Not at all." She simply wouldn't let him get the better of her this time. But she hadn't realized that he would lay his loaf of bread out for her in all its swelled, baked splendor.

"I'm wounded. Perhaps next time you will look at your husband. For comparative purposes, of course. Do sit down and allow me to cut a piece of delicious warm bread off for you. I should prefer staying above the middle, of course, at least for the moment."

She opened her eyes and stared down at her bread man and its enormous phallus. Her husband was enjoying himself immensely. She tried for a smile and managed one, albeit a very sickly smile. "Yes, of course, but please let me cut myself a piece. Here, give me the knife, or perhaps I should just tear off a bit. Yes, I will do that." And she did. She tried desperately not to laugh when her husband groaned. She handed him the piece of warm bread and watched him smear butter and honey on it.

Then he turned and offered it to her. "Shall I tell you how to eat it, my dear?"

"I imagine that I put it in my mouth and bite down, then chew, then swallow. Is that the correct procedure?"

He flinched, grimacing in pain. "You aren't one for imagery, I see."

"Whatever do you mean?"

He gave her that incredibly wicked grin, all white-toothed and gleaming. "Well, since we're married, I suppose there's no harm in educating you. This might shock you, Victoria, but the imagery involves my own, er, masculine self and my—and his—desire for your mouth.''

She simply stared at him, at sea.

Rafael sighed and gave it up. It was beyond him to draw it out. He would show her, and he devoutly hoped that when he did, she would be feeling far differently from the way she felt now.

He tore himself off a piece, all the while watching her nibble at her bread. She looked delicious, he thought, and sweet, and he became hard once more. He shook his head at himself. No, he would wait; he could and would be noble. She had to be very sore, after all.

He continued watching her beneath his lowered lashes. There was no reason he couldn't pleasure her, though. He was old enough to wait his turn. And her pleasure was very intriguing to him. He found that he reveled in the way her eyes glazed and became vague, and in those marvelous cries and shouts she made before, during, and after her climax. No, he amended to himself, not cries after her climax, soft whimpers and little gasps.

She was splendid. He was a lucky fellow. All would be well once she forgot her pique. He would make it all up to her.

Since together they had consumed an entire loaf of bread during the afternoon, they didn't give dinner a thought. Rafael suggested a stroll and Victoria agreed. She was frankly bored with her own company, and despite her husband's perfidy, and his boundless oblivion, he did make her laugh—when she didn't want to smash a board on his head.

He took her hand when they reached the narrow garden path behind Honeycutt Cottage, and his touch sent immediate recognition throughout her body. She saw them on the kitchen floor, like two wild people; he was bucking and roaring on top of her, and she, unmindful of anything save him and the feelings that were flooding through her, was doing everything she could to encourage him, to become one with him, to experience everything with and through him and herself.

At least he hadn't seen her thigh. Her drawers, now the possessor of a tear along the entire central seam, still had intact frilly legs. No, he hadn't found her "malformed toe."

The sun was lowering now but the slight breeze was warm, the air redolent of honeysuckle and hyacinth. There was a low stone wall that ran beside the orchard path down to a small pond. It was there Rafael took her, pausing occasionally to sniff at a rose or any other bloom that took his fancy.

"It's lovely," he said.

He didn't wait for her reply, merely eased down, pulling her with him and stretching his long legs out before him. Victoria settled herself beside him, keeping her legs well covered with her pale yellow muslin skirts.

"There are a lot of frogs and water reeds," she said.

"Hmmm." He lay on his back, pillowing his head on his arms.

To keep herself from staring at him, Victoria said abruptly, even as she forced herself to keep her eyes on the water reeds, "Where in Cornwall do you wish to build your house?"

"*Our* house?"

"Well, yes, I suppose. If you wish."

"Not very close to Drago Hall. I was thinking about the northern coast. Perhaps near St. Agnes. Have you ever visited there?"

"Yes." She turned her head to look down at him. "I have, and I find it beautiful. Wild and savage and untamed. I suppose it's a lot like you."

"Is that a compliment, I wonder?" He cocked open one silver-gray eye.

"Then why must we stay at Drago Hall at all?"

It was a reasonable query, he thought, wishing he'd kept his plans more indefinite. He supposed he should tell her that he already had a house in mind. No, he would wait. He said, "I told you that I hadn't been home in a long time. I wish to visit Drago Hall. It's unfortunate that my brother and his wife are in residence, but we will make do."

"It won't be easy."

"I am your husband. Do just as I tell you, look to me for advice and protection—and nightly diversions, of course—and all will be well."

She hissed air out between gritted teeth. "I think you're an ass, an—"

"Don't insult me, Victoria, or I'll make love to you right here, right now."

He'd spoken ever so softly, but she believed him and she was afraid that she would fight him for only a very short time before yielding. She lowered her head, feeling like a fool, feeling like the wild, untamed, savage one. She felt tears sting the back of her eyes. He didn't care for her, not one whit, and now, since he knew her weakness for him, he would manipulate her to his heart's delight.

Two tears rolled down her cheeks.

She wasn't aware of them until she tasted the salt on her lips.

He said in that same soft, relaxed voice, "Why are you crying?"

"I'm not crying."

"You are so delightfully perverse. You will talk to me or I will make—" He paused, frowning at himself. "Forget that. What's wrong?"

"Nothing." She jumped to her feet, and to her mortification, her leg crumpled and she went down in a graceless heap. It was all too much. She lowered her face to the sweet-smelling grass, wrapped her arms around her middle, tasted dirt, and didn't care.

For a long moment Rafael didn't move. He was confused. Slowly he came up to his knees and clasped her shoulders. He gently pulled her back against him. "It's all right, truly, love. Did you hurt yourself when you stumbled?"

She shook her head and he felt her loosened hair brush against his chin. He leaned against a maple tree and pulled her onto his lap. She felt limp, boneless, without will. It disturbed him. He wanted his fighter back.

He held her tightly, felt her hiccup against his shoulder. He smiled over her head. "It's very odd, you know. Life, that is. A month ago I didn't know of your existence, and now I'm irrevocably leg-shackled to you."

"I'm the one who is leg-shackled," she said between hiccups, her voice sliding into bitterness. "Not only married, but as poor as I was before. At least you are leg-shackled and rich."

"I was already rich. Your money is mine by the law of the land, but I really have no need for it. However, I would have done about anything to keep that money out of Damien's greedy hands."

"You did do 'about anything.' You were forced to leg-shackle yourself. And all your talk about fate is nonsense, Rafael. We would have met eventually, when you finally returned to Drago Hall."

"I wonder if Damien would have succeeded in ravishing you by then." He tensed, wanting his brother's neck between his hands. He also realized that he hadn't given a thought to the *Seawitch* in several days. Or Rob or Blick or Flash or any of the other men who had sailed with him. He rubbed his cheek against the top of Victoria's head. She seemed to have lost her anger and was once again nestled against him in what he chose to think was a trusting position.

"No, you wouldn't have been there. You would have run away, just as you did. And what would have become of you? I shudder to think. But I found you. You're a very lucky wench, Victoria Carstairs."

The problem was, Victoria decided, that he mixed perfect truth with nonsense. It was nearly beyond her to combat him.

Rafael's mind skipped ahead when she remained silent. He had so damned much to do. And frankly, he realized that what he would truly like was at least a month alone with his bride. His ardor seemed inexhaustible to him, and he would enjoy a problem-free period to indulge himself and her.

"Rafael?"

"Yes?"

"I want to go back to the cottage now."

"I don't make a comfortable enough chair for you?"

She heard the laughter in his voice and realized this was one of those times when she wanted to hit him. She wanted to jump off him, but she was suddenly afraid that her leg would lead her to more humiliation. He had to assist her.

"Could you help me, please?"

That was an odd request, but he quickly agreed.

He stood, holding her close, and eased her to her feet. "Did you hurt yourself when you stumbled?"

She shook her head, her eyes on a level with his throat.

"I'd like to go back now, please."

It wasn't, however, until much later that evening that Victoria knew the meaning of true humiliation.

15

Are you sick or are you sullen?
—SAMUEL JOHNSON

"Excuse me," Victoria said, striving for a calm she was decades away from feeling. She quickly shoved back her chair before Rafael could respond, and rose.

"Why? What the devil is wrong with you, Victoria?"

"Nothing. I'll be back shortly. Please continue with your dinner." And she was gone.

Rafael frowned into his crystal glass of deep red wine, wondering what was wrong. She didn't seem precisely ill, yet since she'd come down for dinner she'd been quiet and withdrawn. It bothered him no end.

He took another bite of perfectly baked ham and chewed thoughtfully.

Victoria paused in the middle of her bedchamber and wrapped her arms around herself. Her belly was cramping and she had nothing to relieve the discomfort. She searched yet again for some laudanum. At least she could dose herself with that and sleep away the cramps. It was unusual for her to feel any discomfort at all with her monthly flow. It was marriage that had done it to her, she thought, grimacing at a particularly vicious cramp. She was unsuccessful in her search. She drew a deep breath and walked back downstairs.

She paused in the open doorway until her husband looked up at her. "I'm tired," she said, as if she were a reciting schoolgirl, "and I wish to retire now. I don't feel really well, Rafael, so I would appreciate your not coming—" Her voice fell like a flat stone from a cliff.

He looked at her a moment, his expression bland. He said in his sea captain's voice, and his father's, had he but known it, "What's wrong?" In the past, it was that tone that had always exacted instant obedience.

Victoria nearly blurted out the truth in that instant, but managed in the nick of time to keep her mouth shut. She just stood there looking at him.

"Victoria, I asked you a question," he said now, his voice filled with virtuous determination. "You will answer me, if you please, now."

"It's nothing at all of any importance. I simply need to sleep. I'll be fine in the morning." That was nothing but the truth. She fidgeted a moment with the narrow bracelet on her wrist. "Do you have any laudanum, Rafael?"

That brought him out of his chair. He strode across the dining room and was appalled when she flinched backward. He stopped cold in his tracks.

"Why do you want laudanum? What the devil is wrong?"

She quickly slithered past him out the dining-room door. "It's not important. Good night."

"If you take one more step, I'll bare your bottom and thrash you."

All the wretched tears, she thought inconsequentially at that moment. It was her monthly flow that was making her so emotional, a stupid watering pot. She hated it even as she felt the tears now, brimming in her eyes. "You can't do that," she said, thrusting up her chin. He took a step toward her. "You can't. You have all my money, why can't you be satisfied? Why must you torment me?"

"Torment? I assumed that my behavior was motivated by caring and concern for your welfare. But I see that you don't wish that. Very well. You are ill? Well, then, go away and hide and bear it, please, in silence. I don't wish to be bothered. By the way, I don't have any laudanum." With that, he turned on his heel and strode back into the dining room.

Victoria picked up her skirts and ran back to her bedchamber.

It was just past ten o'clock that night and Rafael was pacing the small library downstairs. He wasn't drunk, not even close. He'd consumed only a third of a bottle of brandy. Smuggled French brandy, of course. Excellent stuff. He paused in his perambulations and looked upward. What if she was truly ill? Bosh, he thought, shaking his head, she was too thick-headed and too stubborn to be sick. She had run, quite literally. She had run away from him, hadn't she? Still, it nagged at the edges of his mind, goading him until he couldn't bear himself anymore.

He changed from his clothes into his dressing gown, snuffed the candles in his bedchamber, and very quietly entered her bedchamber through the adjoining door. She hadn't drawn the draperies across the windows—she'd showed some sense—and he could dimly see her outline in the center of her bed. His intention, he told himself yet again, was merely to see that she was all right.

He stood over her, so still that he could have been an errant shadow. It didn't take him long to realize that she was fully awake. He said softly, still not moving, "Victoria, where do you hurt?"

"Please go away, Rafael," she said, moving a bit farther away from him on the bed. Slowly she eased her arms away from her belly, praying that he wouldn't notice.

It was a prayer in vain. "Your stomach? Your stomach hurts? Something you ate?" Then he touched her very gently, his fingers curling around her upper arm.

"No. Unlike you, I am different, and things happen to me that never happen to you."

"Well, that's true," he said slowly, taking apart her words in his mind and reshaping them to give them their true meaning. It wasn't long in coming.

"Ah," he said.

Oh, well, it couldn't be helped. She gritted her teeth, hoping against hope that just this once he would keep still.

He didn't. Instead, she felt him lift the covers and slip in beside her. His big warm body was quite naked.

"No, I can't."

"Hush, Victoria. I'm a very weary, concerned husband. Let me hold you. You'll feel better in the morning—you're right about that."

And that was that.

She didn't say a word when he pulled her back

against his chest, fitting her bottom against his belly, nor did she do anything but suck in her breath when his large hand lay lightly over her belly. The warmth was marvelous, and she sighed deeply.

Rafael listened to her even breathing in sleep and smiled to himself. He kissed her ear and tried to make himself more comfortable. Poor little tyke.

They left the following day just after luncheon, as Rafael had planned, after Mrs. Ripple's last attempt at a luncheon.

"How, I wonder," Rafael said pensively, "can a body ruin perfectly good ham? Ham, I am compelled to add, that you and I had already baked to perfection?"

"Perhaps, it was the overabundance of some herb."

"You're right. It was dill, I believe. Gallons of it. Perhaps I should have made her one of my special bread men, changed the direction of her culinary thinking—it could have only improved the outcome, I think."

"Ah, here's Tom," said Victoria, laughter in her voice.

Rafael heard it, and gave her a quick look. He studied her face for signs of any discomfort, but found none. Her color was healthy, her eyes bright. He lightly touched his fingertips to her cheek. "You are feeling just the thing again?"

"Yes, certainly," she said as she quickly climbed up into the carriage, not waiting for either Tom Merrifield or Rafael to assist her.

Rafael stuck his head in the open window. "Feel free to call a halt whenever you wish to. All right?"

"Yes," she said. "Oh, Rafael, does Damien know that we are arriving in two days at Drago Hall?"

Rafael studied his York tan gloves for a moment, then said, "Of course. I wrote to him. I'm certain he'll welcome us as politely as a vicar."

"I just bet he will," she retorted. "As for Elaine, she will doubtless give a ball in our honor."

"Not a bad idea," Rafael said thoughtfully. Indeed it wasn't. He needed to reacquaint himself with all the hot-blooded young gentry who abounded in the area. He needed to discover the identity of the Ram. A ball seemed the perfect start. "I'll speak to Damien about it very soon."

She shook her head at him. "I was jesting, but I see that you aren't." She wondered what he was up to. Something, of that she was certain. He had a purpose for returning to Drago Hall, one that involved more than a simple pilgrimage to his ancestral home. How would she pry it out of him? She was fast learning that when he wasn't busy charming her and others, he could be as closemouthed as a clam.

"We will leave Tom Merrifield at Axmouth. Do you remember my telling you about Flash Savory?"

"Yes, the fastest pickpocket in all of London."

"He's the one. He will meet us at Axmouth, at the Sir Francis Drake Inn. We will keep Mr. Mouls's carriage and horses until we reach Drago Hall."

"Flash will stay with us at Drago Hall?"

"Yes. I believe he will be of value to me."

He was up to something, Victoria thought again as she watched him mount his stallion. Why else would he have this young man, Flash, at Drago Hall?

Flash was a young man of many talents, Rafael was thinking as he rode easily, his body swaying in harmony with Gadfly's canter, his thoughts roving outward to plans of attack once they reached Drago Hall. He would probably simply have to become one of them, he decided. Become a member of their ridiculous Hellfire Club. It seemed to him at the moment to be the only way.

And keep the peace, somehow, at Drago Hall. And protect Victoria.

They reached Drago Hall early Sunday afternoon. Rafael hadn't intended to feel anything at the sight of his boyhood home, but he did, deep stirring feelings that made him want to cry with the loss of it. Nothing had changed, he thought, gazing about him.

The main hall was early Elizabethan, built by the first Baron Drago, Arkley Carstairs, in 1564 or thereabouts. Successive barons had added three wings to the central hall. It could have looked a rambling monstrosity, but Drago Hall didn't. It did go on, but in a compact, *reasonable* way, at least that was how Rafael's father had described it. Thank God, Rafael thought as he looked wistfully at a grooved and nicked maple tree he had carved on as a boy; the barons had all used the same soft red stone quarried in Stenalees.

Rafael's father had been content to widen the portico and the drive that curved in front of the Hall. He'd spared the oak and maple trees—indeed, Rafael recalled his being quite adamant about that, and the resulting drive wasn't at all the same width from beginning to end. It curved in here and there to protect a tree, and the effect was odd but charming.

Rafael's mother had believed Drago Hall to be too stark, too forbidding, and had planted every flower known to the southern coast of Cornwall. It had been a successful endeavor. Color abounded, softening the lines of the Hall, casting a welcoming aura over its rather severe facade.

"This is what I call a rich cove's dish," said Flash, looking about him.

Rafael smiled. "We should be comfortable enough for the short time we'll be here."

Flash just looked at him, wondering what the captain was up to this time. He supposed he'd be told soon enough. The captain did things his way and there was no use prying at him until he was ready. Now, the captain taking a bride, that was something else. Flash looked over his shoulder for just a moment, and sure enough, there was Mrs. Carstairs leaning out the window, taking everything in. Pretty girl, and saucy, giving the captain his gravy when it suited her. When he'd first met her the day before in Axmouth, he wondered if she thought he'd steal the silverware at Drago Hall, her greeting was so wary. Then Captain Carstairs had said, a wicked gleam in his eyes, "Now, Victoria, Flash here has promised me that he won't knobble a thing. Drago Hall is quite safe, I promise you."

She was embarrassed to have her thought so baldly set on the table, Flash thought, but she'd quickly recovered and sauced the captain up quick as any general. "And what will he lift? Perhaps my valise?"

"He means 'steal,' ma'am," Flash said.

"I know what he means, Flash. It's just that he's a wicked tease. I'm glad to know you." She thrust out her hand and he took it. "I look to you for information about him. I haven't known him all that long and I begin to believe there is a very perverse streak running the length of him."

"Aye, that's a fact," Flash said comfortably. "Maybe I can do me a spot of blackmail, eh, Captain?"

"Flash, my boy, you do a spot of anything, and I'll nail your hide to the stable door."

A fine good laugh that had brought, once Mrs. Carstairs had realized it was a jest.

"Let's go right to the stables," Rafael said now to Flash. "Over there, to the east."

The stableboy who was in the yard, a boy Rafael hadn't ever seen before, instantly called him Baron, and Rafael grinned. "Make that Captain, boy. What is your name?"

"Everyone calls me Lobo, sir, er, Captain—Baron, sir."

Rafael merely shook his head, smiling that charming smile of his. He assisted Victoria from the carriage. She was a bit pale. "Don't worry, it will be all right. You are a married woman now, not a helpless, unprotected girl. Will you trust me?"

She didn't reply, and he felt a bit miffed at her. He heard Flash explaining to Lobo that he, Rafael, was not Baron Drago.

He repeated himself. "Victoria, you aren't still afraid, are you?"

"Yes, a bit," she admitted finally. He felt her slip her hand into his and it pleased him inordinately. He gave her his brilliant white smile and she returned it, albeit a bit hesitantly.

"Well, the prodigal, or should I say prodigals, have come home to roost."

Victoria felt again the confusion and bewilderment upon seeing Damien and Rafael together. She looked from one to the other and back again. They were so remarkably alike that it was eerie, particularly now that Rafael's tan had faded. From their inky black hair, worn a bit long, to their silver-gray eyes, to their high cheekbones and straight noses, to the strong chins. It was disconcerting, even a bit frightening that two people could so closely resemble each other. Why, she wondered blankly, did she feel such revulsion for Damien? And his brother, his identical twin, had but to smile down at her, lightly kiss her or caress her, and she was ready to take on Napoleon single-handed.

"Good day to you, twin," Rafael said, still holding Victoria's hand against his side. "The Hall still looks the same. Magnificent. You are a good manager. Oh, incidentally, this is my man, Flash. Flash, this is Baron Drago."

Amazing, thought Flash. Scary it was. He nodded, saying not a word.

So, Victoria thought, amazed at the ways of gentlemen, her husband was simply going to ignore the fact that he'd seen his brother in London and, for that matter, wanted to skin him.

Damien inclined his head. "You said in your rather brief missive that you wished to stay here until you decided where to build or buy your own home. I suppose," he continued, his voice pensive as his gaze traveled slowly over Victoria, "that Victoria also wanted to return to Drago Hall?"

"Victoria—my wife—is of course delighted to accompany her husband anywhere. She naturally feels quite safe with me, as is proper."

Two cocks facing off against each other in the hen yard, thought Victoria. She glanced over at Flash and saw that he was gazing from one to the other, a curious expression on his face. She liked him, she realized, probably had liked him from the moment Rafael had told her about him. He was thin, about her own age, with very intelligent brown eyes and curly brown hair. His smile was wicked and gave him an expression fit for a needy orphan.

"Of course Victoria is not the same girl she was when she so precipitately left such a short time ago, is she?"

"No," Rafael said in a matter-of-fact voice, even though he wanted to slam his fist into his twin's jaw, "she is my wife."

"Ah, my love," Damien called to Elaine, "come meet my brother and his charming wife, who just happens to be your cousin whom you haven't seen for many weeks now."

Rafael studied Elaine Carstairs as she walked gracefully down the worn stone steps of Drago Hall toward them. She was tall, with dark hair—as dark as her husband's—and really quite lovely. Her chin was a bit too pointed for Rafael's taste, and as for her figure, it was impossible to tell, for she was well into her pregnancy. She seemed to be having a very difficult time smiling, he saw, feeling unholy amusement, particularly at Victoria.

And like Victoria, she stared openmouthed from him to his brother and back again. "It's amazing," she said at last. "Rafael, welcome back to Drago Hall." She extended a very white hand to him and he dutifully kissed it.

"How is Damaris?"

Elaine looked at her as if she'd just crawled out of the swamp that was some two miles due east of Drago Hall—Penhale Swamp it was called. "Hello, Victoria. My husband tells me you have enjoyed yourself since leaving here."

"I'm not certain if it was all enjoyment," Rafael said, easing quickly into the breach. "I trust Victoria believes it was—at least since her marriage to me."

"Oh, yes, certainly," said Victoria. "Damaris, Elaine? She is all right?"

"I don't know why you should care—you left her quickly enough, after all. But yes, the child is fine."

"Shall we go into the Hall, Rafael, ladies?"

Rafael nodded. He turned to Flash. "See to the horses, then come to the Hall. The butler, Ligger, will tell you where my room is and where you'll be housed."

"Why did you run away, Victoria?"

Straight and to the point, Victoria thought, turning her head to look at her cousin. She waited until the two men had strolled well ahead of them before answering. She had given this some thought, of course, and managed to say easily enough, "I discovered that I was an heiress, Elaine, something neither you nor Damien thought necessary to tell me. I was on my way to London to see the solicitor. That is all."

"That's what Damien said."

She didn't sound pleased with the duplication of reasons. Could Elaine know of her husband's attempted rape?

"I don't know why you simply didn't ask Damien about it."

"It didn't occur to me to ask because neither of you had bothered to even hint that I was more than a poor relation."

"Your precious money was perfectly safe, Victoria. Damien was going to tell you when you came of age."

Victoria could but stare at her. "I wouldn't have gotten my money, unless I married, until the age of twenty-five. Is that the age you're referring to, Elaine? And a husband—ah, I can just imagine how Damien would have handled that. Just as he handled David. I cannot believe that you, my own cousin, could have been so perfidious."

"Don't be ridiculous. You were always treated as one of the family." She paused a moment, pale now. "Besides, I didn't know about your inheritance."

Victoria just looked at her. "No," she said slowly, "I don't suppose you did."

"Shall we go to the drawing room?" Damien's voice. He'd come to a halt in the thick-beamed central hall.

Victoria nodded, her eyes now on Rafael. He was standing very still, looking about. Victoria followed his gaze from the cavernous fireplace, black and deep as a pit, large enough to roast an oxen, to the suits of armor—English, French, Flemish—many of them terribly rusted, along the far walls, to the banners and crests of every Carstairs generation since the sixteenth century.

"It's still the same," Rafael said.

"Don't get too close to those wretched knights in their armor," Elaine said. "They're dangerous, you know. The maids, silly wenches, won't dust them or clean them properly. They say that there are ghosts, and the ghosts hide in the armor. It's stupid, of course, but what can one do?"

That was neutral enough, and the four of them trooped into the drawing room. Here Rafael saw change. Elaine, he supposed. It was an improvement. All the dark, heavy furnishings were gone, to be replaced by some marvelous light Queen Anne pieces. The draperies were nearly transparent, with the sunlight bursting through them. A light blue Aubusson carpet with wide creamy swirls covered the center of the floor.

"Very nice," Rafael said, turning to smile at Elaine. "My God, Ligger," he said, seeing the old retainer on the threshold. "Hello, dear fellow, you are looking just the same."

"Thank you, sir. May I say, sir, that it is very gratifying to see you again."

"Yes, I'm gratified to be here, actually. Did you know, Ligger, that Miss Victoria and I are married?"

Ligger knew, of course. Every servant at Drago Hall knew. It had been a choice topic of conversation for nearly a week now. And Ligger also knew why Miss Victoria had run away. That fact he had kept to himself. His loyalty was to the family, after all, no matter how despicably the current master might behave. Now, Master Rafael—a hell-raiser, that one was, but straightforward and honest. A man people could trust, that was master Rafael.

"Tea, please, Ligger."

"It is coming directly, my lady." Ligger turned to direct two house maids bringing in a huge silver service and a trolley with cakes and biscuits and small sandwiches artfully displayed.

There was silence until the servants left the drawing room in Ligger's majestic wake.

"You are home to stay, Rafael?"

Rafael smiled at Elaine. "Yes, I believe so. My shipping interests shouldn't suffer, however. My first mate, a fellow with excellent training and judgment, will captain the *Seawitch* now. However, I don't intend to become a gentleman of leisure." He paused a moment and leaned back against the settle. "I've worked too many years to enjoy a life of leisure. I suppose I shall continue directing my enterprises from here. Of course, Victoria and I will also raise our family here."

"So," said Damien, "you have earned enough

money over the past five years to buy your own estate? Or," he continued, his voice soft, a bit contemptous, "do you plan to use Victoria's funds to get what you want?"

"Both," said Rafael, the smile never slipping. "The other half of Victoria's money is soon to be in trust for our children." The lovely smile now was directed toward Victoria. It didn't reach his beautiful gray eyes, she saw.

"How noble of you, Rafael," said Elaine, her voice on the shrill side.

"Not at all," he said easily. "It's simply that I have no pressing need for her funds. Indeed, I would have married her if she hadn't had a sou."

Liar. Victoria's expressive eyes told him. Bloody liar. She kept her mouth shut, however, and he was profoundly thankful for small favors. "A young woman as lovely as Victoria," he continued, "shouldn't be left in the world without protection. She was much in need of a husband and I trust that she isn't disappointed with the bargain she made."

Victoria, bless her sweet, reasonable self, dutifully nodded, a bright smile pinned firmly on her lips.

Rafael took a sip of tea, wondering about Elaine. He'd overheard some of her conversation with Victoria and he imagined that she knew quite a bit more about her husband's dishonor than she let on. She was wary of Victoria and she appeared to dislike her. Could it be, his thinking continued, that she simply resented not having a poor relation to do her bidding anymore?

He said with a smile, "Congratulations are in order, I see. An heir, Damien?"

"Yes, undoubtedly. Just after Christmas, Dr. Ludcott tells me. And Elaine is in the pink of health, as you can see."

Suddenly Victoria rose from her chair. "I think I shall go to the nursery and see Damaris."

"Damaris is sleeping," Elaine said sharply. "You know how Nanny Black is—at least you should remember how very *territorial* that old woman acts."

"Actually, I believe I should like to go to our room now, if you don't mind, Elaine." Rafael rose as he spoke, reaching out his hand to Victoria. She came to stand beside him.

"I believe," Damien said, "that Elaine has put you in the Pewter Room."

Victoria stared at her cousin for a moment, shocked. It was a beautiful room, all shades of silver and gray. Three decades before, it had been used as the master bedchamber, and wasn't used now, for no guests were considered worthy. This was indeed a surprise.

As for Rafael, he saw that Elaine hadn't assigned this room to them. Damien had. Indeed, she looked angry. Now, why, he wondered, would his brother assign him and Victoria such a grand suite? Could it be that his errant twin wanted to make peace?

No, that was doubtful in the extreme.

Some minutes later, Victoria was looking about the large, airy room with something akin to awe. "I don't understand," she said, more to herself than to Rafael. "Goodness, I have never seen so many beautiful shades of gray. Even though the gray silk on this chair is a bit worn, it is still exquisite, don't you think?"

"Yes. Actually, I don't understand either. And Elaine didn't assign us this suite, Victoria, it was Damien, I'm quite certain. Another mystery I've got on my hands."

"What do you mean by *another* mystery?"

He recovered quickly. He stepped closer to her and gently clasped her shoulders in his hands. "You, Victoria, are a veritable bundle of mysteries. First of all, you have yet to regale me with your famous or infamous confession, as the case may be. Second, you have yet to show me your malformed toe." He stared over her head toward the wide windows that gave toward the sea. "And now my twin. Very invigorating, don't you agree?" He didn't add the damnable mystery of the Hellfire Club, regenerated, as Lord Walton called it. He'd been a fool to agree. He came back to his senses and the Pewter Room to see Victoria looking up at him hungrily.

"Don't do that." His voice was sharp, harsh. "That look makes me want to ravish you, right here, right now." He gave her a pained smile. "But I can't, so don't tempt me."

"But I didn't do anything. I can't help the way I look. Truly."

She tried to pull away from him. He wouldn't release her. "No, don't be embarrassed, Victoria. It's healthy to feel desire for your husband, makes your husband feel like the grandest lover in the world. What's more, I like it excessively."

"I don't like you, Rafael."

Again his good humor flowed over her, like warm, smooth honey. "Why ever not? Don't wound me, Victoria. Tell me you forgive me for my moment, my very brief moment, of male stupidity."

"You never believed me. How can I forgive you that?"

He was on the point of telling her flatly that a

woman's duty was to be the forgiving one, since men weren't. But he saw the pain in her eyes, the disappointment, the confusion and uncertainty. "Truly," he said, very softly now, "I am sorry, Victoria. Shall I go slay a dragon for you to prove what a contrite fellow I am?"

"You know there are no dragons, so your offer is quite meaningless."

"You are a hard woman to satisfy," he said, then immediately added, his tone wicked, "No, I didn't mean that at all." She slammed him in the stomach with her fist. He grunted obligingly. "What I meant, dear one, was that I shall have to come up with another daring deed that will prove my abject sincerity."

"*Abject* sincerity?"

His inexhaustible supply of good humor and his easy wit were wearing her down. He knew it, of course. She knew that he knew it, curse him.

"I'm tired," she said, on a big yawn.

"Let's nap together, all right? I always wanted to sleep in that grand bed. As boys, Damien and I weren't allowed in here. I'll wager that bed is raised a good three feet off the floor. Shall we close the draperies at night?"

She was on the point of telling him that the evening air was quite healthy, when she realized he'd offered her complete and utter darkness to hide in.

"Yes, I should like that very much. It will be like we are the only two people on earth."

He listened to the brightness of her voice, and quickly realized that he'd offered her a way around his seeing her body. And her ugliness. He sighed. He couldn't very well retract now. It was all becoming too ridiculous. He wondered if the kitchen at

Drago Hall was ever emptied of servants. The kitchen floor at Honeycutt Cottage had made him sing hallelujahs.

"Dinner is at six o'clock, if I remember rightly."

"You remember. We dress for dinner. Elaine insists upon it."

"Wear your peach silk, Victoria. You look more edible than a strawberry tart."

"Tart." She sent her fist into his stomach again, but he was laughing so hard he didn't grunt for her.

He was wiping his eyes, still chuckling. "Shall I help you with that gown, Victoria?"

"Yes, please." It was one that Lucia had chosen, assuming that she would have a maid, which she didn't, nor did she expect to have one now.

She felt his warm hands on her, and responded quickly. Would it always be like this? she wondered, and devoutly prayed it would be. She held herself perfectly still.

She walked quickly to the painted Indian screen in the far corner of the mammoth bedchamber, a magnificent piece brought from Ceylon by a great-great uncle, and eased off her traveling gown. She peeked about the edge of the screen. "Rafael, could you please hand me my dressing gown? It's on the bed."

Some ten minutes later they lay together on the huge bed. Rafael yawned. "Come here and let me hug you. It's been far too long."

It sounded a fine idea, and she complied. It had been too long, since last night. Much too long.

She fell asleep with her head on his shoulder, her palm over his heart.

16

I am the very pink of courtesy.
—SHAKESPEARE

Victoria was being warm, excessively polite, and altogether adorable, Rafael thought as he listened to her wax enthusiastic about the wonders of the Pewter Room, an innocuous enough topic to pursue while the servants were serving dinner. "So utterly magnificent," she finished, eyeing the very generous helping of red mullet Jeffrey had given her.

Rafael was watching Damien's face while she spoke, but his twin's expression remained that of a mildly interested host.

"More wine, sir?"

Rafael nodded and said nothing until the footman, Jeffrey, had resumed his post by the dining room's double doors.

"I do wonder, brother," Rafael said at last, "why you honored my wife and me with such splendid lodgings. Remember as boys we got hided once for tracking mud onto the carpet?"

"And told—rather, ordered—never to set our grubby feet in that room again. Yes, I remember quite well. As for giving you and Victoria that room, why not? I trust you no longer have grubby feet or hands?"

"Upon occasion, but I shall be on my best behavior." Rafael turned to Elaine and continued smoothly, "I look forward to meeting my niece."

"How unusual," Elaine said, and helped herself to a crimped salmon with hollandaise sauce.

"Why?" Rafael's black brow shot up a good inch.

"Gentlemen don't particularly wish to be bothered with children." She looked down at the expanse of table toward Damien. "Particularly little girl children."

"Damaris is fine," Damien said easily. "And soon she will have a little brother to play with."

"And your precious heir for Drago Hall," Elaine added, and Victoria thought she heard a touch of bitterness in her cousin's voice. But why? Any man with property and a title to pass on must have an heir.

"Why, certainly," said Damien easily. Conversation died. Victoria could think of nothing at all to say, so she merely kept her head down and continued chewing on her red mullet and her *ris de veau aux tomates*.

She raised her eyes after a few moments and saw that Damien was looking at her. He made her very aware that her shoulders were bare and her breasts were pushed up high, with only a confection of fine blonde lace keeping her bosom in place. Rafael, who'd assisted her to dress for dinner, had told her she looked delicious as creamy blancmange, since she didn't appear to care for comparisons having to do with tarts. She'd fashioned her hair on top of her head, threaded a pale peach ribbon through the curls, and brushed two thick curls over her shoulder. She thought she looked well enough and was pleased. Pleased until they'd joined Damien and Elaine in the drawing room and Damien had looked at her as if she were naked. She stuck close to Rafael's side, but if he wondered at her sudden and uncommon wifely clinging, he made no comment.

Victoria tried to keep her face expressionless and merely nodded toward Damien. Dinner continued with haunch of venison, boiled capon, oysters, and green peas.

Damien gave a nod, and the servants silently left the dining room.

"This room is positively medieval," Rafael said, eyeing the heavy dark furnishing that filled the long, rather narrow room. Dark wainscoting climbed up three walls, and one could easily imagine flambeaux with rushlight torches on the walls rather than the modern classic, elegant chandelier above the mahogany table.

Elaine merely nodded to Rafael, then said without preamble to Victoria, "You look different."

"It's the gown. I am no longer wearing schoolgirl clothes. Lady Lucia picked it out for me."

"I was under the impression when you were here that you wished to wear schoolgirl clothes, as you call them."

"Elaine, my clothes were fine, really. It's just that Lady Lucia believed I should wear different materials and styles, since I was no longer so young."

"Who, pray, is Lady Lucia?"

"I spent my time in London with her. I stayed at her town house. She's a grand old lady."

"I've never heard of Lady Lucia," Elaine said. "Why ever would she take you in?"

"Lady Lucia took Victoria in because I asked her to," Rafael said mildly. "She's always had a great deal of fondness for me," he lied with the smoothness of a swindler of the first order. "Of course she quickly came to great fondness for Victoria as well. She stayed with Lucia until we were wed, as Damien knows."

Elaine's eyes flew to her husband. He was eating with single-minded concentration, seemingly ignoring the conversation at his table.

"Damien? You knew?"

So, Victoria thought, Elaine knows nothing of what he has done. She waited, peas poised on her fork tines, to see what he would say.

"Yes, my dear. I wasn't able to attend the small wedding, but I was present afterward. To give my best wishes to the bride and groom, of course. Indeed, it was incumbent upon me, as Victoria's guardian, to give my brother permission to wed her."

"Of course," said Rafael.

Gentlemen, Victoria thought again. Why, they'd nearly come to blows.

"You know, brother," Rafael said as he gently ran his fingertip along the crystal edge of his wineglass, "as a wedding present, would you consider giving us a ball? That way Victoria could see all her neighbors and friends, and I could renew old acquaintances. Five years is a long time, and it would take me an age were I forced to make morning calls."

Elaine lost her belligerent look in an instant and exclaimed, "Oh, yes, Damien. That would be grand. We haven't had a ball since—"

"—since the night before Victoria so precipitately left Drago Hall," Damien finished, never batting an eye. "And she didn't have the opportunity to attend that one."

"But she couldn't. I told you that she wouldn't want to. After all, she is quite—"

"No, my dear, she isn't at all. I don't believe she cared for the ball gown I selected for her. Did you, Victoria?"

Rafael hadn't been paying too much attention, but he was now. Victoria was quite what? What he saw at that moment was that his wife was quite without color. He assumed it was because of Damien's ill-disguised attempts to embarrass her. He would give his twin a new direction for his thoughts, on the morrow.

"I had decided to leave," Victoria said at last. "I didn't want to be distracted with a ball."

"The gown is still in your closet, I believe," Elaine said. "A ball. I think it an excellent idea, Damien. You wouldn't wish to be at all backward in your attentions."

"Not at all. I agree. When would you wish to hold this ball?"

"Next Friday, perhaps?" Rafael said.

Victoria looked toward Elaine, expecting her to shout out *lame and ugly leg* at any minute. But Elaine was still looking at Damien. She said at last, "Yes, I believe we could manage. Ligger will marshal the servants like a field general. He dearly loves to entertain, you know," she added to Rafael.

Victoria was vastly relieved at Elaine's silence, unwitting or not. She could dance without her leg collapsing under her, just not at great length. She asked her husband, "Are you a good dancer, Rafael?"

"Excellent," he said. He leaned close to her and

added, "Not as excellent a dancer as a lover, but close, Victoria, quite close. Dancing with me will provide you pleasure, just not the same sort as I give you in bed—or on the kitchen floor."

She opened her mouth, snapped it closed, and clutched her fork in a death grip. "You will stop that," she said, wishing she could smack that white-toothed smile off his face. "You are wicked as Satan. All you need is a forked tail and no one would doubt your identity even if you smiled that beautiful smile of yours."

He gave a shout of laughter. "Satan, huh? Only I am firmly of this earth, Victoria, and all its earthly delights. What could be more delightful than a very responsive, very passionate wife? Now, about this tail business—"

"What are you saying?"

"Nothing of any particular interest, Elaine," Rafael said easily, straightening back up in his chair. "Victoria agrees that Friday next would be charming."

"I believe Victoria and I will excuse ourselves now, gentlemen." With those few words Elaine rose and looked pointedly at Victoria. Victoria wanted to tell her that she was still hungry, but she dutifully followed her cousin from the dining room.

In the huge entryway, beside a rusted suit of Flemish armor, Victoria said lightly, "Ligger will be upset that you didn't wait for him to pull back your chair, Elaine. Remember how he gave you those looks when we first came to Drago Hall?"

"I didn't wish to wait any longer." She gave Victoria a look that could only be described as contemptuous and said, "It appeared that your husband was ready to toss up your skirts right there. I didn't wish to be witness to any further improper behavior. On second thought, I think you would have unfastened his breeches without a by-your-leave."

Victoria stared at her, stunned.

"Oh, yes, I can imagine what you do with him. I imagine he uses you in unnatural and—"

"You will be quiet. You are a silly prig." Victoria felt washed clean as the words left her mouth. Finally she'd said exactly what she wanted to. She held her head high and marched into the drawing room, her heels clicking loudly on the black marble tile. If she thought she'd done her cousin in, she was soon to be shown her mistake.

"Don't think you can return here and try to seduce my husband again."

Victoria closed her eyes a moment. She'd never heard Elaine speak in such a low, dangerous tone. So she *had* guessed. Thus the reason for her attacks. Why not tell Elaine the truth of the matter? She shook her head. She'd always heard that pregnant women should be spared unpleasantness. It could cause miscarriages and other dire results. To relieve her own spleen simply wasn't worth the possible consequences.

"Elaine," she said instead as she slowly turned to face her cousin, "I don't even like Damien, at least as nothing more than a brother-in-law. Why do you say that?"

"Of course you like him. You married a man who is his very image. You couldn't have Damien, so you settled for his twin. It is all very obvious to me, Victoria."

"I married Rafael despite the fact that he and Damien are mirror images. You are being ridiculous,

Elaine. I'm not lying, you know. Oh, no more, please. Won't you play the pianoforte for me? I haven't heard anyone who plays as well as you since I left."

"Even you must realize that Rafael married you only for your money. And we know well why you married him. God, I wish you hadn't come back." When Victoria said nothing, Elaine gave her white shoulders a petulant shrug and strode like a small ship with a heavy cargo to the pianoforte in the corner of the drawing room.

She was playing Mozart's C Major sonata when the gentlemen came in. Rafael paused, clearly startled. He had expected Elaine to be inept in all things, accomplished primarily in gossip and pettiness. She played beautifully. That would teach him, he thought, to make snap judgments about people. He sat beside his wife and took her hand in his and laid it on his thigh.

He whispered in her ear, "How many more nights am I to be celibate?"

He sighed, raised his left hand, and began to count off on his fingers.

Elaine executed a brilliant arpeggio and crashed down on a final chord.

"Two," Rafael said, and clapped with great enthusiasm.

"That was beautiful, Elaine," Victoria called out. "Please, play one of your French ballads."

Elaine sang too, and Rafael found himself again surprised. Her voice was clear and strong. He watched his brother stroll to the piano and join his wife, his own tenor voice as melodious as hers.

"Are you also talented?" Victoria asked her husband.

"No, I sound like a rusty wheel."

"So, you get ill riding in a closed carriage and you have no musical talent. I'm beginning to wonder about the wisdom of my bargain, Rafael."

"Unfortunately I'm constrained to wait to prove to you that your decision to wed me is the wisest one you will ever make."

"They are really quite good together," Victoria said, ignoring him. Bitterness crept into her voice. "If Damien would but realize it."

"I don't care, but he will realize soon enough that he can't have you."

Victoria believed him. "He must realize that he will have to leave me alone now. Besides," she added, her voice hardening, "I'm no longer a young virgin to be victimized. Surely he can't still be interested."

"I would be," Rafael said, his voice as serious as she'd ever heard. "What the devil does virginity have to do with anything? Actually, discovering you were a virgin was frightening. I was concerned about hurting you. No, very little fun at all."

"Bosh. I don't believe you. Had I not been a virgin, you would have berated me until I was deaf, then sent me to a moldering estate in Northumberland."

"Along with some chicken blood," he said.

"It's not amusing, Rafael."

"All right, a bit of what you said does have a small grain of truth, but the theory is valid, I swear. Now, truly, Victoria, all I have to do is look at you and I want you. It's amazing, really. I've never felt anything like it in all my blighted years."

Victoria didn't believe him. She turned her attention back to Damien and Elaine.

The Ram was pleased. He sat a bit apart from his acolytes, a term he dared not use in front of the eight

men. They were all sitting near to the fireplace, snif-
ters of brandy warming between their hands, and
their male bodies were well sated. All of them
thought they were so very wicked, carrying on in the
black of night, the Ram thought, garbed in their black
capes and black hoods. But not one of them had
asked why the girl wasn't wide awake during her
woman's offering, as the Ram had named this ritual.

No, they'd simply taken their turns, plowed her
thoroughly, and now perhaps they would consent to
whatever he, the Ram, wished them to do. His surprise had pleased them, of that there could be no
doubt. It was a pity, though, that the girl couldn't
have been procured in the same very proper way as
the others. It could prove to be a bother. Possibly.

But who would believe a fourteen-year-old girl?
Who would pay any attention to a girl's mother who
had no husband and no sons?

The Ram dismissed the group. Their next meeting
would be All Hallows' night. Johnny laughed and
jested about flying a broom to the hunting lodge.
Vincent wondered if he should bring a caldron and
three witches. Let them laugh, the Ram thought. It
was a ritual he was teaching them, and they would
attend him. Yes, they would. They went with wide
yawns, and he could imagine their disinterest in the
girl who lay sprawled spread-eagled on the oak table.

Of course he had taught them that she was a vessel, nothing more. An unconscious vessel. He would
have preferred that she be awake during her initiation, but what was done was done. He didn't wish
to, but he bathed the blood and seed from her and
dressed her again.

It was close to an hour later that the Ram reached
the girl's small house in St. Austell. The house was

filled with light and there were men milling about. He cursed to himself, thought a moment, then left the girl in a narrow ditch some fifty yards away.

He rode home slowly, feeling anticipation for the morrow.

The following morning at ten o'clock, Victoria opened the door to the nursery.

"Torie! Torie!"

Damaris jumped to her feet and scurried toward Victoria. Victoria quickly leaned down and hugged her tightly.

"Torie, I've missed you—where did you go? Nanny said you wouldn't come back and then she huffed and said you married the master's twin, of all the strange things, and—"

"I'm back, Damie. That's all that matters."

Suddenly the child stiffened and whispered, "Papa."

Rafael smiled at the little girl. "Hello, Damaris."

"You're not my papa. Who are you?"

"She is direct, if nothing else," Victoria said, ruffling Damaris's silky black hair, her father's hair, Rafael's hair. And his face. "How do you know he's not your father, Damie? Doesn't he look just like your father?"

"No."

"Have I just been mortally insulted?" Rafael didn't wait for an answer to his rhetorical question. He dropped to his knees in front of the little girl. "I'm your uncle Rafael. Can you say my name?"

"It's a funny name. Mine isn't."

"Oh, I don't know. Damaris is rather unusual, just like Rafael."

"Rafull," Damie said. "It's easy. Papa never comes here."

Rafael looked up at Victoria, a brow arched in question. When she merely shook her head, he asked Damaris, "Do you mind if I visit you here?"

"No, if Nanny doesn't mind, but mind you, she has to be in a good temper."

"This, Rafael, is Nanny Black," Victoria said, smiling toward the dour old woman. "Nanny, my husband, Captain Rafael Carstairs. Nanny came with Elaine upon her marriage to your brother."

"Bark off the same tree," said Nanny Black with a disapproving eye as the young man rose to his feet and offered her his hand. She took it.

"Not according to Damaris," said Rafael. "She knew immediately I wasn't her father."

"Only because the baron never visits the nursery."

Victoria said to Damaris, who was tugging on her skirt for attention, "Should you like to go riding with your uncle Rafael and me?"

The little girl shouted with glee. "Nanny, I want to go. I will go."

"Little terror," said Nanny Black fondly.

"Have you a proper mount, Victoria?"

"Toddy's well enough. Since I carry Damaris in front of me, I wouldn't want to ride that ill- humored brute of yours, Rafael."

"Gadfly isn't ill-humored, he's simply spirited, like my bride. He knows I'm his master and he obeys me, just as—"

"I don't think Damaris will need a coat, Nanny," Victoria said quickly, cutting him off.

"Should you like me to be your servant until we get downstairs?" With his words, Rafael swung the little girl up on his shoulders. He settled her thin legs on either side of his face and grinned at his wife. "Ready?"

"Damaris," Victoria said in a clear, very sweet voice, "be certain to hold on tight—to your uncle's hair."

Rafael howled, more for Damaris's benefit than from scalp pain.

"Little terror," said Nanny Black.

The three of them were met by Elaine in the entryway downstairs. "Where are you taking her?"

"Riding," said Victoria.

"Mama," said Damaris, and tugged on Rafael's hair, "this isn't Papa, it's Uncle Rafill."

Elaine, Victoria noted, looked a bit pale this morning, and there were shadows beneath her eyes. She said, quickly, "Are you feeling all right?"

"No," said Elaine. "I'm increasing, you know, Victoria."

"Yes, I'm sorry. It's just that you look so beautiful, I tend to forget."

Elaine relaxed visibly. "Do take good care of my daughter, Rafael."

Rafael winced at a particularly enthusiastic tug on his hair. "If she doesn't do me in first."

"Little terror," said Victoria in her best imitation of Nanny Black, and Damaris went into gales of laughter.

"She does know how to control herself, does she not?" Rafael suddenly looked a bit worried.

Victoria said with a perfectly straight face, "For the most part. Only if she gets excited will she forget—"

Elaine interrupted, "Of course she is perfectly fine, Rafael. Really, Victoria, you shouldn't tease him so."

"He deserves it," said Victoria. "We're going to Fletcher's Pond, Elaine, and will have lunch there. I'll have Damaris back in time for her nap."

It was Flash who lifted Damaris up to Victoria.

"Your name is odd, like Uncle Rafull's," Damaris told him from her perch in front of Victoria.

"Rifall, hmmm," said Flash, giving his captain a drawing smile. "Well, then, little miss, you shall call me Mr. Savory. Doesn't that add a certain dignity? I'm a proper dignified person, you know."

"You're funny," said Damaris. "I'm ready, Uncle Refill."

"Yes, ma'am. We will see you later, Mr. Savory."

Victoria let Rafael go where he wished to. He drew his stallion to a halt every few minutes to view a prospect that he remembered from bygone years. At one point he turned to Victoria and said, "I believe Squire Esterbridge lives just over there. Should you like to visit him and his sterling specimen of a son? Old David, the bully-coward and spineless sod?"

She shook her head, frowning at him. What an odd thing to call David. He'd certainly been gullible, but he'd always been nice enough to her before that long-ago afternoon at Fletcher's Pond.

They rode finally into St. Austell.

"Ah, nothing has changed, nothing at all," Rafael said, drawing his stallion in beside Toddy. "What's happening? Look at that crowd, Victoria."

Victoria click-clicked Toddy forward and they drew nearer to the crowd congregated just at the edge of the town.

"Stay here," Rafael said, and Victoria immediately urged Toddy forward, saying over her shoulder, "I know these people. I'll find out what's going on."

Rafael frowned after her, but knew she was right. Actually, when one of the people in the crowd—Mr. Josiah Frogwell—an ancient relic who owned a local inn, spotted Rafael, he immediately said something to the man next to him.

Rafael heard the whispers and the calls: "Baron Drago . . . It's the baron."

"Mr. Frogwell," Rafael called out in a loud voice, "I'm not the baron. I'm Rafael Carstairs, his twin."

The man's face immediately broke into a smile and Rafael wondered at it. Had his twin alienated the people of St. Austell? How? he wondered. What the devil had he done?

"Welcome home, Master Rafael."

"The young master's home."

Rafael grinned, then spotted young Ralph Bicton, a childhood playmate and the son of the local butcher. He was wearing a bloodied long apron and Rafael guessed he was now in his father's place.

"Is it really you, Rafael?" Ralph called, striding forward, wiping his hands, thankfully, as he did so.

Their greeting was boisterous until Ralph seemed to recall the difference in their stations. He withdrew a bit, allowing others to come forward. Victoria smiled and spoke, and responded easily even when confronted by Widow Meneburle, a garrulous sausage-curled matron of uncertain years and equally uncertain temper.

Finally, when Victoria could get in a word, she asked, "Why are you all gathered here, Mrs. Meneburle? Is something wrong?"

Mrs. Meneburle, her sausage curls bouncing beside her plump cheeks, stepped close to Toddy and said in a stage whisper that Rafael had no difficulty at all in overhearing, "It's those ruffians, Miss Victoria . . . rather, Mrs. Carstairs"—this was said with an arch look—"aye those ne'er-do-wells have ravished poor little Joan Newdowns. Left her in a ditch. Awful, perfectly awful, and the girl can't tell who they were. They *drugged* her." Mrs. Meneburle was excessively pleased at Victoria's gasp of horror, and added, coming even closer, "Do you know there were horrible bruises on the girl's wrists and ankles? They'd tied her down and treated her like a trollop. Poor, poor child."

"But why is everyone standing here?"

Mr. Meledor, St. Austell's mayor, a florid, balding man who loved nothing more than to hear himself pontificate, said in his rich baritone, "I'm trying to gather information, Mrs. Rafael. We shall discover the identity of these dreadful men."

"You attribute this rape to the group calling themselves the Hellfire Club?" Rafael asked quietly.

"Aye, Master Rafael, we do. They ravish young girls—how many, we have no idea, for you see, they pay the girls' fathers to do it. Legal, I suppose, but revolting just the same. But then there was the young lady—a real mistake there—she wasn't just a simple maid but a peer's daughter, and that made everyone mad as hornets, and now poor little Joan Newdowns. The little maid really didn't understand, but her ma did and called for Dr. Ludcott. They'd washed her clean, as one might say, but Dr. Ludcott said she weren't a virgin anymore and there were still signs of blood and men's seed. It's got to stop, Master Rafael, yes, sir, it will stop."

"Don't forget those bruises," Mrs. Meneburle said, her eyes glittering.

"Yes," said Rafael, "it must stop."

Damaris began to fidget and Victoria quickly said, "Shall we be off now, Rafael? It's time for luncheon, and Fletcher's Pond is a good twenty-minute ride from here."

He looked at her a moment, then said quietly, "I should like to speak to some old acquaintances, Victoria. Would you take Damaris to Fletcher's Pond? I will join you within thirty minutes."

She cocked her head to one side, but said quickly enough, "Certainly. We're off, Damie."

Victoria heard murmurs as she eased Toddy into a trot. "Aye, Master Rafael will put a stop to this nonsense." "Good thing the lads back—a long time away." "But what of the baron?"

"What a mare's nest," Rafael said to George Trelion, a young man who now owned his own farm. "I heard that this poor girl was simply the latest in a long line."

"Aye," said George, a man of few words. "Hard to know how many." Rafael now remembered that George had also been a boy of few words as well. He changed the topic, inquiring after George's family. He managed to ease his way back to the mayor, Mr. Meledor. He remembered how he and Damien used to steal fruit from Meledor's orchard, and the round of buckshot that had barely missed them one late summer's night.

"Aye, a horrible thing it is, Mr. Rafael."

"Have you any ideas at all of the identity of the men involved?"

"Not a clue. There's a great deal of speculation, of course, always is in these sorts of situations. It's still everyone's belief, even the magistrate's, Sir Jasper Casworth—can you remember Sir Jasper?"

Rafael nodded, picturing a desiccated, bent old man who habitually pursed his lips.

"Well, yes, Sir Jasper believes that all the members of this so-called new Hellfire Club wear masks so that even the members don't know who the other members are."

"That would seem wise," Rafael said, but he couldn't believe that they didn't know each other. Impossible, that, but he didn't disagree.

"Indeed, my boy, indeed."

"Have they done anything else save rape young girls?"

"They did murder," said Mr. Meledor in his most portentous voice. "Yes, murder, and that's how we found out about them paying fathers to rape their daughters. One of the girls died, bled to death, and the father was very upset, you might say."

"He didn't say who had paid him for his daughter?"

"He didn't know," said Mr. Meledor in some disgust. "Said it was all done through letters. Stupid man."

"Does anyone have any idea of how many men are involved in this new Hellfire Club?"

Mayor Meledor cleared his throat, a flush creeping up his fleshy jowls. "Well, after that one girl died, another started talking. She said eight men had had her."

After a while Rafael shook the mayor's hand, nodded to other folk he recognized, spoke to some old friends, then took his leave. He pushed his stallion as fast as he could gallop toward Fletcher's Pond.

As for Victoria, she'd managed to dismount from Toddy's back without oversetting either herself or Damaris. It was a glorious early October day. "Careful not to fall into the pond, Damie," she told the wriggling small girl, a litany that Victoria doubted ever penetrated the child's head.

"I want to feed Clarence," said Damaris.

"You will, love, you will. I can hear him."

Victoria spread out a blanket beside the tablecloth to wait for Rafael. She was thinking about the horrible rape when she heard his stallion approach.

He dismounted Gadfly beside Toddy and tethered him to a low yew bush.

"Hi, Victoria. Hey, Damaris, do you need more bread for those greedy ducks?"

Victoria said as she looked up at him, "Did you hear the people saying that you would put a stop to all of this?"

"Yes, I heard them."

"You're very popular. I can't imagine why no one ever spoke of you to me during the past five years."

"I can." After giving Damaris more bread for the ducks, he eased down beside Victoria. "It's easy enough to understand. You were Damien's ward. It was known that Damien and I parted on neutral terms, at the very best. No one would dare speak of me to you, particularly since Damien appears to have inspired resentment. It's really that simple." He paused a moment, pulling up a blade of grass and rubbing it between his long fingers. "I heard people referring to Damien. It seemed to me that they disliked him, perhaps feared him, certainly didn't trust him. Do you know what he has done to inspire such feelings?"

She shook her head. "People in St. Austell have always been kind to me and to Elaine, only just a bit more standoffish with her. I really don't know."

"I shall have to find out, I see."

"Before you become a detective, should you like to eat your luncheon?"

Rafael gave her that smile of his and nodded. He once again counted on his fingers, sighed, and held up one finger.

"It's just one, Victoria. How would you like to—"

"Rafael. Don't you dare say what you are thinking."

17

*The stupidities begin when one
takes men seriously.*
—JEAN GIONO

Rafael was abstracted. Normally, Victoria reflected, whenever he played her lady's maid, he would kiss her neck, light nipping kisses, and his hands would rove over and around the button fastenings. This evening, however, he planted only one rather perfunctory kiss on her left earlobe, straightened, and absented his mind.

When she sat down in front of her dressing table, she eyed him in her mirror. "All right, what's bothering you?"

He actually looked startled. "However can you think that anything is wrong?"

She laughed at his bewilderment. "Do you think I'm blind? Do you think I have no knowledge of you at all? It's rather obvious to me, Rafael. If nothing were bothering you, you would be bothering me until I was swatting at your hands as fast as I could."

"Ah." He grinned, and managed something of his normal lecherous look.

"Tell me. Is it the incident with this Hellfire Club?"

Rafael gave it up. He might as well tell her a bit of it. She might have some ideas. "Yes. I just happened to see Dr. Ludcott. He spoke to me of it. It turns out that the girl, Joan, remembers a roomful of people dressed all in black, their heads and faces also covered in black. Then she was being laid on a long table and went to sleep. Obviously they drugged her." He paused a moment, looked at the Aubusson carpet intently, and added, "Did you know that Joan Newdowns is fourteen years old?"

Victoria winced. "I knew she was young, but . . .

"Oh, God, that's awful, Rafael. Did she recognize any of their voices? Can she remember anything that might help?"

He looked at her for a long moment, then said, much to her astonishment, "Yes, she did."

"You're jesting. Truly?"

"Yes. She's not certain, of course, but just before she went to sleep, she heard all of them talking—arguing, she thinks. She told her mother she heard David Esterbridge. Dr. Ludcott, when Mrs. Newdowns told him of it, nearly dropped with apoplexy on the spot. He doesn't know what to do, which is why he cornered me. Who, he was whining, would believe a fourteen-year-old girl?"

"Everyone would if it were anyone other than Squire Esterbridge's son. Their family's been practically an institution for generations, and the squire—well, everyone likes him immensely."

"Exactly. An interesting problem." Rafael paused, looked at Victoria with a serious expression, and said quite calmly, "As I told Dr. Ludcott, no one would possibly imagine a bunch of hooligans or lower-class ruffians raping a girl the way this was done. Or the way any of the others were done. First, such a group wouldn't have the money to pay the fathers. No, the ritual and the outward secrecy of the black masks makes it very unlikely. Ludcott agreed, but was very unhappy about it, as you can well imagine. I also suggested to him that he keep quiet about it for the moment. Impossible to confront either David or Squire Esterbridge. A waste of time, certainly, and it would cause an unlimited amount of bad feeling. One also has to wonder why they chose to call themselves the Hellfire Club, aping that infamous group of men some forty years ago. No, it's wild young men hereabouts who are responsible. And they must be stopped. Thus my obvious distraction, Victoria, at least to you."

"You're forgiven. Did Joan Newdowns recognize anyone else's voice?"

"No. Then again, Esterbridge is one of the few young bloods hereabouts who spends a bit of time in St. Austell. Joan's mother does sewing for Mrs. Lemarth on Front Street, and Joan visits her quite a bit. It's natural that she would see and hear David Esterbridge." He paused a moment, looking thoughtful. "As a matter of fact, it's possible that David is the one who spotted Joan Newdowns as their next rape victim."

"So this is why you wanted a ball."

"I doubt your mind spends much time in the shade, sweetheart. Let's say that it will give me the opportunity to see all these wild gentlemen and plant, shall we say, a few seeds of my own hellfire."

"You wanted the ball *before* this occurred to Joan Newdowns."

He cursed softly, then tried for an indifferent grin.

He failed, of course. Victoria watched him shrug himself into an exquisite coat of black satin.

"And since you wanted the ball before this occurred, it's obvious to me that someone in London asked you to involve yourself in this Hellfire Club business. Am I right?"

Rafael negligently straightened his cravat, his example of the Oriental, and not excessively successful. He didn't say a word; in fact, he started humming.

"You were asked to involve yourself because of the peer's daughter. I assume that simple peasant girls wouldn't receive such attention, but a peer's daughter? Yes, indeed, so you agreed to look into the matter."

He turned then and she found herself momentarily forgetting everything except him. His linen and cravat were snowy white. He looked delicious to Victoria. She imagined herself undressing him very slowly, her fingers finally on the buttons of his breeches, and she shivered with her fantasy.

"What is that all about?" Rafael asked, smiling at the dreamy expression on her face. To his surprise, she flushed deeply. "Oh ho. I must know now, Victoria. Could it be that you are thinking about what I'm going to do to you at dawn tomorrow?"

"If you would know," she said finally, giving him a look of great dislike, "I was thinking about what I would do to you." There, she thought, seeing that he was clearly taken aback, she'd finally gotten the last word.

"Tell me," he said. His voice was deep and smooth, his gray eyes intent on her face. "Tell me what you were thinking."

She lowered her eyes a moment, shaken by his intensity. "It wasn't all that complete. Truly."

"What had you completed?"

"Very well, I was picturing myself taking off your clothes very slowly and looking at you very thoroughly."

His eyes silvered and darkened.

"And unbuttoning your breeches."

It was some moments before he managed to say, "I did ask you, didn't I? Let's go down to dinner before I let you and before I ravish you with but half a day to go." He offered her his arm.

She said as she slipped her hand through the crook of his arm, "I want you to promise me that you will be careful. I would appreciate your telling me all about your, er, assignment, but I'm patient. Will you be careful?"

"I'm always careful," he said. And that, Victoria thought, was that.

Before joining Elaine and Damien in the drawing room, Victoria and Rafael visited Damaris.

"Torie."

"Yes, love, oh how very sweet you smell. Did Nanny Black give you your bath?"

"Yes, and it's you again, Uncle Rafill."

"Perhaps you'd best just call me Uncle, Damaris."

"Uncle," the child dutifully repeated. She threw her arms round Victoria's legs, then allowed Rafael to lift her high in his arms and toss her into the air. The squealing brought Nanny Black quickly into the nursery.

"Oh, it's you, Master Rafael, Miss Victoria. The child was a grubby mess, but she could speak of nothing but all her fun. Time for your bed, little miss. Come along now."

Damaris didn't have any intention of docilely following Nanny Black to bed. She set up a tantrum that would have shortly brought every servant to the nursery, believing murder was being committed.

"Enough, young lady."

Damaris stopped mid-yell. She stared at Rafael. She tried one final cry, only to be cut off. "I said, Damaris Carstairs, that your performance is ended. You will kiss me and Victoria good night. Then you will obey Nanny Black. And that is the end of it, my child."

To Victoria's absolute astonishment, Damaris gave Rafael a very brief pouting frown, then grinned at him. She followed his orders to the letter.

"Goodness, that was impressive," said Victoria as Rafael led her out of the nursery.

"Like sailors, children need to know their limits," said Captain Carstairs. "What is appropriate on board ship—or in the nursery—and what is not."

"As reigning adult in the nursery just now, you decided she'd gone beyond the limits."

"Yes."

"I can't quibble about that," Victoria said, and sighed.

"That also applies to women."

"I beg your pardon?"

"Limits, Victoria, limits. On board ship, in the nursery, in the bedroom, limits are the essence of control."

"I'm going to hit you with that naked marble statue of Diana."

Rafael merely smiled, then said abruptly, "I don't care for 'Torie.' I don't like it. I shall have to come up with something else, something quite original, of course."

"Oh, dear," Victoria said, "I dread to hear it. Have you any ideas as yet?"

"Nary a one, but I will contrive."

Dinner at Drago Hall that evening was enlivened by Rafael's telling of young Joan Newdowns' rape by men in a new, revived Hellfire Club. He was doing it on purpose, of course, Victoria thought.

"Unfortunately, the child didn't recognize any of the bastards, er, excuse me, Elaine—"

"That's all right. I fully agree with you. They are animals, crude, malicious, sadistic beasts."

"All that, my dear? Admittedly, it was not at all well done of them, but surely it was some sort of lark."

So, Rafael thought, Damien also believed it the work of moneyed young gentlemen.

Victoria stared at Damien. Even though she'd experienced attempted rape at his hands, she was still shocked that any man wouldn't condemn such an act, at least overtly, in civilized company.

"Age really doesn't matter," Rafael said easily, "but the child was, after all, only fourteen years old. I wonder what kind of man would find it a *lark* to ravish a child?"

"A very twisted, sick man," said Elaine. "Would you care for some salmi of grouse, Rafael?"

"I wonder if there have been other incidents?" Victoria said, waiting to hear what Damien would say. Two could play this game, she wanted to say to her husband.

Rafael found himself looking from beneath his lashes at his brother. He too had been appalled to hear Damien speak so cavalierly about the girl's rape.

Damien said nothing until he took a long drink of his wine. "Actually," he said easily, "I barely remember the incident. It was quite a few months ago, wasn't it, my dear?"

"Yes, but one doesn't tend to forget something like

that so easily. Do you think it's related to this incident? Do you think it's a bizarre revival of the infamous Hellfire Club?"

Damien looked bored, an unusual reaction, his brother thought, given the subject matter. "I neither know nor particularly care, Elaine. It has nothing to do with me. Rafael, may I have a bit more of the stewed partridge?"

Victoria couldn't keep her tongue still. She said, "But it has to do with all of us. No one could possibly condone what was done to that child. My god, Damien, Dr. Ludcott said that she had been drugged and that many men raped her."

Damien gave her a twisted smile. "I shouldn't have wanted to be the last." He quickly held up his hand. "Acquit me, brother, ladies. I was only jesting—"

"—a very poor jest."

"Yes, well, I meant nothing by it. But really, all of you, the girl is of little importance, after all. Just a village girl, just—"

"I believe that's quite enough," Rafael said quietly, in the same tone he'd used with Damaris. "You're upsetting both Victoria and Elaine."

"I certainly wouldn't wish to do that," said Damien, giving his pregnant wife a fond smile. "My heir must be kept safe and healthy at any cost. Elaine knows that, as do I."

"Tomorrow," Rafael said abruptly, "Victoria and I will travel to St. Agnes. There is a property there I wish to inspect. Oddly enough, there are the remains of a medieval castle still there, and the name still visible—Wolfeton. Of course, a manor house is on another section of the property, built in the early seventeenth century, I believe, by offshoot scions of the De Moreton family."

"They were Norman," said Victoria.

"Yes. A very old name. The family must have been marvelously healthy to enjoy such longevity. I understand the direct line didn't die out until the mid-fifteen-hundreds. Their name now is Demoreton, still close to the original, just a bit more English-sounding."

"Why is the property for sale?" Damien asked idly.

"The usual reason. Money. Rather, the lack of it. The family was cursed with a series of wastrels. The last Demoreton, Albert by name, managed to gamble away his entire patrimony by the age of twenty-five, then killed himself, leaving his family to suffer the consequences. If Victoria and I are pleased with it, I think we'll make an excellent bargain. Do you care to be the mistress of the manor at Wolfeton, Victoria?"

"Wolfeton. It's a very romantic name," Victoria said. She found herself staring at Rafael as he calmly finished off his hazelnut pudding. He'd said nothing to her about a specific property. And he appeared to know everything about it.

"St. Agnes," she said aloud. "Don't you remember, Elaine? Damien had business in St. Agnes and you and I went with him. It was four years ago. It's on the northern coast of Cornwall. The country is so beautifully savage and untamed. And remember how very fierce the sea winds could be? And the trees—so bowed and bent and twisted all along the coastline."

Rafael was smiling at her enthusiasm. "I believe," he said, once she had run down, "that I have come across an area that appeals to you."

"Oh, yes."

"I remember St. Agnes and St. Agnes Head," Elaine said, her voice tart. "You were only fifteen years old, Victoria, and you seem to have forgotten that awful storm. I thought we should be swept over that cliff."

"Victoria was more a mountain goat in those years than a young girl," Damien said.

"How long will you be gone?"

Rafael answered Elaine easily, "I believe we'll travel there in slow stages. After all, I haven't seen Cornwall in quite a while. We'll spend tomorrow night in Truro, spend the following night in St. Agnes, then return the next evening. That should be a sufficient amount of time."

Victoria looked at him, wondering why he didn't wish to spend more time there. It certainly didn't seem all that sufficient to her. After all, his entire purpose for bringing her back here to Drago Hall was ostensibly to use it as a base. Now it seemed that he couldn't bear to be gone for any length of time from Drago Hall. But then, it really didn't seem all that odd to her. He was here to ferret out this Hellfire Club business, she was certain of it. She felt a frisson of alarm, and clamped her mouth tightly closed.

"I'm glad you're returning in good time," said Elaine, looking at Victoria. "Your ball will require a great deal of work."

"We'll be your slaves." Rafael turned to his brother. "Is Gwithian Inn still doing business in Truro?"

"Indeed it is. Old man Fooge still serves the finest smuggled French brandy and his wife still makes the most delicious stargazy pie." Damien grinned maliciously. "Ah, I forget, you detest stargazy pie."

"So do I," said Victoria with great conviction. "All those poor pilchards with their heads sticking up."

Rafael said to his wife, "Actually, my dislike comes

from a specific incident in my misspent youth. When I was ten or so, my dear twin offered to share some of his pie with me. Unfortunately, just as I speared a bite, the pilchard wiggled off my fork. I tried to murder Damien, was foiled by our tutor, Mr. Mac-Pherson, and never looked another stargazy pie in the pilchard's eye again."

There was general laughter, then Damien asked, "This property you speak of—are there tin mines?"

"Yes, all could be in excellent working order. Money will have to be spent to bring the equipment back up to par. The water pumps for the most part need to be replaced, and as for the engine houses, many of them are falling apart. I understand the miners are in a bad way. They don't wish to continue mining when the shafts could flood at any time."

It would cost quite a bit of money, Victoria thought, if the situation were as grim as Rafael had painted it. A lot of her money. But he sounded genuinely interested in the tin mines. Perhaps he would be content on land and not want to return to his ship and the sea.

Later that evening, in the Pewter Room, Victoria asked Rafael once again to tell her the truth, but he merely smiled at her and shook his head. "I've said too much already." Then he began undressing, remaining infuriatingly obtuse, and silent as a clam. "You know," he said thoughtfully as she was frowning at him in impotent silence, "if you weren't being so damned womanly at the moment, I could have stopped this argument before it progressed to the first raised-voice octave."

"I simply want to know the extent of your involvement," she repeated.

"No danger. Come and let me unfasten that

gown." She turned her back to him, and in a moment felt his lips lightly caress the nape of her neck. She bowed her head, wanting him to continue.

She felt his hands come around her waist and pull her back against him. "Much too long a time for us," he said, his breath warm on her neck. "Of course, the truth be told, a day is too long. Don't you agree?"

She would have agreed with just about anything at that moment. His hands had roved upward and were cupping her breasts. He was filling his open palms with her. She arched her back, leaning her head against his shoulder. She made a small mewling sound and Rafael closed his eyes with the pleasure of it.

"Would you like me to give you release, Victoria?" Even as he spoke, she felt his hand glide down her belly, lower, until he was pressing against her. He could feel the heat of her through her layers of underthings and her gown. And, unbeknownst to her, she was pressing her hips forward, against his fingers. He was delighted.

She felt immense desire mixed with embarrassment. To stand here against him while his fingers— She simply couldn't allow that.

It hurt, truly, but she slowly pulled away from him. "No," she said, her voice just above a croak.

"Why not? You want me to."

"No. I can't."

She didn't see his grin, merely felt his arms come around her very gently. "Give me but another month as your husband, and you will forget what a lady should or shouldn't want or like or allow. And then, Victoria, I'll give you pleasure whenever and wherever the spirit moves either of us. All right?"

"I don't know. It's embarrassing."

"It's the truth, that's all. Now, sweetheart, let's

climb into our nest, ring down the curtains, and enjoy our frustrated dreams."

Amid the cluster of grapes exquisitely carved in the upper-right-hand corner of the fireplace frieze, a very small wooden panel slipped noiselessly back into place. To see her naked and writhing in Rafael's arms, that was what he wanted to see, but this brief prologue had been exciting, immensely exciting. He could still picture her arched back against Rafael, while his hand was stroking her. He sucked in his breath, painfully aroused. He eased back along the narrow, cobwebbed passage, finally pressed a button, and slipped into the small estate room at the back of Drago Hall. He stood silently for a moment, shivering just a bit, for the passage was damp and clammy. Soon, he thought.

"Oh. The Almighty save me. My lord. I didn't know anyone was in here."

Damien looked up at Ligger, seeing that his butler's face was utterly without color, one hand over his chest. He could well imagine the old man's shock.

"I am ready to seek out my bed now, Ligger. Go to bed yourself. I will ensure that all the lights are doused downstairs and the doors bolted."

"Yes, my lord. Thank you, my lord," said Ligger, who tottered out of the room he would have sworn was empty but five minutes before.

Damien smiled without much humor, unconsciously eased his clothes, and made his way upstairs to his wife's bedchamber.

Victoria felt as if a weight had been suddenly lifted from her shoulders the moment their carriage bowled out of the Drago Hall drive. She patted Rafael's arm when he slammed his cane head on the roof of the carriage not five minutes later to have Flash pull over.

"Sorry, but you know this weakness of mine."

"It's not one of my favorite pastimes to ride with a green-faced man," she said.

And he was gone, to mount his stallion, Gadfly.

She shook her head and settled back against the soft leather squabs. Damien's carriage was very comfortable and luxurious; she would give him that.

They arrived in the bustling market town of Truro late in the afternoon, Rafael having made innumerable stops along the way. He'd spoken to a tin-mine owner in Trevelland and visited a mine just two miles east of Truro itself. The Gwithian Inn was doing a fine business and Rafael was greeted warmly by Mr. Fooge, who believed him at first to be the Baron Drago.

"Ah, Master Rafael," he said, rubbing his fat hands together upon correction, "so alike you and your brother are. And this is your lovely wife? A pleasure, ma'am, such a pleasure. Do come along, Master Rafael."

"As loquacious as ever," Rafael said once he and Victoria were shown to their large airy bedchamber some minutes later.

She smiled at him, and immediately made her way to the window that looked toward the market square. Today wasn't a market day, and the stalls were empty, looking somehow abandoned and forlorn. Rafael came up behind her and said softly, "Do you know what day this is, Victoria?"

"Your birthday?"

"No, my birthday is in January. I trust you won't forget. No, today is a day of celebration."

"Ah," she said, feeling at once excited and embarrassed and very eager, the truth be told.

Rafael wasn't blind or unversed in the moods of women. He smiled down at his bride, knowing very well that the reins of control were firmly in his two strong hands. He wondered just how long he would tease her. Perhaps it would lessen the amount of time she would feel embarrassed around him in the future.

"Shall we change for dinner?"

Victoria could only stare up at him. "What?"

"Change for dinner," he repeated patiently.

"But I thought that—"

"What, my dear?"

But Victoria hadn't been raised to baldly state that she wanted her husband in her bed.

"You're a bully," she said, and pulled away from him.

"Very well, Victoria. I wish to speak to Mr. Rinsey for a few minutes before we dine. He is the Demoreton solicitor with whom I have been dealing." He flicked a finger over her cheek and was gone.

18

Nature made him,
and then broke the mould.
— LUDOVICO ARISTO

Perversity, Victoria thought as she ate her delicious roast lamb and suet dumplings across the small oak table from her husband, was more the prerogative of the male than the female. Rafael was regaling her, with all the enthusiasm of a male very pleased with himself, about this Mr. Rinsey, a bespectacled, stoop-shouldered gentleman who couldn't manage to disguise the urgency of the sale of the Demoreton property.

Finally, when Mrs. Fooge had given them their rich apricot blancmange dessert, Rafael came to a final halt in his endless monologue. He cocked a black brow at Victoria

"Did you say something, Victoria?"

"Me? Say something? Speak when you are declaiming fit for the diplomatic service? Actually, I have been enjoying a fascinating internal conversation." She broke off, her thoughts flying forward. She lowered her head and her hands fisted in her lap. It simply had to stop. It had to. There were no thick, full hangings on their bed upstairs. There was even a wide window that admitted, she well imagined, a surfeit of moonlight. And there was a brilliant half-moon this evening.

But she was still furious at him for his damnable distrust. He didn't deserve any explanation from her, even though it should sink him in guilt. And perhaps revulsion. She knew at that moment that she wouldn't be able to bear it if he looked at her leg and felt sickened. And she would know, no matter how he would try to hide it.

He hadn't touched her sexually during the past five nights, save for holding her while she slept, and of course she'd worn a full flannel nightgown. But tonight, if he were to make love to her in the blackest pit on earth, he would still feel the dreadful ridged scar along the outside of her left thigh. She also knew that tonight he was impatient with her so-called ugliness and would touch every inch of her.

In an unconscious gesture her fingers went unerringly to the scar and slowly she began to knead the muscles through her gown and petticoats.

When she realized what she was doing, her eyes went to her husband's face and she said, her voice sounding distressed to Rafael's ears, "I'm very tired, Rafael."

He wasn't certain what kind of game she was playing with him, but he only smiled, refusing to join in. "You may nod off over your blancmange." He gave an ostentatious look at his watch. "I will give you fifteen minutes, no more."

She was more than aware of the determination in his voice.

"Stop it!" She jumped to her feet, her chair skidding over and falling with a muffled thud on Mrs. Fooge's thick wool rug.

Her yell sounded very loud in the small private parlor and neither of them was surprised to hear Mr. Fooge call from outside the closed door, "Is anything wrong, Master Rafael?"

"Everything is fine, Mr. Fooge. My wife merely slipped, but she is unhurt."

They heard a grunt, a flurry of low voices, then Mr. Fooge's retreating footsteps.

Rafael regarded her from beneath lowered eyelashes. She was excessively upset, as if she'd just recalled something that bothered her immensely. What could it be? Before, she'd wanted to bed him. Impossible for him to be mistaken about that.

"What has changed, Victoria?" He started, surprised that he'd spoken aloud.

"Changed? What do you mean?"

"I mean that you quite clearly wanted me earlier, but now you seem—well, terrified of bedding me. I am just a man, my dear, and am feeling confused."

Victoria looked him straight in his beautiful eyes. "I don't want you. Now, that is. I'm tired. Truly. I'm going to bed."

He said nothing for many moments, merely looked at her. "Very well," he said at last, stretching his arms above his head and leaning his head back. "Good night, Victoria. Sleep well. I'll wake you early. Mr. Rinsey will be meeting us at the Demoreton property at eleven o'clock in the morning."

She stood there staring at him, feeling like a reefed

sail on calm water. She wasn't quite certain what she'd expected him to say or do after her announcement, but utter disinterest wasn't on her list.

"Must I give you a good-night kiss?"

She fled from the private parlor, his voice echoing in her mind.

Victoria didn't fall asleep for a very long time. It seemed to her at least a fortnight, but as she had no watch, she had no way of knowing.

Rafael looked down at her outline, clear in the moonlight from the window. She was sleeping soundly on her left side. Her hair was loose and fanned about her head on the pillow. Her right leg was drawn up, and that made him grin. It seemed that even in her sleep, Victoria's body wanted to yield to him, to give him an unmistakable, quite splendid invitation.

He was quickly naked, his clothing folded neatly over the back of the single chair. As quietly as he could, he slipped under the covers beside her. The bed was thankfully firm and didn't form a trough in the middle as he eased over next to her. She remained asleep, still on her left side. Slowly he began to inch up her nightgown.

"Silly little wench," he whispered. She muttered something in her sleep and obligingly shifted her weight when he eased her nightgown over her thighs.

He gazed down at her long slender legs and her quite delicious hips. Round and soft, so inviting that he couldn't keep his hands off her. He touched her as lightly as a moth's wings, and when he couldn't bear it any longer, he pressed his middle finger gently between her parted thighs, entering her finally. She was incredibly small, and he closed his eyes and groaned.

He eased down beside her and slowly guided himself into her. He couldn't believe the feelings that slashed through him as she took more and more of him. Her smallness, the unconscious squeezing of her muscles that held him firmly, drew him deeper, made him wild with lust. He wanted her awake now, and began to knead her belly with his right hand as he slipped his left arm beneath her.

"Victoria," he said between light, nipping kisses on her right earlobe, her throat, her cheek. "Come on, love, wake up for me, feel me, yell for me."

Victoria woke up. She was stunned. She didn't move, but it was just for an instant. He was inside her and his fingers were now roving down her belly to touch her She was flooded with the most wonderful feelings imaginable. "Oh," she whispered.

Rafael pressed his palm against her, pushing her hips back against him, driving deeper. When his fingers found her, her breath exploded from her throat and she tried to twist around so he could kiss her.

"I can't, Victoria. Shove back with your hips. That's right. Now, just enjoy. You like this, don't you?" His fingers deepened their rhythmic pressure.

"Don't you?"

"Yes—I do like—"

"And this?" She felt his finger press inward, and she cried out, an eager cry that made him feel like the lord and master of all the world.

He felt her near her climax and concentrated on her. When she broke, arching madly against him, he thought he would yell himself from the wonder of it. Slowly he eased and soothed her; then, just when she calmed, he increased the pressure again.

To his immense pleasure, he felt her quicken and respond fully and naturally. And again he brought her to pleasure, only this time he joined her.

"You're delightfully sweaty."

Victoria heard him just outside her right ear. She wondered if she could speak. She could barely think. Her breasts were still heaving, as if she were starved for air. "Am I really?"

Well, three words that did make some sense wasn't a bad beginning.

"Yes, you are." He kissed her cheek and her throat. He was still deep inside her. "And you're wonderful. You enjoyed yourself, Victoria."

"Perhaps."

"Twice, actually. I fear the walls of our room are rather thin. If we have neighbors, I do wonder what they are now doing. Or thinking."

"Be quiet. I still don't like you at all."

"No liking, truly? And here I am still a part of you, a very deep part."

Victoria grinned in the darkness. Then she remembered her leg. Her breath caught in her throat. It was some moments before she realized that she was lying on her left side, that she'd been on her left side the entire time. He hadn't touched her there, he hadn't been able to. She'd been safe yet another time.

"I prefer to think of it as a wifely duty," she said, and pushed against his groin. She felt him tense and said, "Forgive me, I'm simply getting more comfortable."

He laughed, kissed the back of her ear, cuddled closer, and was soon deeply asleep.

Victoria wasn't. She felt him leaving her, slowly, but still he held her very close. She felt the thick hair of his chest against her smooth back. It felt good. Everything about him felt good. And exciting. And tantalizing. His legs were curved into the hollows of hers. She sighed.

"But I can't be on my left side all my life," she said in a small, very tired whisper to the now-silent bedchamber.

"Hmmm? Go back to sleep, Victoria," came Rafael's voice. "It's still dark. We don't have to get up yet."

They reached the town of St. Agnes in good time the following morning. As Flash negotiated the narrow cobbled streets with more enthusiasm than skill, Victoria was leaning halfway out the carriage window, interested in everything.

Rafael pulled Gadfly alongside the carriage. "Look yon, Victoria. This is called the Stippy-Stappy—those long-stepped terraces of tin miners' cottages. The men set off to work their shifts in West Kitty, Wheal Kitty, Blue Hills, just to name a few of the larger tin mines."

"How do you know so much about these mines? Stippy-Stappy and the names?"

"I'm a manly man and thus automatically know these things," he said.

"And that book I see in your pocket?"

The cobbled street narrowed and Rafael was forced to pull Gadfly ahead of the carriage. They turned onto High Street and Victoria marveled at the row after row of slate and granite cottages.

It was but a short distance to St. Agnes Head and the Demoreton property. Flash turned the carriage off the narrow country road some ten minutes later and they bowled down a narrow weed-infested drive to a Queen Anne manor house that was so entangled with ivy that Victoria felt a flood of depression. However would the interior look? she wondered, sinking fast in gloom.

Mr. Rinsey was just as Rafael had described him, and the manor house was a dismal place, to be sure, the Demoreton family having moved out some three months before, when another party had offered for the house, then met an untimely end before the sale could be finalized.

"So, unfortunately, the house has been empty," said Mr. Rinsey apologetically. He was sweating profusely, Victoria noted, feeling quite sorry for him.

She said to Rafael, "It has possibilities if one hires a good dozen gardeners with shears to clear away all the ivy."

"I agree. A baker's dozen. Come inside and let's see what's in store for us there."

They toured the house. The rooms on the ground floor were dark and gloomy, but with the removal of the ghastly cabbage-rose wall coverings in the main drawing room and the burning of the intensely ugly puce brocade draperies that hovered over nearly every downstairs window, the main floor would become charming. As for the rooms above stairs, they were, to Victoria's mind, nearly ready for occupation, save for the musty, closed-up smell. The master bedchamber was a huge L-shaped room filled with light and a clear prospect of the distant cliff and the ocean.

"I think our bed should go right there," Rafael said in her ear, pointing. "We could wake up and go to sleep looking at the ocean."

"That's a wonderful place," she said, and gave him a smile that made him want to toss Mr. Rinsey out on his solicitor's ear and toss his wife onto her back.

The grounds hadn't seen a gardener's hand in many a month, but again, Victoria thought, there were possibilities. Excitement grew within her. Drago Hall wasn't hers, never had been. But this could be hers and she could place her mark on it.

"Where are the ruins of that castle?" Victoria said.

"Wolfeton? Just over there, if I'm not mistaken. Excuse me, Mr. Rinsey. We'll return shortly."

It had been a mighty medieval keep, the east tower the only one of the four not completely crumbled. Massive and tall it was. And dangerous.

"This was the inner bailey," Rafael said, "and that was where the great oak doors used to be. Can't you just imagine the lord riding his huge destrier going into battle yelling 'De Moreton! De Moreton!'"

Victoria's eyes were as dreamy as her husband's voice. "Yes, and I recall that keeps of this size housed literally hundreds of people. Is there a graveyard hereabouts?"

"Probably, but I don't know where."

"It will cost us a lot of money to refurbish the manor house," Victoria said, stopping to look up at Rafael.

"Yes, and even more money to get the tin mines back to full operation."

"We would need the ongoing income from the tin mines for the upkeep of the property."

He smiled down at her. Smart lady, his wife. No problem with tin mining, even though it smacked of trade. He had a great deal of contempt for those gentlemen who turned up their blue-blooded noses at men like himself who had earned their own fortunes. It appeared his wife held his views.

Victoria fell silent. They walked to St. Agnes Head along the well-worn footpath. Rafael sucked in his breath and pointed. "It's at least a thirty-mile sweep of the Atlantic coast and we can see all of it. That is

St. Ives, and far distant is Trevose Head. It's exquisite, isn't it?"

"Yes, and untamed and savage and exciting. I should like to live here, Rafael."

"Should you, now, Victoria? Well, perhaps we can manage it."

"Do you wish to take the part of my inheritance from the trust for our children? We could put it to better use now, I believe."

He gave her a very affectionate, tender smile. "You and I will sit down and make out interminable lists. Then we will see what amounts we need. All right?"

She nodded happily, and walked to the very edge of the cliff. She said over her shoulder, "Do you truly believe you would be happy here, managing our tin mines and not captaining the *Seawitch*?"

"To faraway, exotic places where beautiful women abound?"

"I wish you would let out your brain another notch."

"Very well, ma'am. Yes, I think so."

Victoria smiled at him, and he watched her run her hand over a stunted bowed tree just to her left. He watched her draw in deep breaths of the wonderfully sharp ocean breeze.

He wanted to tell her in that instant that he knew he could be content anywhere so long as she was with him.

Rafael stood where he was, saying nothing, continuing to watch his wife. She was proving to be an ideal mate, he reflected. Passionate in his bed, sharing his tastes and his dreams. Yes, all was going just as he wanted. Except for that damned confession of hers. And that ugly malformed toe—or whatever the devil she considered ugly about her body. He'd meant to look early that morning before she'd awakened, but she'd been awake and dressed before he'd cracked an eye open.

"I've decided to keep you, despite everything."

He'd come up noiselessly behind her. She felt him draw her against his back, and relaxed against him.

"Why?"

"If I told you the truth, the complete sequence of my male thoughts, I'm afraid you might try to hit me over the head and toss me down the cliff."

She turned in his arms and grinned impishly up at him. "What did you mean by 'despite everything'?"

"Well, there is still the unresolved puzzle over your malformed toe."

"Oh, I see Mr. Rinsey coming and he's still perspiring profusely. Poor man, what will you tell him?"

"The man has excellent timing," Rafael said, "at least for you."

Rafael, with a wink to Victoria, left her a moment to speak to Mr. Rinsey. He made an offer on the property. Mr. Rinsey, mopping his perspiring brow with a fine linen handkerchief, said he would visit with the Demoreton family on the morrow and give them Captain Carstairs's offer. "They are currently living in Newquay. If I may venture to say so, Captain Carstairs, my feeling is that they will accept. You and your wife are still at Drago Hall?"

Given the affirmative and a firm handshake, Mr. Rinsey took his leave. As they walked back to their carriage, Rafael said, "Like that first De Moreton, perhaps we also will begin a dynasty that will endure hundreds of years."

"You are a very grand thinker. A dynasty."

"Indeed. That will require your cooperation, of course, and your, er, fertility."

She poked him in the ribs, then tickled him, but his lecherous grin never slipped.

It very quickly became obvious to Victoria that Rafael was anxious to return to St. Austell and Drago Hall. They took their leave of the property after Flash, who hadn't waited to have his opinion asked, told Rafael that he approved of the *cove's roost* as long as Rafael didn't insist that he, Flash, remain here with him for more than six months out of the year.

"A Proserpine arrangement," Victoria said, grinning.

As that sounded like a poisonous sort of foreign snake to Flash, he immediately said that was the furthest thing from his mind.

At least, Victoria thought that evening when they at last reached Drago Hall at ten o'clock, we will be sleeping in our darkened nest again. Only Ligger was up to greet them. Rafael quickly dismissed him, and taking Victoria's arm, assisted her upstairs.

"You're exhausted," he said as they climbed the staircase. He sounded worried, which surprised her. She didn't realize that there were shadows beneath her eyes and that her face was as pale as Cook's clabbered milk. Flash had set a brisk pace, and her stomach, none too pleased with a lunch of cold beef and dressed cucumber, had rebelled.

"And no," he added, a slight smile creasing his lips, "I won't let you have your way with me tonight. Tomorrow morning, however—well, that's an entirely different matter."

That sounded a fine plan to Victoria. Only Rafael

didn't know that Victoria had no intention of allowing him to strip her and love her in full daylight.

If Rafael was at all angered by her early-morning defection, he gave no hint of it. Indeed, he spent little time with her the following day.

Victoria polished silver under Ligger's benign direction, assisted with floral arrangements, helped the footman carry a potted palm into the ballroom, and made three trips into St. Austell for immediate necessities, those items deemed by Elaine to be of premier importance.

On her third trip into St. Austell, this one made on Toddy's back, she saw Rafael coming from Dr. Ludcott's house on Raymond Street. What the devil was he doing there? Was he ill? Her forehead creased with worry. She approached him a few minutes later, waving wildly to get his attention.

His look of abstraction was replaced by an expression of chagrin at the unexpected sight of her, immediately becoming a wolfish welcome. "You look lovely, Victoria. Elaine isn't working you too hard, is she?"

"Not at all. Why were you visiting Dr. Ludcott? You're not ill, are you?"

He looked suitably surprised and Victoria relaxed. Then he looked evasive. She quickly held up her hand. "No, if you're not going to tell me the truth, don't bother making up an elaborate tale."

"It wouldn't be all that elaborate," he said. "I'm only a man, after all."

"Very well, it doubtless concerns this Hellfire Club business, and poor Joan Newdowns' rape. Now, which gown shall I wear to the ball?"

"The rich cream silk," he said without hesitation.

"You look wonderful in it—and yes, it does—but I don't wish to speak of it, all right?"

"All right," she agreed on a sigh.

"What are you doing here?"

"Another errand for Elaine. I'm to see the caterer, Mrs. Cutmere."

They parted company, and Victoria looked over her shoulder to see Rafael stroll into the Gribbin Head Inn. Perhaps he simply wanted to catch up on local gossip, certainly all the loquacious fellows in St. Austell could be found in the Gribbin Head, but that didn't seem at all likely. Oh, no, her husband had much more in his kettle than just plain water. Much more.

That evening Victoria had no need to worry about anything. Rafael was so very hungry for her that no sooner had they enclosed themselves in the huge bed than he was yanking up her nightgown, his hands and mouth frantic and urgent on her body and mouth. Her own need was just as great and their mating was wild and quickly done. She did remember, however, to put her nightgown back on before she fell asleep in her husband's arms.

And, of course, she was up before him the following morning. It was Friday, the day of the ball. Hectic, bordering on bedlam, she was to think many times during the day.

At precisely seven o'clock that evening she was gowned at last and sitting in front of her dressing table.

"You look exquisite."

Victoria looked at her husband's reflection in her mirror. He himself looked beautiful, she thought, and said it aloud. He leaned over and kissed her shoulders. "All mine," he said, more to himself than to her, his eyes intent on her shoulders. "Cream silk and white velvet. Now don't move. I have something for you"

He drew a pink-velvet-lined box from his pocket and handed it to her.

Slowly Victoria opened the jeweler's box. It was a string of beautifully matched pearls, nearly as pink as the velvet upon which they lay. She sucked in her breath. "Oh."

"Lovely with the cream silk, don't you think?"

"I've never seen anything so beautiful. I've never even owned any jewelry save the broach and ring my mother left me."

Her matter-of-fact words made him close his eyes a moment. He felt his guts twist with anger at Damien and Elaine, and tenderness. Nonsense, he told himself, and said quickly, his voice as leering as his expression was now, "Equally as lovely with your white-velvet hide, I think."

"You're dealing in fantasy now, Rafael. White velvet, indeed."

He merely smiled and fastened the pearls about her neck. She stared at herself, then at him and his intent expression. He was such a beautiful man, warm and giving, not cruel like his brother.

"Thank you," she said. "Thank you very much."

"You, my beautiful bride, will be the most enviable lady at this blasted ball."

"What you really mean to say is that the other ladies will want to tear my hair out once they see you."

"You think so?" He was preening at the thought, and she laughed at him.

But what he was really thinking as he walked beside her down the wide staircase was how easily he would manage to be mistaken for his twin.

19

*I will find you twenty lascivious tur-
tles ere one chaste man.*
—SHAKESPEARE

Johnny Tregonnet, a wastrel and a greedy little
snitch since the age of eight years old, tossed down
his third glass of brandy and slapped Rafael on the
shoulder one more time.

"So long, old fellow! Glad you're home, yes, indeed. Another brandy!"

Rafael had no doubt that Johnny was just the sort
of fool to be involved with the Hellfire Club riffraff.
Yes, just the sort of bastard to rape children, he
added to himself, thinking of poor little Joan
Newdowns.

"God, I can't believe you two! It's like looking in
a bloody mirror." Johnny glanced swiftly from Rafael
to Damien, who stood some twenty feet away speaking to another young aspiring rake, Charles St. Clement, whose father was a dour, overly stern magistrate.

"I suppose you and Damien are much alike in other ways, huh, Rafe?"

Rafael had always hated the shortening of his name, but he didn't bother to correct Johnny. He was far too interested in the lecherous tone to discourage his prey. "What do you mean, Johnny? The, ah, ladies?"

Johnny Tregonnet went off on a shout of laughter. "Ladies," he gasped, nearly choking on his hilarity. "Ladies! Ha, different kinds of petticoats, I tell you. Just because we're stuck here in Cornwall, Rafael, it doesn't mean there aren't enough pleasures for us, I can tell you."

"Certainly I enjoy all sorts of females," Rafael said easily, hoping Johnny would keep chatting.

"Of course, you just got yourself leg-shackled. Now, Victoria is quite a little looker, that's for certain. Keep a husband home at night, she would. David wanted her, if I remember aright, but then nothing came of it." Johnny paused a moment, swishing the brandy in its snifter. "I remember David muttering that he'd never trust another woman, that they were all— Well, never you mind. I suppose that doesn't matter in the least now."

Rafael devoutly hoped that Johnny's mouth wouldn't lead him to say something so insulting about Victoria that he wouldn't be able to ignore it. Then he would be forced to kill the fool, or at the very least beat him to a bloody pulp.

"No," Rafael said, "it doesn't matter." What had he meant about David and his distrust of all women?

Fortunately, Johnny, in his twenty-five years, had honed his sense of self-preservation.

"About these other, er, diversions. I suppose you're probably not interested for a while, huh?"

"One never knows, does one?" Rafael said blandly. "A man is a man, isn't he? If he isn't interested, he's dead or too old to do anything about it." He clapped Johnny on the back this time, and strolled off. He'd give old Johnny an hour to consume another three brandies, then give him another opportunity to be indiscreet. Perhaps just one more brandy would be sufficient; he could hear Johnny giggling at what he'd said.

Victoria smiled and chatted with friends and neighbors, gracefully accepting congratulations on her marriage and ignoring some covert glances at her waistline by several sly matrons, all the while watching her husband as he greeted young men he hadn't seen in years. But she realized there was more to it than simply reacquainting himself. He was spending his time with the worst of the lot, and not nice young men like Richard Porthtowan, for example, or Timothy Botelet. Surely he would have known them as a boy, spent time with them, and not with such dissolute wastrels as Paul Keason and Johnny Tregonnet.

David Esterbridge swam into her ken for the first time that evening, eyed her stiffly, and muttered, "I suppose I should dance with you. It would be rude not to."

Victoria would have much liked to laugh in his sullen face, but she forced herself to say with just a bit of irony, "I'll wager that your father sent you over to do your duty."

David shrugged, not bothering to deny it. "Yes, he's a stickler for what's proper, and you are Elaine's cousin, after all."

Victoria looked over at Squire Esterbridge, who was standing alone for the moment, and she smiled at him. He was regarding her intently, and nodded,

and she wondered what he was thinking. She had
known him since she had come to Drago Hall five
years before, and he'd always showed kindness to
her. He also held David in firm tow, she knew, still,
despite David's twenty-three years. The squire was a
smallish man, slight, balding on the very top of his
head. His eyes, though, were as intense and vivid as
they must have been in his youth—a bright moss
green, slightly tilted up at the corners.

David added, as he saw the direction of her attention, "I see you married the other Carstairs."

"It appears so," she said, waving toward the squire
before turning back to David.

"Why? Because he looks like your damned lover?"

"No."

"Are you pregnant? Do both of them share you
now, Victoria?"

"No and no."

He looked ready to spit. "God, how could I be so
wrong about you? You don't even bother to deny it."

It was difficult, but Victoria didn't slap him hard.
"Didn't I just say no and no? Deny what, David?
Deny that you have a foul mind? Deny that you have
an equally foul and mean mouth? Of course, that
would be impossible to deny."

"Curse you, Victoria. Oh, the devil. I might as well
dance with you now. My father's giving me one of
his damned looks, and I'd never hear the end of it
if—"

Her smile never faltered, but it grew more obviously a mockery. "You are such a useless ass,
David," she smoothly interrupted him. She gave him
a small, insolent wave of her hand. "and a complete
fool, of course." She turned on her heel and
walked away.

He stared after her, his lips thinning in fury. The damned little trollop. No longer was she interested in him. He would have married her if Damien hadn't saved him, told him the truth. He made his way to Baron Drago, who was at the moment unoccupied by the punch bowl.

"David," said Damien, and offered him a glass of Elaine's champagne punch.

David tossed down the punch in one long gulp.

"I saw you speaking with Victoria," Damien continued, his eyes resting on Victoria for a brief moment. "You don't look very pleased."

"No," said David. "Do you know," he added viciously, "that she didn't even bother to deny that both you and your brother are her lovers?"

Now, that was a surprise, thought Damien, his expression never changing. Why was Victoria toying with the young fool? "Really?"

"Yes," David downed another glass of champagne punch. "Does your brother know the truth about his wife?"

"An excellent question," Damien said thoughtfully. "I really can't say. I would say, though, that if you want to keep your nice teeth intact and in your mouth, you will not say anything to him in the nature of an insult to his bride."

"I'm not a fool."

Are you not? Damien thought, but said nothing. He watched David Esterbridge dutifully make his way back to his father, that miserable old martinet. Elaine came to him at that moment, smiling quite contentedly. "Everything is a success," she said with great satisfaction.

"Yes, thanks to your brilliant organization and Ligger's execution," Damien said.

"Everyone is asking me about Rafael and his plans. I'm telling them to talk to you or to him." Damien nodded, and she continued, her voice lowered suitably. "Would you look at her."

"At her? Who? Marissa Larrick? She looks no more sallow than usual, though she really shouldn't wear that particular shade of yellow."

"No, Victoria. She is trying to take over, Damien, from me. But I shan't allow it."

To be honest about it, Damien thought, Victoria hadn't done a single thing he could think of to so ruffle Elaine's feathers. He merely arched a black brow and waited. He waited only a moment.

"She has upset David Esterbridge. I saw her give him a very mocking look and walk away from him. And she is dancing with simply all the men."

"Why shouldn't she?"

"What about her husband? She hasn't danced a single time with him. She's flirting quite shamelessly." As Damien gave no more reply than a bored nod, Elaine added, "I hope her leg gives way under her. It should, if she continues the way she has for the past hour."

Jealousy lessened Elaine's prettiness, Damien thought as he watched his wife's creased brow and her pursed lips. Thank God for the arrival of the Countess of Lantivet. Elaine turned immediately charming, ensuring that the countess was superbly content.

As for Victoria, she wasn't stupid. She was as gracious as she could be in turning down Oscar Killivose, the fourth son of a viscount, for the next set. She made her way as unobtrusively as possible to a sofa that was set behind the potted palm she and the footman had brought into the ballroom just that morning. Unconsciously she rubbed her thigh, all the while humming to the sound of the country dance the orchestra was playing.

"You have suddenly become a matron?"

She looked over her shoulder and saw her husband grinning at her. "A matron?"

"Sitting out such a lively dance. Or perhaps you're hiding from an overly ardent suitor?"

"You have found me out," Victoria managed in a suitably mournful voice. She gave a delightful little shudder that made him instantly randy. "Ah, Oliver should find me shortly. You know how it is, I am certain, Rafael. Thrust and parry, advance, retreat."

His gray eyes glittered. "Oh, yes, Victoria, I know."

She laughed and patted the pale blue sofa cushion beside her. "Stay with me a moment, unless, that is, you are promised to another lady?"

"Very well," he said easily, "and no, I am as free as you are for this set." He sat down beside her, stretching his black, satin-clad legs in front of him. "You're feeling just the thing, aren't you?"

"Certainly. The ball is quite a success, isn't it? Elaine should be quite pleased."

"Yes, she should. The next dance is a waltz. Would you indulge me?"

A waltz, with Rafael. "Yes," she said, praying at the same time that her leg would hold steady.

"Should you like me to bring you something to drink?"

She shook her head. "No, thank you. I've been watching you, you know."

He arched a thick brow and waited. It was a ploy identical to his twin's, but somehow when Rafael did it, she wanted to smooth his eyebrow and grin like a besotted idiot at him. She managed to conceal her besottedness and said in a light voice, "You have been spending time with every young rotter from the entire area. Ugh, that Vincent Landower, with his loose mouth and shifty eyes, makes my flesh crawl."

"I haven't paid all that much attention to dear Vincent yet. Remiss of me. Now, what makes you think that I'm ignoring the moral cream of the neighborhood?"

"Would you please stop treating me like an idiot? How much longer must I wait for you to confide in me? Completely, not just your tantalizing little morsels."

She was far too perceptive, he thought, keeping his expression impassive with some difficulty. "Soon, I promise. Tell me about Lincoln Penhallow."

"He's a baronet's son, around twenty-five or twenty-six years old. He's a trial to his parents, so I hear, and is on the edge of being disowned for his irresponsible behavior. He gambles and keeps a barque of frailty—that is your gentleman's expression, is it not?—in Falmouth. Haven't you been able to sound him out as yet either?"

"Ah, Victoria, a waltz at last. Come along. We'll make a striking couple."

And they did. The only problem was that several people were convinced that Victoria was dancing with her brother-in-law, Damien Carstairs, Baron Drago.

Rafael was terribly nice to dance with, causing Victoria little strain. Her leg held and after the waltz was done, it was time for supper.

"You're an excellent dancer," Victoria said as she slipped her hand in the crook of his arm.

"So are you. I'm starved. Once I've taken care of my stomach, perhaps I can convince you to see to my other needs." His lecherous grin, replete with a display of lovely teeth, robbed his words of anything but amusing nonsense. He squeezed her hand.

"You're being outrageous"—this said with a giggle—"and you really should stop it."

"What did you say, Victoria?"

She heard Elaine behind her, her voice sharp and suspicious. She turned to smile, saw the fury in her cousin's eyes, and cocked her head to one side. "Come along, Damien," chided Elaine. "You're taking me to dinner, remember?"

Victoria had the poor judgment to giggle again. "This is Rafael, Elaine."

Elaine sucked in her breath, staring at Rafael. "But I—that is, Mrs. Madees told me that—ha, never mind. There's Damien."

"Quite a problem there," said Rafael thoughtfully.

"Yes. But Damien has done nothing since we've returned."

"Not even a hair out of line?"

"No, he is probably well and completely over whatever it was he felt toward me."

"It's true that you're no longer a virgin. Perhaps that was the obsession he had with you."

"I heard Elaine say once to Damien that she feared that as her time neared he would lose interest in her."

"If my twin does lose interest in his pregnant wife, I hope he has his survival enough at heart to stay away from you."

Victoria paused a moment and looked up at him. "If the Demoretons accept our offer, then we can leave Drago Hall as early as next week."

"Well, actually—no, not really, Victoria."

"Ah, out at last. Come now, husband, I've been

patient with you, but you—" She didn't miss a beat.
"Oh, hello, Lady Columb. How lovely you look tonight. How is Lord Columb?"

Rafael stood with an interested smile plastered on
his face as the two ladies conversed, his attention on
the various young men he'd spoken with throughout
the evening. He would wager the *Seawitch* that each
and every one of them was part of the Hellfire Club.
But what annoyed him no end was the realization
that none of them had the brains to organize such a
venture. The one who had done that—the Ram—was
no Johnny Tregonnet or Lincoln Penhallow or any of
the other young wastrels. But Johnny, with his surfeit
of brandy, was the weak link. Rafael determined to
push Johnny before the end of the ball.

"I'm starving," Victoria said, tugging on his sleeve.
"Lady Columb decided I really wasn't pregnant, and
went off to mind somebody else's business."

"I'm trying, Victoria, I'm trying. Allow me to seat
you and I'll fetch you a plate. I see that is the way
it is done. The gentlemen are the waiters."

"All right. Why don't I sit with Lincoln Penhallow
and Miss Joyce Kernick? Shouldn't you like to get
reacquainted with Lincoln?"

"Ah, yes, gentlemen are but waiters and studs and
the butts of their fond wives' jests." He flicked a
careless finger over her cheek, then escorted her to
where Lincoln and Joyce Kernick, a young plain-
faced girl endowed with a dowry the size to render
her quite comely to the most critical eye, were seated.

Baron Drago and his lovely, very pregnant baroness were alone for a moment at their table. "I made
an utter fool of myself," Elaine said, her hand fretting
over her stomach.

"Oh?" Damien looked away, waving at Lord and

Lady Merther. "They will join us momentarily," he added. "I trust that in your present condition, my lord Merther will have the decency to keep his hand off your knee."

Elaine waved that away as being of no interest. "I thought Rafael was you. And Victoria was laughing with him and he was touching her and I—well, I was furious."

"We've been married for five years. You can't tell me apart from my twin?"

Elaine studied his handsome face. Perhaps he wasn't quite as lean as his twin, but it was difficult to tell unless he was naked. His eyes were the same brilliant silver gray, the nose straight, the cheekbones high. And the lustrous black hair—no difference at all there, nor in the beautiful mouth that smiled identically, or grinned just offside, so very charmingly. But there was one difference, noticeable only when either of the twins laughed immoderately. Both were possessed of perfect white teeth, but Damien had a gold tooth toward the back of his mouth.

"No," she said at last. "It would take me a few minutes of speaking with you before I would truly be certain." She continued studying him for another minute or so. "If you wished to make me believe you were Rafael, I don't know how long it would take me to realize that you weren't."

"I shall tell Rafael to hold his tongue around you, then, my dear. Ah, my lady, please allow me to assist you." And Damien was on his feet, helping the very obese Lady Merther into a chair that he prayed would hold her considerable weight. Her breasts, shoved up ridiculously high, in a gown that was too youthfully styled for her, were nearly fully exposed.

He saw the blue veins and the stretch marks from her four pregnancies. He never stopped smiling.

Rafael waited until nearly three o'clock in the morning before smoothly easing Johnny Tregonnet into a corner. "What is this?" Johnny inquired, looking with an owlish expression at Rafael. "You're Rafael, ain't you?"

"Yes, I am."

"Didn't think you was Damien, he ain't all that friendly most of the time. There'd be no reason for him to want to talk to me here anyway."

"I want you to tell me about the Hellfire Club, Johnny. I think I just might like to become one of you."

Johnny stared at him, his wits gone begging after seven brandies. He looked wildly about for help, but saw none. "How d'you know about that?"

"I know you're a member, and Vincent Landower, and Lincoln Penhallow, to name a few. Tell me how I can get in touch with the Ram. I would join you, Johnny."

"I, ah—" He stopped, looked agonized, then said, "I'll tell the Ram. He'll have to decide. All right?"

"Do tell the Ram that he'll be able to count on me, as a member, to ravish all the young virgins in the county, but if I'm turned down, I'll turn quickly nasty. You understand that, Johnny?"

"I don't know," said Johnny.

"I'll take you down, Johnny—oh, yes, I'll take you down so fast you won't know how it happened. Talk to the Ram for me. Make him see things correctly. Do you understand?"

"Yes."

Rafael nodded and watched him weave away.

Three couples stayed at Drago Hall, for their homes were too far distant to make the journey in one day. The ball itself didn't end until just before dawn. Elaine, pleased and so weary she could scarcely climb the stairs, was even nodding and smiling to Victoria.

Ligger, bless his efficient calm soul, saw to the guests, smoothing everyone's way.

Rafael and Victoria collapsed fully dressed upon their canopied bed. "Ah, what an evening."

"You drank too much champagne punch," Rafael said, and leaning up on his elbow beside her, kissed her soundly.

"It will be dawn soon."

His gray eyes shone silver. "Yes," he said, and gently cupped his hand over her breast. "Yes," he said again, and began kissing her even as his fingers kneaded her. He gauged her response and felt like the greatest male alive. He raised his head, and without a word flipped her over onto her stomach. Victoria turned to look at him, but he simply shook his head. She felt his fingers on the fastenings of her gown.

When he turned her over again onto her back, he very slowly pulled her gown down, baring her breasts. "Ah, how very nice," he said with great inadequate sincerity. He leaned down and began kissing her, his tongue soft and hot on her flesh.

"I've thought about doing this all evening," he said, his fingers replacing his mouth. "And I've thought a great deal about this ugliness you're hiding from me. Do you know that I have yet to see you naked, Victoria? Completely naked just for me?"

He saw the flash of fear in her eyes, felt her stiffen, withdraw from him. "There is something you're ashamed of, isn't there?" There was surprise in his voice. "Is there truly, Victoria?"

"Yes."

"Tell me."

She shook her head, not looking at him.

"Then I shall simply have to discover this so-called ugliness for myself." He began to pull down her gown. Victoria took him off guard, twisting suddenly upward and rolling away from him as she sat up.

"No." She eased off the end of the bed and stood staring at him, holding her gown up over her breasts. "Please, Rafael, no, no."

He didn't move. "This is crazy, Victoria. You are my wife. Do you intend to hide from me for the next fifty years?"

She looked at him helplessly.

"I'm not a particularly cruel man, nor am I a wife-beater," he said, his voice cold now. He got up from the bed and began pulling off his evening garb, ignoring her completely.

She would tell him when she wanted to. He would not beg her. He would not force her. However, he could and would be as angry with her as he liked, damn her.

What the devil was this blasted ugliness? he wondered over and over before he fell asleep, Victoria's uneven breaths sounding in the silence of their bedchamber.

The guests were slow to rise the following morning, but Victoria was up early. She fetched Damaris from Nanny Black and took her to the stable. She wanted the child's uncritical company. Flash was shaking his head as he saddled Toddy for her. "All those bleedin' rich coves," he said in the most mournful voice she'd ever heard. "And here I was with itching fingers the whole night long. I keep telling the captain that I've got to keep my hand in."

Victoria tried to commiserate as best she could, going so far as to offer her own pockets for his practice. Flash thanked her gravely for her offer and said he would think about it. Victoria promised that she would carry something of value in her pockets to make it worth his while. They parted amicably.

They rode to Fletcher's Pond, and Victoria watched Damaris feed the squawking ducks. Clarence, the fat old fellow—at least Victoria assumed he was a fellow, since he was certainly perverse and obnoxious enough to be one—pecked at the little girl's legs when he felt he wasn't getting his share of bread.

Damaris shrieked in delight.

Victoria smiled and lay back, breathing in the sweet-smelling grass. Soon the Indian summer would be over and winter would settle over Cornwall. Next week it would be All Hallows' Night. Perhaps next week she and Rafael could leave Drago Hall. It was a wonderful thought. Her brow furrowed. He was furious with her because she was hiding the truth from him. She had to resolve the matter, she simply had no choice, not anymore. . . .

Victoria jerked awake, momentarily disoriented. She shook her head, calling out at the same time, "Damie! Damie!"

She jumped to her feet. "Oh, my God. Damaris!"

How long had she slept? A moment . . . an hour? She felt terror wash over her and forced herself to take several deep breaths. She looked out over Fletcher's Pond. Not a ripple. No, she would have heard if Damaris had fallen in. And the water was so very shallow, even for a three-year-old child.

She called her name several more times. No Damaris. With shaking hands Victoria untethered Toddy's reins and hoisted herself onto her mare's back. Stay calm, Victoria, for God's sake, stay calm. Damaris couldn't have gone far.

What if she fell into Fletcher's Pond?

Victoria shook her head at the unspoken thought. No, she thought, no, she couldn't accept that. She urged Toddy forward and began to make a small circle about Fletcher's Pond. The maple and beech trees were still summer-thick, the leaves just beginning to turn into riotous colors. Every few moments, Victoria called Damaris's name.

Suddenly she drew Toddy to a halt. Just beyond the woods to her right was the property line. And a fence. And just beyond that fence was Sir James Holywell's prize bull.

Damaris was fascinated by that mean, surly old bull. Victoria had told her at least a dozen times that she was never, ever to go near the fence.

She kicked Toddy unceremoniously in the sides. Toddy jumped forward. Within three minutes Victoria pulled her to a halt beside the fence.

She saw the bull. Then she saw Damaris.

A scream froze in her throat. The child was walking slowly and quite fearlessly toward the bull, her small hand held out, a piece of bread on her palm.

"Damaris," she called, trying to keep the abject terror from her voice, "Damaris, come here."

"I want to pat the bull, Torie," Damaris called back, not slowing one little bit. "I'll feed him, just like Clarence."

Victoria leapt from Toddy's back, vowing if she could but get Damaris to safety, she would spank her but good. She scrambled over the fence and jumped to the hard ground on the other side. "Damaris," she called again, her voice as cajoling as she could make it, "come here and help me, won't you? That bull doesn't like children, nor does he like bread."

"No, Torie," called Damaris. "He'll like me just like Clarence does."

At that moment the bull saw the child. He snorted loudly and pawed the rocky ground with one huge hoof. He was ready to charge.

Victoria began running toward the bull, yelling at the top of her lungs to get his attention from Damaris. She ripped off a piece of her petticoat as she ran, and began waving it frantically, yelling like a Bedlamite.

She stumbled suddenly on a sharp, outcropping rock, and fell hard, onto her knees. She felt a searing pain shoot up her left thigh. She ignored it, coming up again to her feet and waving the material at the bull.

Finally he turned to face her.

"Run, Damaris! Run, do you hear me? The bull isn't like Clarence, he hates you. Run!"

The child finally paid her some attention. Still, she just stood there, looking undecided.

At that moment Rafael came from the line of beech trees along the perimeter of Fletcher's Pond. He heard Victoria yelling, saw the bull, saw Damaris, and felt his blood run cold. He wheeled Gadfly about, then turned him sharply and dug in his heels. Gadfly sailed gracefully over the fence, landing on the other side not too far from the bull.

"Victoria," Rafael called, "run. Grab Damaris and get over that fence."

She wanted to tell him that she couldn't, but her fear clamped down on her pain, and she began running, like an awkward lame duck, dragging her leg, forcing it to move. She could feel tears stinging the back of her eyes, could feel the salty liquid coursing down her cheeks. She didn't slow until she'd grabbed Damaris, tucked her under one arm, and run once again toward the fence. She heaved the child through the narrow rails, then dropped like a stone to her knees. A searing pain lanced through her. She was too large to squeeze through the rails and there wasn't a chance in the world that she could climb over the fence. She sat there helpless and watched Rafael distract Sir James's prize bull.

Finally the bull backed away from the man and horse, turned, and ambled toward a huge elm tree, tail swishing.

Rafael turned Gadfly about and rode him toward the fence. He let the stallion take the fence at his own pace, then immediately pulled him up and dismounted. He dropped to his knees beside Damaris. He looked her over carefully, clasped her small shoulders, and said, "You will stay right here. If you move, I will spank your backside until you are yelling all the way to Truro. What you have done is more stupid than I can say. Don't move. Do you understand me, Damaris?"

Two huge tears fell down the child's cheeks.

"Do you understand?"

"Y-yes, Uncle."

"Don't move."

He climbed over the fence and dropped beside Victoria on the other side.

"Are you all right?" he asked, his voice calm, dreadfully so.

"Yes."

But she wasn't. He saw the tears on her cheeks,

saw the pain in her eyes. "Where did you hurt yourself, Victoria?"

"No place new," she said, and let herself lean toward him. He put his arms around her. He held her, saying nothing, until he became aware that she was rubbing her leg. He frowned.

"No place new," he repeated. Slowly he eased her against a fencepost. "Don't move," he said. He pushed her hand away, then began to pull up her riding skirt.

"No, please, Rafael—"

"Shut up, damn you."

There was no hope for it now. She closed her eyes against the awful pain and the censure and revulsion she was certain she would see in his eyes once he bared that leg.

She heard the rip of her underthings. She heard him suck in his breath.

"Oh, my God."

20

What cannot be altered must be borne.
—THOMAS FULLER

The pain of his words cut more deeply than the pain in her thigh. His shock, his disbelief, and now his silence. Victoria didn't speak. She was beyond words. She turned her head away from him, tightly closing her eyes. He would do what he would do and there was nothing she could say to change things. She waited.

Rafael saw the tensing of her shoulders, saw her flinch, and recognized pain in those silent, rippling shudders. Slowly he eased down beside her. She whimpered softly, trying to pull away, but he merely eased her gently onto his legs and supported her against his chest. He held her still with one arm and with the other bared her thigh completely. Her hand raised, a defeated gesture for him to stop, then dropped limply back to her lap. Slowly he began kneading and massaging the convulsed and knotting muscles.

He heard her suck in her breath, but he didn't stop. He kept to his rhythm, his strong fingers probing deeply at the protesting muscles. He turned once to see that Damaris was still where he'd left her. The child, bless her heart, hadn't moved an inch.

It was many minutes before he felt Victoria begin to relax, felt her pain begin to ease. He paused a moment, studying the jagged red scar against her pale flesh. The muscles were no longer knotting, no longer rippling beneath that scar.

He continued to knead her thigh, but more gently now, his rhythm slower. "Is that better?"

The sound of his voice after the endless minutes of silence made her jump. She forced herself to nod against his shoulder. The awful tearing pain was under control now, the spasms had lessened to small wayward ripples beneath her flesh. As the pain had receded, she'd found that she hadn't known what to think, that, indeed, she was afraid to say anything to him, afraid to hear what he would say back to her.

"If I help you, can you ride Gadfly?"

"Yes." Was that her voice, that thin, thready sound?

She said more strongly, forcing herself to pull away from him, "Yes, of course."

Rafael straightened her torn underthings as best he could and pulled down her riding skirt. Slowly, supporting her with one arm, he managed to stand up, bringing her with him, taking most of her weight himself. He studied her pale face a moment, her downcast eyes, and said, "Now, I'm going to help you climb that fence. When you're at the top, I'll go over, then lift you down. You can do it, Victoria. All right?"

"Yes," she said again, her eyes on the rocky ground in front of her. "Yes, I can do it."

When he'd gotten Victoria to the top rail of the fence, he climbed over and held out his arms to her. Her face was still pale, her lips now a thin line. He knew her leg was hurting more now. But he knew he had to get her back to the Hall.

"Victoria," he said, "just one more step up, that's all."

He saw the sudden determination darken her eyes. "Yes," she said. "Just one more step."

He didn't say another word. He watched as she dragged herself up, then closed his hands under her arms, lifting her over the top wooden rail. He brought all her weight against him as he lifted her down. He held her close a moment, feeling the slow, steady thud of her heart. "You did well. We will have to leave Toddy here. Now, I'm going to put you astride Gadfly. Will that make your leg hurt more than if you ride sidesaddle?"

"No."

He lifted her onto Gadfly's back, then went for Damaris. "Come, child." She was chastened, that much was obvious, and he wished he could comfort her without lessening the impact of the scold he'd given her. "Damie, I'm going to set you in front of Victoria. I want you to sit very quietly and carefully. I want you to take care of her. All right?"

"Yes, Uncle. What's wrong, Torie?"

"Nothing, love, nothing, I promise."

Once he'd placed Damaris in front of a very silent Victoria, Rafael climbed on behind them. Gadfly wasn't at all pleased with the additional weight and promptly began dancing sideways, snorting as he did so. Rafael cursed him, held tight to Victoria, and finally Gadfly calmed.

"Don't worry about Toddy. I'll send Flash for her."

Victoria didn't say anything. She concentrated on holding Damaris, this time keeping the child safe. Her thigh throbbed and hummed as the muscles rippled and deepened their knotting. She wouldn't cry, no she wouldn't.

Ten minutes later Rafael pulled Gadfly to a stop in front of Drago Hall. The last of the guests had left a half-hour before and now no one was about to see them. For that he was grateful. He dismounted with great care, then accepted Damaris from Victoria.

What to do with the child?

Bless Ligger. At that moment the great oak doors of Drago Hall opened and he appeared, thick white hair lifting off his forehead in the stiff breeze.

"Master Rafael? Is there a problem, sir?"

"Yes," Rafael called back. "Would you please take Damaris to Nanny Black?" At Ligger's nod, Rafael kissed the child's cheek and said softly, "All is well now, my dear. Victoria and I will be up later to see you. All right?"

"All right, Uncle."

He grinned at her and handed her over to Ligger.

"Now, its your turn, wife."

Victoria willingly stretched out her arms, wrapping them about his neck as he lifted her off Gadfly's back into his arms.

"I'll tell you the same thing—it's all right now, Victoria."

Certainly it was all right, everything was marvelously all right, she thought with hopeless sarcasm, allowing herself the all-too-brief opportunity to relax in her husband's arms. He was strong, she thought vaguely, and her leg hurt like the very devil.

Rafael saw Molly, one of the maids, come around a corner. Of all things, her mobcap was crooked on her head, giving her a demented look. He said crisply, "Fetch me a very hot towel, Molly. Then bring me another one in fifteen minutes."

The girl blinked at that, but nodded.

"Have you ever tried a hot towel on the leg?" he asked as he climbed the staircase.

"No, but hot baths have helped in the past."

"Well, we'll try it. It can't hurt. I remember my physician, Blick, using heat on a man who'd severely strained his leg. It helped."

Unfortunately, at least in Victoria's view, they passed Elaine in the second-floor corridor. Elaine stopped cold in her tracks and gave them the most disapproving look she could muster. "Whatever is the matter with you, Victoria? Why is Rafael carrying you like that?" Then her disapproving look lightened a bit and she added, "Did you hurt your leg? I imagine you did. You danced so very much last night, didn't you? I said to Damien that you danced with every man. Indeed, I—"

"We'll see you later, Elaine," Rafael said mildly, cutting her off as he opened their bedchamber door, then kicked it closed behind him. He carried Victoria to the immense bed and very gently laid her on her back.

"The hot towel should be arriving soon. Let me help you off with your clothes."

Victoria said nothing. He was gentle, she granted him that, but her leg gave a particularly vicious spasm when he tugged off her riding boot, and she heard herself groaning, clutching at the leg, and rolling onto her side. Rafael watched, not knowing what to do. He had to get her wretched clothes off, that was the most important thing. Then the hot towel, then some laudanum.

"Come, just a few more minutes. You'll feel better soon, Victoria, I swear."

She was pretending to believe him, he thought as he quickly and efficiently stripped her down to her shift. He'd just pulled a blanket over her when there was a tap on the bedchamber door.

It was Molly, her mobcap at an even more precarious angle now, and she was carrying the hot towel wrapped in between several other towels. He didn't ask her how she'd managed. He was simply grateful that she had. He thanked her and sent her after another.

He walked to the bed and stared down at Victoria for a moment. She was rubbing her thigh, her eyes closed.

"Let's try this now," he said. He sat beside her and as gently as he could wrapped the very hot towel around her thigh. "Now, we'll keep the heat in with some blankets."

She sucked in her breath, flinching at the heat.

Rafael eased down beside her, slipping his right arm beneath her shoulders, and began to knead the muscles through the hot towel in the same deep way he'd done before. "I know that must burn, but try to bear it. It will lessen. And you will feel better soon." His damned litany, he thought.

To Victoria's immense thankfulness, by the time the third towel was wrapped about her thigh, she felt only a slight twinge. The pain was gone.

"I'm all right now." There was a good deal of wonder in her voice.

"Excellent. Keep this towel on for a few more minutes." He didn't lie beside her this time, merely stood by the bed, looking down at her. "Would you like some laudanum?"

"No, I don't like to use it, only when I've really hurt myself."

He was silent once again. Victoria closed her eyes. He was behaving very well. She could see no distaste, no revulsion in his expression.

She jerked when he said suddenly, his voice harsh, "Why didn't you tell me? It appears that everyone else knows of your problem except me. I find that peculiar, since I'm your husband."

She struggled with herself.

"Why, Victoria? I assume this is your ugliness? Is this also your confession? Why the hell didn't you tell me?"

Angry, she thought, he was very angry. She opened her eyes and turned her head on the pillow to face him. No, she thought, he was beyond anger, she could see that. He was furious, coldly and calmly furious.

"Yes," she said slowly, "it is my ugliness and you can't deny that it is dreadful. And yes, it was my confession."

"Why didn't you tell me? On our wedding night? Hell, before we were married?"

"I wanted to tell you on our wedding night, but when I tried, you assumed that my confession was that I'd already lost my virginity to your brother. You didn't deserve the truth then."

He said nothing to that. Finally he said, "So many things have become miraculously clear to me in the past hour. I remember the night I rescued you from those smugglers. You were running from me and you tripped. You obviously hurt your leg, but you refused to admit anything to me. There were several other times as well, as I recall. You were terrified I would discover that you were, ah, not whole."

She flinched.

"So you decided to punish me with silence. Did you ever intend to tell me? Was I never to be allowed to see my wife's body?"

"I was going to tell you," she said dully.

He said something very crude.

"It's the truth." She felt her own anger spark at his words. She came up on her elbows. "How dare you, Rafael. How dare you assume that I had been with your brother when I told you I had a confession to make? You were horrible to me, why should I have told you the truth? You deserved nothing from me. Nothing, damn you."

He said very calmly, "The last time we made love, if I recall aright, you were lying on your left side. You were very responsive to me, no, more than that, you were wild for me. But you were protected, were you not, Victoria? I never demanded that you turn onto your back or your stomach. I never demanded to touch all of you, to kiss all of you."

"I was afraid," she said, "I was afraid you would be repelled if you knew, if you saw me."

"What makes you think I'm not?"

She sucked in her breath on a cry of pain. Not pain from her leg, but pain from deep inside her. "Go away," she said, knowing that she was beyond her tether. "Just go away."

"Yes," he said slowly, "I believe I shall. But before I do, I'll finish what I started." He sat down beside her, pulled off the blankets and the towel. He looked down at her thigh, reddened now from the hot towels, then gently probed along the long jagged scar. "No more muscle spasms," he said.

She held herself silent.

He merely nodded, and covered her again. He stood, looking down at her for a brief moment, his expression distant. "You should sleep now," he said. He turned on his heel and left the bedchamber.

She stared at the closed door. Slowly, out of long-ingrained habit, she began to massage her left thigh.

She didn't sleep, nor had she any intention of sleeping. After a few more minutes she raised herself and swung her legs over the side of the bed. No pain in her thigh. She put her weight on her leg. Still no pain. It was over, this time.

Within ten minutes she was dressed again. She imagined that Toddy wasn't yet back at the stables. It didn't matter. She would walk to Fletcher's Pond.

She fell quickly asleep against the trunk of a maple tree, Clarence's irritated squawking sounding in her ears. She hadn't thought to bring bread, and now she was to be punished. His cousins joined in the din, and there was a smile on her lips as she dozed off.

She awoke suddenly, clearheaded. She shivered slightly, for the sun wasn't shining on her anymore. In that instant before she opened her eyes, she knew that Rafael was standing over her, blocking the sun. She opened her eyes. His legs were spread, his hands on his hips. The buckskin breeches became him, she thought, her eyes traveling down the length of him. He was hard and muscular and lean, and no matter how furious she ever was at him, she was at the same time fully aware of his male beauty. His Hessians glistened as black as his hair, with the sun haloing his head, and his eyes were a rich and vivid gray.

He said very quietly, "However can you sleep with all this racket?"

"I'm used to Clarence. He's angry at me for forgetting his bread."

"Clarence?"

"As in the Duke of Clarence. That very substantial fellow over there, howling the loudest."

Rafael chuckled. "As in fat and waddles. Our royal duke wouldn't be pleased."

"He's amiable when fed sufficient bread."

"Yes," Rafael said. Silence fell between them. Clarence waddled back to the bank of the pond, then slid into the water, not making a sound. Rafael said at last, "Tell me about it."

She merely stared up at him.

"Tell me about how and when it happened."

He sat beside her, leaning back against the trunk of the maple tree. He said nothing more, merely looked straight ahead at Clarence and his family members.

"I was eight years old. I was riding, always riding, and I was quite good. I had no groom, indeed, I considered myself quite grown-up at eight. I was also unlucky that day. My pony was stung by a bee, so ridiculous really, and he threw me against a fence. Unfortunately there was a nail sticking out from the fence and it slashed down my leg." She paused for a moment, remembering and feeling again that awful pain, the shock that followed, making her white and dizzy.

"And then?"

"I rode back to Abermarle Manor. Just as I arrived, I was told that my parents were dead." Her voice was calm, detached, and Rafael wondered at it. "I didn't know what to do. So I did nothing. It was the next morning that my older cousin found me and saw the blood on my gown from my leg. His name was Michael and he must have been all of twenty years old at the time. He took care of me, but it was a bit late. At least I didn't have to have my leg cut off." He flinched at that, but said nothing. Victoria continued in that same calm detached voice, "It was soon after that that I was sent to my uncle Montgomery and his family. Elaine was their youngest and the only child at home. She was only five years older than I. Her father, though, wasn't my guardian, something I've never really understood. Well, my leg healed eventually, but when I overexert or do something stupid, it cramps and knots up."

"You make it sound very inconsequential," he said. He could see the young girl in his mind's eye, riding home on her pony, in terrible pain, only to be greeted with a pain that seared the soul. No, not inconsequential, she'd made him see her pain, but she'd been careful not to let herself hurt him. He drew in a deep breath in response to his thoughts. "How did your parents die?"

"In a carriage accident. A wheel came off, and the carriage, the driver, and the horses all went over a cliff."

"My parents were killed by the French. But I guess you already know that."

"Yes, I know that they were on board an English ship bound for Spain to visit your mother's parents in Seville." She paused a moment, but didn't turn to face him. "I know you haven't just been a simple sea captain, Rafael. I think you've worked for the government, against Napoleon, because of your parents, to avenge them perhaps."

He said finally, "At the beginning it was my primary motive—revenge, that is. Then, as the years passed and I saw that I was indeed making a difference, that what I did actually saved British lives, and in some cases changed the outcome of a battle or the fate of a town, well, my revenge motive lessened its hold on me. I believe it was Francis Bacon who said that revenge is a kind of wild justice. I eventually just let it go. I was finally able to admit to myself that I enjoyed the danger, the matching of wits between me and the enemy, the challenge. But back to you, Victoria. If I hadn't been such a bloody fool on our wedding night, would you truly have told me about your leg?"

"Yes, of course. I was about to. It's true that I was afraid, terribly afraid that you wouldn't want me after you saw me. As for telling you before we wed, I knew I should, but I also knew that I wouldn't. Much too much a coward. I was too convinced that if I did, you would refuse to marry me."

"You're a fool, my girl. Haven't you ever really looked in a mirror?"

"Certainly. But that hasn't much to do with anything. One is born with looks or one is not. It has nothing to do with what's really important—one's character or one's morals or how one deals with others. I thought that you had grown to like me, but I was nearly certain that you didn't like me quite enough for such a revelation."

"I did like you and I still do, for that matter."

"But now? Really? Now that you've seen me?"

He turned to look at her. "Face me, Victoria. Now."

She stalled.

"Now, sweetheart. Look at me."

She obeyed him.

"Do you think I could be such a silly ass of a fellow? Such a shallow human being?"

"You're not shallow. It's just that I didn't know. I don't know. I haven't been around all that many men, you see. I think Damien would hate the ugly scar on my leg, and I don't think he would try to hide his revulsion. What is more, you are perfect. And I am not. You're far more a beautiful man than I am a beautiful woman. It is rather a travesty to mate the unwhole with the whole."

He gave her a long, emotionless look, then waved a negligent hand to send a fly buzzing away. "A travesty—perhaps you're right about that. It would appear then that you took me in. False pretenses, Victoria, I believe a solicitor would say. You should have bared your leg exactly three days before we were wed and allowed me the opportunity to cry off. But you didn't. You wed yourself to me knowing full well that you were taking me in. And now I am well and truly tied to you."

She said nothing. A single tear trickled down her cheek.

Rafael waited a long moment, then said quietly, "You're an utter fool, Victoria. No, I hope I'm not a shallow man. I think you and I will pay a long over-due visit to the *Seawitch*. I would like you to meet Blick, my physician. Should you mind a doctor look-ing at your thigh?"

She would, but all she said was, "What would he do? What *could* he do?"

"I haven't the foggiest notion, but Blick has used many odd-named plants from the most godawful places imaginable. You will like him. And let me make this very clear, Victoria. I don't want you to see Blick because he could perhaps make your leg look better. I'm hopeful that he has a remedy that can lessen your pain when you strain your leg. I don't care how your leg looks. I care only about this awful pain. Now, why don't we go to Falmouth tomorrow? I do need to see how things are progressing, and my men will have the pleasure of meeting my beautiful, stubborn wife."

She gulped down a half-laugh, half-sob. "I've been so very afraid."

"There was no need, of course, but how could you have known that? Particularly after my absurd attack on you on our wedding night." He sighed, then reached for her, pulling her onto his lap. She snuggled against him, her arms twined about his shoulders, her head pressed against his throat. "Remember our extremely satisfying, er, mating on the kitchen floor at Honeycutt Cottage?"

He grinned over her head, knowing she wouldn't say a word.

To his surprise, he heard a very small, "Yes."

He waited a moment, then said, "I should like to take you back to our Pewter room, strip you as naked as the day you emerged from your mother's body, and love you in the full sunlight from our windows. What do you think of that idea?"

What she felt was a tremor deep inside her. He knew that she would want him, want him with all her loving nature. "You want to know what I'm going to do to you? Certainly you do." She responded to love words, he knew now, delighting in how the words fired her own imagination, making her wild for him. Only for him. He kissed her earlobe, then whispered in her ear.

"What?"

"Once I have you naked, I want us to still be standing. I want to lift you, have you wrap your beautiful legs around my hips. I want to come deep inside you and—"

"But that must be impossible, surely."

"Wait and see, Victoria."

Rafael carried her once again in front of him on Gadfly's back. Every few minutes he nibbled on her throat, kissed her mouth, moved his hands higher until they touched the undersides of her breasts. He was driving her distracted, and he knew it. He smiled and kissed her nose. And then he spoke to her softly, into her ear, telling her what he was going to do once he was deep inside her.

Victoria was wildly aroused by the time they returned to Drago Hall.

Damien silently watched the two of them as they swiftly walked the length of the entrance hall and up the staircase. They didn't see him. They'd seen no one. They were aware only of each other.

The panel slid silently open and he peered into the Pewter Room. Rafael was laughing, tickling Victoria as he removed each article of her clothing. And then he was kissing each spot of flesh he uncovered. Her breasts—bared and glistening—were full and white as cream silk, her nipples taut and deep rose. And he, Rafael, was enjoying her, caressing those magnificent breasts, sucking her nipples, making her want him. She arched her back, offering herself more fully to him, and moaned, ever so softly, tangling her fingers in his black hair, pulling him closer to her.

Then Rafael was laughing again, cupping her glorious breasts, pushing them upward, lowering his head for more kisses. Her eyes were dark with pleasure, and she was laughing and moaning as he played with her. He watched her hands, her slender white hands, slip below the waist of Rafael's buckskins, saw his eyes widen, his pupils dilate.

Then she was naked, her clothes strewn about her feet on the floor, her chemise half-torn in Rafael's hand. And she was so very lovely that it was painful to look at her. And to watch Rafael enjoying her. But she was protesting now, laughing, poking him in the stomach.

"This isn't fair. Come, it's my turn. This won't be like the kitchen again at Honeycutt Cottage."

And her nimble hands were unfastening buttons, pulling off his coat and his frilled white shirt. Soon he was sitting in a chair, Victoria's naked bottom toward him, and she was tugging at his boots, laughing, and he was chuckling, and touching her buttocks, splaying his fingers over her, leaning forward to kiss the white flesh, running his hands down her thighs.

There was the jagged scar on her left thigh.

Ugly, he supposed, but her legs were long and slender, sleekly muscled. Beautiful as the soft nest of hair between her thighs, covering her, waiting to be probed by a man's hands and a man's mouth.

The boots were off and soon Rafael was as naked as she. They came together, she on her tiptoes, fitting herself tightly against him, her arms around his neck, pulling him down to kiss him more thoroughly. And there were her cries, her moans, and Rafael's hands all over her, kneading her, then lifting her, fitting her legs around his waist.

He pulsed and swelled himself, and ached with wild pain, wishing it were he, hating Rafael for being the one to possess her.

He sucked in his breath as Rafael lifted her suddenly, his hand going between her thighs, parting her, he knew, and then without warning he came deeply into her and she screamed—not in pain—throwing her head back, her hair, loose now, a veil of pure chestnut down her back. Her legs hugged him, and her hands were frantic on his chest, his arms. And he was working her, plunging deep, then withdrawing himself, only to return completely into her.

She cried out, beyond herself, again and again.

He hurt now, a lusting pain so great that he moaned softly to himself.

Then Rafael pulled her tightly against him, drawing on lost control, he knew. More kisses and murmurs, and Rafael saying to her something about wanting her so much, about his mouth on her. Then she was on her back on the bed, her legs parted, and Rafael was coming over her, covering her, his hand between them, finding her.

And she climaxed wildly, endlessly.

God, he couldn't bear it. He slid the panel closed, feeling the small wooden knob slip. His fingers were slippery with sweat. His forehead was beaded with sweat. His pants were distended with his need.

He fled down the dark, narrow passage, his breathing harsh in his own ears.

"Love," Rafael said, "I can't wait."

She drew him deeper, and it seemed in that moment that she would want him forever. She told him she loved him and his eyes gleamed at her words, and she watched the cords tighten in his strong throat, his eyes close, his back arch, and felt him filling her.

And she held him, holding him so closely that they were one, and he was now a part of her and she of him. She didn't want it to end, ever.

He was breathing hard, as if he'd been running. He was beyond words, beyond thought. He collapsed atop her, his head on the pillow beside hers. Never had he felt such profound joy.

The Ram read Johnny Tregonnet's letter once again, trying to make sense of the less-than-cogent recital of Rafael's approach to Johnny the previous night at the ball. Stupid sod, he thought, crumpling the single sheet of paper in rage. So Captain Carstairs wanted to join their little group, did he? Or he would destroy everything? That was his threat.

The Ram sat back in his comfortable leather chair and stared at the glowing embers in the fireplace. He was briefly tempted to let the captain loose on his threatened rampage. He would doubtless learn the identity of every member—if he hadn't already guessed who they were. Except one. No one, not a single member, knew the identity of the Ram. The men thought the black hoods were all a lark, a ploy to pretend that they were anonymous so that their inhibitions were nearly nonexistent. But of course they all knew each other with or without the hoods. No, the black hoods were to protect his, the Ram's, identity.

This was the first occasion the hidden box for messages had ever been used. The Ram had on an afterthought sent his man to the box to check. And there was the letter. At least Johnny had sobered up enough to remember the existence of the box. Now, what was he to do?

He remembered the one terrible mistake. That

damned viscount's daughter. It was more than a possibility that Captain Carstairs was here on behalf of the viscount, and if that were the case, there was no doubt that the captain was out to destroy him, regardless of the nonsense he'd told Johnny.

What to do? He rose from his chair, stretched his aching muscles, and poured himself a brandy.

He supposed there was only one thing to do. Not that he really wanted to; he'd never before considered himself that sort of man.

But there was the fact that Victoria would be dependent again, vulnerable, with no man to protect her. It was heady, that thought. He wanted her, had wanted her for so very long.

Still, he must move slowly, carefully. There must be no mistakes. He wouldn't take the risk of informing any of the members of his plans. One of the fools just might ruin everything.

21

*No man ever became extremely
wicked all at once.*

—JUVENAL

Victoria stood outside the stable door, listening to
Flash recount to Jem, a stable lad of great credu-
lity, one of his more outrageous adventures in London's Soho. He finished with, "So, you see, Jemmy
boy, if a mort's attention flies away from you, if you
ken what I mean, then whosh! And it's yours, every
coin the cove's carrying. Nimble fingers and fast feet,
that's what's needed, yes, sir. Did I tell you about
the time I tried to lighten the captain's purse?"

"What is this?"

She turned and smiled, a dazzling smile that made
him draw in his breath. "Rafael. I thought you'd
gone to St. Austell. Well, as near as I can tell, Flash
is telling Jem all about the marvels of picking pockets
in Lunnon town, and how's it to be done, if you ken
my meaning. His story of how he tried to relieve you

of your sovereigns is next. I suppose I shouldn't be eavesdropping, but—"

He waved a negligent hand. "Actually, I just got back from St. Austell and—"

"I know, now you want us to prepare to leave for Falmouth. After luncheon? I do look forward to seeing your ship and meeting your people."

"Er, yes. Actually, what I was going to say," he continued, his voice lowered, "is that every time I think of yesterday afternoon, I want you again. Every time, Victoria, very much."

She turned red, murmured unintelligible words, and scuffed the toe of her riding boots in the dirt.

"You're enchanting, I've told you that many times. It isn't yet time for luncheon, and even though I haven't a kitchen floor like the one at Honeycutt Cottage, I do know of a very private glade, the ground covered with moss and soft grass, the area hemmed in with huge maple trees."

Her heart began to pound. She licked her lower lip unconsciously, and he grew instantly hard. He wanted to grab her, tear her clothes off, and be damned. Instead, he held himself in iron control.

He wanted to kiss her here, now. They were not in clear view, but on the eastern side of the stable, no one in sight. "Victoria, come here."

She came to him willingly, her expression one of anticipation. She slid her arms around his waist and stood on her tiptoes. His hands went from her arms around her back, bringing her even closer. Slowly he lowered his head and kissed her. Fiercely. Then he gentled, his tongue lightly stroking her bottom lip.

Victoria was stunned. She kissed him back, parting her lips, but still felt nothing. What had happened?

What was wrong?

"Rafael?"

He thrust his tongue into her mouth, probing, finding her tongue, and she drew back, her brow knitted as she stared in confusion up at him.

"I want you now, Victoria. Come along."

"But this isn't right," she said, looking up at him. "No."

He grabbed her wrist suddenly, pulling her off balance, and she fell against him. She felt his hardness against her belly, through her clothes, and saw the gleam of purpose in his eyes.

"Damien. I would that you speak to your brother. Would you look at him and Victoria, just look. There, by the stable, nearly making love for all to see."

He stopped dead in his tracks. "What are you talking about, Elaine?"

"I'm talking about Rafael and Victoria. I know they are married, but still, they shouldn't be so very loose, don't you agree?"

He stared at her, then quickly strode to the window. There was no sign of them.

"Damien? Whatever is the matter?"

"Nothing," he said shortly. "Nothing at all. Your loose cousin and my brother have probably gone into the hayloft."

Damien pulled her in his wake behind the stable, never loosening his grip on her wrist.

"Let me go, damn you. Now."

"Victoria, love, come along. You know you want me—"

"I know, Damien, I know it's you." She jerked free of him, wiping the back of her hand across her mouth. "You're despicable. Why, you've even taken his jacket and tied your neckcloth as he does. Did you sneak into our room?"

Damien tried to smile, but it was difficult. He'd failed. "How?" he asked, not moving, his body aching with need for her. "How did you know I wasn't Rafael?"

She looked at him squarely, and her voice was icy calm. "I felt nothing when you touched me. I felt nothing when you kissed me. Then I felt disgust when your tongue touched my mouth. With Rafael, I feel everything that is wonderful. Go away. You're a pig, Damien."

His look was ugly. "You're lying, Victoria. You wanted me. Oh, yes, I know you're wild with my twin, and you will be as wild with me."

She slapped him, hard. His head flew to the side with the power of her blow. Neither of them moved. Damien lightly stroked his fingertips over his cheek. He said very softly, "You will pay for that."

But Victoria paid no attention. She grabbed her riding skirts and ran full-tilt from the stable toward Drago Hall. Her breath was coming in short gasps. She was trembling. It had been Damien, Damien all along. He'd worn Rafael's clothes, he'd spoken of Honeycutt Cottage, the kitchen—

She stopped dead in her tracks, the edifice of Drago Hall looming over her. She closed her eyes, feeling such fear and humiliation that she couldn't think straight.

"Come with me."

She blinked, and stared at Rafael, who was standing on the top stone step of the Hall.

"Rafael?" Her voice sounded tentative, uncertain, and he frowned fiercely down at her.

A black brow arched upward and his tone was snide. "Who did you think it was, Victoria? My twin, for example?"

"I couldn't be all that certain. You see—"

He slashed a hand through the air. "Enough. I said to come with me. Now." And he turned on his heel and strode through the great front doors, not looking back.

Victoria stared after him; her back stiffened, anger filling her. What was wrong with him? She followed him, but saw that he was turning toward the small estate room. She ignored him, and picked up her skirts again, dashed up the stairs, her destination the nursery and Damaris.

Rafael turned, once inside the estate room. "Now, Victoria, I believe you have quite a bit of explain—" His jaw dropped. She was nowhere to be seen. How dare she. He felt rage pour through him. But he controlled it at the sight of his twin, in his shirtsleeves now, walking across the entrance hall, his head lowered in profound thought.

"Damien."

"Hello, twin. What are you doing in my estate room?"

He wanted to kill Damien, he wanted to strangle him with his bare hands. But he hadn't seen him and Victoria together, no, just Elaine had seen them, supposedly. He said mildly, "Just looking about. You're very neat, Damien." He looked about at the tidy desktop, the rows of books on the shelves. "Where is your coat?"

"I was overly warm," Damien said, shrugging. "I removed it and left it somewhere, I suppose."

"And I was with your wife."

"What is that supposed to mean, brother? More cryptic wit of yours?"

"She was upset that I was with my wife, making love to her in front of God and the stable lads, but you see, it wasn't me, it was you."

"I don't know what you're talking about," Damien said easily. He walked across the Aubusson carpet to the narrow sideboard and poured himself a brandy. "Would you care for some?"

"No, all I care for at this moment is an answer from you. Tell me, Damien."

"Elaine is nearing her time. She also tends toward hysteria, just like her mother in that respect, and it's magnified when she is pregnant. I really haven't the faintest idea what you're talking about. I shall speak to Elaine if you wish."

"Yes," Rafael said slowly, "yes, you do that. And I will speak to Victoria."

Rafael walked slowly up the staircase, down the long eastern corridor to the Pewter Room. There was no one there save Molly, who was cleaning out the grate. This time her mobcap was neatly set atop her light brown braids. She smiled shyly at him.

He nodded to her and retreated. It was some time later that he entered the nursery. Damaris shrieked at the sight of him and dashed forward to clutch at his legs. Victoria remained seated on the floor, a row of dolls in front of her.

"Torie and I are playing dolls. Do you want to? I'll give you Queen Bess."

That was obviously quite a concession. "No, not just now," Rafael said, his eyes searching his wife's face. She looked very pale, frightened. He stiffened. She had no reason to be afraid of him, did she?

"Victoria, I have decided that we will travel to Falmouth on the morrow. Is that all right with you?"

She nodded, saying nothing. He saw her lift one of the dolls and hold it close to her chest.

His lips thinned. He hugged Damaris, set her away from him, and left the nursery, not looking back.

Victoria didn't move. She watched him, listened to his footsteps as they retreated down the long corridor. What would he have done if she'd been alone? What would he do when he learned the truth? She shivered. She disliked Damien profoundly, but she liked her cousin, at least most of the time she did.

She didn't want Elaine hurt.

It was late afternoon and he was lying in wait. He despised himself for what he intended, but at the same time he was determined. His very stubborn jaw grew more so.

He saw her coming toward him, walking slowly, her head lowered. What was she thinking? Feeling?

"Victoria."

She stopped abruptly, but didn't look directly at him. No, she was looking toward the ridiculous gaggle of ducks marching about Fletcher's Pond.

"I've been waiting for you. I was told that you come here a lot."

That got her attention. She looked at him, her face calm, then puzzled.

"What do you mean?" she asked, not coming closer.

He walked to her. "I mean that your husband told me of your preference for the ducks and the pond."

"I see. What do you want, Damien?"

"Why, my love, I want to finish what we began this morning. Isn't that also your wish?" He reached out his hand and lightly stroked his fingertips over her wrist. She jumped, pulling back her hand.

She felt as cold as an ember in July. So that was the way of it. Slowly she nodded, and looked up at him. "Yes," she said, her voice low and as seductive as she could make it. "Yes, I should very much like to finish what we began." She put her hands, palms flat, on his shoulders and gave him a smile that would melt a stone. "You no longer think badly of me for turning you down this morning? I had to, you know. Rafael could have been anywhere, quite close even. Yes, but now that I know we're alone, I want you."

He sucked in his breath, then let the air hiss through his teeth. "Victoria," he whispered, and leaned down to kiss her.

The instant his mouth touched hers, Victoria, despite her rage, felt intense pleasure. Didn't he know? She wondered, furious now, more furious by the minute. Why couldn't he simply believe her? She smiled and melted against him. Her lips parted and she yielded, every part of her giving and wanting.

"Oh, yes," she whispered into his mouth, her breath warm and gentle. "I want you so very much, Damien."

She felt him stiffen at her words, and she pressed her belly against him. His hands were on her hips, kneading her, then lifting her against him. She made no demur, indeed, she clasped him more tightly to her.

He wedged his hand between her thighs, touching her, caressing her through her clothing.

Suddenly, without warning, she jerked away. She kicked him hard in the shin. He yelped, jumping on his right foot.

"You bastard. You miserable, unmitigated bastard. I shall never forgive you this, Rafael. Never."

"Victoria." He felt bizarre, as if he'd walked onto the stage of a play he himself had penned, only to have his leading lady go off on a tangent. And find him out. But when? At what point?

He saw her ready for another attack and yelled, "Stop."

"You may go directly to the devil, Rafael."

The instant she'd flung the words at him, she was running away. "Your leg." He called after her. "Take care."

"Ha."

Her sneering voice floated back to him, but he remained where he was. Well, that was that. He rubbed his shin, then straightened, only to see Clarence eyeing him.

"Sorry, Duke, no bread for you today."

Clarence squawked.

"And no nothing for me today either." He turned slowly and began his walk back to Drago Hall.

"I must speak to you, Victoria."

"Go away."

"No. I will tie you down if I must. We have to talk."

Victoria straightened from her task. She slowly put down the feather duster and laid the volume of Voltaire back on the shelf. "Very well, if you must. Get it over with, if you please." She paused a moment and gave him a thoroughly disgusted look. "This will probably be magnificent. Your other performance was certainly sterling enough."

"I was wrong, at least I assume that I was. You threw me."

"If only I had been stronger, you would have been in Fletcher's Pond."

"Elaine told me she saw you and me making love by the stable. She thought I was Damien. She thought the man kissing you was me. I decided to put it to the test after you refused to talk to me. I'm not proud of it, Victoria, but I had to."

"Yet again," she said mildly, idly dusting a tabletop. "Again you chose to believe anyone, except me."

"But you responded to me so freely, you said you wanted me, and you—"

"You are a great fool. I also find you excessively boring, Rafael. Have you nothing at all to do with yourself except test your wife to see if she's virtuous?"

"Tell me you did it on purpose. Tell me you knew all along that I was pretending to be Damien."

"I will tell you nothing. Nothing at all. Who knows what conclusions you will draw now? Certainly I expect to come out in the wrong. It appears that is inevitable when you are involved. I should like to kick your other shin."

She tossed the duster at him. "I'm going to dress for dinner." Then she stopped cold and turned back to him. "Actually, we must leave the Pewter Room."

"Why?"

"When Damien was pretending to be you, he spoke of things like Honeycutt Cottage and the kitchen. He also said that he was wild for me, particularly after yesterday afternoon." She stopped, watching his face.

He paled; then his face flooded with furious color. "That damned bastard."

"Yes," she said.

"So that is why we were assigned the Pewter

Room. There must be a peephole in there, and Damien was watching us." He stopped, so incoherent with rage that he could find no words.

"Yes," she said again.

He got hold of himself, but it was a powerful effort. "Let's find that peephole," he said, took her hand, and dragged her after him.

It took only fifteen minutes to find it. "In the middle of a grape," Rafael said with disgust. "Look, Victoria."

She looked at the fireplace mantel, at the swags of fruits sculptured on the frieze. "Do you think there could also be a passageway behind the fireplace? Connecting other rooms, perhaps?"

"That would be logical. I can't believe I never knew about this. Obviously Damien discovered it after I was gone. Let's see if there's an opening."

It was the turning of an orange counterclockwise that did it. A narrow panel just to the right of the fireplace slid noiselessly back. The two of them simply stared into the black space. "Goodness," Victoria managed, then stepped forward. "Let's explore and see where it goes?"

"No fear?"

"No, just fury. I should like to do something awful to your brother. I can't stand to think of him watching us."

"I know. Let's explore, then."

Rafael fetched a candle and stepped into the narrow passageway, bowing his head, for the ceiling was low. "All right," he said over his shoulder to Victoria. She paused just inside the passageway. Quietly she turned a small wooden knob, and a panel slid open. She looked into the Pewter Room. She shuddered, then moved aside for Rafael to look.

He cursed quietly. He felt Victoria's hand on his arm and turned away toward the dark tunnel. He breathed in deeply, a damp musty smell filling his nostrils. He watched Victoria stop at the next narrow door. She turned a small wooden knob just like the one that gave onto the Pewter Room.

It was Elaine's bedchamber. And Elaine was dressed only in her underthings. Her belly was huge; she was rubbing the small of her back, her eyes closed.

Victoria quickly closed the panel.

"Elaine?"

"Yes."

Rafael could now picture the twists and turns of the passageway. He wondered idly if his parents had known about it. But no, had his father known, he would have made a great game of it with his two boys. How had Damien discovered it?

Rafael opened the next panel and saw that it gave onto one of the guest chambers. The room wasn't empty. Damien and the maid Molly were on the bed, the girl's skirts about her face, her legs widespread, and Damien pumping into her. Rafael remembered Molly's crooked mobcap. Had she just come from a tryst with her employer? He drew a deep breath and slid the panel shut.

"What is this room?" Victoria asked from behind him.

"Just a guest chamber," Rafael said, trying his best to sound nonchalant.

"What did you see, Rafael?"

He turned slowly and said, "I saw Damien and Molly on the bed. Now, let's keep going."

They continued their descent. There was an opening into the main drawing room and one into the estate room. Rafael slipped through the opening in the estate room, then gave his hand to Victoria. They were standing just in front of the now closed panel when Ligger entered and gasped.

"Hello, Ligger."

"But, Master Rafael. I—didn't know— Oh, dear, this is very confusing."

"Let me show you, Ligger." Rafael opened the panel, the knob behind some carved maple leaves. The butler stared and Rafael saw comprehension come into his eyes. So he'd seen Damien where he hadn't expected to, and wondered about it. Well, no more. No more secret passageways in Drago Hall. He would ensure that every servant, every guest in the vicinity would know about it. Damien would hold no more power, not this kind, anyway.

"The passage winds upstairs and there are peepholes and entrances into many of the upstairs rooms. The estate room here and the drawing room are the only ones downstairs. The passage stops just a few feet beyond the estate room. If I've got my thinking aright, the door leads into the east garden. It is probably well-covered with ivy on the outside."

Ligger nodded slowly. He looked at Victoria, then at Rafael. He said quietly, "What would you like to do about this, Captain?"

"Why, Ligger, I think you should tell all the servants about this, every one of them. Tell everyone. If you like, feel free to tour the passageway. I will, of course, discuss this with the baron."

Ligger nodded and Victoria felt herself go warm with embarrassment at the understanding in the old man's eyes.

"Let's go back to the Pewter Room now," Rafael said, and nodding to Ligger, he took Victoria's hand

and together they disappeared into the dim passage. The panel slid shut soundlessly behind them.

Rafael was leading the way. He was holding the candle high, and at a bend in the path its flickering light fell upon something neatly folded on top of a very old trunk. It was black, velvet or satin, he thought. Later, he decided. Later he would come back. He didn't want Victoria involved in this.

Once back in their bedchamber, Rafael sat in the high-backed wing chair, steepled his fingers, and stared off at nothing in particular.

Victoria watched him for a moment; then looked back to the grape cluster. She shivered. Was Damien planning to come and watch them again? Soon now?

"First of all," her husband said finally, still not looking at her, "you must have another name. Vic, I think, is charming and will suit our purpose quite nicely. Whenever I come upon you, I will call you Vic."

"Vic? I have an even better idea. Let us simply leave Drago Hall tomorrow. We can go to Falmouth, then to St. Agnes, to our new home."

"We don't as yet know if it is our new home."

"You know the family will accept. You continue to delay, Rafael. Why do you wish to remain here at Drago Hall? Oh, damn, it's this Hellfire Club business and you are the one to put a stop to it. Just say yes, and I will say no more."

"Yes," he said very quietly.

"Then what are we to do about your brother? I have no wish to provide him with more entertainment."

"No, we shan't. I want to kill him for what he's done, and that scares me, Victoria. That scares the hell out of me. He is, after all, my brother, my

damned twin. Well, Ligger will begin to spread the
news of the passageway. That should enrage Damien.
I shall board up our cluster of grapes over there.
Then I must decide what to do."

"All right." She sighed. "It's a mess."

"Victoria, will you forgive me just one more time?
I am sorry, you know. Kick me again if you wish,
but forgive me."

She didn't say anything for a very long time. Rafael fidgeted, opened his mouth, then closed it.

Suddenly, Victoria drew back her fist and hit him
in the belly. "I forgive you."

He left her then, shaking his head and smiling, to
return surreptitiously to the passage, and some thirty
minutes later he found her speaking to Flash. "Let's
leave for Falmouth, say, in a half-hour? I'll think of
something, er, plausible, before we return."

She cocked her head at his sudden change of plans.
Something had happened, something he wasn't
going to tell her about. She saw Flash smiling widely,
pleased to the tips of his boots that they were returning to the *Seawitch*.

Victoria forced a smile. "I'll be ready in thirty
minutes."

"Thank you, Victoria." He caressed her cheek with
his knuckles, then turned to Flash.

Victoria walked back to the Hall, furiously thinking. She would pry it out of him somehow.

Two afternoons later, Rafael sat on the uncomfortable scarred bench in the oak-beamed ale room of
the Ostrich. The inn was older than anyone cared to
remember, save for Pimberton, the landlord, who
told stories of how King John had stopped at the
Ostrich way back in 1215 on his way to Runnymede.

No one had bothered to tell him that the Ostrich wasn't exactly on the direct route to Runnymede.

Rafael was alone at the Ostrich in Carnon Downs. He'd left Victoria yesterday on the *Seawitch* in the care of Blick and Rollo. As for Flash, he'd been so excited to be back on board, he'd chattered like a magpie. Carnon Downs was just southeast of Truro, only two hours from Falmouth. He, of course, hadn't told Victoria a thing, simply said he had some business to conduct, but she'd looked at him, that I-know-you're-up-to-something look, shrugged, and taken Blick's arm for a stroll on the deck.

As Rafael nursed his mug of ale, he heard Pimberton talking now about the Black Prince. "—Aye, you may wonder," Pimberton was saying, rubbing his hands over the coat that covered his immense stomach, "wonder indeed that the prince brought King John of France with him—and he was met by Edward III, right here, at the Ostrich—aye, in this very room. 'Twas in 1355, aye, indeed. History, sirs, that's what we have here."

Rafael grinned, then went very still when he heard the loud voice calling out, "Pimmby, your best ale, if you please."

Johnny Tregonnet had come, just as the note had said.

"Here you are, Master John," said Pimberton, beaming at the young man whose father owned a vast part of Carnon Downs.

"Hello, Damien."

"Glad you're here early," Rafael said, and indeed he was. Were Damien to arrive now, everything would be well and truly lost. "I've lots of business to conduct. How are you, Johnny?"

"I'm well as always. Why are you being so civil,

Damien? You've never done much of anything for me except sneer."

Rafael waved a negligent hand. "I'm feeling quite mellow, old fellow. Now, what is it you want?"

"Your brother. He knows about us. He threatened me at your ball. He wants to join our group or else he'll do us all in. I sent a note to the Ram, but I haven't heard a thing."

"What did the Ram say when you told him about Rafael?"

Johnny stared at him. "You know there's no one who knows who the Ram is. I left a message at the hidden box, you know, the one at the crossroads at Pellway. What's wrong with you, Damien?"

"Ah," said Rafael, and called out quickly, "Pimmby, more ale for my friend here." Damnation, he thought, so none of the members knew the identity of the Ram. Well, at least something should happen soon, since Johnny had sent the man a message about him.

"Hey, just you wait a second," Johnny shouted, shoving back his chair. "You ain't Damien!"

"Very good, Johnny. I'm not. Ah, here's our good innkeeper with your ale." Johnny lurched toward him, and Rafael very smoothly threw a right into Johnny's belly, following it with a left to his jaw. He slouched to the floor without a sound.

Mr. Pimberton, a mug of ale in hand, stared down at the unconscious man. "Goodness, Baron, shouldn't ye—"

"Yes, I should," said Rafael mildly. He took the mug of ale and poured it onto Johnny's face.

"That should do it," said Mr. Pimberton. "I'll get me missis to clean him up."

"Excellent. Thank you, sir," said Rafael. He gave

Mr. Pimberton a brief salute, took one last look at a now-stirring and moaning Johnny Tregonnet, and took his leave. As he walked out of the inn, he saw Damien riding his rawboned bay, coming from the opposite direction. "You will have an interesting time of it, brother," he said quietly.

He now had no regrets that he'd threatened Johnny Tregonnet at the ball rather than pretending to be interested in joining his club. He was alert, ready, for he knew the Ram would have to do something.

22

Love is often a consequence of marriage.

—MOLIÉRE

Victoria sat patiently on the edge of Rafael's bunk in the captain's cabin, listening to Blick give his opinion to Rafael. "There's not a thing I can do to prevent the muscles going into spasm. However, when it happens, there's no reason for Victoria to have to endure the pain for so very long. Your idea of the hot towels is a good one, but still it takes time to get the muscles back under control."

Rafael smiled at his wife. "Didn't I tell you he would come up with something to help? Have you got an esoteric plant from, say, the southern coast of China?"

"Sorry, the West Indies. What I propose is that we use two plants together—the cheddah and the cawapate, both of which we can replenish from Martinique. Victoria, with the cheddah you will heat the leaves and use them as a compress. The cawapate you'll use in tea. Now, there's also another use for the cheddah. If Rafael here becomes a thorn in your side, you can mix some cheddah in his tea and he will, after some hours, end up with the most pristine innards imaginable."

Rafael groaned. "I believe I will be the one to oversee the preparation of your concoctions, Blick."

"Thank you," Victoria said, giving Blick her hand as he rose to take his leave.

"My pleasure." Blick took her slender fingers and smiled down at her. "It is also my pleasure to see Rafael so content. He's traveled the seas, enjoyed enough adventure and danger for three men, and emerged whole-hide. He is fortunate, yes indeed. As are you, my dear. He is also a strong, honorable, kind man. I will see both of you at dinner."

"I am content, Victoria," said Rafael.

"Don't be content yet, not until you tell me where you—the strong, honorable, kind man—were, and what you were doing. All of it now, Rafael."

"You're a hard woman, Victoria. Nothing for it, eh? Very well, I was involved in bringing things to a head. Hopefully. I found a note to Damien from Johnny Tregonnet—it was in the hidden passageway, in Damien's black cloak."

She nodded sadly. "Unfortunately, I'm not really surprised. So Damien is really involved with the Hellfire group?"

"Yes, he is." Rafael sighed, and plowed his fingers through his hair. Hair on end, he proceeded to pour himself a brandy. "The group is headed by a man who calls himself the Ram. I can name you every one of the members; I could have done that at the ball after reacquainting myself with all the more objectionable fellows of my boyhood. I imagine you could have done the same. However, dammit, the Ram's identity is unknown, even by the members. I have made well-placed threats. We will see what happens."

"Where were you today?"

"At an inn called the Ostrich, meeting Johnny Tregonnet. I played Damien, and that is how I learned that no one knows the Ram's identity. Damn and blast."

"So," Victoria said slowly, "it's now the Ram's move. What was your threat?"

"That I would destroy their filthy little club if I wasn't allowed to join them. A lie, of course, and I wonder why I even bothered with it. The Ram certainly can't be such a fool."

She laid her hand lightly on his forearm. "Rafael, I trust you will be careful."

"Didn't Blick or Rollo tell you that I'm like the proverbial bad copper? I come skittering back, always. You, madam, will never be rid of me. Besides, you can be certain I shall be careful as a blind monk in a nunnery. I love my wife, you see, and she adores and worships me. Our life, with a modicum of good fortune, will be sweet."

A slow smile sent the corners of Victoria's mouth upward. "All that?"

"Yes, all that. Now, will you let me have my way with you? It has been an age, after all."

She laughed. "Since last night?" Even as she spoke, she savored his words in her mind. He loved her.

"That long ago?"

"Yes." He held her and kissed her, and she responded as she always did with him—immediately, utterly, and sweetly.

"Oh, Lord, Victoria, you're a marvel," he said, drawing her up hard against him.

At nearly midnight, Rafael was still thinking she was a marvel. He was lying on his back in his bunk, Victoria curled up against his side. He smiled in the darkness, reveling in the fact that he had exhausted his young wife. She was limp, so very soft against him. Life, he silently agreed with himself, was sweet, and he trusted it would become even sweeter.

He wasn't certain exactly when he'd given it up. But given it up he had. He was now, he supposed, becoming used to the jumble of feelings—some very calm and serene, others wild and frantic—but he accepted them, all of them, enjoying their flow through his mind and body. Holding Victoria, making love to her, fighting and laughing with her—why, they were experiences he wouldn't trade for anything this earth had to offer him.

When he'd married her it hadn't occurred to him that she would become so vital to him. But she was, and he no longer bothered to fight the inevitable. He dropped a light kiss on the tip of her nose, stretched just a bit, and promptly fell asleep.

Victoria pulled her muffin apart and spread sweet butter and honey on it. "What are we going to do now?"

"*We*, sweetheart? Don't alarm me like that. Do you think that I would ever take the chance of placing you in danger? Oh, no." Her brow furrowed into a fierce frown as he spoke. He tried to smile as he added, "I look at you and realize that you are mine, all mine, and I want to yell to the world that it is so. Forgive my male possessiveness, but I can't help it."

"You will most certainly help it."

"Would you believe that I didn't quite mean what I said just then?"

"Certainly. I'm a very reasonable woman. I'm also your wife and I'm to share things with you. You can't shut me out, Rafael. It isn't fair. And don't you forget that you are also mine, and what is mine I guard."

"I shan't forget that." He gave her his patented white-toothed grin that could charm the serpent and all the serpent's cousins from Eden, and she felt herself slipping. She gulped, looked at her muffin as if it were a lifeline, and said firmly, "No, sir. Now, what have you in mind?"

"I plan to have a very serious talk with my twin. It's time, you know, past time if the truth be told. He has given himself free rein to be as reprehensible as he wishes, and I have allowed it by neither doing nor saying anything in return. All Damien and I have done since you and I arrived at Drago Hall is fence. It must be stopped, all of it."

"Will you beat him to a pulp?"

"There is a lot of relish in your voice at that prospect. Actually, I hope it won't come to that. We will see."

When his eyes slid away from her face, she pounced immediately. "There is more you plan. Tell me."

"Flash will follow Johnny Tregonnet everywhere. Our infamous Soho pickpocket will become the infamous Cornwall shadower."

"You don't think it's possible that Damien is this leader of the group, this Ram, do you?"

"I doubt it, since there was that note to him from

Johnny. In other words, Johnny knows him as a member. No one knows the Ram."

"Well, that is something."

"Amen to that."

"You will be very careful, you swear?"

"I already promised you that I would."

"And when you need my help, you won't hesitate to ask?"

"I won't hesitate for an instant," he agreed with immediate untruth.

They returned to Drago Hall the following day to discover that the Demoreton family had accepted their offer. Elaine was very happy to celebrate with them. Victoria imagined that her cousin would be delighted when she and Rafael were well and truly gone. As for Damien, he said the right words, but he looked distracted.

When Elaine gently inquired when they would leave, Rafael replied easily enough, "Next Monday, I think. Does that sound all right to you, Victoria?"

She nodded. It gave them four days to bring things to a conclusion. She wished devoutly it was Monday already and they were gone from here. Then she thought about Damaris and her heart gave a lurch. It was sometimes uncomfortable being an adult, she reflected as her third glass of champagne was making her thoughts more and more profound. One had to face unpleasant things, like leaving her one very small cousin whom she adored.

Before going to their bedchamber, Rafael looked directly at his twin and said mildly, "I assume you've spoken to Ligger about the secret passageway and the peepholes?"

Damien didn't blink. "Yes. Interesting that you discovered the passageway. I myself came across it quite by accident during a vicious storm. It must have created a sort of echo effect. I happened to turn the correct piece of fruit on the frieze."

"Have you had the carpenter board it up as yet?"

"No."

"I think it time to do so," Rafael said, took Victoria's hand, and led her from the drawing room.

They went to the Pewter Room. Rafael hung his jacket over the cluster of grapes on the frieze.

"I will ensure it's done tomorrow."

"When we leave, Damien will probably have it unboarded again."

"With all the servants knowing about the passageway? I imagine that he might find himself with a problem—the servants just might use the passageway for their own trysts."

Rafael didn't tell Victoria when he was going to speak to Damien. He simply waited until she went to the nursery to visit Damaris. He ran his twin to ground in his estate room. As he closed the door quietly behind him, Damien turned from his position at the window. His expression was thoughtful, his arms crossed over his chest.

He said nothing, merely watched Rafael stride to the single leather chair beside the small marble fireplace, sit down, and stretch his long legs out in front of him. "We must talk."

"Do you really think so?"

Rafael kept firm control of his temper. He steepled his fingers, saying easily, "It's time for home truths, Damien. I was sorely tempted to kill you for your lies about Victoria. I was sorely tempted to kill for your seductive playacting with my wife. I was sorely tempted to kill you once I realized you had watched

Victoria and me making love. Regardless of my own personal feelings toward you, I've nonetheless always believed you a complex man, and no matter what wickedness you did, I still believed you held some honor dear. But your actions toward both Victoria and myself have been distasteful, reprehensible, and dishonorable."

"What did she tell you? Did she claim I'd tried to seduce her? I find that mightily amusing, Rafael, particularly since all I've tried to do is warn—"

"I suggest you shut up," Rafael said. "Really, Damien, you are very close to physical harm at this moment. There's no more reason to lie to me about Victoria, about anything."

"This is how you repay my hospitality? You attack me? Insult me?"

Rafael could only stare at his twin. "You're amazing, truly. Victoria and I will leave on Monday, but before we do, I must have done with your unorthodox and quite filthy little club. I assume you spoke with Johnny Tregonnet after I took my leave of him at the Ostrich. I trust I didn't break his jaw."

Damien merely shook his head, turning his back on his brother to stare out the window onto the western lawn. Two gardeners were scything the now thinning fall grass, their movements practiced and graceful.

"I suppose I was a fool," Damien said in a meditative voice, "to keep that note from Johnny. But who would have thought that you, brother, would discover the passageway?"

"Suffice it to say that I did."

"May I inquire why you are so terribly intent on destroying our private little club?"

"Did you know, Damien, for the past five years or

so I've been something in the nature of a spy for England against the French? No, I guess there was no reason for you to imagine such a thing. Well, in any case, it no longer matters because my skulduggery days are over. I accepted just one last assignment from Lord Walton at the ministry. You see, no one would have ever bothered about this ridiculous little Hellfire Club if you hadn't raped Viscount Bainbridge's daughter by mistake. It was the fatal error. Now your little club must be disbanded, the Ram— that phallic ass—brought to justice."

Damien scoffed. "Brought to justice? All the world is to know that Viscount Bainbridge's precious daughter was raped by eight men? You jest, Rafael. No father would want that public."

"I suppose I should have been more specific. Once I discover the identity of the Ram I will tell Lord Walton, who will in turn tell the viscount. The Ram will be given two choices: first, he can leave England forever, or second, he will die. Removed from this earth like the scum he is, no duel, nothing that could smack of honorable differences between gentlemen. No, removed, quickly." Rafael paused a moment, closely watching his brother's face. He read little there, frustration perhaps, and a touch of fear and maybe aggression. But not a single great emotion to sweep all others before it.

"No one will grieve for him, you know, not for a twisted evil creature like him. I don't really want you dead, Damien. No matter that you've more than likely enjoyed yourself mightily raping young girls. But it will stop. You will stop."

Damien said nothing. He picked up a silver letter knife from his desktop. He gently slid the razor-sharp edge along the pad of his thumb.

"What about Elaine? Have you no feeling for her at all? You also have an adorable daughter, and an heir to be born shortly. What the hell is the matter with you, Damien? Why have you continued to play the satyr? Oh, yes, two can use the peepholes, you know. I saw you and Molly. I had wondered the day before why the girl's mobcap was crooked and there was a vacuous smile on her face. Why, Damien?"

Damien raised his head from concentrated study of the letter knife. He looked at his brother squarely. "Boredom," he said. "Pure and simple boredom." He laughed at Rafael's incredulous expression. "You believe I should be satisfied being Baron Drago, owning Drago Hall and all its damned antiquity? You believe I should continue deliriously happy with a woman whose only claim to my affections is the yearly dowry payments made me by her damnable father?

"You believe I should be content wandering about my acres, counting the trees that dot my land? You believe it the best of all possible outcomes for me to have wed at the age of twenty-two? Lord, I hadn't even begun to live, and there I was with a damned wife. Surely you can't be that blind, brother, you who prevented boredom quite effectively through your spying adventures, you who had no worries about how to maintain this hideous pile of stone, no damned responsibilities toward the Carstairs line. Even now, you thumb your nose at me, at all the aristocracy, and calmly enter the tin-mine trade after making a fortune as a merchant. Even now, you find yourself married to a woman who has brought you fifty thousand pounds.

"I have resented you for many years now, Rafael, more years than I care to consider. I know you must sometimes remember Patricia—yes, I recall her as well, the silly little fool, though her last name eludes me. I enjoyed taking her from you. I enjoyed plowing her, knowing that you watched. You were always much too much the careful, sincere lover when what dear Patricia wanted was forcefulness and dominance. But that was years ago, too many to dredge up now."

"Far too many," Rafael said.

"I will leave Victoria alone. Her leg is quite ugly with its ridged red scar. It was simple sport that last time—seeing if I could fool her into my bed. No, I don't want her."

Rafael stiffened, fists clenching. "It is enough, Damien. Surely it is enough."

Damien shrugged, an elaborate motion that was identical to his twin's. "You know, I do believe that I will give you the Ram."

"I beg your pardon?"

"I said I will give you the Ram."

"Why?"

Damien laughed at the incredulous look on his twin's face. "Let's just say that I'm—bored with the nasty little club, as you call it. The others really are rather paltry fellows, you know. Do you doubt me? Not that I would blame you, of course. Suspicion would be wise, I should say. But I'll do it. Why not? Perhaps to prove to myself that I have some honor left." He paused a moment, shaking his head. "Perhaps it is a bit of retribution to my merchant brother."

"Trade isn't synonymous with vulgarity, Damien."

"Oh? Well, perhaps that is true for plain Mr. Carstairs or even for Captain Carstairs, but for Baron Drago? It makes the blood congeal even to consider it, no matter how briefly. No, that is something the baron could not do."

"*Would* not do, you mean. Were I Baron Drago, I wouldn't hesitate."

"Ah, the noble twin again. Just like our father, with your noble streak. Only thing about our father, he wasn't all that clever a businessman. But at least he didn't gamble my inheritance away. He did leave me something, perhaps even enough. And who knows, perhaps my heir, my as-yet-unborn-son, will become a cit in his thinking, if not in his breeding. Perhaps he will be like his uncle and wallow in trade."

"Drop it, Damien. Drop all of it. We are still brothers."

"More's the pity, that's what you're thinking. Well, since your face is mine, damn you, I can't dispute the fact for even an instant. Incidentally," Damien added as he made for the estate-room door, "I appreciate your not killing me. Fratricide wouldn't sit well on the English hero's shoulders. No, indeed. I will tell you how we will get the Ram. Soon."

Rafael didn't move for some time after his brother left him alone.

It was All Hallows' night, the eve of All Saints' Day. There was no full moon, but there were jack-o'-lanterns aplenty, including two that Damaris had carved with the help of Victoria and Elaine, with Nanny Black making dire predictions throughout the process.

"We will set both of them in the window to welcome friends and scare off ugly goblins," said Elaine in an excellent conspiratorial voice as she carefully placed lighted candles in each carved-out pumpkin.

"Look, Torie, look!"

"Hmmm? Oh, yes, they look grand, Damie."

Elaine gave her cousin a look, then shrugged. "You will be leaving in two days," she said.

"Yes, we will. If you would like me to take care of Damaris while you are confined, I should be delighted."

"No, I think not. Nanny Black will be sufficient. Oh, Lord, I just wish the child would make his appearance and be done with it."

Victoria gave her a perfunctory smile, kissed Damaris good night, and left the nursery, Elaine in her wake.

"What's the matter with you, Victoria?"

"Nothing." But there was; she just couldn't put her finger on it. She was very sensitive to Rafael and his moods. Although he'd tried, she sensed a tension in him throughout the day, a barely leashed excitement that, even controlled as he was, made his eyes glitter silver. "All right, husband," she'd said to him after luncheon that day, "what are you planning? No, don't tell me I'm imagining things, for I know that I'm not. Tonight is All Hallows' Eve. What is going to happen?"

"Victoria, love," Rafael said, closing his hands over her forearms, "the only thing I'm planning is to exhaust you so completely you will not rise until noon on the morrow."

"Rafael, you can't get around me with promises like that."

He laughed, leaned down, and kissed her hard.

"Promises, huh?"

"You know what I mean. Now, tell me what you're up to."

He looked at her thoughtfully then, but shook his

head. "You will be in my company all evening, my dear, and all night. Oh, Victoria, I always keep my promises."

He left her and she stood staring after him, wishing she had something to throw at him.

For once the two ladies were first to arrive in the drawing room. "I shall surely roast Rafael for this," Victoria said, sipping her sherry.

"Damien won't join us this evening," Rafael said from the doorway. "He had business to attend to, I'm afraid."

"Business?" Victoria repeated blankly. "Tonight? But that is ridiculous."

"I agree, but nonetheless, that is what he said. Ah, here is your husband."

Well, Victoria thought, giving him a brilliant smile. He hadn't lied to her about being here. He looked lovely in his black evening clothes, her favorite of his vests—a soft pearl gray—contrasting with the black of his coat and the snow white of his linen.

"Do you know where Damien has gone, Rafael?" Elaine asked, rising ponderously.

"Some business he had to attend to."

Victoria snorted. "Nonsense," she said. "I think there is some sort of conspiracy here, Elaine. I shall take this husband of mine away and pry it out of him."

"No, I pray not, Victoria. I'm hungry. Ligger, bless you, old man. Is dinner ready?"

"Yes, Master Rafael."

Conversation over dinner was light, amusing, and Victoria found herself forgetting, for a few moments at a stretch, that it was All Hallows' Eve, a night when this Ram fellow would more than likely indulge in some wickedness. How could she really worry, though, for her husband was here, safe as could be, across from her, chewing on some delicious stewed venison.

After dinner Victoria was delighted to see that Rafael didn't remain in splendid isolation in the dining room with port. He assisted Elaine from her chair, offered each lady an arm, and escorted them back to the drawing room. Victoria begged Elaine to play.

"A Beethoven sonata, if you please," said Victoria. "He has such passion. I heard you practicing the other morning. All right, Elaine?"

Elaine settled herself, barely able to reach the keyboard now that her belly was so large. Her hands came down with impressive drama on a C-minor chord.

It was at that exact instant that there was the sound of shattering glass from behind Victoria. Just as she jerked about, a shot rang out. Victoria saw Rafael slam back against the wall, stand very still for what seemed an eternity, then very gracefully, slowly, slide to the floor.

She heard a hoarse, ugly cry. A scream, and it was from her own mouth.

23

*Truth and hope will always
come to the surface.*
—SPANISH PROVERB

The Ram was pleased. Soon, very soon now, his success would be confirmed. He'd sent his trusted and loyal man Deevers to Drago Hall. He looked toward the baron, who was chatting easily with Vincent Landower. He had no doubt that the baron would eventually approve of what had had to be done. Even if the baron didn't approve, he would keep his mouth shut—oh, yes, he would, because he was as deeply embroiled as every other wicked young fool in this room.

The Ram was aware of tremendous elation tonight, for it was Satan's night, and thus, his own night. He'd worked long and hard refining his rules, his beautiful rituals, delighting in their near-perfection, molding the men in this room into the image he desired. Oh, yes, it was a wonderful feeling he had.

"Gentlemen," he said, gaining their attention. "It

is symbolic that we meet on All Hallows' Eve to toast our brotherhood and our continued success. We're becoming known. Soon the Hellfire Club will be infamous, its members an elite who are feared and respected and held in awe, in short, envied by all men. Gentlemen, a toast to our continuation, to our surpassing the infamy of the original Hellfire Club."

There were cheers, a few grunts, but general head-nodding, and everyone drank the rich brandy from the cups. The Ram wished he could take a whip to all of them. They should have been shouting at the top of their bloody lungs. Damned fools. The Ram then saw Baron Drago rise slowly from his chair. He saw him turn and look at the girl who lay in a drugged stupor on the long table, her arms and legs spread away from her slight body, bound at the wrist and ankle, awaiting her initiation.

"Something troubles you?"

"No, not for very much longer."

Then, to the Ram's consternation, the baron slowly drew off his hood and tossed it to the floor. Then he ground the soft velvet beneath the heel of his boot.

"Stop," the Ram roared, his fists on the arms of his high-backed chair. "That's against the rules. Your hood must be on at all times during our meetings."

"Why?"

"Damien, what ails you? Are you foxed? You continue in this disrespectful manner, and you will be chastised."

The baron laughed. "Really? But why can't all my friends see me? Why can't I see them? I want them all to study my face when I thrust into that girl over there. She is all of thirteen years old. I want them all to see how much I enjoy raping a senseless child, how much I will delight in making that small heap of humanity bleed and shudder in pain."

"Shut up, you young fool. Have you lost your bloody mind?"

Johnny Tregonnet jumped to his feet, his brandy snifter falling unheeded to the floor beside him. "You're not Damien. Damn you, you're Rafael."

Very smoothly Rafael drew a pistol from the pocket of his capacious black cloak. "You're right about that, Johnny." Rafael turned slowly toward the Ram. "I have tried to place your voice. It's familiar to me, but you are disguising it effectively." He shrugged and smiled, a very bad smile. He turned back to the members. "Now, dear friends, I want all of you to remove your hoods. I want us all to see each other. Now."

No one moved. They all appeared black apparitions frozen in a moment of time.

"If you don't immediately obey me, I will shoot the Ram." Very calmly Rafael raised the pistol, aiming it in the center of the Ram's forehead. "It would be excellent riddance and certainly clear the air of its foul stench."

"Take them off," the Ram said.

They did.

"Throw them into the fire."

As the black velvet hoods landed in the fireplace, they smothered the flames for a moment, sending black smoke gushing upward, then burst into bright orange.

"We all know each other. No reason for the non-sense of hoods. Hello, Charlie, Paul, Linc." Rafael saw that they had difficulty meeting his eyes. Not that he blamed them. It was worse than being caught with your breeches down. He continued around the group, calling out each name in a jovial voice, watching their embarrassed reactions. Then he frowned, pausing. David Esterbridge wasn't here. His frown deepened as he remembered that young Joan Newdowns had claimed to have heard David's voice. If that were true, where was he? He said aloud to Vincent Landowner, "Vinnie, don't you wish to know the identity of the Ram?"

Vincent raised rather bulging blue eyes to Rafael's face. "It's not allowed," he said simply.

"I asked you if you would like to know."

"Yes," Vincent said. "All of us would, I guess."

"No. It's not allowed. I'm the leader here, you young bastard. You will stop this, immediately."

Rafael looked around the circle of lowered heads. "Why?" he said. "Why do you allow him to make you do these things? Charlie, you have a sister, Claire. She's fifteen. Should you like to see her drugged, tied down, and raped?"

"Damn you, Rafael, Claire's a child."

"And the girl lying there, Charlie?"

"She counts for nothing," Paul Keason said, his voice sounding a sullen litany.

"Ah, is that so? It appears to me that you're willing to swallow any swill that the Ram feeds you. Did the young lady—the daughter of the viscount—did she also count for nothing?"

"We didn't know at the time," Johnny cried. "We didn't know until later."

"Ah, she didn't tell you who she was?"

"Yes," said Paul Keason, "but of course we didn't believe her."

Lincoln said, "That was a mistake. The wretched

girl was dressed like a peasant and had no groom with her."

"Every evil has its excuse ready," said Rafael. "Charlie, doesn't your little sister Claire occasionally take walks without her groom?"

Charles St. Clement swallowed painfully, but said nothing.

"Perhaps little Claire even takes walks wearing an old gown? To go berrying, perhaps?"

"Stop it, Rafael."

"All right, I believe you do see the point. Now, all of you listen. I will tell you the truth. I was asked by the ministry to put a stop to this foolishness. Yes, gentlemen, you gained the attention of high-placed men when you ravished the viscount's daughter. So you see, it will stop. Now. If all of you swear to return to something resembling a path of righteousness, you won't be punished. This gentleman, however, this Ram, well, he will be taken care of in another way."

"There are seven of you and but one of him. Kill him."

"Flash."

" 'Ere, Cap'n. None of ye fancy coves move, now."

No one budged.

"Thank you, Flash," Rafael said quietly. "Would you please see to our young friend on the table? Untie her and see that she's breathing all right."

Flash moved to the young girl and efficiently unbound her. "She's all right, Cap'n. In fact, she should be awake very soon."

"Ah, yes, of course," said Rafael, turning back to the Ram. He said contemptuously, "You want her to be somewhat awake when all your obedient little lads rape her."

The Ram rose slowly to his feet. His voice trembled as he spoke. "You have desecrated this place. You have sneered and threatened. I am the leader here. This is All Hallows' Eve. This is my night of triumph." His eyes shifted, and in that instant, Rafael knew. He whirled about but he wasn't quite fast enough.

"Cap'n!"

The pistol butt came down, not on the base of his skull, but on his right shoulder, and he reeled with the force of it and the blinding pain. His own gun went flying across the old wool rug, and he lurched toward it.

"No, Captain, don't try it or Deever will kill you."

Rafael, panting, straightened and looked at the bulbous-nosed individual who was pointing a pistol at his chest. He stilled, cursing himself silently, closing his mind to the pain, regaining control.

"This, my dear Rafael, is Deevers. You, Flash, come here by your captain. Yes, that's better. Now, gentlemen, let us tie up these two interlopers."

Rafael looked Johnny Tregonnt in the face. "I, an interloper?" he said very softly. "Because it revolts me that you have somehow convinced these men to perform acts that normally they would find equally repulsive?"

"Shut up, Captain. Sit down, now."

Rafael sat willingly, motioning Flash beside him.

"Tie him, Johnny, Vincent."

"Yes, do," Rafael said easily. "Then you can draw lots to see who rapes that child first. An exciting prospect. I should hurry if I were you."

"Deever, if he says another word, put a bullet in his brain."

"Look here, Ram," Johnny Tregonnet said, stepping back rather than forward, "you'll not kill him. I shan't allow it."

"You'll not allow it, Johnny? You young ass, you have no say in anything I choose to do."

Johnny turned pugnacious, a sight that surprised Rafael and made a surge of relief wash through him. Johnny and the others were his only hope now.

"I think the others agree with me, Ram. Vinnie? Linc? Charlie?"

"But what are we to do?" Vinnie said, his voice a bewildered low whine.

"Lookee here," said Flash, "you 'eard the cap'n. He said not'ing would 'appen to you."

"Kill him." The Ram screamed at Deever.

Deever whipped the pistol around toward Flash. In that instant Johnny Tregonnet and Charlie St. Clement rushed forward, Rafael with them. Soon all the others were piled on top of Deever. The pistol was wrested from his meaty hand. He was pummeled and kicked until Rafael called a halt.

"No," Rafael said, "the Ram is the important one, not this pathetic bastard." He rose a bit unsteadily, aware of the pain numbing his shoulder. "Now, Ram, take off your hood. All of us want a good look at you."

The Ram backed away slowly, his body curiously still even as he walked.

"Now," Rafael said, "or I shall remove it for you."

The Ram cursed, and even Flash, who had heard the most lurid of speech on his mother's knee, was shocked.

"Who are you?" Rafael said. "David, is it you? Joan Newdowns recognized your voice, at least she thought it was you. Is it you, you miserable little bully?"

The Ram drew up straight as a rod. Slowly he raised his hands. The hood slid upward, then back and off.

There was complete silence. Everyone stared in disbelief at Squire Gilbert Esterbridge.

"An old man . . ."

"David's father."

"Jesus, I don't believe this . . ."

"So Joan was nearly right, closer than any of us," said Rafael. "Well, Squire, what have you to say? Does David have any idea of your perverted activities?"

"David wanted to join us," Linc Penhallow said, shaking his head. "And the Ram here said no. Only eight members there were to be. No more, no less."

"He was always making up rules," said Johnny. "Rules and more rules. Like my damned father."

Rafael said nothing. He wanted to beat Johnny and the others to a pulp, but knew the pleasure would be denied him. He needed the dishonorable little bastards.

"Yes," said Charlie St. Clement, "even rules for the girls. We weren't to fondle their breasts, not even to see their breasts. Their only use is what's between their legs. Vessels, that's all they were, that's what he called them."

Rafael listened to each of them complaining, but he was watching the squire's face. His complexion was ruddy, and his eyes, an odd shade of green, were glittering, intense, and suddenly Rafael felt a frisson of fear.

He had to regain control, of himself and the situation. He said, shutting off Paul Keason, "As I said before, Squire, only you are to be punished. You have a choice. You may leave England forever or you may die. The viscount won't meet you, for that would be an honorable acknowledgment. No, sir, he will have you killed. It's that simple. The decision is yours."

If anything, the squire's complexion grew even ruddier. He said, throwing back his head, squaring his meager shoulders, "I am Squire Esterbridge. I have lived here all my life, my father and his father before him. This is my land, my people. You, you sneering bastard, have no say. This is even my hunting lodge. I purchased it. You are trespassing. Get out."

Rafael smiled. "You amaze me, Squire. Indeed you do. I will be delighted to leave for I have told you of your choices. Take heed, Squire, for if you do remain in Cornwall, in England, you won't awake one day. And your son will become Squire Esterbridge." That, Rafael guessed, was the most devastating consequence he could offer the man.

The squire said nothing more. Rafael nodded to the other men, then said to Flash, "Let's tie old Deever up. The squire can release him once we are all away from this place."

Flash, quick as his nickname, did the deed. Rafael walked to the table, took off his cloak, and wrapped the girl in it.

"Who is she, Squire?"

The squire sneered and said nothing.

"I will take her to Dr. Ludcott. He will know." Even as he lifted the slight little figure in his arms, he said to the other men, "Have I your word that this club is well and truly done with?"

They all nodded, and Johnny said a furious, "Dammit all to hell, I can't believe we were all so gulled by this—this—"

He couldn't find a word, and Vinnie smoothly said, "This old curmudgeon? Crazy old Bedlamite?"

"Cursed sodding bastard."

The Ram didn't move, didn't change expression. He said to Rafael, "You won't be smiling much longer, Captain."

Rafael froze for an instant at the squire's very soft, taunting voice. "What the hell do you mean?"

The squire shook his head. He said nothing.

Rafael and Flash were both elated and weary. They rode side by side to the Drago Hall stables. "I wonder if Damien succeeded in fooling my wife."

It was a rhetorical question and Flash said nothing.

"I threatened him, you know. The only way she would question his identity is if he touched her. He swore he wouldn't, swore he would be the soul of honor, that his new leaf was well turned over, as of tonight. Well, we will soon see, won't we?"

Rafael took his leave of Flash and walked toward the Hall. "Good sport, Cap'n," Flash called after him. "Aye, excellent sport."

Rafael grinned as he walked toward the Hall. It was late, very late, yet all the windows still blazed with light. He frowned. He suddenly remembered the squire's words, and broke into a run.

He flung the oak front doors open. "Ligger. What the hell is going on?"

Ligger stood gape-mouthed, mute with distress.

"Out with it, man." Rafael stepped quickly forward and grasped the butler's narrow shoulders. "What happened, Ligger?"

Ligger stared up at him, finally managing, "Are you the baron or Captain Rafael?"

"I'm me, Rafael."

Ligger moaned softly. "Someone shot the baron. We thought it was you, sir. Your wife, well, she—"

"Is my brother dead?"

Ligger shook his head. "Dr. Ludcott is with him, but—"

Rafael didn't wait a moment longer. He took the stairs two at a time. He ran down the long eastern corridor toward the master suite, realized his mistake, and turned back toward the Pewter Room.

He was still some distance down the corridor when he saw Victoria standing beside the closed door, leaning against the wall, her head bowed. She looked unutterably weary. Softly he called, "Victoria."

Her eyes flew open. "Damien. Thank God you're back. He's hurt badly and I—"

"Victoria, love."

She grew very still, her eyes wide and haunted on his face. He was striding toward her.

"Damien, I don't under—"

"Hush, love. Hush, it's I." He drew her into his arms.

"Rafael?" Her voice was a thin cry.

"Yes." She threw herself into him, wrapping her arms as tightly as she could about his back, burrowing her face against his shoulder.

"I'm all right, love," he said over and over. "Tell me about Damien."

"I thought he was you. So did Elaine. So did everyone. Oh, God, I can't bear it." She stopped and drew in a deep breath. "Dr. Ludcott sent me out. He's digging out the bullet, it's deep in Damien's shoulder. He's unconscious, thank the Lord, but I just don't know."

Rafael gently shook her shoulders. "Listen to me, Victoria. I want you to go speak to Elaine and tell her what's happened. I will see to Damien. Are you all right? Can you manage?"

She nodded, gave him another fierce hug, and picking up her skirts, dashed down the corridor toward the master suite.

Rafael quietly let himself into the Pewter Room. Dr. Ludcott looked up, his expression grim and strained. "Baron, you're back. Your brother, I'm relieved to say, is a vital, very strong man. He will survive this."

"I'm Rafael Carstairs. This is the baron."

The doctor looked from the unconscious man on the bed to Rafael. "Amazing," he said, and shook his head.

"I took a young girl to your house. She was to have been raped by the Hellfire Club. It's over now, all of it."

Dr. Ludcott merely stared at him, silent for many moments. "I'm relieved," he said at last. "There's a lot you will not tell me, if I read you aright, Captain."

"Yes, perhaps."

There was a moan from Damien. At that moment Elaine came into the bedchamber, her face as white as January snow, her belly huge, molded closely by her fitted dressing gown.

"Now, now, my lady," Dr. Ludcott said quickly, striding toward her. "Your husband will survive this. He will. You must stay calm, for the child's sake. You must."

"He was playing you, Rafael," she said, her fingers stroking her husband's hand.

"Yes, this time I knew exactly what he was doing, Elaine. Neither of us guessed that something like this would happen. I'm sorry, so very sorry."

"Why?" she asked helplessly.

Damien opened his eyes at that moment to see his

wife staring down at him. "Hello," he said. "Where is Rafael?"

"I'm here. All is taken care of. All of it."

"Good," said Damien. "We succeeded." He closed his eyes, but his fingers tightened on his wife's hand. "I'll be all right," he said, then fell into a stupor.

Victoria tugged at Rafael's sleeve. "Tell me," she said.

"Elaine, would you like to remain with him?"

"Yes," she said. She gave Rafael one long look, then turned to speak to Dr. Ludcott.

Rafael and Victoria walked silently, side by side, down the corridor. "Why did you do it?"

"To protect you," he said simply, hearing the anger in her voice, understanding the awful fear she must have experienced, and sorry for it. "I had to make you believe I was here and not away. I knew you would do everything, move heaven and hell, to help me, otherwise. I wasn't about to take a chance with your safety, Victoria."

"And that is that?"

"Yes, it is. The Ram—you will never guess who he is."

"No, since I wasn't allowed to help draw the curtain down on this intrigue, I couldn't possibly guess."

"Squire Esterbridge."

That silenced her. She stared up at him, incredulous. "And David?"

"No part of the filthy little group. His father evidently wouldn't let him join. He knew David would recognize him sooner or later."

"You and Damien planned this, then?"

"Yes."

Victoria stopped suddenly, grabbed his arm, and pulled him about to face her. "I have never been so frightened in my entire life. The bullet . . . it slammed you—rather, Damien—against the wall. I was useless. I screamed and cried. You're probably right to have kept me from your plans. I would have ruined everything."

He grinned, that heart-pounding, white-toothed grin that made her want to kiss his face again and again. "You love me," he said. "You proved that you can't live without me."

She gave him a look of acute dislike. "You, or Damien, as it turns out, made an awful mess. That was probably what scared me so much. All that ghastly blood."

He frowned at that. "Hmmm."

She poked him hard in the stomach. "What did you do with the squire?"

"Nothing. It's his choice. If he isn't too batty, he will leave England immediately, but he's floundering mentally."

"Poor David."

"Poor David, ha. That callous little bully doesn't deserve any kind words from you, love. But I do. Just look at me, Victoria. A weary but triumphant warrior returned to you from the wars. I need succoring at your soft breast, and you could—"

"Make you a cup of tea, perhaps?"

"That's all you're offering to a hero?" he said, and that damned smile of his was hovering, ready to burst forth in full force and do her in.

"I can put brandy in your tea."

"Is that so? You know what I was just thinking, Victoria? We have brought the Ram to a kind of justice. Now, about this fellow who's called the Bishop, you know, that smuggler. What do you say we journey to Axmouth again, and use you for bait, and try to find out— Hey, where are you going?"

"To see Flash. I propose to leave you and go to the *Seawitch*. I plan to get more herbs from Blick. Particularly more of the one that ensures clean innards."

He grabbed his belly. "I don't feel well already. I need succor now."

Victoria looked at him, her hands on her hips. His smile broke through, showering her fully, and she couldn't help herself. She cursed, even as she grinned back at him. "I don't know, you wretched creature, I just don't know."

I feel the same way. Come here, Victoria. We'll succor together."

Epilogue

Carstairs Manor, Cornwall, England, January 1814

*It is not enough to conquer;
one must know how to seduce.*
—SHAKESPEARE

"Our table will collapse under the weight of all the food and consequence. Mrs. Beel's delicious stuffed quail will be buried beneath the brussels sprouts."

Victoria laughed at her husband's words and looked around at their guests. "Rafael is quite right, you know. We've never been so coroneted and peered."

Hawk, the Earl of Rothermere, said to his wife, Frances, "I think that if Victoria wishes to be condescended to properly, we should immediately write to my father. He and Lucia together, with Didier in their wake, could out-consequence the Regent."

Diana Ashton, Countess of Saint Leven, swallowed a bite of her artichoke bottom, then shook her head ruefully. "I'm still reeling from the shock. Lucia marrying the marquess."

"My father," said Hawk, "informed me that Lucia reads aloud her gothic novels to him. At night. In bed."

Frances giggled, unable to help herself.

"All right, I'll tell them the rest of it," Hawk said. "My father also let slip that Lucia is marvelously inventive. If the plot of the novel doesn't suit her purposes, in other words, if it isn't sufficiently wicked, she alters it without my father even realizing it."

"Then everyone is content," Frances said. "No, no, Hawk, don't you dare say another word. You've already gone beyond what is acceptable dinner conversation."

"She's turning boring and proper on me in her old age," said Hawk. "Where's that wild Scottish girl I dragged into the tackroom and—"

"Hawk. Philip. Whoever you are, stop now."

Hawk raised a hand. "I apologize. I am now a pious fellow, nearly a Methodist. Please pass me some of that plum pudding, Diana. Frances, my love, your face is a charming shade of red."

Frances said, "I wonder about Lucia's tatting since she married the marquess."

Rafael said, "I want to know what you, Diana, do when you wish to punish yourself. Do you tat with as much energy and determination as Lucia?"

Diana was grinning shamelessly into her own plum pudding, and Rafael added, "I was good enough to bring Victoria to Lucia as a replacement penance, so to speak. Victoria came into the drawing room and the tatting went underneath Lucia's chair for the duration, so Didier told me."

"I have a feeling that Victoria will serve you up for that remark, Rafael," Diana said. "As for what I do for a penance, let me see—"

"She makes me do her penance," said Lyon Ashton, Earl of Saint Leven. "The rounder her belly becomes, the more outrageous the demands she makes. 'Lyon, darling, would you *please* fetch me just one small strawberry tart? And perhaps just a *tiny* bit of whipped cream on top of it? It's only three o'clock in the morning, Lyon *dear*. Please? I have three more months of this.' "

Hawk leaned forward, waving his fork. "Lyon, that's nothing at all. Let me tell you what Frances did that scared the very devil out of me this past August. She dressed up like a boy and actually rode in a race at Newmarket. Another jockey didn't like the fact that he was losing, and thus took his whip to her. She very nearly fell, and, well, if anyone had discovered the truth, she would have been roundly ostracized."

"Ha. Your father thought it a marvelous lark," Frances said. "I always wanted to ride Flying Davie, in a real race where it really counted. It was worth pulling the proverbial wool over your eyes, my lord. As for that other jockey—Dorking was his name—you forgot to mention that he received his just deserts."

"What did you do?" Victoria asked.

"I didn't waste an instant. I brought my whip down across his face. He howled and pulled away fast enough, let me tell you."

"Yes," said Hawk. "Then he sent three bully-boys around our stables to beat up the jockey who had struck him."

"I know what happened," said Lyon. "The jockey

had disappeared. No doubt he was once again wearing a lovely gown and flirting with the Earl of Rothermere."

"Exactly," said Frances, sitting back and looking quite pleased with herself. "And Flying Davie won."

"Bravo!" shouted the three ladies.

To Lyon's delight, strawberry tarts were served for dessert. "Enough whipped cream for you, sweetheart? Perhaps just a little bit more to cover any latenight cravings you just might develop?"

Diana said slowly, "You know, Lyon, even with the whipped cream, it simply doesn't look appetizing to me anymore."

Lyon groaned loudly. "Show me the shortest route to your kitchen, Victoria. I shall probably be roaming about during the night."

The gentlemen didn't linger over their port, but soon joined the ladies in the drawing room.

Victoria was soon telling them about the very old castle ruins. "We considered naming the manor Wolfeton, after the old castle, but since Rafael wants to begin his own dynasty, we decided Carstairs Manor was more fitting."

Rafael smiled at her. "Victoria would give about anything to have a medieval ghost lurking about. I'm even willing to build her a fake abbey, blight it enough to give it an eerie look on foggy nights, and then put out an invitation to all monkly ghosts to come for a visit."

"Your two wonderful little joys would like that, Hawk," said Frances. "Our children," she added.

"The little pestilences would probably scare any promising spirit across the Channel."

"He's a doting father," said Frances.

"You have done wonderfully with the house," said

Diana. "Everything is so light and cheerful, even in January."

"There was enough ivy removed to cover all the colleges at Oxford," said Rafael. "Next, though, our project is to begin the Carstairs dynasty, as my demanding wife said. She has set her mind on producing enough progeny to outlast the Demoreton line."

"Do recall," said Hawk, "that Frances and I have two absolutely wonderful children. Anyone interested in marriage contracts?"

"Hmmm," said Lyon, eyeing his wife's belly. "I have my mind made up for a little girl. Is your Charles promising, Hawk?"

"He is the very image of me," said Hawk. "Do you know what my father said? He said I was getting my comeuppance through Charles. He's right. I found a gray hair just last week."

"I think we should wait until Diana brings her daughter into the world," said Frances. "Then we will see. Now, Rafael, please do finish telling us about this Hellfire Club and your twin brother."

"Well, there's really not much more after what I've already told you. The Ram—Squire Esterbridge, surprisingly enough—left the country. None of us expected him to, for he'd grown really quite unbalanced. But one morning, not even a week later, he was gone, his man Deevers with him. To his son's fury, he also took every bit of money he could get his hands on.

"As for my identical twin, Damien, well, he isn't any longer."

"What do you mean?" Hawk asked.

Victoria said, "It's fascinating, really. After Damien recovered from the gunshot wound, a shock of white hair suddenly appeared. Now there is no more confusion, nor," Victoria said in a lowered voice to her husband, "will you ever again be able to fool me and go off on your own."

"No more need of that," said Rafael easily. "Behold a man whose energies all go to his tin mines and to the satisfaction of his wife."

"Rafael."

"I forgot to add that as of nearly a month ago, I am again an uncle. My brother's wife gave him his heir. Who knows? Maybe Damien, with his wicked streak of white hair, will become the model father and landlord. Now. Frances, would you please play the pianoforte for us?"

Scottish ballads demanded by everyone, Frances seated herself gracefully at the pianoforte. She played until teatime, to everyone's delight.

"To think," said Hawk, shaking his head as he looked at his wife, "that once I believed she played so badly all the crystal would break."

"I think," Diana said, "that I am developing a craving for marrow pudding. Lyon, my dearest sweetheart?"

Lyon shuddered. "That's disgusting."

"With perhaps some whipped cream?"

Hawk moaned and held his stomach.

Diana clapped her hands. "I've got it—a dash of ginger. Yes, that's it, ginger."

Rafael said to Victoria, "I think we're coming very close to clean innards here."

"No, not ginger. A gooseberry sauce."

"Oh, my God," said Lyon, and collapsed in a heap, his head on his wife's bountiful lap.

"Now, Lyon, if that offends you, then I will simply make do with—let me see—"

"Victoria," said Rafael, "I'm taking you upstairs. Give poor Lyon here a map of the kitchen. His distress bothers me. I can't bear to witness it further."

"Your turn will come," Lyon shouted after them. "Just you wait, Rafael." To Diana he said fondly, "Now, my dearest, why not some parsnips with some delicious onion sauce?"